GODS AND MONSTERS

GODS AND MONSTERS

RUTHLESS BOOK 2

D. J. Rintoul

Podium

For Bryan and Sara,
who filled Orlando, Florida, with happy memories.

Podium

GODS AND MONSTERS

CHAPTER ONE

Empty Planet

Mina looked around cautiously.

The System had dropped her in a strange place. A frozen environment. Snow covered the ground everywhere she looked, a white blanket broken only by a smattering of other people, a few small buildings, and evergreen trees in the distance.

Immediately, she pressed her arms against her chest. *So cold!*

Some warning would have been nice. Jumping from Florida to this place wasn't her idea of a good time. But at least she had warm clothes in her bag. These Mage robes were helpful, but they weren't doing nearly enough. Others were changing clothes around her, but Mina couldn't see a modest way to switch from robes to one of her warmer outfits. And she wasn't *that* cold.

"Sis! You're here!" Yulia ran up to her from among the crowd of people. Mina smiled broadly despite the frosty weather. They embraced a little awkwardly, but warmly, around Mina's pregnant belly.

"Good to see you made it here too! Let's see if we can find James!"

The two spent the next several minutes searching. At first, they looked down on the crowd from atop a small hill. Then they walked among the crowd to cover areas they hadn't been able to see from the hill. Their hopes were disappointed again and again.

Must be strong for Yulia. But she couldn't keep her lip from quivering. James didn't seem to be anywhere. She was afraid for herself, for Yulia, for the baby.

Where are you? We need you.

She resisted the urge to call his name. *I can't afford to draw attention for being isolated. Think like James. He would survive no matter what.* She surreptitiously patted her jacket over her shoulder.

At least I still have the gun. And Yulia must have James's gun in her bag. She didn't want to ask Yulia out loud. A pregnant woman and a teenager would automatically be targets in a place like this. If the people around knew that they were armed, someone would try to take their guns at some point.

But for the moment, everyone was just milling around. Mina couldn't detect anyone paying undue attention to her or Yulia.

She allowed herself to shift her worry back to James for a moment. *You didn't land here with us, so where did you end up? What are they doing to you?*

[Welcome to your Orientation, my fortunate members of the Class of 2042!]

A voice interrupted her train of thought. It sounded soft, feminine, mischievous.

Suddenly, Mina noticed movement in the corner of her eye. She whipped her head around and saw a female figure dressed in green and red, wearing what looked like a Judy mask from a Punch and Judy puppet show. Instinctively, she knew this was the source of the voice.

The people closest to him were giving the figure a wide berth. Those who were slightly further away, like Mina, seemed to have largely failed to notice her. *How can someone just appear like that?* She thought of what the homunculus Roger had told her about the System. *Magic, maybe?*

Identify!

[Cyrilla Cygnus, Lv. ????]

[I am your proctor, citizens of the world chosen for today's induction! It is your privilege and my responsibility to begin this initiation of the 73rd Earth into the System that binds the other surviving member worlds. Over the next ninety days, you will have the chance to grow stronger to face the danger that threatens your world. The Earth itself will be fairly dangerous once the System has completed its construction work there, so consider this your opportunity to adapt to a generally heightened level of danger.]

Just hearing the voice was nerve-wracking for Mina. She imagined endless stress and danger. *Ninety days? I can't wait that long to see James again. And I'll have given birth!* After a moment of feeling her pulse race, she took deep, calming breaths to try and slow her heart back down. She and Yulia stood transfixed, staring, holding hands and waiting for the next pronouncement.

[There are opportunities beyond the chance to grow stronger available here, however. Those are up to you to interpret and discover. This Orientation will take all of your tenacity, ferocity, and cunning to survive. It is calculated that only the fittest of humans are likely to make it through the challenge that presents itself to you. Fitness takes many forms. The System

has a way of balancing things out, so do not despair, those of you who may be physically impaired.]

The last sentence felt a bit directed at her, although there was also at least one person here in a wheelchair. The words weren't especially comforting, coming as they did against the backdrop of what appeared to be a frozen wasteland.

[This Orientation is a unique experience. It offers you an opportunity and a question. Humans are a uniquely adaptable species. How best should such a species try to survive an almost empty planet, with limited resources? Is it better to live and die together, working in collaboration, and share in the fate of your group? Or to fight tooth and nail against other humans and perhaps guarantee your own survival at another person's expense?]

Mina felt fear's icy grip take hold of her. *Why are you telling us we might have to fight each other?* She had already accepted the possibility in her heart, but by mentioning it, the proctor seemed almost to be encouraging people to take a dog-eat-dog approach.

She began slowly and firmly pulling Yulia back from the crowd in anticipation of the potential violence that could break out at any moment. Mina's eyes darted all over as she tried to avoid being caught off guard by any sudden movements.

[Only you can decide what is best. There are no rules for how you survive Orientation. Just live, and there will be rewards commensurate with performance.]

Mina turned toward one of the small buildings that lined the perimeter of the clearing. Yulia clearly understood what her sister intended and moved along beside her until they reached a doorway. Despite their leaving the area where the figure stood, making her announcement, they continued to hear her words in their heads with startling clarity.

[Yes, this will be a difficult challenge. This Orientation is more difficult than others, in some ways. Although there is no formal requirement that any of the population here die, the next ninety days will be difficult to survive. In previous instances, there have been occasions when almost the entire population has been killed by the end. We have included a few features to make your challenge less imposing than it might be. First, you will have a counter in your System screen that will help you keep track of population numbers.]

A number appeared in the corner of Mina's vision, and she took a quick look at it.

[3,397/3,397 Survivors]

Hopefully, people don't take this as a challenge about killing each other, Mina thought. She knew that many of those in the clearing would be on edge already and that a single spark could set off a powder keg of violence. *We might have actually been better off if the proctor hadn't said a single word. People don't naturally want to kill each other.*

Mina looked around the building they'd just entered. She didn't see anyone else inside with them. From the outside, the building had been an unremarkable, unpainted two-story structure. Each of the buildings she had seen was identical. Boring. Plain planks of wood solidly nailed together, but nothing Mina would have looked twice at in the pre-System world.

From the inside, the setting looked like an inn from a fantasy story. Two dozen or so tables, a liquor bar, and a roaring fire in the fireplace. She wanted to just sit and warm up by the fire, but that wasn't what they were here for.

"Let's look for supplies in here while we're the only ones," Mina said quietly. "We have enough food in our bags to survive for a week or two, so we'll try to find warm blankets first."

In case the clearing descends into violence, we need to be able to hide out further away from this place while we wait for things to settle down. There was a set of stairs in one corner that Mina guessed led to the rooms in this inn. That was where she expected to find the blankets.

According to Roger, the homunculus, the Small Bag of Deceptive Dimensions that they each had should be able to contain a vast amount of equipment. If she had time, Mina would love for them to be able to examine this whole place and strip it bare. But she knew they would not have time. Mina silently pointed at where she wanted them to go, and they headed up the stairs. Fortunately, they could still hear the proctor. Distance didn't seem to be a factor.

[The second thing is that we will provide some resources. Weapons and opportunities to increase your powers. Challenges that will test your resourcefulness. If you perform well, you will increase the odds of survival for yourself and your group. The first scheduled challenge will be tomorrow morning.]

Interesting. Maybe these challenges would even the odds for the physically disabled people in the Orientation. If there were battles of wits, Mina was confident that she would be a good performer, even with occasional bouts of pregnancy brain.

As they reached the top of the stairs, Mina and Yulia peered around the corner. The first thing Mina noticed was that there were about a dozen doors lining the hallway. The second thing was the sound of movement. Someone was up here with them. *Rummaging through one of the rooms?*

"It looks like someone beat us here," Mina said. "We should probably go back down."

But Yulia darted past her, up the last step and quickly, quietly into one of the rooms.

She decided to go in alone because she knows I would only slow her down, Mina immediately understood. It was a good decision, though she hadn't wanted to let her baby sister go in by herself. Who knew when another person might try to enter the room that Yulia was in? There was a high potential for conflict.

Of all the times to be pregnant! At least I can keep watch. She turned her head to make sure no one was coming up the stairs behind her, and then she looked back down the hall toward where the rummaging sounds were coming from. The noises seemed to be growing quieter.

[Third, although the population of wild creatures in this Orientation is relatively small, there are some monsters here. They will generally not enter this settlement area, barring certain exceptions that will not be explained. The monsters are similar to those you'll find once you've returned to your Earth, so it may be worthwhile to seek them out. You can give them experience if they kill you, and they can give you experience, and possibly loot, if you kill them. This is how you get those weapons I mentioned, and they may serve as another food source in this treacherous environment. For now, I bid you farewell and good luck!]

Well, I suppose that's useful information. A little annoying that I suddenly couldn't hear anything except the proctor's voice, though. She poked her head up to peek down the hall past the stairs again, but at that moment, another set of words popped up in front of her face.

[Quest unlocked: Survive the Orientation!]

Mina stared at the quest for a moment, then a further description appeared.

[Survive the Orientation: You have entered the System's culling grounds for the new world, the Orientation. Find a way to survive until this Orientation concludes. Reward for Quest Success: Variable dependent on contributions. Penalty for Failure: Death.]

Well, of course the penalty for failure to survive is death! Useless! She dismissed the quest irritably.

And she saw a tall, olive-toned man had appeared at the end of the hall.

He was standing still, looking into the air, just like her. Mina quickly darted back into the stairwell. *Did he see me or was he looking at the quest?*

She thought of the kitchen knife and then drew it from the Small Bag of Deceptive Dimensions. As the homunculus had patiently explained during the tutorial, all she had to do to remove an item from it was think of what she wanted and open the bag.

Mina held the weapon carefully at her side, her arm slightly raised. She slowly backed away from the opening of the stairwell to give herself adequate warning in case the man moved to descend. Her breathing was slow and steady, but her knife hand shook slightly. She consciously tried to steady it. She didn't want to drop the weapon.

Then she heard the man moving down the hall toward her. *He's getting close to Yulia!*

She clutched the knife tightly and braced herself to see the man's head pop up around the corner. But there was nothing.

She waited a few seconds, pulse pounding in her ears. Nothing.

Then Yulia poked her head around the corner.

"I got some stuff," she mouthed. She began descending the stairs, and Mina forced herself to lower the knife. Her heart rate began to slow.

The two of them walked back down the stairs slowly and quietly, holding hands tightly.

"Did you see a man up there?" Mina whispered as they retreated.

Yulia just shook her head.

Once they'd made it down the stairs, Mina put away her knife. The two of them were able to sneak back out to the crowd, where people were discussing the announcements.

"What do you suppose the challenges will be like?" a woman was asking a man. She had dark skin and long, straight black hair.

"Probably tests of our physical abilities and so forth," a man replied. He had an Australian accent and kept his blond mop of hair long and messy.

He sounded excited, Mina couldn't help noticing. *Probably has a lot of faith in his physical abilities.*

"I wouldn't count on that," Mina said, approaching the two. If the crowd wasn't breaking down into violence yet, she was going to see about making inroads with other people.

"Oh no?" the man asked, looking her up and down. Mina felt immediately uncomfortable but forced her face to keep a blank expression. "What do you think the tests are, then?"

"Testing everything, naturally," Mina said. "Everything that humans need to survive. It's not because human beings are stronger and faster than the animals that we rule the world."

"You're a sharp one, missy," the man said grudgingly. "Guess I was hoping it would be something easy! The name's Kyle Dannager."

"It's a pleasure," Mina said, smiling with an enthusiasm that she did not feel "And you?" She turned to the woman.

"Priyanka Dani," the other woman said.

"Nice to meet you," Mina said, smiling more genuinely. "This is my sister, Yulia."

"Nice to meet you both," Yulia echoed.

"Has anyone made any suggestion yet about what we're doing with the rest of the day?" Mina asked. "I know there's a lot of discussion going on."

"Quite right," Kyle said. "A lot of discussion, mainly led by that bloke there!"

He pointed his thumb at a tall man who seemed to be the center of attention for a number of other people, though the vast majority were broken off into smaller groups and talking among themselves.

The tall man wore a suit and tie. He looked physically strong and intelligent, insofar as Mina could tell that by his appearance. Certainly confident.

I don't think he'll end well, though, she assessed. She wasn't completely sure why she felt that way. But it was a very strong intuition. Perhaps it was the imprudence of drawing this much attention at such an early point in the Orientation. *James would have said someone like that will either end up king of the hill or buried at the bottom.*

Mina resolved to keep a careful distance from that man. She excused herself and Yulia and said that they were going to keep looking around for her husband.

"Do you know where James is?" Yulia asked once they were out of earshot.

"No, he's not here," Mina said. "After we met those two people I realized it's only people with last names like ours, starting with 'Da,' in this place."

"Then why . . . ?"

"We have to meet more people than just those two if we're going to do well here, sweet." She tried to infuse her voice with an excitement she did not feel. "Let's network!"

Hopefully, once the challenges began, she could show her worth. Until then, connecting with people was her only way of being seen as something other than a liability.

Everyone acted friendly enough as they walked around, but Mina didn't trust them. Quick sidelong glances from men and women alike revealed their skepticism, though she pretended not to notice. What value could a pregnant woman and a scrawny teenager bring to a survival competition, after all? And even those who were warmer and more welcoming could not be expected to maintain that stance once the realities of the competition hit.

Mina had seen firsthand how people—and, in her experience, particularly women—could backstab each other and maintain a smiling face while doing it. She just hoped that she wouldn't have to behave the same way to stay alive here.

The networking didn't last long. It came to its end when the self-appointed leader of the group called for everyone's attention.

"We've been discussing what to do going forward, and although there are many issues still up in the air, we've resolved one thing. As far as accommodations for this evening are concerned, we've agreed that men will be on this side"—he gestured to the buildings on his left—"and women will stay over there." He gestured toward the buildings to his right.

There were a few quiet grumbles from people who hadn't been in on that conversation and had their own opinions, but most people readily complied.

He's taken the first step toward seizing control of this situation, Mina thought. *Hopefully, he's competent beyond being able to fill a power vacuum.* She wished again that James was there.

But at least the rest of the evening passed quietly.

Mina and Yulia made several acquaintances among the women who'd selected the same building as them to sleep in.

They split a room with an elderly woman and her teenage granddaughter, whom Yulia seemed to get along with. They had to sleep two to a mattress in the twin beds, but Mina and her sisters had done that for years growing up. Even with the baby bump, it was comfortable enough.

It was cozy.

"What do you think tomorrow will be like?" Yulia asked in whispered Bulgarian.

"I think you'll have the chance to show some of your athletic talents," Mina replied back, also in their native tongue. "Probably they're going to have athletic competitions. They'll let you choose between tennis and soccer. And maybe I'll sit down with a blanket over a game of chess."

Quiet snickering came from Yulia, who clearly did not believe any of that. *But I'm also not sure why she thinks I might know what's coming next.* Yulia would have to get used to her sister not having all the answers anymore.

"What?" Mina pretended to be offended at the laughter. "Chess is a completely real sport!"

"Seriously, though. Um, do you think we're going to get home?" She swallowed nervously. "Whatever you tell me, I'll believe you. I know you're the smart one in the family." For once, there wasn't a trace of resentment in the pronouncement.

"I was the one who was good at studying in the family," Mina replied gently but firmly. "I never wanted you to feel like you were dumb just because you didn't get all As! You're good at so many things, sweet. Some of them are things the intelligence tests don't measure. You're kind and thoughtful. You see the best in people." She was surprised to find a few tears at the corners of her eyes as she spoke. *Stupid hormones . . .*

"Well, I know you at least meant some of that," Yulia said softly. Mina could hear from her tone that Yulia felt quite small.

Stop that or you'll make me cry, she thought.

"You're one of my favorite people in the world, and you know I don't like dummies!" Mina said. That provoked another round of quiet snickers. Some of the tension seemed to leave the bed.

"As for whether we'll get home," Mina added, "I don't want to sugarcoat things. We're in trouble. This is a scary place, and people aren't going to be nice to us, no matter how they seemed today. I think we will get home, but only if you and I look out for each other. That means thinking carefully before we do things. And please, do as I say if I tell you to do anything. Especially if I do not say please!"

Slowly, the conversation drifted to less serious things. People they'd met that day. How they felt about the weather—both were excited to see snow for the first time since they'd moved to Florida, but nervous too because they knew how inconvenient it could be from their years in Bulgaria. What James was probably doing right at that moment—thinking about them, of course! How Yulia's school friends would be doing in the apocalypse. She had some strong opinions on that.

They whispered back and forth until, gradually, the conversation slowed down and sleep overtook them.

When Mina awakened the next morning, the population counter greeted her.
[3,396/3,397 Survivors]

CHAPTER TWO

Unfinished Business

Who the hell was that guy?" Officer Ross wondered aloud, staring into the deep darkness that had swallowed up the intruder and Jan Roest. Beyond some invisible line, he couldn't see a thing. It wasn't like the fading of objects as they fall into darkness normally. It was as if they were simply yanked out of existence.

The disturbing thing was that Perception was one of his higher Stats. He should be able to see them. But there was something *off* about that black void.

"Who cares?" Rostov replied glibly. "No one else has survived being thrown into that darkness, right?"

Ross shook his head slowly. They had already thrown one prisoner over the cliff's edge experimentally, when Rostov had felt they'd had enough of a surplus to waste a human life.

They'd never seen the prisoner again. They hadn't even heard him strike bottom. The inky blackness below seemed endless and impenetrable. No one was eager to explore it further after that.

Moloch had apparently informed Rostov after the fact that the area was the edge of the Orientation terrain. There should be nothing beyond it, or so Rostov claimed.

But if Moloch really knows so much, why did we do the experiment of throwing somebody in? Ross questioned. *Moloch seems to be on the line to Rostov every few hours, considering the rate at which he makes public pronouncements about the wishes of his god. But how much of that is Moloch, and how much is Rostov? And how much does Moloch have the ability to tell us, anyway? If that void is a place the sun don't shine . . .*

"Are you coming, Officer?"

Ross turned his head to face the swordswoman who had just been fighting alongside him.

"I guess so, Hilda. It just doesn't sit right with me to leave things unfinished." He gestured at the black void. "We have no way of knowing if he's dead. I'd hate for that guy to come back."

"Does your ability still detect him, then?" she asked, her tone betraying a slight curiosity.

"Well, no," he admitted.

"Then don't make trouble for yourself. He's dead. You still have to live." She turned away, marching to catch up with the rest of the group.

Ross recalled that Hilda Rohm had been one of the more reluctant of those recruited by Rostov. The Prophet had his ways of persuading each of them, or they would have been left behind in the clearing when the wolves came. But she was the last one to begrudgingly follow him, despite whatever he'd whispered in her ear.

She's probably giving me advice for my own good. I'm sure she hates Rostov as much as I do. He turned and gave the cliff's edge one last look.

Still, somehow I don't think we've heard the last of this shithead.

Mitzi Roget felt and heard her joints creak noticeably as she rose from within the tent she shared with her husband. She was trying not to wake him for now, so the noise was annoying.

Not as annoying as it was before this all started, she noted. Before, the limbs had sounded like teenagers stepping on dry twigs in a slasher movie. The volume was much more muted after several points invested in Fortitude, which seemed to have improved her overall physical health as well as increased her Health bar.

Alan didn't stir.

Mitzi walked out toward the edge of camp. Dawn was barely breaking, the sun just beginning to peek over the horizon. No one was nearby except a teenager and a mother on shift for guard duty. She exchanged quiet greetings with them as she passed. She stopped in a place where the trees began to grow too thickly for a person to easily walk through.

She stared off into the distance. He had been so confident he would return alive, come what may. But she saw nothing.

"Come on," she said to herself quietly. "Be there. Somewhere."

Mitzi looked around, as if she would need to be especially vigilant to spot James when *and if* he appeared. As if he wouldn't make a big spectacle of himself. She smiled thinking of the way he had returned from his spider hunt. She swallowed nervously.

Don't make us give your family this news!

But she waited there for almost an hour, and the camp's leader did not appear.

At last, Alan came and found her. He took her softly by the hand, and she let him lead her back to the center of camp, where people were now breaking their fast.

Mitzi ate the meat without tasting it. She hoped they would have all their usual food groups again soon. And she couldn't help but think that James had probably killed whatever animal they were eating now.

"We think it's time that we all meet and talk."

She turned and looked up to see Cliff standing behind her, looking down at her and Alan.

"Oh, you mean the leadership group?" Alan asked, his tone ironic.

Cliff either missed it or chose not to engage. Hard to say for sure which it was, knowing him.

"Who's 'we'?" Mitzi asked.

"Me, Chava," Cliff replied. He seemed a bit impatient this morning, though Mitzi couldn't particularly fathom why. He should be in a great mood; there was a power vacuum for him to try and fill.

"I suppose you're right," Alan said. He sighed. "I wish it could be under other circumstances."

You're writing James off, Mitzi realized. *I never thought Alan would. I know I said it was a suicide mission, but I suppose everyone else thought so too. Somehow, I thought we were all waiting for him to come back at any moment.*

They finished their food quickly and convened a meeting of the council of elders in Chava's tent.

"We're meeting this morning because our dear leader has failed to return from his mission of mercy in the most dangerous area we know of in the forest," Cliff said.

"We must decide what to do next," Chava concurred.

"I don't think there's much deciding to do, personally," Cliff added. "It was clear what James wanted us to do, and I think he was right."

"You mean we leave?" Alan asked.

And Cliff simply nodded.

I don't think James has ever mentioned having any kind of tracking Skill. If he had one, killing the spiders would have probably been much quicker. So we're abandoning any chance of him ever finding us if we leave! We're abandoning him.

"I don't think this is right," Mitzi said slowly. "James is—I can't easily put words to everything James has done. But I think it's fair to say that none of us would have had a shot at surviving this place if we hadn't met him. The three of us"—here she looked from Cliff to Alan—"had no clue how to survive in this place. We almost died fighting a couple of wolves. The Rodriguezes were bottled up in a small, isolated place with no food, and he risked his life to save you." She was surprised to find tears pressing at the corners of her eyes. "You're leaving him for dead!" Her voice broke, and she had to exhale a deep breath.

"It's what he wanted," Cliff broke in quickly. "He didn't do all of that crap just to let us die—"

"Missy is right," Camila interrupted, drawing a smile from Mitzi. "We cannot leave James behind. I don't know him well, but I already know what he would do for strangers, let alone his friends. I can't believe you could abandon him after a single night! You'd leave him to fend for himself, and I think he would die for any of you! Maybe we could organize a rescue mission."

"A rescue mission for the rescue mission?" Cliff asked. He tried to sound skeptical, but Mitzi just found his tone nasty. Almost like he wanted to laugh but held it back.

This is why I wanted James to be the leader and not you! she thought. *You would sacrifice any of us to save yourself. And James, whatever his faults, isn't that way. If the way he's behaved in recent days is any indication of his character, he really would die to save us. With a smile on his face.*

Mitzi took a deep breath and prepared to rebuke Cliff. But Alan spoke first.

"I think what my friend here is trying to say is that James has been very good to us. He's a hero, no doubt about that. And I'll never forget him for as long as I live. But he's probably dead now. He almost certainly died while trying to do the right thing, which is laudable. He wouldn't want the whole Rodriguez family to die with him.

"The problem we have is that we have to think of the living here." He fixed Mitzi in his gaze. "Staying here means putting the Rodriguez family in danger. That's why James thought we should move on and get further away from this evil cult"—Alan turned to Camila—"and sending a rescue party after James would only get us noticed by the cult more quickly.

"Unless we're prepared to send everyone there and go to war with a group of people who defeated James, we wouldn't stand a chance. I don't think it's wise to throw away everyone else's lives to save one man. Even an indispensable man."

Mitzi wanted to argue further, but she knew her husband was right. He was being the rational one this time. But she wished he could be swept up in his emotions, as he had been at other times in this forest. She wished the two of them could go, even on a suicide mission, and rescue the young man who had been their protector.

And she hated to see the smug look of satisfaction that passed over Cliff's face as Alan spoke.

"It's resolved, then, that we will prepare to move camp away from this threat?" Chava half-asked, half-stated.

There were three reluctant nods, and one nod with very little hesitation from Cliff.

* * *

Nikolai Rostov sat uncomfortably, staring into the fire.

The longer he served as Moloch's instrument, the more accustomed he became to the searing pain in his eyes, the numbness in his ass cheeks from sitting on unforgiving surfaces for long periods, and the way his limbs fell asleep after lengthy stretches of time spent conferring with the god.

What he had not yet accustomed himself to, however, was the effect on his brain.

It was more than merely uncomfortable to stare into the flames and connect with his god. Every contact with Moloch left him slightly diminished. Old memories burned away. He could no longer remember his father's face. He was fairly certain that in one session connecting with Moloch he had lost his ability to cook.

The effects were intense enough that Rostov could only bear to connect with Moloch once per day.

Fortunately, thus far, the things he'd lost were not things that Rostov would miss. He wasn't sentimental about his deadbeat dad, and he now had attendants who jumped at his command—and who naturally brought him his every meal. But he was conscious that, at some point, he would begin losing things that mattered to him.

The god hadn't warned him about this but had said something along the lines of "Use this power sparingly." Rostov sometimes wondered if Moloch had thought he would've rejected the Class and Job if he'd known that they carried such dangers to his mind. That the power he held came with terrible trade-offs. His candle burning twice as bright for half as long and so on.

But no.

Moloch had to know him better than that!

Rostov finally rose, and two of his acolytes leaped to his side.

"Prophet, what is your will?" asked one. Her name was a bit hazy to Rostov just now—hopefully not something permanently lost because she was rather appealing. Freckled, with attractive facial features, in a pointy sort of way. Strawberry blonde. Perky breasts.

The other acolyte, while a little older, was also attractive. But she was forbidden fruit. Officer Ross's wife, Catherine. He couldn't touch her and maintain the balance of his camp. Not without killing Officer Ross, who remained useful and kept onside only barely, through the influence of the very same wife.

So many complicated considerations one must balance as a leader, Rostov thought, bemused. *But I think I'll reward myself with the blonde girl tonight. I can at least do that much. I can imagine that Catherine is there with us.*

He had been very well-behaved since arriving in Orientation, but his interpretation of Moloch's will did not exclude the odd bit of fun.

He did not hesitate in issuing a command. "A new sacrifice for Moloch. No, make it two sacrifices today! That is His will. We must maintain His favor." He didn't really think losing Moloch's favor was a danger, but he knew where his bread was buttered.

Rostov strode away from the fire, searching for one of his trusted lieutenants. "Ah, Kassim!" he said. "How did the check for the prisoners go?"

He had ordered a headcount for the prisoners just before going into his trance. He assumed they should all be there, but no sense in getting sloppy. A few days ago, Moloch had informed him that a group of humans was heading his way, running away from the Dead Marsh. With any luck, he would have the opportunity to acquire some new sacrifices. It simply wouldn't do to have prisoners running loose, potentially warning others away from the Rostov camp.

And it turned out, contrary to his expectations, there were in fact prisoners running loose.

"My Prophet." Kassim wiped his forehead nervously.

Officer Ross, who was standing nearby, visibly rolled his eyes.

"Speak your truth, Kassim," Rostov said, a little more impatiently than he had intended, slightly needled at seeing Ross.

"My Prophet, the prisoners are, uh, *almost* all accounted for. You have my word that we will track the other few down."

Rostov resisted the urge to ask how other prisoners had escaped. There would be enough time later to find and flay the incompetent guard who had let them slip away while Rostov and his finest fighters had chased the intruder.

"You have dispatched a search group, then?" he asked.

"Of course, Prophet!" Kassim sounded relieved at the question.

"Good. It is of the utmost importance that they not warn others, or we will be forced to migrate and take our hunt on the road." He rounded on Ross. "And you, why haven't you accompanied the searchers? With your Skill, I assume you could be of some use?"

"You know very well that isn't how my tracking Skill works." He sounded distinctly unimpressed by Rostov's annoyance. "I have to mark the person first. It's not about following a trail like some hunting dog. What about you, anyway? Did you manage to find out what happened to our intruder? Or where our trio of guests from yesterday happen to have ended up?"

"The intruder is dead," Rostov lied. "And Moloch shows me that the elderly couple and their young friend are far from here. They were not involved in the night attack on our camp."

In truth, he had no way of knowing this information. The Solar Sight that Moloch had granted him allowed him to see the world as Moloch saw it, from the perspective of the sun looking down on the world, but it still took time to find what he was looking for.

Rostov had been able to appear omniscient during the early days of Orientation. He could navigate perfectly to where they were going, avoid danger as long as they only moved during the day, and find easy kills for the group. His perfect information and powerful abilities were made more effective by Moloch helping him select the correct people to join him. He had created an unquestioning following. But it was much easier to have seemingly perfect information when he only had to focus on finding things in a specific area, as opposed to when he was conducting a broad search.

"I suppose you want me to just take that on faith," Ross said. "Well, don't forget, I know exactly where you came from, pal."

"Everyone knows where I come from, Officer," Rostov countered smoothly. "It's made no difference to anyone but you."

I dearly wish I could sacrifice him, he thought. *Get rid of a headache and increase my enjoyment of this place in one fell swoop. Moloch thinks I still need him. But perhaps if we run low on sacrifices, I'll have to make a tough executive decision.*

He smiled at the thought.

Mitzi stood with her back to the camp once more. Everyone was in the last stages of packing up the camp, and the sun was just about to set. They planned to move at night so Moloch would not be able to see their activities, increasing their odds of getting far away from any potential reprisals.

But Mitzi still wasn't ready to leave. She wouldn't let go of her lingering hopes. She wanted to see a big figure come lumbering through the trees, smiling and perhaps slightly apologetic about taking so long to return.

Maybe, just maybe . . .

And suddenly she saw a figure moving toward the camp through the trees!

She rejoiced for a moment, but then her blood chilled.

There were several figures, and none of them looked like James.

CHAPTER THREE

Beyond Borders

As they fell into darkness, James threw his head back and laughed. It was a horrible, ragged noise thanks to the hole in one lung, but that didn't stop him.

"What the fuck is wrong with you?" Jan Roest screamed, struggling helplessly to get out of James's grip. "And why the fuck are you laughing?!"

James paused his laughter long enough to hiss, "That's for me to know and you to never find out!"

"We're going to die, you crazy bastard!"

"One of us sooner than the other!"

James tightened the arm that he still had wrapped around Roest's neck and then twisted with all his strength until he heard the ding.

Pillage. It was almost a reflex now. He selected Talent, opened his magic satchel, and directed everything inside.

[Talent obtained: Flame Affinity!]

Um, I already had that one. System, are you trying to cheat me? Or was that really the only Talent he had? He knew people were bound to have a smaller variety of Talents than Skills. That was why he usually Pillaged Skills. But to think that all he got out of the attack on the Rostov camp in material terms was the gear on Jan Roest's body was a bit outrageous. There was that cool flaming spear Roest had stabbed him with, but it still felt like a raw deal.

He tried not to think about the other elements of his failure. *All those people condemned to be tortured and burned alive because I was reckless.*

He couldn't afford to fixate on his regrets too much in that moment, though.

He was wounded and falling headfirst, further and further into a pit so deep and black that he couldn't see the bottom.

He finally relaxed his battle-weary body. Allowed himself to fully feel the horrible, searing pain in his chest. Pressed his free hand over the opening in his body just above his lung. Cast Laying on Hands to close up that single gaping wound.

Now, how to solve my other problems? James thought. He used Roest's body for leverage to flip over in midair and look back up at where he'd left the other enemies. And saw nothing.

Just impenetrable blackness.

Wasn't there a full moon tonight? And I can't see the cliff I fell from anymore either. Clearly this is no ordinary darkness . . .

As he noticed this, he felt himself beginning to fall again, but there was something off about the pull of gravity. As if it was just a little slower than he remembered. As soon as he had the thought, he was falling faster, moving past Roest's body.

This is impossible. Physics isn't working properly. Not only that, did it just respond to my thoughts? He realized he didn't feel the rush of air moving past his skin as he fell either. Just the vague sensation of falling.

He tentatively thought of moving through the murkiness with his own willpower, and suddenly, his body jolted to a halt. He tried thinking of moving through the darkness again, but nothing more happened. He just hung there, suspended.

Fine, then, I'll figure it out in a minute. He used Laying on Hands with the last of his Mana to repair the worst of his remaining injuries. It took a few minutes, but with Stem Cell Production already working, his injuries had been partly repaired before he'd started. The lung had been the biggest outstanding issue. And nothing he'd suffered was nearly as bad as losing a whole limb.

That done, and his Mana depleted, he returned to the big question.

How do I get out of this place?

The environment around him seemed to respond to his thoughts, and he observed himself being pulled through the gloom, getting further from the landmark of Roest's body, which simply floated in place.

Where he was going, he couldn't tell. This place had not behaved in a predictable way thus far. But it felt like he was moving deeper into the void.

That's not what I wanted, he thought. *Need to focus on what will actually get me out of here. Or maybe . . .* He recalled the thought he'd had before he jumped. *Maybe I need to think like a spider. Think like Anansi.*

He put his hand on his chin, stroked just above where his goatee was, and focused on the problem. *If I were a spider, what would this place be to me? Spiders like the dark. And this place has me trapped. So, a place to find prey?* He would hate to be found by anything while he was stranded here.

As he had that thought, his body began moving in a different direction. This time, though, he ignored it.

How does a spider web trap insects? It's sticky, but that's not the only thing. Most of the time, the more the bug struggles, the more it entraps itself. The web just pulls it further in while it's trying to get out. By the time the spider gets there, it barely has to do anything.

If this is the place off the edge of the map where Anansi told me to look for him, maybe it's acting like a spider's web. It moves me around when I think about wanting to be moved or to stop moving. But just like a web, it's not moving the way I want it to. It seems to be doing the exact opposite of what I think in my head. Like a spider's web, if he wanted to get out, it would just suck him further in.

It was a strange idea, but it was all he had to go on. If he didn't come up with something, he'd eventually starve in there. And almost on cue, his stomach growled as he realized this.

Fine. Take me far away from Anansi! As far from him as possible! James focused on the thought.

And he began moving through the dark in a new direction. It seemed to be composed of strange, spiraling twists, sudden shifts in path, and headlong motions straight down. Like a nightmare roller coaster in complete darkness.

Like an extreme version of Space Mountain, he thought. He resisted the pull of his mind toward nausea. If he thought about being sick, this place would actually go out of its way to make him vomit.

Take me far away from Anansi, he silently repeated. *Away from Anansi!*

As he dropped straight down once more and felt his stomach fly up into his throat, he passed Jan Roest and saw the body beginning to fade away. *Literally impossible for me to pass him again unless this place is a continuous loop in some way.* He was certain he'd left the body some distance away, in the opposite direction from the one he was traveling in.

But back to his mantra.

Away from Anansi! Away from Anansi! Away from Anansi!

And something came into view in the distance. Not Jan Roest. A shape that was glowing with bright golden light. He had to keep himself from speculating about what this might be in his own mind. He wanted to avoid thinking any stupid thoughts that would send him in the wrong direction.

But James felt an uncontrollable surge of relief. He kept his thoughts largely restrained, but he couldn't resist wishing, *Hope it's a soft landing!*

Suddenly, he accelerated at an impossible rate. He found himself zipping toward the golden glow—a golden web, he had only a second to notice—and before he could think the correct thoughts, he felt his body slam into the web with all the speed and force of a bullet train smacking into the side of a mountain.

His head struck first. The spider exoskeleton mask shattered on impact, and the pieces flew off into the distance behind him.

Then James felt his nose strike a thick golden thread—the strand of webbing had a similar diameter to a human wrist—and he heard the bone snap before he felt it. *I've had worse*, he thought for a split second.

Finally, the rest of his body hit the web. The broken wrist and the broken rib he'd just repaired both bent painfully, then snapped. Then his right femur. Thankfully, the web hadn't smashed his balls. But pain screamed out from almost every corner of his body as he struck the hard structure at what seemed to be near-sonic speed.

An involuntary series of noises leaked from his lips: grunts, gasps, and a sickening groan.

He bit into his lip until he drew blood, trying to focus his mind and bring the pain under control. He could feel it was almost enough, even through Pain Resistance, to knock him out. And in truth, he wanted to succumb to unconsciousness now.

But first, one step to make sure he was in better condition when he woke up.

Skill Fusion. He combined Stem Cell Production and Healing Aura, setting this fusion as permanent. Ideally, that would juice up the healing speed. Stem Cell Production hadn't impressed him much so far. He could still heal other people's injuries with Laying on Hands anyway. And hopefully, Enhanced Stem Cell Production would serve him much better.

Then he succumbed to the darkness clawing at his vision.

When James awakened, he could tell that hours had gone by. Through Pain Resistance, he could still sense terrible discomfort in all of the regions of his body where bones had been broken. But an experimental wiggle of his limbs confirmed that the injuries seemed to be more or less healed. *Probably at the stage where I'd be joking about this now in regular life and people would be asking to sign my cast. I can definitely walk if I have to.*

As he finished the physical self-check, he felt vibrations beneath him. Movement on the web.

Perhaps that was what had woken him.

He swallowed drily. *Really hope this is actually Anansi's web. I'm not sure I'm in proper condition to fight Shelob right now.*

"Hey, something landed in the web," a male voice said.

"Do you think it's food?" a deeper male voice asked.

"You always think with your stomach, Afudohwedohwe," the first voice said. "We have no reason to think it's food! Things float here through the darkness all the time."

"Maybe it's another human," Afudohwedohwe said. "I think of food because there's never enough to fill my belly, Ntikuma. You know that!"

Oh crap. A pair of talking monsters! They must be high level. Need to heal faster.

He tried to sit up, only to realize the golden thread held him fast. And as he struggled against the pull of the golden thread, he heard the voices moving closer.

"Well, if it's a human, you can have him," Ntikuma said. "That last one was far too greasy for my taste. He made my belly ache!"

Shit!

James still couldn't escape from the sticky threads, so he did the only thing he could think of. *Natural Camouflage!*

Hopefully, his body would somehow camouflage against the backdrops of the black void and the golden web. He wasn't optimistic, but he was helpless to do anything else. He couldn't even see who was approaching him, since he was stuck to the web lying face down.

Finally, the vibrations drew close enough that he was certain they must be standing almost right on top of him.

There were a few long moments of silence.

"Say, brother, you said I could eat this one, right?" Afudohwedohwe said finally.

"Yes, that's right. He looks a lot healthier than the last one too. Hurry up and grab him before I change my mind."

James instantly felt a hand grasp him from behind the neck.

"Wait!" he yelped. "Anansi! I'm here to see Anansi!"

The hand that had grabbed his neck very smoothly pulled him away from the golden web, seemingly effortlessly.

"Here to see Pop, you say?"

James was pulled through the air and turned toward the two figures.

They were a pair of the strangest people—if that was the correct word—that he'd ever seen.

One of the two, the one not holding him, was a giant black spider standing on his hind legs, with a male human head attached where the spider's head would be. The one holding James was even stranger: a male humanoid figure with six arms, a pot belly, and a black spider's head. Both of the brothers had dark colored skin.

"The children of Anansi, I presume?" James managed to squawk.

"That's right," said the one holding him. James recognized by his voice that he was Afudohwedohwe.

"I'm here to see Anansi. He asked me to come," James repeated, desperately hoping that he was in the right web.

"Well, Pop didn't say anything about visitors, did he?" Afudohwedohwe asked, turning his head to Ntikuma.

"He did, actually," Ntikuma said, rolling his eyes. "You were just too busy stuffing your face while he was talking. Still"—he looked at James closely—"I don't know if you're really him. Pop said there was a smart human coming. You don't look too clever."

"How many humans do you think are looking for Anansi's web out here?" James asked, gesturing frustratedly at the void around him.

"You sure I can't eat him?" Afudohwedohwe asked, still looking at Ntikuma rather than at James.

"Well, let's not say I'm totally sure yet," Ntikuma said. Afudohwedohwe gave James a gluttonous look. "We should test him to see if he's worthy of Pop's attention."

"All right, big brother," Afudohwedohwe said. He looked pleased, as if he was sure James would fail this test and become dinner.

At least I'm not dead yet, James thought. He was not entirely confident that both of these brothers wanted to give him a fair shake, though.

"I agree to be tested," James said, "even though your father specifically requested that I come as his guest and didn't name any such conditions. However, I'll only do it if the one to test me is Ntikuma."

"What's that about?" Afudohwedohwe asked, tilting his head and giving James what seemed like a hard look. He sounded incensed, although it was hard to read his emotions when the words were coming out of a giant spider head.

"What he said," Ntikuma agreed, a stern expression on his face. "Are you questioning my brother's honor, kid?"

"Not at all," James quickly lied. "But I'm an important guest of Anansi. I deserve the older brother's attention, not the younger!"

The two brothers exchanged a glance, and then both burst out laughing so hard they clutched their sides.

"I think I'm going to like this one. Maybe there's something to his story after all."

"I can sort of see what Pop might see in him."

James nervously chuckled along with them until the laughter faded.

Then the two brothers began to walk away from the edge of the golden web, where James had been suspended. James was still gripped on the back of the neck by a single one of Afudohwedohwe's massive hands, as if he were a toy in the grasp of an over-large child.

As they reached the center of the web, an alert popped up for James.

[Dungeon entered! You have arrived in Dungeon: Anansi's House!]

CHAPTER FOUR

The Witness

Mina awakened, blinked her eyes at the sunlight streaming in through the window, and looked out at the snow shimmering on the rooftops visible outside.

That wasn't there yesterday, she noted. *So, it snowed last night?* She filed this environmental detail away—it snows here, therefore it's dangerous to spend the night outside even in seemingly good conditions—while noting the beauty.

She was still smiling softly, looking through the window at the early morning light, when her sister stirred beside her a few minutes later.

"You seem happy, sis."

"I had a nice dream," Mina said. "James was there."

Yulia half-smiled in return. "Was he all right?"

Mina snorted. "He seemed all right. He was actually worried about us." She frowned for a moment, as if just then realizing that it had been *only* a dream. "That was the best sign. Wherever he was, however he was doing, he had space to worry about us."

Then she noticed the population counter. She'd seen it when she first woke up, but she hadn't registered its meaning, as her mind still lingered on the dream world.

[3,396/3,397 Survivors]

The numbers don't match, she thought in a daze. Then, *Something's seriously wrong.*

Someone had died during the night on the very first day. *It has to be murder, right? No, maybe it was an accident.* She could hope, at least.

"Sweet, let's get ready for the day and get outside as quickly as we can," Mina said.

She didn't want to alarm her sister, but she wanted—no, needed!—to find out what had happened. *Maybe it was an accident*, she told herself again. *Stay calm. Don't scare Yulia . . .*

Both sisters rushed through the application of makeup, Mina giving Yulia side-eye until the latter finished. Then they stormed outside, dressed in their warmest clothes. The brisk air made Mina glad that they'd packed clothes for all weather.

Yulia was looking at Mina curiously. She definitely knew that something was up from how Mina had rushed her, but Mina was hoping she hadn't noticed the change to the population counter. She didn't want Yulia alarmed unless there was a good reason for it.

Maybe they would find out that someone had gone for a moonlit stroll and slipped on the ice.

But then again, maybe not.

As they left their little building, they saw a crowd of around thirty people had gathered. Mina took in the crowd for a moment, noticed how their breath fogged the air as they spoke among themselves, and how they all appeared to be looking at something at their center. Then, hoping not to stand out, Mina and Yulia gently tried to insert themselves in the closest part of the circle.

Mina was a bit less than graceful; with her belly as swollen as it was, she waddled more than walked. But fortunately, people weren't pushing and shoving. They were staring, quietly murmuring among themselves, at a thick greatcoat that lay on the ground. Mina saw immediately that there was a thick layer of dried blood around the neck, staining the otherwise pure black with an ugly reddish brown.

Her first, absurd thought was that now that coat would go to waste. It could have kept someone warm, but some careless person had spilled blood all over it.

As the reality hit her, she felt a little twinge of nausea at her own thought process. *Someone died in that coat! I wouldn't want to wear it unless I was freezing to death.* After a moment's delay, a more sober thought occurred to her. *I can no longer assume there was some sort of accident.*

Then she wondered, *Where is the body? Surely someone was murdered, based on the population count and this obvious physical evidence. But what happened to the body?*

"Excuse me, pardon me, comin' through!" A business-like male voice from Mina's left side caused her to step aside. A moment later, a man stepped through the gap that she'd left.

"Thanks, sweetheart," he said, flashing her a friendly smile.

She forced herself to smile back at the stranger. She wasn't his sweetheart.

He turned and moved toward the coat, and she couldn't help wondering who he was.

Just an inch or so taller than her, around fifty, bald as a cue ball, with a thin mustache and olive-toned skin. And wearing a greatcoat like the victim's, but in deep blue rather than jet black. Despite the fact that he was now crouching over a dead man's coat, he seemed to brim with confidence. As if he'd seen this all before.

Perhaps he had.

The bald man rose. He flashed a badge from one of his coat pockets.

"I'm Detective DaSilva," he said. "Since I seem to be the only law enforcement officer anyone could find in here, I'll be taking charge of this investigation. Does anyone know where we can find a medical examiner or other medical professional?"

Someone standing behind him tentatively raised his hand but seemed too shy to speak up, so Mina caught DaSilva's eye and pointed behind him. DaSilva turned and saw the bashful young man.

"You a medical examiner?" DaSilva asked.

The man shook his head. "I kn-know where I can find one, though!"

"Fine, go fetch me whoever you can," DaSilva said. He turned away from the man again, and the shy fellow ran away. "Next, I'd like to take witness statements. Anyone who saw anything or believes they know anything that might be pertinent to the investigation, please step forward. Everyone who doesn't know anything or hasn't seen anything, please disperse."

Mina didn't want to stand out any more than she had to on day two of Orientation, but she also felt that knowing what was going on in the investigation of this murder could be directly relevant to her and Yulia's safety, so she was reluctant to leave.

Most of the others started to walk away, but she stood her ground. She quietly asked Yulia to walk back to the inn on her own, but her sister gave her a stubborn look.

"I'm not leaving you," she mouthed.

"Fine," Mina whispered. "Just stay out of people's way."

Yulia inclined her head slightly as if to agree, but Mina thought she caught her rolling her eyes at that.

Once all but a few were gone, DaSilva looked at the four people surrounding him and said, "All right. Who's first?"

As he looked at Mina, a young Black woman with her hair in cornrows came running up.

"You were, hah, looking for, hah, a medical examiner?" she asked, panting.

He looked at her quietly for a moment, then nodded.

"Are you her?" he asked.

"I'm new, but yeah. I haven't done a lot."

He sighed. "And I know we don't have the kind of equipment you'd like to work with." He pointed to the neck of the greatcoat on the ground. "We know that this person bled a significant amount from the neck just from the stain there. I'm hoping you can enlighten me on the injuries, whether they were fatal and any other likely wounds besides the neck." He paused, then spoke again as if expressing an afterthought. "By the way, I'm Detective Leon DaSilva."

"Nice to meet you. I'm Adelaide Davis." She awkwardly nodded to the others gathered around.

They shook hands, and then he turned away from the medical examiner. "The first question I have for my witnesses, since I was called here a while after the coat was found, is where the rest of the blood is. And the body. If anybody knows." He looked around as if hoping someone would raise their hand to tell him.

"I f-f-found the c-coat," a voice said.

Mina looked at the figure, and Detective DaSilva turned around to see her too. A small tanned blonde woman, around two inches shorter than Mina's height. Early twenties, by Mina's guess. She stuttered with either cold or nervousness. Mina could easily have believed either explanation since the woman was wearing shorts and a midriff-baring shirt, hugging her arms against her chest.

"Is this the place where you found it?" DaSilva asked.

The woman shook her head.

"Show me where," DaSilva ordered immediately.

The few people who remained around DaSilva and the medical examiner, including Mina and Yulia, followed the blonde woman. She walked through the space between two of the inn-like buildings, and she led them to a patch of snowy ground that was stained reddish brown.

"The coat was over here," she said, gesturing at the ground.

"I can see that," DaSilva replied. "Thank you. What was your name, young lady?"

"Cara Dahlhaus," the blonde woman said.

"Cara, pleasure to meet you," he said. The detective turned back to the others. "Any of the rest of you here when this discovery happened? Or see anything additional?"

One of the two men with them shook his head.

The other, a dark-skinned man with close-cropped black hair, said, "I was with Cara when she made the discovery."

DaSilva looked hard at him. "You were with her. And the coat wasn't hidden at all?"

The man shook his head.

Mina heard Detective DaSilva mutter something like, "So much for the person who discovered the body," to himself. His voice trailed off so that she couldn't hear the last few words after "body."

Then he cleared his throat. "All right. And nobody saw a body? Not even any parts of a body, besides blood?"

More head shaking.

Then a silky voice interrupted the conversation.

[Good morning, everyone! Congratulations to all of you on surviving the first night. Please prepare yourselves for the first of our challenges. The winners will receive provisions as a prize, so you will want to do well here! There will be a timer in your System interface counting down from now until the challenge begins.]

DaSilva looked extremely irritated at the interruption. "All right, then. I suppose you all can go if you have nothing additional to say. We seem to be on a timer again, and I don't suppose this 'System' waits for law enforcement to do its job. Cara, I will want to get a written statement from you as soon as we can. Are you available later today?"

She nodded.

"Good, good." He appeared to be distracted by something hanging invisibly in the air. "You stay in which building?"

While Dahlhaus was giving her answer, Mina looked to the corner of her vision, and she saw that a timer had appeared while she was focused on DaSilva and Dahlhaus. As she watched, it ticked down. **[00:07:32]**.

I'm not ready for whatever this is, she thought to herself. *Nor is Yulia.* But they would have to be. Then she noticed that the witnesses besides herself and Yulia were walking away.

"And what did you two stay for?" DaSilva's voice had a slight air of menace now. "Just to catch a glimpse of the investigation? Or did you witness something you didn't want to share in front of the others?"

Mina had already thought through her response.

"Forgive me for not sharing in front of the others," she said. "I just have a suggestion, based on my understanding of how the System works. The System has placed us in a game-like setting. Whoever killed this person would have received experience from it. They might have leveled up already, and there won't be a lot of people who will have done that on the first night. You could get volunteers using Identify to figure out who leveled up on the first night. It might help narrow your suspect list down a bit."

"Hm," DaSilva grunted, but it sounded affected to Mina. Like he was trying to pretend he was unimpressed. "That assumes the killer was a human at all. This is apparently a whole other world . . . But well, I suppose I'll look into it. It's not as if I have other leads to chase. You two had better get back to the center of this little settlement before the proctor comes." He looked at the medical examiner. "Adelaide and I will see what we can make of this scene."

Mina and Yulia returned to the settlement, and they saw that a much larger crowd had gathered now. No one was standing near the greatcoat, but everyone was chattering. Some, Mina could hear, were talking about the murder. Others were focused on the challenge ahead of them.

As the timer ticked down, Mina explained to Yulia why she'd felt the need for the two of them to learn what had happened to the murder victim.

"The police were already imperfect in the world we knew," Mina said. "Now we have to try and take care of ourselves. If we can, I would like to help Detective DaSilva track down this killer. Otherwise, we could end up next." She sighed. "I was hoping I could do that without making us stand out, but I don't know if I've come close to succeeding. The killer might think we witnessed something now."

"I think you did the right thing, sis," Yulia said. "That detective seemed pretty clueless. It was nice of you to give him a hand."

Mina found herself laughing in little snorts at that. "Hopefully not as clueless as you think." She shook her head.

They turned to face the crowd again. More people had poured out of the buildings as the last minute began ticking down on the clock. This included the self-appointed leader who had been practicing his public speaking yesterday by assigning rooms.

And then Mina suddenly realized the proctor was among them. The same masked figure in green and red that they had seen yesterday. She was just *there*, standing atop the greatcoat that no one else had been willing to go near. Mina didn't see anything until there was a presence in her peripheral vision.

Cygnus, she remembered. *The proctor, she said. How can she do that? Just appear out of nowhere?* But no answers seemed likely to be forthcoming.

[Thank you for gathering so well, residents of Earth-73! Nearly all of you are here.]

The proctor's head moved; she seemed to be looking down.

[On second thought, perhaps all of you are here. Someone was quite unlucky on the first night, I suppose.]

"Hey!" someone yelled. "That shit's not funny! One of us is dead, and what are you going to do about it?"

The proctor straightened up.

[It is not my concern what the population of the Orientation chooses to do to each other here. I am not law enforcement. As long as you follow the rules I set, I will not interfere. However, if you interrupt me again, Jeffrey Danvers, I will kill you myself.]

There was a quiet rush of wind from a collective gasp at that.

The self-appointed leader tried speaking up next, much more politely and with a winning smile. "I'm sorry, proctor. We understand you're not the police, but couldn't you at least tell us who or what killed this person? Our actual law enforcement is working on it, but any information from you would help."

Mina looked to the crowd, to see if anyone reacted to the prospect of the proctor passing on information to the humans. There were a few reactions, but it was hard to read, and then the proctor spoke and changed the focus of the tension completely.

[**No further interruptions of this announcement will be tolerated.**]

Cygnus seemed to ignore the substance of what the leader—who Identify noted was Paul Dawson—had said. She sounded irritated, as if she didn't think they were taking her seriously. Mina looked at Yulia and put a finger to her lips.

She felt certain that the next person who spoke up other than the proctor would suffer an immediate death. The System and its representatives hadn't overtly lied about anything yet.

Fortunately, everyone clammed up at that.

[**The first challenge will be a marksmanship competition. The System will supply each participant with a bow and a handful of arrows. You can keep the bows and any unused arrows for future use. You are to organize yourselves into teams of ten to twelve people. There will be no time limit in shooting. Each team will get to fire a total of twenty-four shots. The teams that perform best will receive food and access to better dwellings than those we initially provided.**]

[**There is another thing you should know. Although we provided food for you in your current dwellings, it's not plausible that the food provided could last for more than a week. Therefore, failing to participate in these competitions could diminish your ability to obtain food.**]

It's starting to feel as if the System wants us to kill each other, Mina thought. *Despite what the proctor said on the first day, that would be the easiest way to survive here. Kill people who win and steal their food. Right? And now she's made it explicit that there are no penalties . . .* She wondered how James was holding up. If this Orientation had already included one death, and Cygnus hadn't batted an eye, there was no telling how his Orientation was going.

The proctor paused, and Mina saw there was a young Hispanic woman raising her hand.

[**Go ahead and ask your question.**]

"Thank you, ma'am," the woman said. She looked very nervous. "Are we allowed to use magic?"

[**Excellent question. Absolutely. You may use any projectile you wish. Feel free to be creative. But individual bursts of magic or thrown objects large enough to destroy a target will each count as a single shot out of your twenty-four, just like your arrows. Are there any other questions about the competition?**]

There was silence.

[**Very well. You will have a quarter of an hour to pick your team members.**

Stand with your group as the timer concludes to be recognized as one of them.]

The timer reappeared in the corner of Mina's vision. **[00:15:00]**.

Then she noticed that Cygnus had disappeared again.

And a thin bead of sweat trickled down Mina's neck. Her worry about the murderer on the loose receded into the back of her mind, and she became much more concerned about the present moment. *What kind of people will want to team up with me and Yulia?*

CHAPTER FIVE

Through the Looking Glass

As James passed through the opening, the alerts kept coming.

[Dungeon entered! You have arrived in Dungeon: Anansi's House!]
[First human of Earth-73 to enter Dungeon: Anansi's House!]

So, at least my System Pioneer bonuses will be active, James thought. *For whatever a ten percent boost to everything is worth. I could be forced to fight something leagues beyond my abilities, and I wouldn't be able to do anything about it except bemoan my fate, even with a ten percent boost.*

"Um, could you put me down?" James asked quietly. "I can walk on my own."

He'd gotten his first look at his surroundings. Somehow, despite this place being located at the bottom of a black void beside a cliff, the golden web had led into what looked like a vast African savanna. He had never visited the continent, and he was embarrassed to realize he only recognized what the general landscape looked like from some old cartoon movie he'd watched as a kid.

"We have a little ways to go, chicken-legs," Afudohwedohwe said. "I doubt your scrawny human muscles could keep up! Be glad I have a fair number of hands and can spare one to carry you."

"Fine, then," James said. "My name is James, by the way." He didn't like not being in control of the situation even to the point of not doing his own walking, but he could see where they were probably going. There were some buildings in the distance. And rather than walking miles to reach those buildings, it probably *was* best for him to just recover his Health and Stamina as much as he could.

But that was assuming James actually planned to complete the brothers' test as promised. That had not been his real plan. If Afudohwedohwe never put him down, he would never have a good opportunity to escape. Not until he was all the way in the middle of that apparent village.

The brothers made good progress, moving almost at a running pace across the savanna.

"Still wish you were walking, human?" Afudohwedohwe asked as he ran.

James gave a noncommittal grunt. *My name is James*, he wanted to remind the spider-headed brother. And he was also mildly surprised that a figure with a pot belly could move this quickly. But then again, Afudohwedohwe was the son of a god. Best not to comment on the "human" remarks, and he probably shouldn't be surprised by anything either of them could do.

The village quickly moved into view: earthen and wattle-and-daub buildings painted in brown and white hues with thatched roofs. It was frankly similar to what James had always imagined a traditional West African village would look like, with the exception that the buildings were much larger, a hundred feet tall or more, and there were fewer of them. There was also some furniture outside, chairs and tables.

I shouldn't be too surprised, I guess. Big house for the big guy, but I suppose he doesn't have too many guests over to the inner sanctum. I imagine I would enjoy my privacy, too, if I were a god. And he keeps some furniture outside because he can probably control the weather in here.

"All right!" Afudohwedohwe said, dropping James to the ground. "Time for your tests."

"Uh, don't I get any recovery time?" James stalled. "My Mana and Stamina are both pretty low after the way I found this place."

"Fine, human," Ntikuma said condescendingly. "Look, we'll even feed you. 'Ey, Ma!" He called the last words out. There were no windows, only openings in the walls of the houses, and the sound seemed to carry. James saw movement within the largest of the structures.

"Our ma is Pop's favorite wife," Afudohwedohwe murmured proudly to James.

He braced himself to see some kind of monster. Instead, a tall, beautiful woman with African features emerged from the house. She had long, thick, curly hair held in a yellow band, and she wore a red, green, and yellow patterned dress.

"What do my sons need?" she asked, smiling broadly. She looked completely unruffled to see James in the company of her children.

Right, I guess I forgot a little of my mythology, James thought. *Anansi liked human women, I guess.*

"Some boiled yams for our guest, please, Ma," Ntikuma asked with a smile. "He is weary, but we need to test him."

"You don't want to let him sleep a bit first?" the woman asked. "And he looks so scrawny, all skin and bones! Maybe we should fatten him up a bit before you test him."

I only look skinny next to your pot-bellied son! James thought incredulously. But he said nothing. Stalling was good. Her taking the time to cook would mean he'd have a little more time to recover from his injuries, regain Stamina and Mana, and plot his escape.

It was a big savanna he'd have to cross to find the Dungeon's exit again, but he thought he could do it if given a little time. The brothers hadn't been that much faster than he was when he made the effort. He just needed to find a way to distract them.

"Please, Ma," Ntikuma said. "We want to test him right away so he can see Pop as soon as possible if he's the right one."

"As you prefer," she said with a shrug.

She swept back into the house, and James couldn't help but notice how gracefully she moved. Her walk was almost a dance, with a grace and rhythm that he'd never been able to match on an actual dance floor himself.

Now, what to do while she's cooking, James thought. But a moment later, his jaw dropped.

"This was all I had in the kitchen," Anansi's wife said apologetically. She carried a massive bowl in one hand. It looked like a big salad bowl to James. The kind used to serve food to a whole table of people.

"That's plenty, Ma," Afudohwedohwe said. "We don't want to spoil him."

Ntikuma kissed their mother on the cheek and took the bowl from her hand.

"Thanks, Ma." He set the bowl down on a table and gestured for James to pull up a chair. He saw that the bowl was full of boiled yams covered in a stew of some sort. The dish smelled extremely rich.

"Uh, thank you, ma'am." James bowed his head at the spiders' mother.

Then he sat down, and although he was very conscious of the eyes on him, he dug in.

The food was delicious. Comforting, yet surprisingly spicy for a stew with yams! Perhaps the most impressive thing was that the cook had him eating vegetables he didn't recognize without giving it much thought. As he ate, he found he was ravenously hungry.

The more of the stew he consumed, the more he wanted. And he noticed something strange happening. He checked his Health, Stamina, and Mana bars, and they were all refilling rapidly. He still hadn't made a study of how quickly he regained those resources in any precise detail, but he knew this wasn't normal. It had to be the food.

So he kept eating, and he pushed escape to the back of his mind for the moment.

Before he knew it, James had finished all of the food, despite how large the bowl had seemed at first glance. And all of his resources were completely full. The pain in his ribs and nose, which he'd been successfully ignoring since he'd met the brothers, had completely disappeared. He felt better than fully healed.

"I love a young man with a healthy appetite," the woman said approvingly. She walked over to James and rested a hand on his head. "You boys don't be too mean to the young man, now."

Am I in an episode of Dragon Ball? James thought wryly. *One where Son Goku gets to hang out with the gods, eat their food, and complete their tests? Maybe I shouldn't be thinking of escaping. Maybe I'm going to get a big power-up out of this!*

"Up and at 'em, human!" Afudohwedohwe said. "Complete the test successfully or we'll eat you!" He sounded annoyed. *Maybe Afudohwedohwe is jealous that I got to eat all of his Ma's cooking? He could have asked for some.*

"All right," James said, rising and brushing himself off. Without realizing it, he'd been a slightly messy eater, and there were bits of yam on his clothes. "And my name is James. Now, which one of you do I have to fight?"

He got into a fighting stance, fists raised like a boxer's.

The two brothers gave each other a look. Ntikuma's face showed bemused surprise.

"This isn't that kind of Dungeon," Ntikuma said finally.

"You wouldn't want to hurt us delicate spiders, would you?" Afudohwedohwe added.

No comment, James thought. He kind of would like to hurt them if he thought he could. They were imposing random requirements on his visit to Anansi that the Spider God hadn't alluded to in their encounter.

How much experience would the son of a god give? Are they really fragile enough that a human could actually hurt them? He doubted it. They had seemed plenty strong when Afudohwedohwe had to carry James across the savanna. It was a feat James could accomplish well enough himself now, in truth. But they were at least strong enough that it was strange to think of them as "delicate" in any way.

"No, Anansi is a god of wisdom, tricks, and storytelling," Ntikuma continued. "We will test your capacity in two of those three areas. First, you will follow us to the maze."

James swiveled his head around, looking for where a maze might be.

"This way, human," Afudohwedohwe said, shoving him from behind.

The two spider-people escorted him to a large square hole in the ground that wasn't noticeable until the three drew close. There was a stone stairway descending straight down.

So, it's going to be an underground maze, then, James thought. *Fascinating. Makes me glad I'm not claustrophobic.*

"Get ready," Ntikuma said. "I'm going to blindfold you and take you to the center of the maze."

"Just a moment," James said. "I need to mentally prepare."

"We don't have all day, human," Afudohwedohwe said.

"My name is James," James repeated, slightly annoyed. "Don't call me 'human' unless you want me to call you guys 'spider-monsters.' I'm not just some random human."

"Fine, whatever-your-name-is," Ntikuma said. "Hurry up and finish your preparations."

James resisted the urge to repeat his name to the brothers yet again and instead closed his eyes. He thought of how he would solve this problem. A maze should be simple enough. He was good at mazes on paper at least. But there'd probably be a time limit.

He opened his eyes again. "What's the time limit for the maze?"

"If you find your way out at all, you can color me impressed," Afudohwedohwe said.

"Half an hour," Ntikuma answered, shooting an annoyed look at Afudohwedohwe.

Who knew how complex the maze would be? Maybe half an hour was an impossible time span to complete it in.

Time to cheat. The perfect method had occurred to him.

He used Skill Fusion, and he combined Natural Camouflage with Silk Production. He set the duration of the fusion to an hour and a half, just in case he ended up needing it for longer than he expected. The result was Camouflage Silk Production, which the System defined as follows:

[Camouflage Silk Production: Develops a set of organs that can be used to naturally and nearly invisibly produce silk of great tensile strength. Silk is extremely difficult to perceive unless produced in large quantities and layered. Silk can be manipulated via Mana. Some forms of manipulation may compromise the silk's quasi-invisibility. Silk quality can be improved by the infusion of Mana or other energies. Consumes caloric energy and Stamina. Consumes additional forms of energy if the user attempts to produce silk beyond a certain threshold without a break.]

Perfect.

James bent down, pretending to adjust his shoes. In fact, he secured an invisible silk thread to the top of the stone steps that led down into the maze, and he began producing more silk to trail behind him as he moved through the maze.

"Ready!" James declared.

"Finally!" Afudohwedohwe exclaimed. "Even for a human, you're slow! Definitely not the clever one Pop was waiting for."

James held his tongue and looked to the older brother.

Moving his legs more quickly than James could completely track, Ntikuma quickly spun a silken blindfold, which he then pulled over James's eyes. Then he scooped James completely off the ground and began walking, first down the stairs and then into the maze. James found that he quickly lost the ability to keep track of all the twists and turns that Ntikuma took. If not for his high Fortitude, he suspected it would be nausea inducing.

It would take a superhuman sense of direction to notice anything about this place, the way Ntikuma navigates!

The only thing he really noticed was how musty the maze smelled. Like a basement that had sat empty for a century. Or one that was infested with a massive population of spiders.

Also, the maze was pleasantly cool. Like a root cellar.

James never stopped producing thread and trailing it behind him as they went. The trail remained unbroken; he was almost certain.

And it would have to be enough. Ntikuma never slowed, and he seemed to walk for a long time.

Finally, James felt the spider-person's grip change, and then Ntikuma lowered him to the ground.

"Count to ten aloud, and then you can remove your blindfold. Good luck, human! If you fail this test, my brother will probably want to eat you afterward. Try to at least make it near the entrance, though. Otherwise, our cousins who live in the maze might get you!"

Oh shit, is this challenge a mix of combat and intelligence test? James questioned. *I'm pretty sure I can get out of here following the thread.* James still felt the tug of it on his wrist. *I hope it's as invisible as I think it is. It would suck to get caught cheating. Or would it?* The Anansi he was familiar with would definitely cheat.

Aloud, he asked, "Am I expected to fight while finding my way out of the maze?"

"Only if you take a long time," came the impatient voice in reply.

"Fine," James said. He would be quick, then. "One." He counted loudly, his voice echoing slightly in what must have been a small space.

He began counting to ten. There was a sound of scuttling that seemed to come from every direction at once, and James couldn't detect which way the spider-person was moving as he left.

Pretty good ability he has, James thought grudgingly. *My superhuman senses couldn't tell where he went at all.*

He finished the count, and he removed his blindfold.

[First Challenge: Escape Anansi's maze before time runs out!]

[00:29:59]

CHAPTER SIX

Secrets and Lies

James looked all around himself. He was in a small circular chamber with three exits. The diameter of the room was roughly equal to double his current height, and the ceiling stood roughly a foot above his head.

The walls were nondescript smooth gray stone. The room was lit by hundreds of glowing green mushrooms that lined the ceiling and the walls.

James spent a moment trying to trace in his head where he'd heard the spider-person's footsteps, but he quickly gave up. The lighting was bad even for his improved vision, and he couldn't detect any foot markings on either floor or ceiling.

All right. Just need to follow my thread now, right? He still felt it dangle, not quite taut, from his wrist, and he could only hope it was intact all the way to the exit. He was optimistic because he'd never felt the thread break, and he knew from experience just how strong it could be. He immediately felt where the thread was pulling him. It was partly stuck to the ground, partly to a wall, leading toward the exit to his left.

Just in case someone was watching him, he pretended to inspect the three exits to the room. He didn't feel eyes on him, but dealing with a trickster god and his children, you never knew. Feigning reluctance, he headed through the leftmost opening the thread pulled him toward. He tried to be subtle about winding up the thread in his hand as he walked, but he was also very conscious of the timer ticking down at the corner of his vision. He decided that as he moved slightly further away from the starting point, he would have to abandon any pretenses and loop it around his wrist.

He passed through the exit and found himself in a narrow tunnel. As with the room he'd started in, the walls and floor were made of stone. There were openings lining the walls. Many different options to confuse someone who wasn't cheating the maze.

And there was one more thing to be distracted by. As he walked, James's foot would occasionally bump into small smooth, round, opaque objects stuck to the ground. He tried not to pay much attention to anything but the path out, but he gradually realized those objects weren't rocks.

They were eggs. Eggs the size of volleyballs.

Identify.

[Divine Realm Spider Eggs, Lv. 0]

He wasn't sure if this was part of his test somehow, to see if he would spare or destroy these eggs. Or maybe they were the monsters he was threatened with in the event that he failed to complete the maze in time.

In either case, he elected to leave them alone. The eggs were the closest thing to an obstacle in the maze. There were no traps that he came across, only twists and forks in the maze and random gaps and doorways in the walls that could have been confusing if he hadn't been guided by the thread.

As he moved through the maze, he grew more confident. The thread was leading him in a clear direction, and it looked less and less likely that it had been snagged somewhere and severed.

If it had been broken, he wouldn't feel so much tension in the line. The other end would be stuck to some dust somewhere rather than a fixed object.

James decided to speed run the rest of the maze, since he didn't know how far down he was, only that he'd used a lot of thread.

Despite knowing exactly which way to go, escaping the maze took almost the rest of the time he had. Some places were almost fully dark, with barely any glowing mushrooms, and he had only the thread to guide him. It didn't stop him from banging his head or bumping into walls occasionally, though the stone walls took more damage from that than James did.

The timer read **[00:04:59]** when James finally spied sunlight.

He strode up the stairs to the exit confidently, and he met the brothers again.

Afudohwedohwe took a half-step backward as James emerged from the darkness, as if he was surprised to see him. But he recovered quickly.

"Nice job, maze runner!" he said sarcastically. Turning to face his brother, he said, "Can you imagine one of us taking twenty-five minutes to get out of Pop's maze?"

James caught the hidden meaning in what Afudohwedohwe was saying and smirked. Before, they'd compared him to other humans they'd encountered. Now, Afudohwedohwe was comparing James to Anansi's children themselves.

Moving the goalposts means I win, he thought.

But for all that Afudohwedohwe seemed to be hiding his reaction poorly, Ntikuma's expression was unreadable, despite his human head.

"Very well, you seem to have completed the challenge," he said after a moment.

[First Challenge completed!]

"Are you ready to move onto the second challenge?" Ntikuma continued. "The first one was clearly too easy, so I assume you do not need another rest."

Ntikuma's all business, James thought. *I barely completed the maze in time even while cheating, though. How would someone else have managed? Smash up the place? Surely that's not what's intended in the Spider God's Dungeon.*

"Yes, I'm ready," James said.

"Very well," Ntikuma said. "Your next challenge is storytelling. Tell my brother and me a story that impresses us. You have as long as you need."

[Second Challenge: Impress Anansi's sons with a story!]

"Uh, any hints as to what impresses you?" James asked.

"Originality. Artful storytelling. Good stories." His tone was flat, and James began to think he might have made the wrong choice about which brother he wanted to judge him. If Ntikuma was determined to remain unaffected by whatever narrative James presented, then he wouldn't be impressed no matter what kind of story James chose to tell.

After a few minutes of quiet thought, James began his story. He chose to stick to something he knew. He told his own life story in third person, with some parts altered, and some secrets and lies where necessary, to either make his protagonist look better or to conceal traits that would make it obvious who it was.

The three sat in the dust outside, and the two brothers patiently listened as James opened himself up to their scrutiny.

He was telling his story for a long time. It felt as if he entered a state of flow, where he was focused on this one task only, and his usual background thoughts and doubts faded. Parallel Minds tried to focus on other things, and James silently deactivated the Skill. He poured himself into this one thing. He had no idea how long the story lasted, except that his Natural Camouflage and Silk Production Skills had more than enough time to diffuse into their original forms. And he went on beyond that.

Ntikuma seemed attentive, though his expression remained stoic throughout.

Afudohwedohwe kept making distracted and distracting movements. Looking off at things behind James or to the side. Scratching himself. Covering his mouth as though he was stifling a yawn, though James wasn't sure if spiders could even yawn. James tried not to let it distract him, and he thought he largely succeeded.

James wasn't sure if the story had won their hearts and minds, but as he told it, he picked up a couple of levels in Politician and in a few of the associated Skills. Apparently, telling a story to the Spider God's children was enough of a challenge to push him to a new tier in his Job.

And whether he'd impressed the brothers or not, James realized it felt good to tell the story. He was unburdening himself with every event conveyed, every sin confessed, every grievance aired, every worry expressed.

So rare to just be able to talk about yourself, he thought at one point, before realizing that he had lapsed into first person for a moment. He caught himself and brought it back, turned the line he'd just spoken into a line of dialogue in the story he was telling about another person. He'd named his protagonist "John." Not the most original name, but it started with the same letter at least, and it was a good name for a hero.

"Enough," Ntikuma said, cutting him off midsentence. "You have failed." His voice was as bored and neutral as if he was reading from a grocery list.

[Second Challenge failed!]

Was it the change in subject? Because I didn't keep to third person? James knew that he would have judged a story poorly if it included a subject change like that without warning.

"I see," James said. "Was the subject of the story not of interest?"

"You're just a bad storyteller, human," Afudohwedohwe said. The spider-person got up from the ground, stretched, and began pacing back and forth. Ntikuma remained seated, facing James, so James remained in place.

"My name is James," James said, a little needled. "I prefer to be called that, not '*human,*' especially when I know you occasionally eat humans."

"My brother is correct, human," Ntikuma said. "It was flawed from the start."

Well, of course, there's no such thing as a perfect story!

"The two of you certainly let me go on for some time despite how poorly I performed from the beginning."

If you didn't like it, why did you let me talk for well over an hour?

"Well, everyone gets a chance," Ntikuma said evenly. He picked up a chunk of earth on the tip of one of his limbs as he spoke. "We gave you your opportunity, and you flubbed it completely. Your story wasn't original in any way. It was picked-apart scraps from your own banal life. That choice destroyed you, I think. You then told the story in a cowardly way, with no spirit. Your prose was lifeless. Perhaps you have no poetry in your soul. You lied about everything that was important or shed any light on your true character, guarding yourself from imagined criticism or some such vain thing. Not the actions of any real kind of storyteller." As he finished speaking, he turned his limb sideways and let the dirt he'd picked up fall back to the ground. There wasn't a moment in his explanation when he didn't sound bored.

James realized that he felt more than a little upset at what the brothers were saying, but he reminded himself that he had no reason to be. Right? *So they didn't like it. So what?*

It was his life; that was "what." Plus, Anansi had invited him there. He shouldn't have needed to be tested to see the god who had invited him. But he couldn't obsess over that.

Orientation was a limited-time opportunity. He had to get back to things that would be more productive than arguing with Ntikuma and Afudohwedohwe.

I should be grateful for the levels I got in Politician, he told himself. But he felt far from grateful.

"Fine. If I can't see Anansi, take me to the exit," he said, his voice thinner and higher than usual.

"I don't know if we should do that," Afudohwedohwe said instantly. "I don't think we ever said we'd take you back to the exit if you failed." James realized the voice came from behind him.

When did Afudohwedohwe get back there? James was tempted to turn and face him, but Ntikuma was still sitting in front of him, and, absurdly, James didn't want to be rude.

"There are penalties for failure," Ntikuma agreed. His deep brown, almost black eyes met James's and held his gaze.

Sweat broke out on James's forehead. A surge of fear roiled his stomach.

He opened his mouth to speak, but Ntikuma began first.

"You cheated on the first test, and you failed the second outright," Ntikuma said, his stare suddenly menacing. "You didn't think we'd missed that invisible thread, did you?"

Shit. I guess I should've known. They're spider people, after all. For once, James was speechless.

"Stupid human," Afudohwedohwe said from behind him. "To think you really believed you could fool us? Our father is the God of Trickery!"

James rolled his eyes. Insistently, he said, "My name—"

Then he felt a sharp pain in the back of his head.

The world collapsed into black.

CHAPTER SEVEN

Innocence

The camp was alive with the sound of murmurs. People were talking quietly among themselves about the newcomers, and almost as much about who wasn't there.

So, you really didn't come back, Sierra thought. The idea was slightly offensive, for some reason, even more than it was frightening. The people who were capable of killing him were still out there. Still a threat. Maybe even more of a threat now.

So, James was supposed to protect you and the group all the way to the end, and then you'd forgive him for killing me, was that it? David's voice chimed in.

Something like that. She'd never put it to herself in such explicit terms, but, in fact, that was more or less exactly how she'd imagined it. But Sierra quickly put her brother's question from her mind. Talking to the voice inside her head wasn't going to help matters.

She approached Alan to get some real answers about the situation.

"What have the new people been saying?" she asked.

"They're shocked they even made it here," Alan said. "Apparently, James broke them out of their prison and fought the whole cult off by himself to give them an opening to escape." He shook his head and smiled sadly. "A handful of the stronger cultists recaptured them inside of five minutes. Then James used some sort of big magic attack on them before half the cult tore off after him. That was when the lucky ones made their escape."

Sierra winced and then smiled. "Yeah. That tracks. So, when do we expect our dear leader back?"

"Our new friends assume he's dead."

"What about you?"

"I don't know. I don't want to believe it. I just—I don't know."

"I won't believe it unless I see a body."

Alan frowned. "Anyway, they didn't even know who he was or what he looked like, so he at least kept his word about disguising himself. They only knew which way to go because he vaguely pointed them toward us and one of them has a tracking Skill. They followed his trail here. Nevertheless, we're all still agreed on moving. Even more set on it, if possible. The cult may be coming after them."

"I think they have to," Sierra said.

Alan looked at her. She didn't elaborate.

He furrowed his brow and fixed her with a stare. She had the sense that she was under the gaze of someone who could outwait her. Someone who could perhaps wait *forever* to get the answer he wanted. *Alan and Mitzi definitely have a daughter out there somewhere.*

She sighed. "If the cult doesn't come after them, they're just guaranteeing that they'll have more trouble luring in new sacrifices. The escaped prisoners will be running around warning people. The remaining population of Orientation could unite against them. It doesn't matter how strong they are. Even if they killed James, there's no way they would want to fight an army."

"Do you think the others remaining in Orientation would actually fight them?" Alan asked. "Most of us probably want the same thing: to escape this place alive."

"It doesn't matter if the others who are left would actually be willing to fight or not," Sierra replied. "The cult has to take the threat seriously and act accordingly. They can't just hope people won't band together against them. Not when that's probably the only thing that could threaten them here. And I'm sure that god they're sacrificing people to won't be too happy about losing out on offerings, even if people wanted to just avoid confronting them."

"Moloch," Alan said, his tone hard.

"Yeah, um, Moloch."

"You may be right. I had hoped we could get away from this place without any more losses."

Well, hope and eleven dollars will get you a drink at Starbucks, she thought.

But she only shook her head.

"Are we leaving now?" she asked.

"As soon as Cliff and his hunting party return," Alan said. "He thought it would be a good idea to gather some food before the journey."

Sierra looked off toward the column of smoke. "And everyone's accepting the new group? No one's suspicious that they're enemy agents or something?"

Alan looked surprised at the thought. "No, we all just figured there was safety in numbers."

Of course you did, Sierra thought. *One thing I could say for James: he wouldn't have automatically trusted people just showing up at camp.*

She didn't try to hide her skepticism.

"When I visited the camp with James, none of these people were outside, participating in it. Not that I saw, anyway. I figured that was because they were in the underground cell James mentioned." But he sounded much less confident now that she'd pointed out the other possibility.

"Oh, yeah, that's probably right," Sierra said. *At least, hopefully.*

Officer Jeffrey Ross crept around the edge of the camp, trying hard to remain unheard. His footsteps traced a less-trodden path to the area where the wards had been activated.

He snuck up on the unknown individuals, and he kept sneaking even after he recognized them.

Finally, he spoke.

"How goes it?" Officer Ross asked.

Three figures jumped at the sudden noise. The fourth just smirked and shook his head.

"Why do you do that, Officer?" Fatemeh Roshan asked.

"Probably boredom," Mustafa Roshan said immediately. He was the only one who hadn't jumped. "Officer, please remember, just because most of the creatures in this place no longer pose a threat to you, it doesn't mean the rest of us aren't on edge. Especially when wandering the woods without the Prophet's guidance."

"Well, you're home now," Ross said. "You all can afford to let down your guards a bit." The words came out a bit more callously than he'd intended. He wasn't sure why he felt so on edge today.

Maybe it was something he didn't want to think about, bubbling up in the back of his mind. He'd gotten better at avoiding those thoughts over the last two weeks, but that didn't mean he could prevent the associated bad mood.

"This camp isn't especially safe anymore either, though, is it?" Leonard Robie asked. He spoke cautiously, in a lowered voice, but the other three members of the search party all looked his way and scowled. "I mean, we got attacked. Probably by *your* old buddy!" He pointed at Ross.

There it was. That was what bothered Ross. James Robard had reminded him of what he already felt: this camp was completely the wrong place for him to be. Every day that he remained, a little more of his sense of self-worth drained away. *But Catherine . . .*

Philippe Rousseau, who had been silent thus far, looked away from Ross. Mustafa and Fatemeh looked right at him as if waiting for his reaction to Robie's provocation.

Ross decided to pick on Robie a bit to distract himself.

"First, it's rude to point," he said. He grabbed the index finger that was pointing at him in one fist. "Second, whoever attacked us is dead. Very dead. He went off the edge of that cliff that overlooks the void! Multiple people saw it happen, and the Prophet confirmed it. Third, he didn't pose that big of a threat in the first place. He killed a few people and burned a couple of tents. Fourth, the attacker was no friend of mine." He squeezed Robie's finger tight and bent it backward until the other man winced. Then he let go, before the finger could break. "And last, everyone saw you running away when we got attacked. You should be careful what you say, *Lenny*. The Prophet occasionally decides people are no longer of use to the group, after all. And a cowardly guard isn't very useful."

Ross saw Robie swallow hard, and the others also looked nervous at those last pronouncements.

"I assume none of you have good news?" Ross asked.

"We'll tell the Prophet what we discovered," Mustafa said brusquely.

Ross walked with the four of them to where Rostov sat; one of his priestesses was sitting in his lap.

Old habits die hard, eh? Ross thought. His expression hardened. *This man ought to be dead, not enjoying himself.* Ross cast his eyes around discreetly. Catherine wasn't nearby.

"I see we have a report coming," Rostov said. He gently shifted the priestess from his lap to the grass beside him. "Tell me what we know. I can already see you didn't recover the prisoners."

"That's correct, Prophet," Mustafa said uncomfortably. "We bring only information. The prisoners have reached a place of refuge. Another camp, with dozens of people, judging from the number of tents. They seem to be mostly Hispanics. Average level of around three to five."

"Weaker than our camp, then," Ross interjected.

Rostov looked surprised that he was chiming in, but then nodded. "Yes, weaker by a fair margin. You didn't feel comfortable simply retaking the prisoners with a sudden attack?"

"Well, n-no," Mustafa said.

"Given their numbers, it wouldn't have made sense," Leonard Robie added defensively. "And Moishe Rose is one of the prisoners who reached them."

"I see. Then I suppose it really was impossible," Rostov said. Ross couldn't read his expression. The extent of Rostov's patience with groups who failed tasks had not been predictable thus far. But he sounded like he genuinely believed the mission had been too difficult for them.

"What do we do now, sir?" Fatemeh asked.

"Simple. The whole camp will have to mobilize. The fight that was impossible for the four of you will be easy enough for the lot of us." He turned to the priestess next to him. "Tell the other acolytes that they should prepare to finish their prayers on the road." She nodded, rose, and walked away. Rostov's eyes lingered on her for a few long moments as she moved.

"What about the rest of us?" Ross asked.

Rostov's gaze shot up to him. Then Rostov reached a hand up, silently asking Ross to help him to his feet. The officer reached down and pulled Rostov up, though he couldn't restrain a look of annoyance as he did so. He hated the petty power games Rostov played. Just another way to remind Ross of his place.

"The rest of you will prepare to move camp, naturally." He pointed a thumb toward the statue of Moloch, ten feet behind him. "I tasked Rick with constructing a cart to transport that. But we'll need our strongest pairs of hands working together to move it onto the cart."

The statue towered over Ross.

I wish I hadn't asked, he thought. Yet he knew he would comply.

Ross was standing by the statue, waiting for Rick to join him in moving it, when Catherine approached. He saw she was walking from the outskirts of camp, carrying some firewood. She wore her long, dark hair in a bun, a few loose strands framing her kind face.

"How are you today, sweetheart?" she asked.

Better if I saw more of you, he thought, smiling despite how unhappy he was with the present situation.

It was strange how the end of the world as they knew it seemed to be pulling them apart. Catherine spent almost all her time among Rostov's priesthood.

"Just about to get my hands dirty moving this giant statue," he said, tapping Moloch's leg with one knuckle. "And then we're apparently going to go pursue some innocent people we can feed to the fire. But you must already know about those plans."

She winced, and his face mirrored her expression.

"I know you don't like that word," Ross said. "But it's the truth. You know it is."

"It's not that I don't like the word," Catherine said. "Innocence is a fine word. But don't you think we're innocent? We're just normal people trying to survive. Against our wishes, we've been pulled into a world where monsters exist. They want to eat us. Some of them want to do worse. And there's a very real god who can protect us."

"I know," Ross said. "I know." They'd had this conversation more than once already.

"Moloch already saved my life once," she said.

"I know. That's why we're still here." *That's why Rostov is still alive.*

She shifted the conversation. "How do you think the kids are doing?"

He resisted the urge to say something snide, like "Can't Rostov tell us?" But the impulse must have shown through on his face.

"Forget it," she said. "I have faith that we'll find out in time. We just have to live through this." She stepped in close to him, then leaned in so their faces were almost touching. "I need you to do what you have to so we live through this and see our kids again." Her tone was serious—and concerned.

Despite her somber tone, Ross felt a little warmth in his face. He could smell her hair. *How does it still smell like strawberries after two weeks in the woods?* He realized he might be blushing. Catherine still had that effect on him, even after fifteen years.

"I'll do what I have to," he managed, slightly flustered. "You know I always do."

She leaned in to speak directly into his ear.

"I know you hate Nikolai," she whispered. "Just try to hide it a little more for now. Look forward to the *end* of Orientation, all right? We won't need his help forever." She nibbled his ear slightly as she finished speaking.

Even the sound of the cult leader's name on her lips couldn't sour the feelings that rose in him then.

"I understand," he said breathlessly.

Catherine pulled back from his ear. Their eyes met. Two pairs of pupils, dilated.

Her hand came around to the back of his neck, and she pulled him in for a long kiss.

"I love you," she said.

"I love you too."

"To hell with the innocent!" The words were a gasp. From her expression, almost an involuntary exclamation.

He bit his lower lip. Looked into her eyes. Found that he either could not or would not fight her on this anymore. Gave her the slightest nod.

To hell with innocence, he thought. *Nothing else matters. Only us.*

CHAPTER EIGHT

Seven Seconds

James awakened to the sound of low voices. He opened his eyes, but he couldn't see much. He was in a dark room with no windows. He tried to move, but his arms were bound to his sides, and his legs were bound together.

He recognized this feeling from when the Wood Spiders had captured him back in the Orientation forest. He was probably tied up with spider thread again. Who knew how strong it must be if it was generated by these two?

"Should we really do this? Pop will be upset—"

"You said it yourself! This human failed the tests, ergo he isn't the right one. Even if he met with Pop, the old man would just be disappointed that this was the human we brought him. Better to wait until a clever human drifts down here. Pop can be patient."

"Still, to cook him and eat him? What if this really is the human Pop was interested in?"

James realized that it was the two spider-people talking. And he noticed another sound in the background: rapidly rolling bubbles.

"Better to have a good meal than a lame human visitor, anyway," Afudohwedohwe said. "What Pop doesn't know won't hurt him. When he asks what's for dinner, we'll just say pork! It tastes just the same. Someday, years from now, if he's still wondering, we can tell him the truth."

"Well, I suppose," Ntikuma said. "Make sure the water in the pot is good and hot."

How the hell do I get myself into these situations? James asked himself, exasperated. He didn't think he'd misinterpreted Anansi's invitation.

But it was a bit hard to believe that the Spider God had invited him here, mentioned his arrival to his monstrous sons, and yet failed to make any efforts to ensure the safety of his guest.

Maybe Anansi had lied to him. Perhaps he had taken the Spider Queen's death more seriously than James had imagined, so he'd decided to just let his sons take care of James for him. Anansi probably knew how they'd behave in the absence of any strict instructions to avoid eating his guest. Or perhaps it was some weird, drawn-out psychological torture designed just to spite him.

Whatever the motives involved, the situation spoke for itself. James was bound tightly. He was a prisoner, not a guest, as far as these spider-people were concerned.

But at least he wasn't completely helpless. *Predator's Armaments!*

His fingernails turned sharp as razor blades, and he easily ripped a hole in the webbing near his hands. It took him several minutes of cutting, but finally, he freed himself completely.

Fortunately, they didn't use the sort of golden thread that giant web was made from, or I'd never have gotten loose. Now, how to get out of here?

Fight or flight time, but he wasn't sure how to do either one. The children of Anansi would surely be much stronger than him, and they had no obvious weaknesses. And if he wanted to flee, he didn't even know how to escape from this room unseen.

In the time that James had been struggling to free himself, he'd heard Afudohwedohwe go over to the pot and check it. James estimated from the sounds of movement that the water was boiling on the other side of the wall near where he lay.

Afudohwedohwe said, "Water needs another few minutes to be hot enough. It only just started really bubbling."

"Fine," Ntikuma said.

From that point on, James didn't hear any further signs of life from the brothers. They could have been just outside the door of the room where James was listening, or they could have wandered off anywhere else. As long as they were trying to walk quietly, he had no confidence that he'd pick them up.

James decided not to risk opening the door to the next room. Instead, he would try Skill Fusion again. This time, he combined Basic Elemental Magic: Earth with Natural Camouflage, producing Camouflaged Earth Magic.

He began casting. He sat in silence for almost a full minute, gathering power. Then he placed his hand on the wall furthest from where the water was boiling, and the material of the wall began to reshape itself according to his Will. A small block of wall separated itself from the rest, and James slowly, quietly pushed it outward. He lowered his hands, and they came to rest on clumps of yellow-green grass.

Thank all the gods but Anansi that this was an exterior-facing wall! he thought. He pushed a bit further until the block was far enough away that he had room to emerge through the hole. He stuck his head out first to get a good look at the surrounding environment.

He was outside of the house, back in the savanna. No spider-people around. No people of any kind. Nor animals.

He pulled himself completely out of the house and did a full 360-degree rotation to make sure there was no obvious threat he was missing. But there was nothing.

He began the long trek back to the exit. He could almost see the point he'd entered from when the brothers carried him in. The big advantage of not having to walk or run the whole way, in retrospect, was that he'd simply watched the scenery. Now that he had to navigate his way back, he found that he remembered many landmarks, despite this having seemed like a nearly flat, almost featureless savanna landscape on first entry.

It had seemed at first almost like stepping into a nature documentary. But his mind remembered more than he would have expected. There was a particularly crooked tree here, an oblong watering hole there, a massive termite mound a bit further on.

Keeping low, he tried to remain hidden in the long grass or behind the occasional tree where he could. And he gained distance quickly. He had no desire to be eaten. The only thing that slowed him down was the priority of remaining unseen. That was critical, given that he was all but certain the brothers could outrun him.

He occasionally stopped and looked back, just to see if there was any sign of pursuit. Every time was the same. No one seemed to be coming after him. But he was sure that the brothers would, eventually. Perhaps they were delayed, because it would surely take time for them to notice he had escaped.

Finally, he began to get closer to his destination. He could actually see the small hole in the sky where Anansi's realm met the Orientation world. It looked like a small target from so far away. But the real problem was below.

James immediately dropped to the ground as soon as he spied them.

Both of them came. Of course they did. They knew this was my only way out.

Afudohwedohwe and Ntikuma stood back-to-back beneath the opening. Blocking his escape route.

Goddamn it! What the fuck?

James had a quiet, contained tantrum. A stream of curses ran through his mind as he looked at the two figures. The only motion he made associated with those feelings was slowly grinding his fist into the dirt beneath him.

Finally, he lowered himself all the way to the ground, and he slowly crawled sideways until he was shielded from view behind a group of rocks.

Okay. How do I get around them now? he asked himself. There was only one idea that immediately presented itself to him as possible. However, attempting this plan would be extremely painful, so he was reluctant.

He reviewed his Skill descriptions just to make sure the idea actually had a chance of working. Seemingly, it did.

Finally, he gritted his teeth and accepted that he didn't have any better options. First, he produced a large quantity of silk, infusing it with Mana to make it as strong and sticky as possible. Then came the painful part. He drew a dagger in his right hand and infused Mana into his left arm. Then he raised the dagger, lifted it over his left arm, and swung it down with as much force as he could.

He chopped the left arm off at the elbow. The pain cut through his resistance, and he almost bit through his tongue as he restrained himself from crying out.

His first order of business was regenerating the lost limb. He accomplished that while gritting his teeth and focusing on his survival.

Then he began manipulating the silk and the severed arm.

"Bro, do you see that?" Afudohwedohwe asked.

"I have exactly two eyes, smartass, and they're both in the front of my head," Ntikuma said without turning. "Maybe you could describe what you're seeing so I don't have to turn my back on the side of the savanna I'm watching."

"Right, right," Afudohwedohwe said. He didn't get insulted anymore when Ntikuma said those things. As his father had told him years ago, his big brother was just jealous that he was the handsome one. "Well, there's someone or something running through the long grass in front of me. It's not exactly close, and it's getting further away. It's keeping low, so I can't see it well. But the skin tone is definitely the same as our visitor's."

"I see what you're saying," Ntikuma said. "You think he saw us out in the open like this and now he's running away."

"Yeah. Where can he really go, though?" Afudohwedohwe asked.

"It's a big world," Ntikuma said. "We can't embarrass Pop by letting this drag on too long, right? You should probably get after him. I'll stay and keep watch here."

"You sure, bro? What if I lose him, and he comes back?"

"You don't think I can handle one solitary guy, little bro? Don't insult me!"

"Fine, whatever you say. I'm going!" Afudohwedohwe said.

And Afudohwedohwe took off into the long grass.

Once Afudohwedohwe left, James took his opportunity.

Ntikuma was no longer standing facing in one direction. He walked in small circles, trying to get a good view of all sides. He was muttering something to himself under his breath, which was indistinct due to the distance that separated them.

As James crawled closer across the ground, he continued listening and watching Ntikuma's lips. When James was halfway to the spider, he finally realized what he was muttering.

"I know you're coming. Hit me with your best shot."

Fine. Not a problem. As long as Afudohwedohwe didn't come back—and James's Flesh and Earth Golem, made from his arm using Monster Generation, indicated it was still being chased—it didn't matter too much if Ntikuma knew he was coming. Let the spider-person focus on James's approach.

It would only increase the likelihood that James's plan would actually work.

He began Silent Spellcasting, gathering wind Mana around himself.

After around thirty seconds of gathering Mana, he deactivated Natural Camouflage. Just to make sure Ntikuma saw him, he rose from his prone position. When James was on his feet, Ntikuma turned fully toward him.

"So, you've finally decided to fight like a man?" Ntikuma asked. His face didn't show a trace of surprise.

They were taunting me the whole time, James thought. *Trying to provoke a fight for some reason. I don't know how I failed to see it sooner.*

"That's right," he said. "Assuming you don't need your brother to bail you out. A one-on-one fight, just you and me."

"Ha! You've got jokes!" Ntikuma snorted. "Did you forget that I was the big brother?"

He took a few steps down from the slightly elevated piece of land he stood on. Then he frowned.

"What did I just step—" He looked down, clearly confused at what he was seeing.

"Gotcha," James said. It was almost under his breath, but it returned Ntikuma's attention to him in an instant.

"You did this!" Ntikuma exclaimed. He tried to lift his leg, and it barely moved. A creature made of silk was wrapped around it, clinging to two legs with one half of its body and a big chunk of rock with the other. The Silk Golem wasn't particularly pretty. It looked like a straw doll, except with eight limbs instead of four. But it wasn't any uglier than the tar baby from the folk tale that had inspired this part of the plan.

James estimated the Silk Golem wouldn't hold Ntikuma for long. *Seven seconds at most?*

He took off, letting the wind carry him up and away, toward the hole in the sky. Below him, he was barely cognizant of Ntikuma's movements. The spider-person was frantically working to dislodge himself from the creature that gripped his legs.

It shouldn't be easy, James thought. The only Skills his creation had inherited from him were Natural Camouflage and Predator's Armored Defense—the fusion of Predator's Armor and Adamant Defense. The Silk Golem wouldn't live for long, but what life it had, it would expend in slowing Ntikuma down.

Ntikuma yelled for his brother while he grappled with the creature. "Afudohwedohwe! Afudohwedohwe, you pot-bellied fool! He's escaping! Get back here!"

James smiled. The Flesh-and-Earth Golem had led Afudohwedohwe on a merry chase. There was no way he would return in time to help Ntikuma.

As he closed in on the portal, he sensed motion beneath him. He looked down without pausing in his forward motion. Ntikuma was leaping up toward him, pulling the Silk Golem and the giant rock that it clung to behind him.

I almost didn't account for how impossibly strong Anansi's children were, James thought. Ntikuma was moving much faster than he was, despite dragging a massive weight behind him. *Seven seconds was a wildly optimistic projection for how long he'd be distracted with the golem.* But despite his overly optimistic projection, James still had a big head start.

The spider-person rocketed upward toward him through the sky.

Ntikuma's long spider limbs came within inches of grabbing James's ankle. He felt the movement of air from around Ntikuma's body. James lifted his ankle slightly, just in case. Just to put himself a little more out of reach of those grasping limbs.

And then James was through the opening.

He found himself in darkness, but it wasn't the darkness of the void. It was the darkness of a thunderstorm, lit by occasional bolts of lightning.

There was the sound of drums, rain sticks, and strings playing coming from all directions.

James's eyes narrowed.

Anansi.

CHAPTER NINE

Limelight

Mina recalled how the System Homunculus had explained magic as she charged her Mana.

It was the first time she'd practiced outside the tutorial. Not counting some fuzzy memories from her dream last night.

Activate the Skill. Basic Elemental Magic: Water! Speak the words that come into your mind. Let your body go with the feelings that rise in it to accompany the words. Hold the image in your head of the shape and the action that you want from the Mana. This is not real water until it materializes from your Will. You control the quantity, the momentum, the shape, the form. Imagine what you require, and let your magic grant your wish.

Mina pictured what she wanted. Her mind had always been sharp. Even with pregnancy-brain making it more difficult to focus, her vision was more specific than the average person's.

She held her hand out, trigger finger pointed outward. She felt the energy concentrate around her fingertip, and she focused on holding it. Aiming it. Using the exact amount of Mana she wanted to spend. Precise. Careful. Controlled.

She released it, and a stream of water shot from her finger at high speed.

It struck the thin branch Mina had been aiming at. She was pleased to see the wood bend, then slowly break under the pressure. The little branch fell to the ground.

Hardly any Mana spent, she thought. *I could do that another ten or fifteen times.*

"Um, that was cool, sis," Yulia said. She sounded a bit bored.

Mina's face colored slightly. "Well, you wanted me to show you."

"I was hoping that if you showed me, I could figure out how to do it too." Yulia's tone was slightly apologetic.

"Well, the way the System Homunculus explained it . . ." Mina described the simple process she'd gone through to conjure the stream of water.

"Uh-huh." Yulia's expression was closed off.

I'm not doing well at teaching this, Mina recognized. Was there another way to explain it that would allow Yulia to actually use magic, or was she going to be stuck with pure healing forever? Certainly, those Skills would make her valuable to the group, but it didn't sound particularly exciting. And it would effectively sideline Yulia in any conflicts, which could be a problem with James off in some other place.

The two women sighed, then looked at each other. Mina chuckled quietly, and Yulia smiled. *At least we have each other.*

"Hey, have you two found a team to work with yet, or are you just standing out here hoping not to be picked?" Detective DaSilva's voice cut through the frosty air.

Mina checked the timer before she answered: **[00:08:38]** remaining. It was probably time to rejoin the group.

"We walked over here to practice our marksmanship," she said. "We want to make sure we're ready for the competition. I'm not assuming we'll have anyone to team up with, but my sister and I will manage, thank you."

"Well, you do actually have interest from at least a couple of people," DaSilva said. He pointed a thumb at himself. Next to him stood the blonde woman from before. *Cara?*

"We think we have a few other people lined up to join us," Cara said. "With you, almost enough for a team maybe?"

"Are we going to join them?" Yulia asked quietly from just behind Mina.

"Why would you want us in your group?" Mina asked. "A pregnant woman and a teenager. Aren't you afraid we'll slow you down?"

"It's just for now," DaSilva said, slightly exasperated at her skepticism. "If it works out, maybe we keep working together. Truth is, you're the only people I'm pretty sure aren't this killer."

That's right, Mina thought. In the excitement of preparing for this competition, she'd almost forgotten there had been a murder last night. Almost. *He can't have many people to trust. Just like us.*

"Identify says you two haven't leveled up yet," DaSilva went on. "We've got our only witnesses here too." He gestured to Cara Dahlhaus. "And I think the medical examiner will be with us. Add a few additional people, and we've got a complete team. It's too early to really know the strengths and weaknesses of the group, plus we don't know what kind of challenges we'll face beyond today. This early it only makes sense to form teams based on the possibility of establishing some kind of mutual trust. For me that boils down to the people I trust to help me with my investigation."

Interesting methodology for picking a team, Mina thought. *Since it helps us, I won't say anything against it.* She felt a little guilty about taking advantage of DaSilva's apparent good nature, but she reminded herself that she didn't have James to lean on here. She would just have to pull her weight on the team and make her inclusion into a genuinely wise choice.

"We will join you, then," she said quickly. "I don't think we introduced ourselves. I'm Mina Danailova, and this is my sister Yulia."

"It's a pleasure to meet you both." The detective gave them a warm smile.

They all walked back to the crowd together. Mina had walked some distance away, in the opposite direction from where the murder victim's coat had been discovered, to avoid anyone seeing her practice her magic. But now it was almost time to compete.

DaSilva waved to someone in the crowd, and Mina saw several people break away and move toward their group.

She recognized Adelaide Davis, a large Black man who shared similar facial features with Adelaide, and the man who had been with Cara when she discovered the dead man's coat. There were a few others who were not familiar to her: two Latino teenagers and two slow-moving senior citizens. Frankly, it didn't look like a very strong crew on the surface.

At least I don't feel as much like I'll be holding them back, Mina thought.

The group from the crowd completed their walk. It felt like a very slow march to Mina as she stood with the others and watched. And the team was complete.

"All right," DaSilva said, looking to the corner of his vision. "Who are our marksmen in the group?" He seemed eager to discuss strategy quickly, and Mina couldn't blame him. Taking the time to recruit her and Yulia had been a strange choice.

[00:06:48] remained. It seemed like enough time, but only if the group actually agreed on a strategy. If they had to argue about who would do what, then even the fifteen minutes of time they'd had at the start might not be enough to settle it.

Mina raised her hand without hesitation, while everyone else shuffled their feet and looked at each other.

"You?" DaSilva couldn't keep the doubt out of his voice. "I mean, I guess it's you and me, then."

"As long as the proctor is telling the truth about no time limit," Mina said. "I'm planning to shoot magic at the targets."

"Oh, okay," DaSilva looked relieved. "You were just practicing that, right? I guess you feel pretty confident?"

Mina simply nodded. She didn't want to say she'd be more comfortable with the gun she had under her jacket, because she didn't want anyone to know about that yet. And she didn't want to waste bullets. The stream of water she'd fired had behaved closely enough to her previous experience with guns that she was confident in her ability to aim accurately.

"We'll take turns, then," DaSilva said. "No one else wants to give it a try, I suppose?" There was little acknowledgement from the other team members. Just grunts and nods.

Mina realized that everyone else was at least as nervous as she and Yulia were. She took deep breaths. *Just relax. You're not any worse off than anyone else here for now. It's a marksmanship competition. Probably the only competition where the physical disadvantages of being pregnant won't be a big deal.*

The child within her wiggled as she took the calming breaths, and Mina smiled to herself and placed a hand over her stomach. *You just stay still while mommy shoots*, she thought.

Friggin' Christ, Leon DaSilva thought as he watched the pregnant woman and her teenager. *It's just me and this lady we have to work with. Still, it could be worse. One thing I already know is that she's not stupid.* Which meant she probably wasn't overestimating herself by much. *We'll probably do all right.*

Whether the team Adelaide and Derek had selected would be any good for future challenges was a separate question. But if they weren't, it was DaSilva's fault for letting two people he barely knew decide who he was tied to.

Time ticked down as DaSilva questioned and doubted everyone in his team but himself, and the proctor reappeared. She stood in the same spot as in her previous appearances.

If someone ever wants to do something like try and kill the proctor as she appears, he thought, *they know exactly where to stand.*

[Hello again, everyone! Congratulations to all of you on forming teams. Please form single-file lines with the members of your team, starting here.]

She gestured at a long gash in the ground, cutting through the snow at her feet. DaSilva had not noticed it before. He suspected it had only appeared when the proctor needed it. *Scary reality-warping powers.*

[Participants in the challenge, you will want to be nearer the front of the line.]

DaSilva gestured for Mina to stand in front of him. *Ladies first*, he thought.

He let the other rabble fall where they might in the line behind them. Their order didn't matter for this challenge. He simply checked once he was in place to make sure they formed a single-file line behind him. Everyone seemed to straighten up a little when he turned to look at them, which was good to see. At least they were taking this seriously. Even the teenagers.

There was a small lag as the less disciplined groups got into line and squabbled over the order they would stand in. Finally, once all was settled, the proctor spoke again.

[Thank you for your quiet compliance. You will be competing with your direct neighbors. Half of the teams participating in this challenge will receive food. And yes, for those of you wondering, it is too late to move now, so I would not waste my energy if I were you. The System has marked your positions, so prepare to be transported.]

Transported? Like we're getting on a bus somewhere, or beam me up, Scot—

DaSilva suddenly found himself in a different place entirely.

—ty? Wait, what the fuck?!

He stood on a cliff's edge. The wind whistled all around him, and he felt compelled to take a step back from the edge, for his own safety. In truth, perhaps there was no real risk of falling. He wasn't that close to the edge, right?

Others in the group murmured in tones of vague alarm as they looked out at the obvious height of the cliff's edge where they were placed.

Why did it have to be at this height? he thought. *Just don't look down. Right? Then it'll be fine.*

He swallowed hard. *Don't look down, don't look down—*

A hand fell on his shoulder, and he quickly spun around. It was Mina.

"Be careful, sneaking up on me like that!" DaSilva exclaimed, louder than he meant to.

"I just wanted to ask if you were all right," she said in her slight Slavic accent. To her credit, she seemed totally unruffled by his reaction.

"I'm not a big fan of heights," he admitted. "Doesn't seem like we'll have much time to adapt, though."

The proctor had just popped into existence directly to his right, and he was suddenly conscious of the other group. They had appeared at some point, on the other side of the proctor. They were also looking around, clearly a bit surprised by the shift in settings.

"Now's a great time to show everyone how brave you are," she said encouragingly. She had a bright smile, and as he looked into her bright, thoughtful, yet trusting eyes, DaSilva felt a little of his calm returning.

"Thank you," he said quietly.

[Participants in the challenge, your targets will begin appearing in the next thirty seconds. They will appear more quickly over time. The goal is for your team to strike the most targets possible before you run out of your twenty-four shots. The amount of force used is irrelevant. Any physical contact will register with the System. Any physical or Mana-constructed object that crosses over the cliff will register as a shot. You will need to take environmental factors into account.]

The proctor gestured at the sky above them, and DaSilva saw that in addition to the wind he'd noticed already, it looked like it was about to rain.

[No one may cross this line during the challenge. Further, you must remain on the cliff for the duration of the competition. No flying, burrowing underground, or otherwise leaving the ground of this cliff. Likewise, you cannot manipulate the earth below you to create additional ground to walk on. Following those parameters, strike as many targets as you can. Once you have run through your team's number of shots, any further projectiles from your side will be stopped by a barrier. If you attempt to fire additional projectiles and activate the barrier, you will be docked points for cheating.]

DaSilva now noticed that there was a white line on the ground that separated his group from the other team. *Thankfully*, he thought. The other team, once he had the chance to actually look at them, turned out to be a bunch of strapping young men of a few different ethnic groups and only two women, both young and healthy-looking.

This group had clearly emphasized physical fitness in selecting their members. DaSilva hoped it wouldn't pay off for them in this challenge.

As he looked at them, one of the other team raised his hand to ask a question.

[What is your question?]

The proctor sounded slightly impatient.

"Is there any punishment for losing?" asked a long-haired blond guy a little nervously.

[The punishment is that you receive no reward, and the setting of this Orientation is a hostile environment with scarce food that would naturally be difficult to survive.]

[With the questions answered and rules established, you may begin!]

Everyone instinctively turned to face the cliff, and the targets began appearing: pale, off-white balloons with bullseyes painted on them. They floated up from below the cliff and then began drifting further away, moving slightly with the breeze.

DaSilva noticed that Mina was gathering a blue aura around herself immediately, and he reacted in kind. She would probably take at least a few seconds to gather enough energy for what they needed.

He pulled his gun from its holster and fired at the furthest balloon he saw. It exploded, and he smiled. *At least the first challenge is something fun. I wonder if I'll be able to line them up and shoot through two at once.*

He only got to fire two more shots.

The pregnant woman surprised him. As he fired his third shot, he sensed rapid movement from his side. When he turned, he caught sight of the first burst of water moving surprisingly fast. It struck a close balloon.

Then another burst of water. Another. And another.

They came almost rapid-fire, and she was consistently accurate.

It was almost scary. If the little bursts of water hadn't been golf ball sized, he would have considered them extremely dangerous. The speed was comparable to a high-pressure water hose.

The negative for the other team was that they had reacted slightly slower, and they were competing for the same targets as Mina and DaSilva.

With Mina wiping out most of the early balloons, the other team ended up having to scramble to get shots off at the balloons that had floated up at more difficult angles. They were also further away, having drifted with the wind.

Mina stopped shooting, breathing heavily and sweating visibly, after thirteen shots. DaSilva was there with a Mana Potion, and he fired a few more shots before she drank the draught and recharged. He was in no rush to empty his pistol, though, considering that Mina had struck every target she'd aimed at, and he had no way to replenish his bullets. *I guess I should expect a lot of pleasant surprises from this lady.*

He wished his own daughter had been willing to learn shooting from him. Wherever Carrie was, she wasn't performing like this stranger, who probably did not have a cop father to show her how to shoot.

Finally, Mina charged her blue Mana again, and she shot their last few shots. She only missed once, which he guessed was probably from fatigue. She was panting like she'd just run a quarter mile by the time she finished, a few drops of sweat sparkling on her temples. He hadn't realized magic would require any effort. But maybe it was a struggle to focus and aim so precisely.

Despite the cost to her physically, the results were remarkable. DaSilva had no doubt their team had won. The other team had shots left, but speed had ended up mattering as much as accuracy here since both teams were shooting at the same pool of targets, and there were only around forty in total. The few targets that remained had already drifted out of easy reach.

DaSilva could hear groans of frustration from the other side of the white line.

"You're a natural," he murmured to Mina appreciatively.

"Spent . . . a lot of time . . . at the firing range with . . . husband," she said as she tried to catch her breath. She slowly lowered herself to the ground and sat.

Ah, if she wasn't so obviously taken, I'd be thinking that she could be the third Mrs. DaSilva.

"Yeah, it really shows," he said.

The other team fired a few more useless shots across the cliffside, including a fireball almost the size of a man, which made DaSilva's eyes pop open.

I doubt Mina could do that, he thought. *It's a good thing this wasn't a contest about destructive power. Or a gladiatorial match . . .*

[The challenge is completed!]

The proctor appeared. She gestured at DaSilva's team.

[Your team is victorious! Congratulations!]
[Heavy Warrior leveled up!]

I hardly did anything, DaSilva thought. But he wouldn't complain about an easy level. It was obvious enough that these would be critical in the days and weeks to come. *I hope my helpers took note of who had levels* before *the challenge . . .*

[In addition to experience and the glory of victory, please enjoy your well-earned provisions!]

Bulging sacks of provisions popped into existence in midair next to each of the members of the winning team.

"Aw, hell yeah!" DaSilva heard one of the teenagers yelling. He shook his head. *No sense in gloating within earshot of the other team. Just asking for trouble.*

[Once the other teams have completed the challenge, you will all be transported back to the Orientation setting.]

The proctor seemed to pop back out of existence again.

Everyone on Mina's team gathered around her.

"Great job, sis!" Yulia exclaimed.

"You were amazing," Cara said.

The elderly couple murmured their agreements.

One of the Latino teenagers started to move as if to punch her arm, then thought better of it and gave her a fist bump instead.

"Well, thank you, folks. I did miss one when the baby kicked," Mina admitted modestly. "And I'm happy we won too. But I really think we should share this." She nodded her head in the direction of the other team.

The mood of the group changed immediately.

"No way!" one of the teenagers said.

"You won it for our team fair and square," the elderly gentleman objected mildly.

"Are you sure about this, ma'am?" DaSilva asked skeptically.

"We need to set a good precedent," Mina said. "We might not win the next competition."

And just as importantly, she thought, *if we don't share now, there's every possibility that they will attack us later to get some food. That's what I would expect James to do in a parallel situation. You can't mess around about food.*

The System, it seemed to her, was trying to force the Orientation participants into that exact situation. That was how they might get a breakdown of order.

That breakdown wouldn't happen if she had anything to say about it.

CHAPTER TEN

The Night Watch

Nikolai Rostov's eyes focused once more.

He blinked twice and tried to clear the frustrated look from his face as quickly as possible. This had been one of his least productive conferences with Moloch since he became the god's Chosen One. Moloch cared little for the happiness of his instruments, as only became more apparent with each contact.

I'd think he would at least be interested in helping me recover the escaped prisoners. But no. If you want something done right . . .

"Where are we in the pursuit?" he asked brusquely.

Beside him on the cart, along with the statue of Moloch, sat Alice, the priestess he'd gotten to know the previous night. Happily, he could remember her name now.

She shifted nervously at his obvious displeasure. "I understand that we are drawing near the enemy's campsite, as pinpointed by our spies, Prophet."

He let out a gentle sigh. "What did I tell you before, Alice?"

"Yes, sir—yes, Nikolai. Niko. I'll call you by your given name when we're alone." She contorted her face into a forced smile. The ugliness of the false gesture on her otherwise charming face brought a scowl to Rostov's lips.

He looked away, not wanting her to realize she'd displeased him further. This relationship was awkward enough without her stumbling over apologies.

Sometimes I think operating a religious organization isn't worth all the headaches. Maybe the Chosen One of Apophis had the better end of things after all. Just go around causing as much chaos and destruction as possible. That, at least, sounds like fun.

"My Prophet, we are closing in on the camp!" Kassim's voice presented itself, and then his face became visible as he rounded the side of the cart.

"I'm ready for action, Kassim," Rostov said. "The priesthood is just waiting for the laity to get results!" He tried to sound peppy and witty, but the tenor of his voice instead felt sour and impatient. It was as if his Charisma had taken a hit with the humiliating attack on their camp. Perhaps it had. Stats were functionally magical, after all, not something that followed logical rules.

"We're onto the enemy camp!" a voice called.

Rostov sat up straighter and looked around.

"They've abandoned it!" another voice reported. The cart that carried Rostov and Alice pulled forward into a cleared area, and then they could see the campsite for themselves.

The Prophet's eyes confirmed the obvious. The grass was flattened everywhere, indicating that a camp had clearly been made there. There were stumps from where humans had removed trees that were in their way. There were even small piles of wood where someone had clearly intended to light or feed a fire.

But there were no tents, no sleeping bags, no burning fires, and no camping supplies of any kind. Nothing but—

What the hell is that doing there?

A single gray fur blanket remained near the middle of the cleared area. It lay almost flat on the ground, slightly ruffled, as if someone had laid it out to sleep on, used it, and then forgotten it when the camp moved on.

Definitely belonged to someone in this camp. Hell, maybe that was our intruder's property. If he left to fight us, he would've known it was probably a one-way trip. Maybe he told his people to move along after he left. He gave them a rendezvous point, and they went on their way. But this blanket was left behind?

There was something wrong with this explanation. *Assuming he was meant to return if he could, why would they leave his property lying there? This man was going on a probable suicide mission. Heroically sacrificing himself to save a bunch of strangers. Yet it seems a distinctly disrespectful way to treat his remaining possession. And if it didn't belong to our intruder, then who left a perfectly good fur—*

His thought process was interrupted by someone stepping into his line of sight. Rick stood there, all six and a half feet of him, looking down at the fur quizzically. He bent—

"No, you idiot, don't!"

But before the words were all the way out of his mouth, the Flame Sprite had picked up the fur by the corner. For a moment, nothing happened. Rick turned his head toward Rostov, as if realizing the warning might have been directed at him. His expression was dumbfounded.

Then there was a bright flash of light.

The whole cult was blinded for a few seconds. Their eyes, adjusted to the twilight haze, were unprepared for the sudden flare-up in their midst.

Rostov was immune to this effect, as were his three higher ranked priests. And Officer Ross seemed unaffected, too, on the other side of the cart from Rostov. He'd been wearing sunglasses despite the low lighting.

"Well, at least now I know why that was left there," Rostov thought aloud.

It means we're on the right track, and they're afraid of being caught. They can't be a very formidable force, if they're worried enough to leave a feeble trap like that. But the prisoners have definitely warned them as to how dangerous we are. Would they have taken the prisoners in? Almost certainly, if they're the same people that produced our intruder. And there's little upside to sending them on their way since the larger group will inevitably produce the easier to follow trail. Not to mention the strength in numbers factor. So, they'll be traveling together . . .

He looked to the setting sun. It had taken them so much time to get here. *Our prey must have a pretty good lead.*

Do I order the group to continue and give chase through the night, hoping that we catch up to them by sunrise? If we catch up to them sooner, they might have an edge over us without the sun as our ally. It might be safer if we camp here and march at first light.

He shook his head irritably at that flicker of doubt.

No, we defeated that intruder despite the cover of darkness! There can hardly be others as exceptional as him in this forest.

"Everyone! Clear your eyes and prepare to move out immediately. I want my trackers to take the lead again. This is a significant group of people moving now. It should be much easier to follow their trail than it was chasing a few prisoners."

"My sincerest apologies, sir, I—" Rick groveled in Rostov's general direction, clearly unable to see where the Prophet was.

"Don't concern yourself about it, Rick. No harm done." Rostov infused his voice with the usual calm, cool tone he'd trained himself to deliver on command. "You've only revealed the other camp's weakness more profoundly than I could've expected."

All according to plan, nothing to worry about, nothing to see here.

"We're really moving out now?" Officer Ross questioned. "You know we might end up having to fight in the dark if we're lucky enough to find them. Or we could lose our trail. Fall into a trap. There are a dozen different things that could go wrong. We're putting ourselves at a big disadvantage by going out when the sun's going down, isn't that right?"

Rostov noted that the officer was actually speaking discreetly, with a lower voice. As if he wanted to ensure the exchange was a private one between the two of them. And he actually appreciated Ross's effort to be somewhat cooperative for a change. So, he decided to pretend to be nice.

"Please, calm yourself, Officer." Rostov tried to be reassuring. "Have a little faith. This is an absolutely necessary mission, and we can't afford to fall far behind our prisoners. If we get close, we'll make a battle plan and figure out how to lay our ambush."

Internally, he was fuming.

We're going to find these fuckers! Rostov thought. *We're going to recover Moloch's sacrifices. Hell, we'll bring back more than we lost! We'll crush whoever's helping them. And we're going to do it, even if it's the longest night of your life!*

"We have a decision to make," Alan said. "Do we make camp around here, or do we try to press on further in the darkness?"

"Do we really have a choice?" Mitzi asked. She looked around them and saw the same things that Alan could see.

The sun had just set. The whole group was exhausted. Everyone wanted to sleep. Some people were already taking out axes and kindling as if they wanted to begin felling trees and making campfires before a decision had been made.

"No fires. They might be watching us through the fires," Chava said, voice ringing through the camp.

"Is it really safe to make camp now *at all*?" Camila's voice echoed after, concerned and wavering.

"Well, they're a sun cult, right?" Chava asked. He sounded uncertain. "Will they really come after us now? At night? We don't even know for sure that they're pursuing us, anyway."

"I think Chava raises a good point—" Cliff began, but he stopped as Ramon stepped forward.

The young Rogue walked up between two trees near where the elders stood. "They set off the trap," he said quietly. "The one that I laid in the blanket we left behind."

All of the elders turned and stared at him.

"You're sure?" Alan was the first to speak.

"Absolutely," Ramon said confidently. "I can only set a certain number of traps. The number doesn't reset unless I use them up. That means I have to deactivate one, or it has to be set off. This one was set off. So, unless someone else stumbled on our last campsite . . ."

"We have no reason to imagine that," Cliff murmured. "So, they're really after us. And they won't stop until they get those prisoners back. If only James hadn't gone to fight the cultists—"

"That's enough of that, Cliff," Alan said. His voice had a flinty edge to it, though he spoke quietly. "Can we please focus on solving the goddamn problem?"

"Sure, sure," Cliff's tone turned mild. He raised his hands as if in surrender. "What do you propose we do now, then?"

"Ramon, would you be able to scout the outskirts of the camp for us?" Camila asked. "Maybe we can't camp for the whole night, but I think most of our family is exhausted and scared. If they could get even a few hours of sleep, they might be able to walk the rest of the night on that."

"Of course I can." Ramon smiled sweetly and took her hand.

"I'll go with him." Moishe Rose stepped out of the shadows. His tone was flat, his expression grim.

No one wanted to contradict him.

"The more, the better," Ramon said after a brief pause. He extended his hand, and Moishe shook it. They introduced themselves. Then they walked away to leave the elders to their planning.

"Hopefully, we can trust that Rose guy," Cliff muttered. "Do we really know that none of these prisoners is a plant?"

Alan just shook his head. *We might all die tonight. But it feels like we're in good hands.*

"Nice to meet you, Ramon," Moishe said as they walked.

"The pleasure is all mine."

"No, if we get to kill some of the cultists, the pleasure will really be all mine," Moishe said.

"Remember that our first job is to warn the camp," Ramon said. "If we have to kill some of the folks who held you captive along the way, I'm glad we can do it. They sound like some real pieces of work. But my family comes before your revenge."

Moishe looked at Ramon levelly for a long, slightly tense moment.

"Of course," he said at last. "No matter how much I want to get back at those bastards for what they did to my sister, I can never forget the debt I owe your leader. Your camp will come first."

"Our leader?" Ramon looked confused for a moment. "Oh, you mean— so you believe James is still alive? The others who came from the cultist camp seemed pretty convinced he died."

"Maybe they couldn't see what I saw in him," Moishe said. "I'm sure he's coming back."

"We'd all like to imagine that's true, I think. But why do you sound so certain?"

"Hm." Moishe tried to sum up the reasons. "I guess just the look in his eyes. Hard as nails. I've known soldiers before. Including special forces guys. His eyes reminded me of theirs. And then he blew up half of that SOB's camp with one crazy spell. That guy's a real badass. And incredibly powerful. I won't believe he's dead unless I see it happen."

"Huh." Ramon had no immediate response. After a few seconds, he said,

"Must be nice to have that much faith in someone." Another pause. "I really hope he comes back."

They walked away from the camp for almost an hour, aware of the need to have a buffer zone between the camp and possible attackers.

Eventually, Ramon called a halt.

"This is far enough," he said. "If we patrol here, we should have plenty of time to run back and warn the camp if we see anything."

"Very good," Moishe said. "I think this is a good place."

Ramon looked at him curiously.

"It's a good place for me to use my ability," Moishe explained. "It's an excellent force multiplier." He drew a knife, and Ramon stepped back as if threatened.

Moishe just shook his head. *He'll see soon enough.* He stabbed his palm with the tip of the knife, then dipped his index finger into the cut. And he began tracing a pattern onto a tree trunk. The pattern he saw in his mind when he used his Skill, Beast Contract Ritual.

"I think we're getting close," Mustafa Roshan murmured.

"Yeah, the trail is definitely fresher than what we've been seeing," Philippe said, sniffing the air. "Can we wake the big guy now?"

"We'll wake the Prophet when we know we're within striking range of the camp," Fatemeh Roshan reminded him sternly.

"We don't want to piss the Prophet off with another failure," Leonard Robie agreed.

"What's that sound?" Mustafa asked.

They all stopped, turned in the same direction, and listened for a moment. They heard a sound like an animal grunting. It was fairly close.

Then, much closer, a sudden sound of choking and pouring blood.

Mustafa turned his head back first.

"Fatemeh!" He fell to his knees beside his collapsed sister instantly. The knife that was embedded in her neck was disappearing. He tried to grab it before it vanished, but it was gone before he could touch it. As if the weapon had only been a trick of the light.

And the blood poured out of her neck, fast and hot all over his hands as he tried to staunch the bleeding. She tried to say something, but all he could hear were gurgles and gasps for breath.

"Get a Healer!" Mustafa barked without looking up from his sister. "One of you assholes, get a Healer now!"

"Phillippe's gone!" Leonard said.

Despite his focus on his sister, that announcement made Mustafa's blood run cold. The vanishing blade. The silent disappearance of Phillippe.

"It's Moishe Rose," he muttered, mostly to himself. Fatemeh nodded in agreement, smiling through the blood that covered her lips. Even as she lay dying, she was trying to help her brother. Giving him a sense of the danger they faced.

Leonard took off running. Mustafa picked his sister up and ran as well, taking a different direction to get to the same place.

They were being hunted now. And only one of them was going to make it back to camp.

CHAPTER ELEVEN

Revelations

"**C**ongratulations, James!**"** The voice was familiar, jovial—and grating, despite having a generally smooth and pleasant sound. A surge of annoyance overtook James with those words from Anansi. He was now certain the Spider God had put him through his recent ordeal.

Which meant that none of it was serious.

Some sort of game? An amusement for a bored god?

"Hello, Anansi," James said, trying to keep his voice neutral. He still couldn't see the Spider God, so he simply spoke into the darkness.

A sudden flash of illumination in the distance showed James that he stood before a staircase. At the top of the stairs there was a throne.

And seated in the throne there was a giant figure. The light faded before James could make out any features, and the two were plunged back into darkness. Though apparently the Spider God could see through it.

"There is no cause to sulk, my friend," Anansi admonished, accurately reading James's emotions. **"Are you upset about what happened on the savanna?"**

"I am questioning the necessity of what happened on the savanna," James corrected.

"Did my boys scare you?" He sounded vaguely amused.

"A bit," James admitted. Anansi seemed to have a good read on him anyway, so there was no point in lying.

"Good. I wanted to make sure that you were actually fooled. It is difficult to be sure whether you will see through a deception or not. You can be incredibly clever sometimes. When you're not being incredibly foolish."

"Why go to the trouble of fooling me? Some kind of game? Are you bored here?" He tried to keep the irritation out of his voice, but he had genuinely feared he might be eaten.

"Less of a game, more of a test. You were never in any real danger, but I had to see how you would behave if faced with an obstacle that you could not overcome. Yes, a test of your character."

"Did you doubt my character when you invited me here?" James asked, struggling to keep from yelling. "You said something about me being your kind of warrior. Was that sincere?"

"If it was not, you would not have made it here. You completed the Dungeon, and if you were anyone else, you would have been given your prizes and escorted out."

A pop-up obscured James's vision as he was about to speak.

[Congratulations! You have cleared Dungeon: Anansi's House!]

[First human of Earth-73 to clear Dungeon: Anansi's House!]

[Politician leveled up!]

He swiped the text away a little angrily.

"Then why the tests at all?" he asked with more heat than he'd intended.

My temper, James thought. *It never used to be this bad. I need to calm down.*

"Your behavior after your battle with the Spider Queen made me doubt my initial judgment of you. At first, when you migrated toward the Moloch worshippers' camp, I thought you were looking for the edge of the map. Maybe you had found me. Then you returned to their camp a second time. I realized you were about to start a fight with that entire group. Alone. I started to think maybe this fellow is not the clever warrior I thought he was. The person I wanted to bless. It could be that my initial character assessment was off. Maybe he only knows how to fight, not how to choose his battles. Maybe he would just get himself killed without my intervention. Maybe I should look elsewhere to find a kindred spirit."

James felt slightly stung by this, but it wasn't as if these were completely alien thoughts. He'd been beating himself up about his decision-making in the prisoner rescue ever since it had become obvious the mission had failed. It was something else to hear the Spider God echo those thoughts.

"Fair enough, then. So, you put me in a situation where I would feel certain I was going to be killed to test my judgment."

"Were you ever a *Star Trek* fan, James?"

"Which one? Well, actually, no. Just no."

"Well, there's a test in the *Star Trek* universe. The Kobayashi Maru. Essentially it tests how you react to an unwinnable situation. Do you fight? Do you lay down and die? Do you run?"

"And what would you have done if I had somehow defeated your kids?"

Side-splitting laughter rolled uncontrollably from the Spider God. James could still only see a vague outline of where he sat, his eyes not having fully adjusted to the darkness. But he saw Anansi pound the armrests of his throne with one of his many limbs. **"You're a thousand years too early to ask that question! You would have to continue growing at your present rate for a millennium to beat any one of my sons in a fair fight."**

How long would I need to keep growing to beat one of them in an unfair *fight?* James couldn't help but wonder.

"No, you missed the whole point," Anansi continued. **"You are admittedly strong for a warrior of your level. You're not the only fighter on Earth with unfair advantages, though. Hundreds of thousands have similar or better natural abilities to yours. The System awards them based on your life experiences, after all. Many of them will die in Orientation, just as you almost died several times. Most of the others will lag behind you even if they survive. Because they don't all have your drive.**

"But no matter how strong you are, you will keep running into the occasional person who is stronger than you. This will continue to happen for some time. You cannot fight them all head-on or you will wind up dead. This would disappoint any god foolish enough to have invested in you. Even more often you will run into groups of people who you should not fight on your own. In that situation, you need to either run or talk your way out. Running has gotten me out of some bad jams in the past. Believe me, it's not pride that keeps a spider alive for thousands of years. So, the purpose of my test was simple. If I was going to back you, I wanted to know I wasn't backing a fool who would only get himself killed the moment I took my eyes off of him."

"Backing me," James said, a bit incredulous. "That's what this is about. Backing me how? And why? What's in it for you?"

"The typical way a god backs a human is with a blessing," Anansi said. **"I believe you already know something about that."**

"Apophis," James acknowledged. "But you're not addressing the why of it."

"Gods all want different things. Some of them sustain their existence through the faith of humans. Others feed on sacrifices to live. Some of us are strongly connected to a particular concept, and the connection to that concept is enough to keep us alive for as long as the thing itself continues to exist. In my case, I am intimately connected specifically to the elemental concept of 'story.' As long as sentient life-forms continue to tell stories, I will continue to exist."

Nice work if you can get it, James thought. *Push the "easy" button to continue to exist.*

"So, you want humans to keep telling stories?" James asked. "That's all?"

"**Humans, elves, dwarves, any other sentient life-forms that happen to exist. Though humans are the best storytellers, in my opinion. You lead such blessedly short lives. Many of you treat stories as a drug. A way of dealing with the pain of knowing you'll die so soon or a way of escaping from your lives.**"

James winced slightly at that description.

"**Not to say that description applies to you, of course,**" Anansi added hurriedly. "**Any part of it. You could live for a very long time! Forever, for all I know. And many humans enjoy stories as a way to slip into another consciousness. Enjoy another person's imagination. To interpret the world, or to imagine alternate worlds.**"

Why does he seem concerned about offending me? He's a god. There's a massive power disparity between us here. Right? But then, he still hasn't answered my question as to why he needs me. Why he wants to back me in particular.

"I think I'm still missing the 'why' of everything," James said.

"**Of course, of course. I want to bless you—no, more than that. I want to make you my Chosen One so that you can protect humanity.**"

What a sales pitch! A god with a hundred percent approval rating, folks! He just wants to protect humanity. What a guy!

"Honestly, that sounds very suspicious," James said. "I guess I get that you want to protect humanity so that we can continue telling stories"—Anansi was nodding along at this—"but why me?"

"**Killing two birds with one stone, honestly,**" Anansi said. "**First of all, I believe humanity needs a clever warrior to lead it through the next phase of its existence. You are one such, or so I hope. Second, you can only be the Chosen One of one god at a time. You can have blessings from as many as you like, but you can only be the Chosen One for one.**"

"Oh, I see. So, the real reason is that you have something against Apophis?"

"**You ask some very sharp questions, James. I don't mind the curiosity.**" The god sounded slightly annoyed despite his words. "**It reminds me of myself. But how would you feel if I started prying into your real reasons for going after the Moloch cultists alone and almost killing yourself?**"

"That was for a constructive purpose, as you know," James said. "To save as many people as I could from a horrible, gruesome death and avoid unnecessarily risking other human lives."

"**I see. My mistake. You failed to rescue the prisoners, possibly endangered your own camp, and fell from a cliff to your likely death constructively.**" There was a mocking edge to the Spider God's tone that James hadn't noticed before. He decided he didn't much care for it.

"The spider, who has many children, might not understand, but we humans are quite fond of each other. We don't necessarily take kindly to others practicing human sacrifice in this day and age."

"Oh, is that the whole reason? Or were you also hoping to recruit more troops for that little army you're building? And by saving them alone, trying to look like a messiah figure?"

James remained silent, a shade of guilt showing on his face. *That thought may have been in the back of my mind. Can he literally divine my intentions? Or am I that typical, that obvious, that he can read me so easily?*

"Relax, my friend," Anansi said. "You and I are alike. We do nothing without more than one motive in our hearts. We are both studies in contradictions. A trickster god who wants to spread knowledge and wisdom through stories. And a shrewd warrior who goes into deadly fights alone. I am not judging your motivations, only your execution. By the same token, please believe that a major part of my motivation is that I am a humanitarian."

Are you really? How strongly could you feel about humans when you were so forgiving about me killing hundreds of your spiders who had the potential for sentience? Perhaps we're all just tools to you. But he couldn't voice that thought.

"Fine. What's your problem with Apophis, then?"

"Must we focus on Apophis? I would rather discuss your many positive qualities that make you an ideal savior of humanity."

James snorted. "I'm sure you would. Let's not lie to each other more than necessary, though, all right? If you wanted to just deceive me, you could probably do it easily and be done with it. You're a Trickster God as well as the God of Knowledge, Wisdom, and Stories. I'm sure you have some powers that make your lies irresistible."

I myself have powers in that vein, though not irresistible ones, James thought.

"This situation doesn't work that way. Not for me. If I trick you into being my Chosen One, it will not fulfill my purpose. I would just turn you into an unpredictable variable. Possibly a future enemy of humanity."

"It sounds like you have to be very careful," James said a little skeptically.

"You have no idea," Anansi said. "But since you understandably do not trust my honesty, why don't I give you your prize for completing my Dungeon first?"

He leaned forward from his throne, and James got his first real look at Anansi's head. It looked to have the shape of a human head, but with spider-like fangs sticking out of the side. Then James realized, with the help of a sudden flash of lightning, that the head he saw was a mask. He couldn't discern the true shape of Anansi's features at all.

He looked down from Anansi's head and realized Anansi had extended one of his long legs to James. On the end of it, two stone rings hung, one white and one gray.

James reached forward and grasped them. Anansi let them slide off of his limb and leaned backward into his throne.

Identify. I hate to look a gift horse in the mouth, but I have to know what these are. He Identified the white ring first.

[Ring of Truth: Extremely durable ring. Allows the wearer to reliably distinguish true statements from false ones. Only effective for oral statements. Only effective where the speaker is communicating in real time. Additionally, amplifies the persuasiveness of true statements by the wearer. Effectiveness of ring functions is unreliable against beings above mortal tier.]

Holy shit! That's a definite game changer. I'll always know who to trust from now on. I could literally just ask, 'Can I trust you?' and I'd have the correct answer. Not to mention a million other, probably more practical, uses. Remind me never to take this off.

He slipped the white ring onto his left pinky finger, right next to his wedding ring. The new ring seemed to shrink slightly to better fit his finger. *Neat.*

Then he Identified the gray ring. Up close, he saw that it was actually gray with red bands running diagonal along the band.

[Ring of Lies: Durable ring. Allows the wearer to more reliably deceive others with false oral statements. Only effective where the speaker is communicating in real time. Additionally amplifies the effectiveness of Skills where they are used to deceive others. Effectiveness of ring functions is unreliable against beings above mortal tier.]

And this is the counterpart, of course. If anything, it's even better. But Anansi's about to turn me into a big fat liar. He knows that, right?

He slipped this ring into his pocket. The temptation to use it was something he would try to grapple with later. Better not to just have it sitting on his finger.

"All right, you've given me the prizes," James said, looking back up at the black outline of Anansi on his throne. "I'm slightly more equipped for this conversation we're having, although I doubt either ring would have any effect on a conversation with a Trickster God such as yourself. Go ahead and make your arguments about Apophis and why I should go with you instead."

"Have it your way. Apophis is an eldritch entity, not a normal god. The rest of the gods, including the evil ones, all agreed to the existence of the System as a way of preserving the multiverse. Even some evil gods, like Moloch, want humanity to persist because they need sacrifices. The people who have discovered Apophis throughout the ages have named him many things—Apep and Jörmungandr are the most popular examples from your universe. But wherever they have worshiped him, he has never answered prayers or provided aid of any kind. All Apophis wants is to unravel the universe. He is barely sentient at all. The god consists only of a semi-conscious desire for destruction, joined to a terrible power.

"Apophis didn't even choose you. You may be the Chosen One of Apophis, as I gathered from the power you displayed in Orientation, but that Title

is assigned randomly whenever the former Chosen One dies. Somehow, he got lucky this time and the Chosen One Title landed on someone who was genuinely dangerous enough to achieve his ends, even though, unlike several other gods, Apophis almost certainly was not watching you personally. He does not cultivate talented individuals; he merely grants power and the temptation toward destruction. Have you not wondered why Apophis doesn't speak to you? Other gods communicate with their Chosen. They grant boons. Assistance. Powers. Advice. If you were my Chosen—or even if you were Loki's Chosen, as he would prefer—he or I would have already aided you in overcoming the challenges you have faced thus far. Perhaps you would not have made your ill-fated decision about fighting the cultists."

Anansi seemed capable of continuing this, perhaps indefinitely, but James had heard enough. He raised a hand, and Anansi stopped.

"I get it," James said. "Evil destruction god. You're better. What would this proposed switch do in terms of my destructive capabilities, though?"

Even though James could only see the outline of Anansi, it was visible to him how the Spider God deflated at this question. He seemed to sink back into his chair, as if he wanted to become invisible.

"You will have to be much more creative," Anansi said at long last. **"No more getting into fights that you can only be certain of winning with a ten-times power multiplier. That sort of boost is not in my repertoire. You can be clever, though. I know that. On the other hand—have you heard the expression, 'Until the lion tells the story, the hunter will always be the hero'?"**

James shook his head.

"How about, 'The pen is mightier than the sword'?"

James nodded reluctantly. Anansi was, it seemed to him, being honest and direct, in defiance of his own nature. James found that he wanted to give the Spider God a chance.

"Well, the power of story is even mightier than the power of the pen. Taken to a high enough level, you redefine reality. Redefining reality is more useful than destroying it. Story and real life intersect in a number of ways that will surprise you when you fully grasp all the connections. If you're willing to consider my offer, I will show you one of your new abilities right now, on a trial basis." He extended a limb toward James. And almost reflexively, James found himself reaching forward.

"Dreamwalk with me."

CHAPTER TWELVE

Date Night

James reached out to Anansi and gripped the extended limb by pure instinct. Something inside him was deeply attracted by those words, "Dreamwalk with me."

And then the whole environment disappeared from around them. James was plunged into what seemed to be almost pure darkness and emptiness. Even the ground beneath his feet seemed to have fallen away. *Like the void.*

The only thing he felt was Anansi's touch. He dimly saw that Anansi was there with him, though it was only the shape of the god that he had seen before and not a fully revealed image.

"Where are we?" James managed after a moment.

"Dreamspace," Anansi replied. **"On our way to the dream of the person you most love."**

James found himself speechless.

"What?" Anansi asked. James could hear a grin in the Spider God's tone. **"Did you forget that I'm married too?"**

And then James found himself in a different place. A brightly lit courtyard framed by two blocky, ugly buildings and bounded by a chain-link fence. His eye was drawn to the window of one of the brutalist structures. He recognized her immediately. He smiled.

Mina. Her eyes were laser focused on the front of the classroom, but there could be no doubt.

It was his wife. As a teenager.

So studious. He wanted to walk up and join her. But he looked down at himself. He was still wearing his battle-shredded cult-fighting outfit. And, for that matter, he was sweaty and dirty from a lengthy fight and days without a proper bath.

I can't let her see me like this.

"You know that you can change what you look like, right?" The voice seemed almost to come from beside his ear. James turned and saw a small spider sitting on his shoulder.

"Wow. Clearly, you're making use of that feature." He snorted.

"I can change my appearance anytime I like, James. Do you think my realm looks like that all the time? On thousands of versions of Earth, different cultures have discovered me. Sometimes on the continent you call Africa. Sometimes in Asia. Sometimes in America. I chose a savanna biome for today because it was a place your mind would associate with my mythology. But you can change your appearance here as you would not be able to without a Skill elsewhere. You can change many things if you wish. This is a dream. Just focus. Become a teenager so you can fit in properly."

"Fine, fine," James said. "Are you going to be here the whole time? No offense. I definitely want to get to know you better, but—"

"I get it," Anansi interrupted, his voice thick with obviously feigned indignance. **"The shoulder spider is cramping your style! I will take my leave. See you when date night is over!"**

He disappeared from James's shoulder.

"Well, I'm glad you get it," James said, a little skeptical that the Spider God was simply gone.

He looked around a bit but couldn't see where Anansi might be. Nor did he imagine he'd be able to find the Spider God in the dream if he didn't want to be found, whether he was there or not. Turning invisible seemed like such a basic divine ability that it would be silly to assume he didn't have it.

Fine. He looked down at himself again, focused on an image of himself as a teenager, and watched as his body and clothing changed.

There we go, he thought. *Now I'll try something harder.*

He closed his eyes and imagined himself outside of Mina's classroom. He opened his eyes, and there he was. Right outside the door. He grabbed the handle. Turned it. Walked in. Willed the teacher to recognize him as if he belonged there.

And the teacher did. He looked at James for a moment, then continued speaking.

James realized the teacher was speaking in Bulgarian. Fortunately, Universal Language Comprehension seemed to still be functioning. The lesson was a physics concept. Torque. *Of course it is. Mina loves that stuff.*

He saw the seat next to her was empty. He slid into it, and she turned to look at him.

"You're cute," she said quietly in Bulgarian. She looked a little confused.

"I'm glad you still like me," he said.

"Have we met? You do look familiar." She leaned in closer to him, ignoring the lecture now.

I guess I have changed quite a bit since high school, James thought. *And she didn't meet me until we were both adults.* Although they had speculated on what their relationship might have been like if they'd met in high school, it was something they'd never actually experienced.

"We met last summer," James invented. He began spinning a story from something Mina had told him once. "We ran into each other volunteering at the elder home."

He could see her mind going along with his story as she listened to him.

"Right, I remember you now, um—"

"James."

"James, yes." She smiled as she said his name.

He willed class to end, and a bell suddenly rang.

"Oh, it's over?" Mina looked around surprised. Everyone else was packing their things away in bags.

"How about I walk you home?" he asked.

She raised an eyebrow, but then said, "Sure."

I can't believe I'm actually nervous, he thought. He wiped his sweaty palms on his jeans.

And then he walked with Mina, out of school, through the town that she'd invented in her mind. Or some impossibly immaculate memory of her hometown.

My dreams are never this detailed, he had time to think at one point.

But mostly he was focused on Mina.

Walking with her. Joking and laughing with her. Listening to her point out significant places. Holding hands. James had never met high school Mina and had never been to Bulgaria, so it was all new to him. All magical.

I miss you so much, he thought. *I can't believe how much longer we have to be apart.* Unless the two of them both completely destroyed their Orientations' challenges, he wouldn't see her again for some time. Not until after the baby was born. Not until after she'd had to face dangers unknown without him.

I've been selfish, just trying to spend time with you. I should be thinking if there's anything I can do to help you survive.

The two of them walked into Mina's house. She didn't seem to notice the slight cloud hanging over James.

"Mom!" Mina called as soon as they'd crossed over the threshold.

"I'm right here, Mina," a middle-aged woman said, poking her head around a corner. "I see you've brought a friend home." She looked a little suspicious of James. That had not been his experience of meeting her in real life, perhaps because Mina had told her things about him before they met.

James decided to let the meeting with Mina's mother play out before he considered changing anything else in the dream. One final fun, imaginary experience before he got down to business.

He introduced himself, and Mrs. Danailova's face curled into a friendly smile.

Mina and James sat down, and her mother brought them some sort of herbal tea. He established his cover story for the dream: he was a foreign exchange student, which was why he didn't look like a member of any Bulgarian ethnic group. And the three of them talked about school, the elder home where he and Mina had supposedly met, and the quality of the tea. James pronounced it delightful, which brought a smile to Mrs. Danailova's face.

He'd always been good with older people.

She left him and Mina alone for a few minutes at one point, and the atmosphere of a high school students' date reasserted itself. She returned to find them holding hands and staring into each other's eyes, although they quickly separated once she was back.

Mrs. Danailova just smiled again, this time a bit mischievously. And she said the only words James remembered her saying to him from when they'd met in real life.

"Be sure to take good care of my daughter, young man."

"Mom! Please!" Mina blushed furiously.

"We should go do some homework," James said.

Mina nodded and practically ran from the room. James rose from the table, and Mrs. Danailova spoke again.

"Really, though. Thank you for taking such good care of her."

When James turned back to Mina's mother, he saw her face had aged to match when he'd last seen her. Not terribly long before she'd passed.

He swallowed. *That's freaky. Might have been my subconscious influencing the dream?*

"It's really my privilege, ma'am." He took her hand for a moment and gently squeezed. "I'm very lucky."

Then he followed where Mina had gone. She was in her bedroom with two younger girls. James stood back and watched without interacting.

Neither child was Yulia, who would have been very small around this time.

"Girls, I need you out of here, now! I—I have to study!" Mina was agitatedly ordering them.

"Fine, fine." The two ran out of the room giggling.

James heard the distant chorus of "Mina has a boyfriend!"

Then Mina closed the door. Her face was blazing red.

"Indecent children!" she muttered, refusing to make eye contact with James for a few seconds.

He snorted, and she finally looked up at him.

"Are you laughing at me?" she asked sharply.

"No, never," he said. "Just the children."

"Well, that's all right, then." She nodded to herself.

Such a serious teenager. I really would have fallen for her if we'd met back then too.

He approached her and took her hands in his. Mina's hands were shaking, and he caught her looking toward the door as if she thought it might open at any moment.

Just to make her less anxious, he walked away and locked the door.

"Um, we can't. I'm not supposed to—" She gestured to the locked door a bit nervously.

Oh my gosh, her mom was such a stickler. Now I know where you get it from!

"Don't worry," he said smoothly, taking her hands again. "I'll unlock it again in a minute."

"All—all right." She looked nervous.

He smiled. "Close your eyes."

Her breathing slowed. Slowly, she closed her eyes. She turned her face up toward his, lips puckered.

I'm going to steal your first kiss, he thought playfully.

He leaned down and kissed her. As he made contact with her lips, he imagined the Mina he remembered. He imagined them both as adults. He pictured them as they'd been only a year ago, before she became pregnant. And he closed his eyes, holding that picture carefully in his mind.

They separated, and both opened their eyes and looked at each other again. Husband and wife.

"So it was you," she said wonderingly.

"Yes. We met early this time."

He imagined them outside again, and the environment melted and changed around them.

Mina never stopped looking at him.

"I'm glad you're all right," she said. "I feel like something happened that I was worried about."

"Orientation," he said. "The System."

Her eyes widened. "That's right!"

"How's that going for you so far?"

"Oh, it's just been a day."

It was his turn to look surprised now. "Only a day? Are you sure?"

"Yes, it's just the start. The System proctor introduced herself. I spent about an hour and a half with a homunculus who kindly explained everything I needed to know about being a Mage. Yulia's a Healer . . ." She spent a minute explaining what her Orientation looked and sounded like, though the thing that struck

James most was how long the System Homunculus had spent with her, helping Mina figure out how to be a Mage.

I guess I really pissed off the homunculus in my tutorial, he thought. *Probably ought to apologize better the next time I see him.*

"So, a snowy Orientation setting, and the competition will be around challenges of some sort," he summed up.

She nodded.

They were walking as they spoke now, on the streets of Orlando. James conjured up an ice cream stand and bought Mina a chocolate cone. She ate it while he discussed his own experience a bit.

The problem is that her Orientation sounds completely different from mine. Depending on what types of challenges she faces, I might give completely bad advice. Maybe that's why Anansi brought me to the past? If she was past day one of Orientation, I might have a better idea of what I was working with here.

He had no way of training her body in her sleep. And with the late stage of her pregnancy, physical training right now seemed like both a lost cause and a bad idea.

Conversely, if a challenge relied on brain power, he had complete confidence she would win with or without any help from him. Mina was the only person he knew who he believed was actually smarter than him.

He tried using Skill Transfer, but it didn't work. Or rather, it seemed to work, but then he reviewed his Stat sheet, and the Skill he had tried to give Mina was still there. Probably because they weren't really in the same physical location. Or even the same dimension.

There was only one thing he could think of that might make a difference in her Orientation and help her survive.

"Why don't we try this?"

He had her use her Basic Elemental Magic: Water for him. He knew she had the Skill from her tutorial. And she was able to use it in her dream when he asked her to. He had no idea whether the result was really correlated with what she could do in real life, but she was chanting just like other Mages.

Hopefully, this doesn't translate into her wetting the bed or something in real life.

And he was also acting out of an optimism that practicing something in her dreams could make her more skillful in real life. This was something he'd never done before, but he'd read somewhere once that it was possible for a person to learn something or make some form of discovery in their sleep. And he knew he'd received inspiration and ideas from dreams before.

Even if I just get her more used to the idea of using magic, I'll have done something that increases her chances of survival, he thought. *I hope.*

There was an indeterminate period where he was just putting her through her paces, getting her to show him everything she could come up with that used her water magic. But before he knew it, he sensed that the dream was drawing near its end. Maybe he recognized the feeling from thousands and thousands of dreams in the past.

"I love you," he said. He pulled her close and held her tight.

"I love you too," she said, nose buried in his chest.

"Give Yulia my love too," he added.

He held her for a long time.

Then the setting faded. Mina faded away. He was back in the void. And Anansi appeared next to him again.

"I hope you enjoyed your time together," the Spider God said somberly.

"Yeah," James replied. "Yeah, I really did."

A bittersweet smile played across his lips.

I hope I get to see her again in real life, he thought.

Then there was a sensation of reality reasserting itself, and James's hand was touching Anansi's spider-limb. Back in the place where they'd met. Back to Anansi's realm.

"Annnnd we're back," Anansi said.

"How do you have those powers?" James asked. "You're not a god of dreams. Are you?"

Anansi shook his head in an indecisive way. **"It's complicated. Dreams are stories. Chaotic, confusing, impossible stories, but stories, nevertheless. So, I have an arrangement with Hypnos, the God of Sleep. Dreams fall under both our jurisdictions, and we share authority in that overlap."**

"Right," James said. "And we traveled back in time?"

Anansi shrugged. **"Dreams are mysterious things. They don't have to follow the usual rules of chronology or cause and effect. That's why déjà vu exists. And there are some questions I can't answer for you."**

"I see," James said. "And now I need to decide if I want to become your Chosen One."

If I do, I can see Mina whenever I like. The thought was irresistibly tempting.

CHAPTER THIRTEEN

The Popular Kids

Gradually, the other members of Mina's group agreed to share with the opposing team.

She observed that the teenager and the older gentleman who had initially objected remained a little reluctant. But they conceded, perhaps because everyone knew that she had been the main actor in solving the challenge.

The huddle broke up, and the victorious team members each grabbed their sack and began dividing the provisions. The other team looked on in what appeared to be confusion.

Mina was the first to approach the white line on the ground. She'd produced a large napkin from within her Small Bag of Deceptive Dimensions, and she now spread it on the ground and placed half of her food on the napkin.

"What's this?" one of the young men from the other team asked, approaching.

Mina looked up at him. The young man looked tall and fit, with a mop of blond hair and a suspicious scowl.

"It's food," Mina said simply. "There's no reason we shouldn't all eat just because the proctor decided to give only one side provisions. So, some of us are sharing. Hopefully, other people will follow the example."

"But why?" another young man on the other side spoke up. He was Hispanic, a little shorter than the first guy, but well-built. His cheeks were pockmarked with acne scars.

"I just said why," Mina replied brightly. She wrapped the napkin up as best she could, and she used a stone she picked up to push the bundle of food across the white line. Cygnus had said earlier that they couldn't cross it, and she didn't want to risk any consequences from doing so herself.

"All right, then," the blond guy said shakily. His eyes were momentarily distracted from Mina as he saw her other team members follow suit and share their provisions.

She rose to her feet slowly and dusted off her clothing.

"Good luck to both of us in the next round," she said. "I would shake your hand, but I still don't know if we can cross the line."

"For sure," the blond guy said. "Oh, and my name is Keith! Forgetting my manners."

He picked up the food Mina had put down with a look of relief. Now that he seemed sure enough that this wasn't a trick, he looked almost embarrassed.

"I'm Mina," she said, "here with my sister Yulia." She gestured to Yulia, who was placing half of her food nearby too.

"Andy," the Hispanic guy said, stepping closer to pick up the food Yulia had given. "And you guys are awesome. I'll compete against you anytime."

"Yeah," Keith said, now fully smiling. "No one has to go hungry, right?"

"That's what I think," Mina said. "Maybe—"

Suddenly, she found herself back in the snowy Orientation space.

"Whoa!" Yulia said from next to her.

"So sudden," Mina said.

And then Cygnus was there again, standing in the same position as before.

[Our sincerest congratulations to the challenge winners! As promised, all provisions have been provided to them. They are yours to do with as you wish, without restrictions or interference from us. New housing has been constructed for our winners.]

The proctor gestured toward new buildings that had somehow been thrown up alongside the old ones. They were similar in exterior appearance but twice the height of the old buildings. And they also looked fresher somehow.

[You will not be able to enter the new housing unless you have successfully won a challenge. Please do not attempt to enter, for your own health.]

"Hey, what about provisions for the rest of us?" someone shouted.

[Those who failed to successfully win the challenge are welcome to hunt for food. Alternatively, you can wait for the next challenge, which will be held in three days.]

"That's bullshit!" that same voice called out again. Mina could see him now: around twenty feet away from her was a small sweaty man with a noticeable gut. *Surely he can't be starving yet*, she thought. *Doesn't he understand how dangerous this situation is?*

[Any further interruptions to these announcements will be met with immediate death.]

"I don't believe you. Hey, guys, this person has a body just like us. We can take h—*yeeaaarghhh!*"

A horrible, inhuman noise filled the air where the man had been standing. An invisible force had come down on him and crushed him into the snow. What was left was a large bloody smear where he'd been and some internal organs and odds and ends of the body that had managed to go flying away from the impact zone. The men and women around the troublemaker looked stricken. Blood and bits of gore caked their clothing and skin.

But they didn't make a sound. A few covered their own or other people's mouths. They didn't want to "interrupt" next.

Something tapped her foot, and Mina looked down to see that an eyeball had managed to roll all the way to her. She covered her mouth to keep from vomiting.

Oh my God! Why would she do that? He was just a loudmouth. He obviously wasn't a threat to her!

[As I was saying, another challenge will be held in three days. You have time to change up the memberships of your teams. We will hear any verbal statements made regarding team structure, and we will take such statements into account. For example, you could tell one member that they are no longer a part of your team, in which case we will assume that they are in a team on their own until someone states otherwise. If you do not make any verbal statements regarding such a change, your team will simply be teleported to the challenge location when the next event arrives. Best of luck, and well done in the first competition!]

And the proctor was gone once again.

Silence ruled the air for a few frozen seconds.

"The System feels more monstrous the more time we spend with it," Mina said to Yulia quietly.

"Yep," Yulia said. The tone carried the connotation, "Duh!"

"Let's go to our new room, sweet. I don't feel entirely safe out here among everyone. People will be on edge after a death right in front of us."

"How about I walk you both to your new housing?" Detective DaSilva said as he approached.

"That would be welcome, sir." Mina smiled gratefully. "Honestly, I feel a bit queasy. Best for me to get behind closed doors."

"Sure," DaSilva said sympathetically. He offered his elbow, and Mina grabbed it. With Yulia on her other side, Mina felt well insulated from the crowd, which had begun to murmur with discontent now.

"Tensions are getting high, Detective," Mina commented quietly.

"I know it, Ms. Danailova. I know it. But what can we do?" he replied.

"There's very little," she granted.

"I think you've already done what was possible, in terms of lowering tensions. I'm starting to realize how wise your choice was. Imagine if you had to try to hold onto all that food now, with no white line separating you from the other team. I'd probably have had to shoot some of those fellows."

"You definitely did the right thing, sis," Yulia agreed. She was looking around—clearly noticing, to Mina's chagrin, the teenaged boys in the crowd around them.

She tried not to groan as she thought of how annoying it would be to keep Yulia apart from the boys in this place. Especially the ones who had won their challenges. There would surely be no sex segregation in the new housing as there had been in the old.

Although Mina hadn't taken a survey of all the winners of the challenge, she had seen that most of those carrying sacks of provisions were men. Not everyone was carrying them openly. Some had stowed them in their Small Bags of Deceptive Dimensions as Mina, Yulia, and DaSilva had after splitting their food with the other competitors. But if the people Mina had seen were at all representative of the challenge-winning population generally, the new housing would be predominantly occupied by males.

As long as the doors lock, it'll be fine, she told herself. *Yulia isn't stupid. She won't let strangers into our space. And I'll make sure to remind her what a bad idea that would be.*

As the three of them drew close to the entrance to one of the new buildings, the murmurs of the crowd broke into shouting.

"You bastards have to share—"

"Get your own!"

"Calm down, everyone!" A voice that had become familiar over the last forty-eight hours broke through the noise. "I'll get to the bottom of this."

Detective DaSilva had turned to look at the tumult, and he let out a small exclamation under his breath.

"Shit!" he swore.

Mina and Yulia turned to see what he was looking at, and they saw the self-appointed leader walking toward them.

I know I've heard his name somewhere before now, Mina thought. Her mind raced, trying to think of what to say when he made it to them. And what he might want.

But the leader closed the distance quickly.

"I'm Paul," he said brusquely. "Don't think we've met. Need to ask you folks a few questions. I'm sure you understand."

He's speaking loudly so that the rest of the mob can hear him, Mina realized. *Making us some kind of scapegoat?*

"Paul, you said?" Mina began.

He didn't acknowledge her question at all. "First question. Is it true?"

"Is what true?" Mina exaggerated her accent slightly. "I sorry, English is not my first language." She spoke at a similarly elevated volume to ensure the crowd would hear her answers to Paul's questions as well.

"Is it true you had extra food that you've shared with the other team from your challenge?" Paul asked hotly.

"Um, no," Mina said. She shook her head and tried to put on a perplexed look. "No extra food."

"Then they're lying?" Paul asked. "This is a serious matter, so be careful how you answer."

"We just shared what the System gave—"

"That's what I'm talking about! Extra food, so you had enough to share! How much did the System give you? Not all of us were given enough to share!" He continued to speak at the top of his voice, as if the conversation included the whole mob of people outside.

"No extra!" Mina said. "Same as them!" She pointed at one of the people who still had a sack of food visible.

"I don't think—"

"Listen, buster!" Detective DaSilva placed himself between Paul and Mina and began poking Paul in the chest with his right index finger as he spoke. "I know the bullshit you're trying to do. It isn't going to work, and you'd better quit it before you get a bullet right here! This situation is already volatile enough, and you're making it worse!"

With his free hand, DaSilva was gesturing for Mina and Yulia to retreat into the champions' quarters. Mina noticed and gently pulled Yulia back with her. As soon as she felt the tug, Yulia moved quickly to retreat into the building without further prompting.

As Mina retreated into the building herself, she heard the sounds of heated argument from more than just the alleged leader and Detective DaSilva. Others had gathered, too, without her noticing until she was on the threshold. She recognized it was unsafe for her to stay any longer, though.

People were angry.

She and Yulia went up the stairs hand in hand. They heard more people entering the building as they neared the top, so they ducked into the first room they came to.

They locked the door behind them and retreated further into the room. They could hear the muffled sounds of people moving in the building behind them, and they didn't want to confront any of these people, whether there were many or a few.

"At least we made it to a room," Mina said, trying and failing to smile.

Yulia wrapped her arms around Mina and buried her face in her sister's shoulder.

Mina felt Yulia's hot tears through her jacket, and she held her little sister close.

Before she could say anything comforting, there was a pounding at the door.
"They're in here!" a male voice proclaimed.

Then there was Detective DaSilva's voice. "Get away from there, asshole!"

"Huh? Who do you think you are?"

There was the sound of someone being struck. A thud. Then several more thuds, increasingly distant.

A few seconds passed. Then another set of knocks on Mina and Yulia's door, much gentler.

"Ladies?" It was DaSilva's voice again. "Coast is clear out here. Fellows got the message and cleared out!"

Mina started to move toward the door, but Yulia was holding her tight.

"What if they're making him say that?" Yulia hissed.

"I'll check the peephole, sweet," Mina said reassuringly.

If they can get into the building, I have no doubt they could break down this door. It's just wood as far as I can tell. Normal wood.

Yulia stayed back, her face red and teary and buried in her hands, while Mina walked slowly toward the door. The baby was starting to move inside her, and she imagined he was agitated by all the noise, the sudden running and shouting, and perhaps his mother's stress.

It'll be all right, little one, she thought. She imagined herself sending calming energy down into her womb, although she realized such thoughts were silly and mystical, even as she had them.

She looked through the peephole. Detective DaSilva looked like he would have a black eye the next day, and he was missing the collar button from his shirt, but he was otherwise all right.

She still felt a bit reluctant to open the door.

"Thank you for protecting us, Detective!" she called through the wood. "Did you get hurt?"

DaSilva smiled. "Nothing I can't handle, ma'am. I've been in my fair share of fights over the years. Even if I occasionally get knocked down, I've never lost yet!"

Probably better not to rely on him too much, Mina couldn't help but think. *A very well-intentioned man, but someone who says things like that will inevitably lose a fight eventually, at exactly the wrong moment.*

"Do you need healing?" Mina asked.

He shook his head, then seemed to remember there was a door between them. "No, ma'am. I just wanted to let you know it's safe out here for now. I'll be staying across the hall from you in case anyone else gets any funny ideas. I might come back a bit later to talk to the two of you. Probably best if we keep a low profile for the next day or so. I'd rather not have to shoot Paul. He's not such a bad fellow, though he made a serious mistake here."

If that's what you call a mistake, I wonder what being a bad fellow would look like!

"Thank you again, Detective! Please let us know if you need anything from us."

"Of course!" Detective DaSilva looked at the door for a moment, then went into the room across the hall from them and stayed there.

I'm glad he didn't ask me to let him in. Yulia could've been right about other people forcing him to talk to us. But refusing would've been awkward.

Mina walked back to Yulia and took the room in afresh. Now that she saw what it was like, it was clear that it was an upgrade from the first room they'd shared. Almost like moving from a motel to a hotel.

There were still two beds, but they were larger. There was charming, old-fashioned furniture: two dark-wood vanities with three mirrors mounted on top and wooden desk chairs placed in front. The window was fairly small like the window to the first room had been, but it was bigger in this one. The room itself was larger as well. And Mina didn't expect they'd need to share the space with anyone. After all, the champions' buildings had at least one extra floor each, based on height. And they would only have half as many occupants as the first buildings had needed to accommodate.

This is a nice reward, Mina thought. *If only people weren't so irrational, we could enjoy it properly . . .*

She put an arm around Yulia again and embraced her. The two lay down and held each other in silence for a long time.

"Why are they treating us like this?" Yulia asked eventually. "You just tried to help people!"

"They're not in control of their situation," Mina said. "They want someone to blame. They think that having someone to blame would mean they have a way of solving the problem. In all times and places I think people behave this way when they're afraid. That Paul probably thought they would turn on him if he didn't solve the problem, so he jumped to attacking us. It was the easiest way he could think of."

She shook her head wearily. The sisters whispered back and forth for a while about less pressing things until they almost forgot Orientation.

And in time, the two of them slept.

CHAPTER FOURTEEN

The Longest Night

Ramon raced through the forest.

Every minute he saved by moving more quickly would add to his family's chances of survival.

I don't know how that Rose fellow thinks he's going to do anything against the cultists, he thought. *But then, it seemed more about revenge for him than anything else. Maybe he's prepared to die for that.*

Whether Moishe would actually succeed in fighting the cultists for very long or not was unclear. But it didn't matter. Ramon couldn't afford to waste whatever distraction he was creating.

Thank you for making this opening for us, man. I'll get the camp far away from here, even if it takes all night!

Mustafa Roshan stopped dead in his tracks.

Moishe Rose had seemingly materialized out of the trees in front of him. He wore a sadistic smile and played with a pair of knives. Mustafa recognized them as the same type of blade that had pierced Fatemeh's throat.

Think this through, Mustafa told himself. *This man is an Assassin. He must have some tactical reason for appearing in front of me. It's not just—wait, maybe he just wants to stall me while Fatemeh bleeds out! He wants revenge, not just efficient kills. How do I make an opening?*

"What's wrong, Mustafa?" Moishe interrupted Mustafa's train of thought, his voice taunting. "You've been sacrificing people for weeks now. You've stared death in the face over and over. And yet you look so nervous."

"You used to be one of us, you son of a bitch! You can't act high and mighty now! You did the same as me, and for the same reasons—"

"Until your Prophet decided to sacrifice my fucking sister!" Anger flashed in Moishe's expression. "Just because he didn't like her Class Evolution! We were loyal! Loyal to your fucking Prophet! None of you cared! I remember who helped him bring her down. And who helped him when I tried to stop it. I remember your faces and your names. I don't forget, and I don't forgive. None of you bastards are getting out of this forest alive." His face returned to the sadistic smirk from before. "Now it's *your* sister on the chopping block. How does it feel?"

"Let me through, you son of a bitch!" Mustafa shifted his sister so that he could hold her with one arm, then drew his sword with his free hand.

He charged. No matter how deadly Moishe was, it had been a mistake to turn this into a face-to-face contest. Mustafa would make him pay for what he'd done to Fatemeh.

There was only a moment's warning from the corner of Mustafa's vision.

He couldn't react quickly enough, and the shape that darted from the trees struck his neck. Mustafa felt a set of sharp fangs sink into his neck, and the sword dropped from his hand almost instantly. Then his body dropped like a sack of bricks.

The world grew dim. The last thing he saw was Moishe Rose's twisted smile approaching.

"Thank you, Cecilia," Moishe murmured.

The viper slithered away from Mustafa's corpse and up Moishe's arm, twisting and positioning herself until she was wrapped around almost his whole upper body. He hadn't known the snake long, but she clearly enjoyed physical contact as a means of showing and receiving affection.

Not the first girl I've known whose love language is touch, but you're definitely the clingiest, he thought.

A ding sounded.

[You killed Fatemeh Roshan, Lv. 9! You gained 200 exp!]

[Assassin leveled up!]

[Beast Tamer leveled up!]

[System-Boosted Human leveled up!]

[A Race Evolution is available. Review? Y/N]

So that was available. But it wasn't something he was interested in right now. He selected "N."

Race Evolution would take hours based on his prior observations. Even though he'd be better prepared for the fight if he was evolved, he would also be hours behind his element of surprise.

If the surprise wasn't spoiled already.

Even if Robie gets through to a sentry and warns that the camp is in danger, I just need to make sure I kill him before he spills how close they are to the Rodriguez camp. The priority is protecting them. Perhaps Robie was the one he should've targeted first since he would've gone down more quickly, without the need to play these games and launch a sneak attack while Mustafa was distracted. Perhaps the desire for revenge had already clouded Moishe's judgment.

No, Mustafa and Fatemeh Roshan were more dangerous and competent anyway. Stop second-guessing yourself. Every second you waste thinking puts the camp in more danger!

He started running in the direction he was pretty sure Robie had retreated to, aiming to cut the coward off from Rostov's camp. Fortunately, in his panic Robie had chosen an indirect route.

The race was on.

Cecilia pressed herself more tightly against his body as Moishe ran through the trees, streamlining her form, trying to cling to him without slowing him down.

She's a good partner, he thought. It was a shame his last companion had been killed when he had his falling out with Rostov's group, but Cecilia was an excellent replacement.

Then there was no thought, only movement.

Moishe sprinted for several minutes. He became increasingly aware as the minutes crept by that the odds he would stop Robie in time were quickly dwindling.

He was uncomfortably close to the enemy camp—he could spy the giant statue of Moloch peeking through the trees in the distance—when he spied a figure running in front of him. The run was more of a jog.

It seems I'm in luck. Robie's cowardice lost out to his lack of Stamina.

Robie had failed to keep the pace needed to get back to his camp before Moishe could catch up.

A voice called into the darkness, "Hey! You there!"

Moishe froze.

Damn it! He made it to the sentries on patrol . . .

Moishe was familiar enough with Rostov's security measures from his time as one of the man's helpers.

But had they spotted him or Robie?

"Hey! You there!" Kassim Roukoz called into the darkness.

A figure froze.

"Friend or foe?" Kassim asked.

"Friend!" a familiar voice called back immediately.

"Leonard? Step into the light, you moron!" Kassim said, relieved. "Why are you back here, anyway? Did the trail change directions?"

Hilda Rohm, also on sentry duty, visibly relaxed next to Kassim.

Leonard Robie's face became visible through the gloom as he took a few steps toward the circle of Kassim's torch light.

"We're under attack," he began.

"What's that?" Kassim demanded, stepping forward. "Who's attacking us?"

Leonard made a sound as if he was about to vomit, and Kassim saw a knife handle seemingly grow out of his throat.

Then the knife disappeared, and the blood began to pour out of Leonard's neck in quick-flowing bursts. The man collapsed to his knees, then fell face first onto the ground.

Kassim's first instinct was to help him, but he held back. He hadn't seen the attacker, and he was wary of another surprise strike.

"Hilda! We need more light!" he called.

She responded instantly, activating one of her Skills. Her body armor began to glow brightly, and the forest suddenly became significantly easier to see.

"There he is!" Kassim exclaimed.

A man was moving, stooped, toward Leonard's position. Obviously planning to finish the job.

"We're under attack!" Kassim yelled as loudly as he could. "Sound the alarm!"

The figure of Moishe Rose was unmistakable. Even if Kassim believed that he and Hilda could take Rose down without difficulty, he didn't want to charge in without sounding the alarm. Rose might have backup waiting somewhere just out of sight.

Rose seemed to freeze in place for a moment, as if he had a sudden case of stage fright. Kassim could dimly hear him hissing something, though he couldn't hear the substance of what was said. But then he noticed a flash of movement.

Something small moved suddenly and quickly toward Leonard's body and then back again toward Rose's. It was too fast, and the surroundings still too dim, for Kassim to be sure what he'd just witnessed.

"Get him!" he called, drawing his sword.

Hilda charged in next to him.

And Moishe smiled—fucking smiled!—before stepping back into the tree line and suddenly disappearing.

What the fuck? I didn't even know he could do that!

Rostov awakened to shouts and a general atmosphere of fear and disorder.

He quickly gathered what had happened from Alice and marched to the edge of camp to speak with Kassim and Hilda personally.

"Where did Rose go?" he asked upon hearing their report.

"He fucking melted into the forest!" Kassim half-screamed, gesturing wildly at the woods.

"That is a *less* than helpful characterization," Rostov hissed, grinding his teeth as he spoke. "Which way did he go? Can you tell us that?"

Kassim shook his head. "I don't know!"

"Hilda?" Rostov looked to the woman in white armor, who seemed slightly more composed than Kassim.

"We weren't able to track his movements once he entered the darkness, sir," she said simply.

"Fine, then." Rostov gritted his teeth and let out a short hiss as he spoke. "What about Leonard? I heard he was the only one of the scouting team who returned alive."

"Uh, yes, Prophet," Kassim said. "He is alive, but he's in bad condition. One of the Healers is tending to him now."

"You, take me to him!" Rostov demanded. He turned to Hilda. "You, grab three more people and return to sentry duty! We must redouble our security precautions!"

I don't know how far away Rose actually moved. Even if I set up wards again, he might not be outside of their range right now. The camp is too big to adequately protect unless we all remain tightly packed. We're a perfect target for an Assassin like him!

Kassim silently guided Rostov to where Catherine Ross was healing Leonard.

"What's taking you, Catherine?!" Rostov questioned. His words came out more impatient than intended, but he didn't apologize. No time. "I only see a cut on his neck. That should be easy work for you, no?"

"Oh, Prophet," she replied, smiling smoothly. She didn't take her hands or gaze away from Leonard as she spoke. "Please forgive the delay—"

"I cannot!" Rostov interrupted. "I'm not worried about how long he'll take to be fully functional; we need answers as to who's ambushing us besides Moishe Rose. We need to know how many they have, what Skills they've demonstrated, and whether the enemy camp has notice of our position already or if Rose was simply one of their perimeter guards. These questions are of critical and immediate importance. Failure is unacceptable!"

Catherine's smile faltered slightly. "Prophet, I don't know if it's possible for him to wake up now! The cut on his neck wasn't the only problem. The wounds are closed up now, but when they brought Leonard to me, he had two puncture marks on his neck. I believe he was bitten by a venomous snake. I've purified him, but I'm not sure when he'll awaken. The healing process is taking a lot out of him—"

"Damn it!" Rostov exclaimed, stamping his foot. "Fuck!" He let out a long sigh, then turned away from Catherine.

"All right! No one sleeps!" he shouted, ensuring his orders would spread more quickly. "From here on, we continue until daylight, when we'll be able to see our enemies properly." He looked at Kassim and lowered his voice. "We lost the trackers, but we still know the proper direction to travel in to reach our enemy, correct?"

"Yes, Prophet," Kassim said simply.

Rostov could tell there was some objection Kassim wanted to raise but was afraid to. He took a deep breath.

"Kassim, do you have some problem with this course of action? I will hear whatever logistical concerns you may have." He forced himself to adopt his more patient, wise, and knowing demeanor for a moment.

"It's just, I doubt that Moishe Rose came here and killed our tracking party and our sentries all by himself. He's skilled, but we know generally what he's capable of. He's not on the same level as the intruder we had the other night."

"So, you think he had help?" Rostov finished.

Kassim simply nodded. And swallowed audibly.

I've made him quite nervous, Rostov thought. *Need to calm down. I will not maintain control over this group if I lead purely by fear.*

"I think you may be right," Rostov said. "We're not far from sunrise, though. A couple more hours. If everyone keeps moving until then, it drastically reduces the odds that Rose or his allies will be able to pick off any more of us. And tomorrow we'll catch up and kill every last one of them!"

"Yes, sir," Kassim said. He smiled weakly. And it was a little out of character for him to call Rostov "sir" instead of "Prophet."

His doubts are showing. And if I lose Kassim, one of the strongest believers . . .

"I know, Kassim," Rostov said, trying to cajole him. "I know. This is turning into the longest night of our lives, eh?"

Kassim smiled more genuinely.

"Yes, Prophet."

"Yes. It's always darkest before dawn, no?" He gestured at the horizon, where the first dim flickers of brightness were already visible. "Soon, our great ally will be able to lend us his assistance again. Once we have Moloch's help once more, we'll be inescapable."

CHAPTER FIFTEEN

A Good Husband

So, I have to choose between my destructive power and your more mysterious set of offerings," James mused.

"**You would not be giving up your offensive power completely,**" Anansi said. "**As I said before, I cannot offer you a massive power boost whenever you destroy something, but some of the advantages that I can grant you will make you deadlier—and in a more targeted way than just blowing things up!**"

"Well, I don't know," James said, hoping the Spider God would offer some further incentive.

Anansi reached up and removed his mask. There was a flash of lightning, and James saw the real head of the Spider God for a moment. *Or at least the version he wants me to see.*

The face was a human one, despite the spider body beneath. *Like Ntikuma.* It had African features, with an almost perfectly round head, and was ageless and free of wrinkles. But the lightning flash had revealed scars on each side of the Spider God's head. James couldn't quite get an idea of what sort of scars they were because the brightness faded too quickly. But they ruined the symmetry of Anansi's face.

Assuming this is a real image of him, James reminded himself. Perhaps this was the image of the Spider God best calculated to win James's respect, sympathies, and loyalty. It was hard to trust anything the Spider God did or said, knowing his reputation. *That would be lonely if it were me.*

"**If you switch patrons and become my Chosen One,**" Anansi said, "**you will have a direct line to me, to receive my help whenever you need it. I will** always keep one of my children with you, ready to carry our messages back and forth. I know Apophis would never provide such support unless you were on the precipice of destroying your world. My responses may not be instant, but my attention is vast, so they should be fairly quick unless we have some form of emergency here."

"Interesting. Are you going to be guiding me through the rest of Orientation, like Moloch does for Rostov? His followers said that he basically knew how things would go before they happened, like he was on a two-way radio with his god."

Anansi slumped backward into his throne.

"That should not be possible. Moloch has no children. He plants no seeds. The only things he grows are cancer cells." He seemed to become lost in thought.

"Well, that doesn't seem quite accurate," James said. "He grows the plants that live on Earth, right?"

"There is more than one Sun God, James," Anansi answered. **"Moloch represents the cruel aspect of Earth's Sun. The scorching heat that strikes the desert, the radiation that damages living tissue. Nyame is the embodiment of the Sun's paternal aspect, giving life. Apollo represents the creative aspect, the light of truth and beauty. And there are others. The Sun has been important enough to enough humans over the millennia to give rise to more gods than one. So, believe me when I say that, from my point of view, Moloch is nothing but destructive."** He paused. **"I think the way he communicates with his Chosen One must be different than what I had imagined. I had not realized the Tyrannical Sun was this desperate. Moloch may be communicating directly into his Chosen's brain."**

"So it *is* possible for you to do that," James said.

"Well, if I was willing to destroy your mind, then yes," Anansi said. His voice sounded agitated.

"Why does this seem to bother you so much?" James asked. "If Moloch is desperate, and Rostov is going to lose his mind or something, that all sounds pretty good for us, right? What am I missing?"

"A desperate god is a dangerous thing, naturally. There have been rumblings for some time about Moloch's situation. In the other universes, he has fewer and fewer worshippers. Sometimes, an evil god will be targeted by other religious groups. Given that Moloch demands human sacrifices, he has never been one of the more popular deities. Gradually, he receives fewer sacrifices as his worshippers are marginalized or killed. This weakens him. I think he was desperate to reestablish his base of sacrifices with the relatively weaker and more vulnerable humans of Earth. He was so desperate that he was willing to burn through a Chosen One and let Rostov's decline be witnessed by all his new followers. Not a good way to spread your religion. But

if he has allowed himself to become that hungry for sacrifices, then he will not restrain himself when using his powers at all."

From what Anansi mentioned earlier and now, it sounds like Moloch could actually fade away—and die?—if his goals in my universe aren't met. Just my luck that it's here where he's apparently making his last stand.

"Sounds like a mad dog. I should stay away, then, and not think about trying to get revenge or rescue prisoners anymore. I don't want to get bitten."

"That is one approach, and a sound one," Anansi granted. He raised a limb as if to forestall any further questions. **"But I do not intend to give you the benefit of any further divine guidance until you decide whether you are willing to be my Chosen One. If not, you can take your prizes from the Dungeon and get out of here. The door is right behind you."** His voice was only slightly playful as he made these last remarks. **"If you are—well, then I have a bit more advice for you, and I would be happy to sweeten the pot with a bit of knowledge up front. Ask any three questions, within reason, and I will answer them."**

He stopped me just when I was going to try and fish for more information. He probably always intended to offer me three questions, but he wanted to get me curious about something first.

"Honorable Spider God Anansi, I accept your gracious offer to make me your Chosen One."

I was already going to accept it before I made it here, honestly. I've been thinking about it, and I definitely prefer the god I used to read about as a kid over the evil chaos god, even if it affects my ability to blow things up.

Anansi stepped down from his throne, closing the distance with James.

James felt, rather than saw, Anansi stare deeply into his eyes. The sound of drums, rain sticks, and strings playing filled his head rather than his ears this time.

[You have been offered the Title of Chosen One of Anansi. In order to accept this Title, you must abandon the Title of Chosen One of Apophis. Accept? Y/N]

James chose "Y" without another thought.

The music that filled his head intensified, and a bright orange spotlight shone down from Anansi to James.

[Required conditions met. Title obtained: Chosen One of Anansi!]

[Patron deity Anansi has granted additional Titles: Storyteller, Dreamweaver, Deceiver, Trickster, Spider-King, Friend of All Spiders, Figure of Destiny, and Living Legend.]

[Required conditions met. Title obtained: Devout Beacon!]

[Required conditions met. Title obtained: A Stitch in Time!]

James felt noticeably *different* for a moment, but not in the way that he had been accustomed to when obtaining previous Titles or Status increases. He didn't feel stronger. Not exactly.

Damn, that's great! I feel more real, *somehow. Like there's more power inside of me, or I've started to grow in a new direction maybe.* It was hard for him to describe the change in a way that would do it justice, even in his own mind. But he had no doubt that it was an improvement. *Which Title did that? Chosen One or one of the others?*

The music and the light faded away, leaving only James and Anansi. The Spider God stepped back, giving him a little room.

"That feels pretty nice," James said, cracking his neck and then flexing his arms. "I'm surprised you didn't mention all those extra Titles when you were selling it to me."

"Better you feel that I over delivered than under," Anansi said. **"Frankly, if I had to sell you on it too hard, it would probably mean we were not such a good match. I like a man who knows his own mind. Otherwise, I would have started dropping the names of other people from your world I have blessed in the past. From Louis IX of France to Shaka Zulu, Alexander the Great, Hannibal Barca, Qin Shi Huang, and Christopher Columbus. I have a great track record for picking winners and helping them get to the finish line."** He cleared his throat. **"That was pre-System for your world, so they didn't have to accept or reject my blessing, and none of them were a Chosen One. It would have been a waste for me to bestow such a Title on a being that would only live a normal human lifespan. The point stands, though."**

"Hm." *Did he bless them before or after they were winners, I wonder . . .*

"Now that you have accepted, you can ask your questions, and I will give you some strategic and tactical advice."

"Let's reverse that," James suggested.

"Good catch," Anansi said. **"I would hate for you to waste your questions on things I would have told you anyway."**

James thought he caught the Spider God winking at him as he put his mask back on and sat back down on his throne.

"First things first, then," Anansi said. **"What do you have on your Status sheet? Give me everything, nothing held back, and I will give you some optimization hacks."**

James rattled off his entire list of Skills, Talents, and Titles, plus his Stat points, Job, and Class.

"You haven't been using Skill Fusion, have you?" Anansi asked immediately.

"I used it for experiments," James said.

"Did you permanently combine any of your Skills?"

"Only one pair," James admitted. "Healing stuff. I wasn't sure if I wanted to commit to permanent fusions for any of my more important Skills. Plus, some of them are really useful by themselves."

"The combined Skills will inevitably be better than most of the non-combined Skills, though."

"I guess, but I can always combine Skills on the fly if I need them."

"Yes, but a newly fused Skill will always start without any levels. If you don't use Skill Fusion for permanent combinations, you will hit a bottleneck in your growth. Basic abilities are not as effective as abilities created through Skill Fusion. Even if it bothers you to lose some of these Skills permanently, most of them besides gravity magic are pretty common. By fusing Skills, you create something uniquely yours, and you only lose something that you can fairly easily replace. You are also accruing so many Skills currently that at some point soon, you will hit the cap for your current mortal body. Then you will either lose some or have to transfer them into other people or items."

"Fine, fine," James said. The Spider was making too much sense for him to argue anymore.

"Second, start using Monster Generation. That is an extremely powerful Skill, and you seem to be treating it like a last resort instead of the kind of reliable tool that it actually is. At its peak, you could have multiple monsters almost as strong as you at your command, or a swarm of tiny creatures with your inherited powers."

"It requires me to use my own biological material—" James began.

"You humans are constantly shedding skin and hair, you personally can produce silk that contains your biological material, and you are even able to quickly regrow lost body parts. That last will come in particularly handy once Pain Resistance turns into Pain Immunity. Anything that comes off your body counts as biological material for purposes of that Skill. There is no need to be so attached to your original limbs; you saw how useful they can be in the Dungeon."

James grimaced at that last suggestion.

"Got it."

"Next are a few suggestions about how you handle the remainder of Orientation. First of all, once you leave here, you will be going out the same way you came in. Moving through the same black void. The void is a bit like dreamspace. It can take you back to where you came out, elsewhere in the Orientation space within reason, or somewhere else. That is a choice you have to make."

"I'm going to respond to what you're saying, and my sentences will include questions," James said. "Please do not count those as a part of the three questions that you promised me."

"**Sure, sure,**" Anansi waved a limb. "**I will wait for you to tell me when you intend to use your questions.**"

"All right. What are the options, specifically?" James asked. The Spider God's statements on the void had been simultaneously vague and tantalizing. "Can it take me back to where I left my group?"

"**No. It can only take you to places that connect to the void. Fortunately, there are other locations that could get you near them. There is also another option.**" Those last words sounded strangely reluctant.

"What are we talking about, Anansi?" James asked, trying not to be impatient.

"**You could travel to another Orientation. For instance, to where your wife is.**"

There was a silence so complete that for a moment, you could've heard a pin drop.

"Why didn't you lead with that?" James asked carefully.

"**I felt I had to bring it up, or you might hold a grudge against me, but I didn't want to. I think it's a bad idea. I am a god of storytelling and tricks, not prophecy. But wisdom is also a part of my purview. I think that if you go to her now, you will only increase the danger to her and your whole family. If you want your loved ones to survive, I believe you need to stay here.**"

James took a deep breath, then slowly exhaled.

"Please explain."

"**Your wife's Orientation is challenge-based. I understand the program is composed largely of non-violent competitions for food. People who fail those competitions can still survive by hunting. Given her wits, I would estimate that she and her sister have a high likelihood of surviving there, as long as they have decent Skills. I detect only one plausible threat to their survival present in their Orientation. The bigger threats to your family once Orientation is over are two life-forms in this Orientation.**"

Two?

"Rostov and who else?" James asked. *I could kill Rostov anytime I catch him alone, I think . . .*

"**Every Orientation has a final boss creature. In your Orientation, the final enemy is a particularly potent one. Any monster that is not defeated and killed by the conclusion of Orientation will return to Earth along with the surviving human participants. Per the System's rules, monsters are treated as equal to other life-forms.**"

"So, I should stay here so I can fight Rostov and one monster?" James said, unimpressed.

"**Do not underestimate the followers of Moloch,**" Anansi cautioned. "**Their strength will only grow with numbers. This is a threat that should be nipped in the bud. As for the Ruler of the Dead Marsh, I cannot tell you**

much about him unless you burn one of your questions for it. What I will say is that he would make a large swathe of your home region effectively uninhabitable within a week of returning to Earth, if he is not exterminated here."

That felt more like a real threat. What kind of biohazard was the Ruler of the Dead Marsh? James gritted his teeth.

"You don't give easy choices, do you?" he said.

"I just make sure you know all the options," Anansi replied.

"Fair, I suppose," James said thoughtfully. "Before we make that decision, though, I should probably use my questions."

He felt an inexplicable sense of time pressure even as he spoke, despite the fact that there was no particular deadline attached to his decisions. *I could be with Mina, protecting her right now . . . Right now, she and Yulia are on their own.* But that might put them in more danger in the future. *What would a good husband do here?*

His darkly pragmatic inner voice spoke up. *Well, do you* believe *in the woman you married, or don't you? You know Rostov is probably more dangerous than anything she's going to face in her Orientation. If you leave him alive, Anansi's as good as saying you'll regret it!*

She's pregnant! She's about to burst! She can't fight! And Yulia's a ninety-pound teenager! Another voice screamed back.

James placed his fingers on his temples, gently massaging them. He felt the beginnings of a headache coming on.

After he had a bit more of a grip on himself, he looked up to where Anansi sat.

The Spider God simply nodded for him to go ahead with his questions.

"First question. If, gods forbid, something should happen to me or Mina or Yulia, or anyone I care about, is it possible to resurrect the dead?"

CHAPTER SIXTEEN

Sick and Evil

Is it possible to resurrect the dead? Not generally," Anansi answered slowly.

"You're not going to give me any more than that, huh?"

"You're not going to use up another question to get a better answer, I suppose," Anansi replied. James felt as if the Spider God was smirking behind his mask. **"Fine. I will give you a freebie. Resurrection in one form or another might be possible, but only if the soul is bound to the physical world at the moment of death."**

It sounded like an answer he'd had to give before.

"That sounds rare," James said. "Thank you for answering more fully."

Need to be more careful how I phrase my next questions.

"The death gods are quite greedy, I'm afraid." Anansi shook his head somberly. **"Because the attributes of the gods are shaped by the collective unconscious of sentient life-forms, including those in worlds with no System, the gods of death are particularly uncompromising. Most humans are not used to taking seriously the possibility of bargaining with death."**

That's very interesting. Feels like I just learned a very useful piece of cosmology, but I don't know how to apply it. He would store it for later.

And he resisted the temptation to ask if death could be cheated, bribed, or tricked. Bargaining was such a specific term that James couldn't help but look for loopholes, but ultimately, this wouldn't be necessary unless someone he loved actually died. He didn't intend to let that happen.

"Well, what are the best decisions I can make, going forward, to achieve the goals that you understand are important to me?" James asked carefully.

"Do not try to lawyer your questions, James. I am no scheming djinn, trying to find ways to cheat you in the specific language of your requests. Ask me like a friend, and I will give you my best answers."

Easy to say, Trickster God, was his first reaction.

But James inhaled and exhaled another deep breath. *Of course he's right. He's given no indicators of hostility, not counting that one time he allowed me to think his kids would eat me. All right. Try something else. Ask a selfish question. I'm good at thinking about myself.*

"How should I pursue my Quest, Path to Immortality?"

The god let out a whistle and shifted his posture in a way James interpreted as surprised.

"You already unlocked that? Impressive! Well, I suppose it was that Enhanced Stem Cell Production Skill. Still, quite an achievement for one so young! You must be one of only a few in your universe to have that Quest now—not counting the elves and dwarves, only the humans."

James resisted the temptation to ask about that. *The elves and dwarves comment is definitely bait. Not going to bite. Not going to use a question on that . . .*

"Well, there are several ways to become less mortal," Anansi continued. **"You can make a contract with a deity affiliated with death. You can Evolve into something that doesn't age, though you already have that covered with your Skill. You could become a completely ageless undead, such as a vampire or a lich. You can become stronger and more difficult to kill in many thousands of different ways. But the most reliable method is to ascend to godhood. A small percentage of humans from the history of your world have ascended, Julius Caesar being a notable example. It requires leaving a lasting legend that carves your memory into the human heart, enough to create faith and leave a mark on mankind's collective unconscious."**

So it is possible to become a god, James thought. *Probably something that would take thousands of years, considering Anansi's comment about how long it would take me to fight his sons and win. But then,* I'll *have time.*

"Thank you for the answers," he said. "At some point, you know I'm going to ask you about the elves and dwarves. But for now, given my three-question limit, I'm going to think carefully about what I need to know right now."

"Take your time. We have as long as we need, right? Why not sit down and relax a bit? You could even take a look at one or two of your new Titles."

James sat down cross-legged and closed his eyes. He tried to dive deep into himself and figure out what kind of question he should ask a god. Anansi wasn't some random deity. He was the God of Knowledge, Stories, Trickery, and Wisdom. Three out of four of those would be useful for giving advice that James would want. But he had to make sure that he didn't waste this last question.

There are a thousand things I'd like to ask. Why is the System the way it is?

Why did it show up now? What's my place in this world? I always wanted to know if there was a real purpose to my life, but I didn't think it was very likely any god existed. Now I actually have one in front of me. I'm skeptical that he could answer that question to my satisfaction, though. Fine. Fuck it. There's probably no good question I can ask.

James decided to look at his new Titles again as Anansi had suggested. He opened his eyes and pulled up his list of Titles. *Of course, I already had Devout Beacon, but there's a pretty good list of Titles there now besides that one . . .*

[Titles
Chosen One of Anansi
Citizen of the Dead Marsh
Deceiver
Devout Beacon
Dreamweaver
Figure of Destiny
Friend of All Spiders
Living Legend
Spider-King
Storyteller
Swiss Army Mage
System Pioneer
Trickster
Xenocide]

The first of the new ones that caught his eye was Dreamweaver, mainly because Anansi had just given him a taste of what powers came with it.

[**Dreamweaver: A Title granted by a god. Anansi has chosen you from among all sentient life-forms to enact his will in the world. You may infiltrate and influence the dreams of others with the Skill Dreamwalk, which is bound to this Title. The god of stories bids you good luck and a happy ending.**]

A little vague, but I might as well try it. If I visit the dream of someone from the Rodriguez camp, that might give me a better idea if the group really needs me back.

"Anansi, I think I want to try Dreamwalking to see if I can gather information."

The Spider God just nodded.

Dreamwalk! James's body instantly grew sluggish and sleepy and slumped to the ground, and after a moment he felt himself drifting through that same black void from before. What Anansi had called "dreamspace."

He focused on connecting with the consciousness of someone whose mind he was already connected to: Chava Rodriguez.

He felt a distinct presence off in the distance once he'd identified whose dream he would enter, and he moved toward that presence. Movement through dreamspace seemed to be a little easier, and a little less contradictory, the more practice he had. This time was easy.

He arrived in a small apartment's living room, facing an archway that led into the kitchen. Chava was sitting at the kitchen table, back turned to James, chatting with a man who looked quite a bit like Chava himself.

"Hello, Chava," James said, walking through the archway into the kitchen.

As the older man turned around in his seat to face James, he noticed how much younger he was here than in real life. *Well, I know dreams can break the rules of reality already.* And he wasn't here to learn about Chava, so he didn't have much interest in investigating the social dynamic at play between Chava and this other person.

Probably his brother.

"You. I'm not supposed to encounter you, uh, yet." Chava squinted and looked confused.

James took the moment when Chava was focused on him and silently ordered the other man to leave the kitchen and go use the bathroom. Then he sat down in that man's place.

"This is a dream, Chava," James said. "I'm checking up on you. You're still following my orders, correct?"

"Yes, of course." Chava's voice turned monotone, and he seemed to visibly age to his real present condition before James's eyes. It was almost sad.

"Very good. How is the family doing?"

"We think it is possible that we are being hunted by that cult you attacked," Chava said.

Damn! So, they really are in danger here.

"What makes you think that?" James asked.

Chava explained what had passed in James's absence.

So, I did free some of the prisoners! Although I could have freed all of them if I had planned it out better, it's encouraging to know my efforts weren't all for nothing.

"Keep running away," James admonished. "Don't fight them if you don't have to. Unless the family gets a lot stronger, you can't win."

"That is the decision everyone made when the matter came up for discussion," Chava said. "I will ensure the family continues to follow your direction."

"Very good. I'm glad we had this chat." James rose from his seat and willed himself out of the dream.

He reappeared in dreamspace again.

That was productive. I think I want to try it again. But where to next?

He decided to visit Mitzi. She and Alan would have been the most worried about his survival. She deserved to know he'd made it.

As soon as he focused on her, he felt a distinct presence again. *Dreamwalking is turning out to be surprisingly easy.*

He popped into her dream, and he saw Mitzi immediately. She was so much younger than the woman he knew that he almost thought he was in the wrong dream for a moment.

Jesus, I guess those memories never completely fade from your subconscious . . .

Mitzi, looking all of twelve years old, was sitting on a sofa in front of James between two adults who James guessed were her parents. At least they looked like her. That was half of how he realized that the young girl in the middle was Mitzi. The man certainly wasn't Alan, and he looked a little too much like adult Mitzi to be unrelated. The woman's resemblance to Mitzi was uncanny. Almost clone level!

"Um, hello, Mitzi?" James tried.

"You're blocking the TV, bozo!" Mitzi exclaimed.

James turned and saw what Mitzi was referring to. There was a modestly sized television behind him, and something called the *Andy Griffith Show* was just starting.

"Black and white television?" he asked with a raised eyebrow. *Mitzi and Alan aren't* that *old! Are they?*

Out of the corner of his eye, he noticed that the girl who would become Mitzi Roget had risen from her seat.

"I think I know you," she said. "Where do I know you from?"

"Um, you know me from Orientation," James tried. He didn't want to completely break the flow of Mitzi's dream, so he wasn't sure how much he should say. It looked like a happy dream. Surely her parents were long dead, so there was no way she saw them in real life. It was possible that she didn't remember what they looked like outside of her dreams.

"I know you from where?" She sounded confused.

"On second thought, I'll come back," James said. "Don't mind me, just enjoy your show!"

He ran away from the bewildered Mitzi into another room so that she wouldn't see him suddenly disappear when he returned to dreamspace. Then he left.

One more dream. I'll tell someone else I'm alive, and then that person can tell Mitzi and anyone else who's wondering.

James thought of his target, identified the distinct feeling of that person, and found that person's dream immediately. Then he navigated there.

But when he entered this dream, things felt *different*.

The setting wasn't a familiar human one at all to his eyes. The space was dark and misty, but James thought it was indoors. At least, he could feel that there were walls and a roof of sorts. The ground was hidden by the mists, and when he tried to focus on a single spot, he could swear that it moved. James turned to his left, and he saw a naked man walking along the ground, apparently lost. James turned again and saw more naked people wandering around at varying distances.

This was a large space, and everyone within was aimless, lost, and, from their facial expressions, miserable. As James tried to get a better idea of the setting, he realized the walls were moving. Not closing in but sliding up and down in places. After a few seconds of this, he recognized that the walls were made up of living snakes. The floor must be too.

What the fuck is this place? How could this be your *dream? What kind of sick, evil shit . . . ?*

A naked man stumbled into James, and he reflexively jumped back. The man went down and struck the writhing floor, and there was a sound of something biting into him, followed by the man wailing.

I don't need to see any more.

James left immediately. Back in dreamspace, he decided to just return to his own body. He didn't want any further surprises like that last dream. And the Rodriguez camp didn't really need to know he was alive. He hadn't even completely decided if he was going back to them. If he didn't return, then knowing he was alive would only give them false hope that he would come to fight beside them. If he did return, then his arrival would be all the more triumphant if it came as a surprise.

Need to figure out what that last dream meant as soon as possible, but visiting other people's dreams won't help me with that.

He sought his own body, and it too had a distinct energy. This one felt like home.

And then he could feel himself again. He lay in an awkward position on Anansi's stone floor, limbs tangled. But he had a fresh resolve.

Need to figure out what's going on with the Rodriguezes. Need to figure out if they really need me more than my family. Need to figure out if I care enough about them to go back to them instead of my family, even if their need is greater. I'll try my second question again with different phrasing.

James opened his eyes, stood up, and stretched his limbs. Anansi remained in place, clearly watching him. James wondered if the god was curious about what James would ask or what he'd seen. From their interactions thus far, he was fairly certain Anansi could not read his mind.

"I suppose that if I asked you a question about a dream I observed, that would count as my final one of the three questions," James said.

"You suppose correctly. That does not mean I will not help you with questions after this. But there are some answers that may be restricted by my divine role. I am bending that for you right now, as a sort of signing bonus for becoming my Chosen."

"Final question, then," James said. "What should I do now?" He raised his hands, palms out, to preempt any objection from the Spider God. "I'm not trying to lawyer this, but given the things I care about, I just want to know: what's the best next move for me? It's hard to be certain about what to do when I just don't know what kind of risks my family faces."

Anansi sighed. **"That's fine, James. I'll give you my best advice. Your last question is appropriate. I just wish I had a better answer for you. The future is always clouded. Anyway, you will be able to ask more questions in the future. I will go ahead and show you a lot of favoritism and bend the rules for you as much as I can. That is what rules are for, right?"** He leaned in and lowered his voice confidentially. **"Even if I can't guide you like Moloch does for Rostov, I know a lot about the way the multiverse works."** He slumped back into his seat.

"Speaking of how the multiverse works," Anansi continued, **"the best single piece of advice I can give you, for both now and the future, is simple. It is also counterintuitive for people like you and me who like to calculate every angle, make promises and then take them back, and generally behave like tricksters. Take decisive action. Even if you do not feel decisive. Choose what your intellect tells you is the best of your bad options and commit without looking back. When Caesar crossed the Rubicon, when Cortes destroyed his ships, when the elves left Earth, they made decisions that could not easily be taken back. But that is how great legends are born, James. Whatever you do, do it decisively. No half measures. Become the legend you were meant to be."**

"Thank you, Anansi."

All right, James thought. That advice was actually much more helpful than the more specific advice Anansi had given him before.

I know that Mina and Yulia are resourceful. And it sounds like their Orientation is a lot less cutthroat than ours. I know what the rational choice is. I know what I need to do.

"Which way is the exit again? I know where I'm going."

CHAPTER SEVENTEEN

Surface Tension

W ake up! Wake up, everyone!" Ramon shouted at the top of his lungs as he came through the camp's perimeter.

Within seconds, the camp was filled with the loud commotion of people rousing, realizing what was going on, and shaking others.

"Is this real, Ramon?" Cliff appeared and asked the obvious groggily. His state of partial dress was off-putting—no pants, though, thankfully, his boxers and sweat-stained button-down shirt concealed everything important.

Ramon kept himself from yelling back at the stupid question and simply said, "Yes! Definitely real. We have to move right away. Moishe is distracting them, but they were on our trail, and they definitely know where we are."

"I see. I'll wake more people!" Cliff took off back toward his own tent, Ramon noticed, not toward anyone else's—he'd probably realized he wanted to put some pants on before speaking to other people.

Ramon continued rousing people himself, going and shaking the tents of the few people who were heavy sleepers. Families gathered and did head counts of their members to make sure no one was missing. People who had already accounted for their relatives' whereabouts began taking down their tents. After the last move, everyone seemed to know what to do to move on quickly.

I hope we don't make a habit of this, Ramon thought. But it seemed like a distressing possibility. What would make the cult leader give up on them?

"Camp's in bad shape," Jeffrey Ross muttered to himself. Three people dead, everyone else tired and wary, expecting the other shoe to drop at any moment as they moved slowly forward. These and the losses they'd taken against the anonymous intruder the other night were the cult's first unplanned deaths since Orientation started.

I warned Rostov about continuing to chase the enemy through the night, and now this happens. If the enemy didn't get a few of us in a situation like this, it would be purely due to their own negligence. Hate to say I told you so . . .

It wasn't exactly a good political move by Rostov to relax in the cart with the Moloch statue while everyone else had to move on foot either. More than one in the slow, bleary mass of cultists threw resentful glances his way. Rostov either didn't notice or didn't care. Jeffrey wouldn't want to bet on which. *Probably both.*

He sought Catherine, who was walking alongside the other priests—all besides Alice, who was in the cart with Rostov and the unconscious figure of Leonard Robie.

She'd let her hair down, and Jeffrey thought she looked beautiful. A little worn down, maybe, but serene. *Unlike Rostov, she actually sort of resembles what I imagine a religious leader would look like*, Jeffrey realized. He snorted at the thought. Pictured her wearing a crown of sunflowers, holding a white staff. She would present a beautiful picture, but the image felt to him like some overgrown teenager experimenting with Wicca.

Then he swallowed nervously as he imagined what the future was actually likely to be. *Christ, the religions of the new world are going to be fucked up! Gods like Moloch and leaders like Rostov. Christ on a cracker . . .*

He stepped closer to his wife, out of the shadows and into the moonlight.

"How's the hunt going, sweetheart?" Catherine asked when she saw him.

With the actual trackers besides Leonard dead, Kassim was directing the group forward with Jeffrey as a backup navigator in case something happened to him.

"We're still walking straight," Jeffrey said, deadpan. "I can confirm that we'll catch them unless they bob and weave a bit. If they get out of the way, though, we might walk past them and never know it."

The Rostov forces were in a more condensed group as they moved now, to dissuade further surprise attacks from the Assassin who had injured Leonard and killed his fellows. Their scouting abilities right now were extremely limited.

Catherine stifled a chuckle, covering her mouth so the other priests didn't see she wanted to laugh. Jeffrey could see because he knew how her face moved when she wanted to laugh.

"Why don't you and I step away and talk for a while?" she suggested once the impulse to laugh had passed.

Jeffrey extended his arm. She grabbed his bicep and pulled herself close to him. Both of them smiled, and they created a bit of distance between themselves and the rest of the group.

The odds that they specifically would be threatened by Moishe Rose were much lower than the odds of him attacking other pairs of people who might try the same thing. Besides Rostov, Jeffrey and Catherine Ross were two of the strongest members of the camp. A knife in the neck wouldn't be as effective as it would be against most of the other members of the camp, and there was a good chance that it wouldn't even land.

"So, what are you thinking about?" Catherine asked, batting her long eyelashes at him.

"I'm thinking about how unhappy the group is," Jeffrey said, not meeting her eyes. "How tired and resentful people are right now."

"You're thinking about how bad of a leader Nikolai is," she said bluntly.

Jeffrey grimaced slightly.

"Well, it's not as if I disagree with you," Catherine said. "It's still night, so we can discuss things a bit more freely. There's no chance of him being able to spy on us."

"Can we kill him now?" Jeffrey asked. "Decapitation, knife in the heart—the method doesn't matter, but he's probably only barely awake if he hasn't fallen asleep. If you got Alice to leave the cart for a few minutes on some pretext, I could get the job done."

"I've been thinking along the same line as you for some time," Catherine admitted. "We'd be much better off without him. He's a poor leader, he abuses his position, and he's slowly but surely losing his marbles." She lowered her voice. "I definitely want to kill him. But here's why we need to wait until the Orientation is over to act on it.

"Moloch is burning through his brain right now. He can barely remember people's names. That means he's only going to become more dependent on us priests. So, my position is only growing more secure, which means there's no urgency to act. The second reason is related to the first. Moloch is literally destroying Nikolai's capacity to think, slowly but surely erasing his brain with these repeated contacts. My understanding is that Moloch wants to ensure the cult survives through to the end of Orientation. After Orientation is over, the level of omniscience Moloch is giving Nikolai right now won't be necessary. The altered Earth will be dangerous, but not nearly as unpredictable as this place. So the next person who takes over as the Chosen One of Moloch won't have to burn through their brain to do it."

Is this something Moloch himself has been telling you? Jeffrey wondered. He didn't know how much contact with Moloch the priests actually had.

"Anyway," Catherine continued, "it's also possible he'll die of natural causes if he keeps overusing Moloch's power as he has. But I'm next in line for the throne, so to speak. If we wait to kill him, I can probably get the Chosen One Title. If we kill him now, though, that would probably come with the burden of accepting the same kind of deterioration Nikolai is suffering now. That's the only way we'd get through Orientation. So, I think we need to wait. Okay?"

Wordless, Jeffrey nodded. *I guess that's one way to do it.* He didn't know what to say to any of that. His wife gave him a long kiss on the lips, which he returned with more fervor than he felt, and then she walked slowly back to the other priests. For once, he didn't watch her walking away.

He felt numb.

Jeffrey had just figured they could off Rostov and steal away in the night like bandits. In this relative chaos, it felt like a perfect opportunity. They wouldn't have to kill other members of the camp to get away. No one would know what had really happened for some time. No one would be likely to come after them until they had a new leader. By then, the Rosses would be long gone.

But that was based on his premise that they were sticking with the cult for pure survival reasons. It seemed that his and Catherine's motives had diverged. He wanted to kill Rostov because Rostov was evil. Full stop. The fact that Rostov was sacrificing people to Moloch was an additional motivator, even though it was hard for Jeffrey to judge the cult for doing so when Moloch had so obviously kept them alive in the deadly Orientation space, where people were dying every day.

But the idea that Catherine would become the new Chosen One of Moloch didn't resolve the dissonance that Jeffrey felt in this situation. It just shifted.

What the hell have I gotten myself into?

The Rostov camp buzzed with nervous activity. Tensions that had festered within individual cultists now began to show on the surface.

From those who were anxious that they had been woken in the night to the individuals who knew what had really happened and feared further reprisals from Moishe Rose, no one looked comfortable. Some clearly looked at Rostov as if they blamed him for their current predicament.

Moishe looked on the scene with grim satisfaction.

Back when I was one of them, they never would've looked at Rostov that way, he thought. *I only wish I could stay and inflict more damage. I really think that if I could keep going without ever being caught, they might eventually turn on him. I was very lucky that I was able to snag my gear when we fled before.*

He backed away from the camp and retreated some distance, outpacing Kassim, who was leading them toward the Rodriguez camp. Despite all of Moishe's efforts, the cultists would certainly find the Rodriguezes if they didn't move quickly enough. It was time for him to catch up to them and make sure they were moving in the right direction, and with the appropriate sense of urgency.

Once he was far enough ahead of Kassim, Moishe began to run at top speed without concern for stealth.

The sun was just beginning to rise. Rostov would be able to track him and the Rodriguezes without difficulty soon enough.

Nikolai Rostov emerged from a trance about an hour after sunrise.

He chuckled madly.

"Excellent, excellent!" Rostov said.

"What's the good news, Niko?" Alice asked with what sounded like genuine enthusiasm.

"With the sunrise, I have laid eyes on the enemy," he replied. "And we have very good news from Moloch. We simply have to continue driving them forward. The region ahead of them is one that Moloch identified for me previously. The Dead Marsh."

Alice frowned. "A marsh? Doesn't that mean it will be difficult for our group to pursue them? Swampy ground is hard to walk through, isn't it? And the cart—"

"We don't have to chase them *through* the Dead Marsh," Rostov interrupted, shaking his head. "The important thing is to get them into the marsh itself. My understanding from Moloch is that it's an incredibly dangerous place. We might be able to destroy our enemy without needing to fight any further." He rubbed his palms together.

"Don't we need sacrifices?" Alice couldn't help asking.

He didn't let her doubt spoil his mood.

"Oh yes," Rostov said, shrugging. "Best to capture some if we can. If not, we'll set up the signal fire and resume our previous strategy. But the Dead Marsh solves a lot of our problems, you see! We don't have to worry about these people getting away from us, warning others about what we're doing, and perhaps uniting with others to fight us. As long as we keep them from escaping the marsh once they've entered, I don't think any of them will survive."

CHAPTER EIGHTEEN

Unknown Subject

Mina woke to the sound of a knock at the door, and she felt instantly anxious.

Her eye jumped straight to the population counter. [**3,395/3,397 Survivors**] *Thank goodness*, she thought. *Only two dead.*

No one had died while she slept. Yulia was still asleep beside her, lightly snoring, chest rising and falling slowly and peacefully. All was right with the world.

Then the knock came again.

This time, Mina only twitched slightly in response. *Not my ideal way to wake up, but I'm sure there's some reason someone wants to see me*—she looked to the window, which was dark and brightened only by the reflected light from flakes of falling snow—*in the middle of the night.* Was that someone moving around outside? Mina thought she saw a large, dark figure dashing through the snow. It could have been a trick of the light—the falling snow was not helping her vision. She blinked and whatever she'd seen was gone.

There was a gentle repeat of the knock.

She rose slowly from the bed, taking care not to wake Yulia up. There was a little part of her that wanted to have Yulia next to her for reinforcement when she spoke to whoever was at the door. She told that little voice to kindly shut up.

The day that I need a teenager half my size to keep my courage up is the day that I stop going outside and hole up in a small room, Mina thought furiously.

Still, she found herself shivering as she crept toward the door across the creaky wooden floorboards. *It's because the floor is cold*, she told herself.

She reached into the Small Bag of Deceptive Dimensions as she got closer to the door, and she put her hand on the kitchen knife she'd brought as a weapon. Then she looked through the peephole, and all the tension drained from the air.

It was just Detective DaSilva again.

Of course it's just DaSilva again, who did you think it would be? Mina chided herself. *Then again, there is a murderer on the loose.*

She pulled the door open slightly. "Detective, what brings you back?"

"I wanted to wait until the coast was clear around here before I spoke with you again," he said in a lowered voice. "This seemed like as good a time as any to update you on the status of the investigation."

She opened the door completely, stepped out, and pulled the door almost shut behind her.

"My sister is sleeping," Mina said. "What's going on?"

"We're still not certain who the killer is, of course," DaSilva said. "No forensics, only one cop, and only one medical examiner in this group makes that difficult. But we followed up on your idea about levels. I went around before the first challenge, and I found volunteers to report on the people who had already somehow obtained their first level before the challenge started. There was one person willing to volunteer for almost every team that formed. People are eager to see this matter resolved. I checked up on the groups where no one volunteered myself. So, we now have a fairly comprehensive list of the people who had leveled up before the challenge started. It's not decisive. There are ninety-two names on the list I compiled."

He reached out and handed her a small folded scrap of paper.

She took it and frowned. "Why are you giving this to me?"

"You're already a part of this investigation. You had the first good idea of anyone, you're clearly sharp, and I'm desperate. So I'm deputizing you. You and just a few other people have my copies of this longhand list. We can't let anyone get a look at it, or we'll have another problem besides the murderer."

"Protecting the innocent." Mina nodded. Back when James was a prosecutor, he used to emphasize that it was law enforcement's duty to protect the innocent from wrongful arrest and incarceration just as much as it was to prosecute criminals.

"Exactly. I know you'll be judicious with this list. Please give me any other lead ideas you come up with, and keep your eyes peeled. Three of the people on this list are also on our own team, so you'll be able to keep an eye on them in particular."

"Yes, Detective," she said seriously. "Is there anything else I should bear in mind?"

"Uh, no, I don't think so," he said thoughtfully. "Um, did you and your sister know about the coats available here?"

"Coats? Where?" Mina asked. Her mind immediately jumped to the blood-stained coat she'd seen on the ground that morning.

"There are lots of coats in the linen closet at the end of the hallway." DaSilva pointed, and Mina noticed a door that was set too close to another room in the inn to be a full room itself. "They were in the original set of buildings, too, but not everyone noticed them. I noticed you, Yulia, and a few other members of our little band of misfits weren't quite dressed for the weather, so I asked around. It turned out the System was looking out for us a bit!"

Hm. I wonder what the System's motive is in providing winter gear.

"Are there enough for everyone, or are they all taken?" Mina asked.

"More than enough," DaSilva said. "Some people were wearing relatively warm clothes anyway, but everyone who's heard about the free clothing has grabbed one as far as I know. Some people still haven't heard—but this building is one of those only for the winners, actually. No one would have raided this closet unless they were a winner."

Mina frowned slightly. "Let me just check." She walked down and opened the closet.

Sure enough, there were a half-dozen thick wool coats just hanging there.

That would've been expensive once. That's awfully convenient. Everything I observe about the System just makes me more suspicious of it, but it is possible this is just an amenity they're providing to make our lives more convenient.

She turned back to the detective. "Speaking of coats, did you ever ask Cara about why she moved the greatcoat the first victim left behind?"

DaSilva nodded. "Yeah. Dumb reason, but believable enough. She thought someone was injured in a fight and lost their coat. She was hoping she'd find the victim alive and be able to help them."

"That does make some sense," Mina said. "Well, how about the matter with the group's leader?" She couldn't keep a scowl from her face as she asked that.

"Leader? Oh, you mean Paul." DaSilva snorted a little at the name. "I gave him a talking to privately, and I don't think he's going to speak so recklessly in future. At the very least, I think he'll keep you and your sister's name out of his mouth."

Mina relaxed a bit, some tension falling away from her shoulders.

"Thank you, Detective," she said. "I really wanted to lie low during—"

Something flickered at the corner of her vision, and her eyes widened.

"The population count just dropped!" DaSilva exclaimed.

[3,394/3,397 Survivors]

Mina grabbed a coat from the closet and another for Yulia. She stopped to dump the coat for Yulia on the bed in their room, and then she accompanied Detective DaSilva downstairs.

As they descended the stairs, there was another flickering movement in the corner of her vision.

[3,393/3,397 Survivors]

Is there a fight going on downstairs? She found herself hoping absurdly that there was some dispute outside between groups of people. Something that would make sense of the two deaths. Something less sinister than a serial killer on the prowl.

But when Mina and DaSilva reached the entrance to the inn, there were no people visible outside. It was quiet. The only thing moving was the slowly falling snow.

The center of the settlement looked and felt empty.

"It has to be the same killer again," DaSilva said after a long silence. "No way we have two murderers killing people at night after a couple of days here."

"What do we do?" Mina asked.

"We can't go after him now. This person just killed two people inside of a few minutes. Whoever it is, he might have us outgunned if the two of us confront him. We have to be careful."

Mina nodded. "Or *whatever* the killer is," she said.

"Right," DaSilva said. "Anything in particular making you think that it's a nonhuman again?"

She elaborated on the figure she thought she'd seen through the window right after DaSilva's knock woke her.

"I don't suppose there's much likelihood that was just a dream," he said slowly, thoughtfully. Mina shook her head. But there didn't seem to be much more to say. They reentered the inn and ascended the stairs once more.

"I wish I understood the limits of the System and what magic can do," DaSilva said thoughtfully as they reached the landing. "Whether the killer is human or monster, I don't know how to catch this unsub."

"Unsub?" Mina asked.

"Oh, 'unknown subject,'" DaSilva said. He sounded surprised, as if he'd forgotten Mina was there and had been talking to himself. "Some people in the FBI use the phrase to talk about a perpetrator. It always pops into my mind whenever I think I'm dealing with a serial killer." He looked a little guilty, as if he was afraid of scaring her. "Of course, usually I've been incorrect when I thought a serial killer might be active in the past. Superficial similarities in killings can get you into some silly Hollywood ideas. This time, though . . . It would be strange if we weren't dealing with a serial killer, given what we know."

"How would you normally catch an unknown subject if you didn't have forensics? Regardless of whether they were a serial killer or not?" Mina asked.

"The basics of criminal investigation are motive, means, and opportunity," DaSilva said. "But here, the means are unclear, and in a world with magic, we don't know what's possible. Anyone might have an opportunity, as far as I know. Maybe the killer is magical and walks through walls. We don't know what everyone's abilities are. Even *you* have magic."

I assume you won't consider me a suspect, since you were with me when these people died, Mina thought.

"So you have to focus on motive, then, no?" she said.

"Right. But who has a motive to go around killing people at night? If we think the killer is a beast, they could be hungry, I guess. This hungry, though? Hungry enough to kill person after person? There are three victims now. So it would have to be more than one creature, in which case it would seem strange that they're killing us without anyone seeing them. If something is this unafraid of humans that it's approaching the settlement over and over this close together—well, I'm no expert on animal behavior, but it seems awfully bold . . .

"And assuming it's a human, I don't know how the motive could be any of the classic murder motives. Revenge, lust, greed, and jealousy don't make sense with what little we know so far. Serial killer motives tend to be weird too. Psychodrama stuff. 'I'm recreating my childhood to get back at Mommy,' or some such nonsense. I have a tendency to believe it's a human, because the killings don't feel entirely rational and calculated to me. And animals are driven by their natures when they kill. A wolf or a lion has a specific hunting method, and they don't typically hunt for fun. But even if it's a human, like my gut's telling me—I'm just not the kind of expert in these killings that we need. I don't know how these people think!"

He sounded agitated, so Mina decided to let the discussion rest for now.

"I'm going back to my room to try and get some sleep," she said. "I suggest you do the same."

"Yeah," he said, not moving. His mind seemed stubbornly fixed on the problem he needed to solve, but Mina decided it wasn't her job to make him feel better right now. Maybe if he obsessed over this, he would solve the crimes more quickly, anyway.

She reentered the room, locked the door behind herself, made sure that Yulia was still unhurt, and went back to sleep.

Or tried to.

She tossed and turned. Her mind couldn't return to the same peace she'd felt before being awakened. But eventually she stole another hour of sleep before sunrise.

At that point, Yulia stretched and yawned loudly beside her, and Mina gave up on sleep.

Mina rose and quietly told Yulia that there was a serial killer out there somewhere. Either that or a ferocious beast—maybe multiple beasts. She did not mention the figure she thought she'd seen outside. In the light of day, that memory was already beginning to feel like some campfire spirit had a hold of her imagination. Yulia seemed to take the news better than Mina would have expected. She was a bit alarmed, but no more than she had been by the first body.

"Maybe I'm too used to serial killer stories from TV," Yulia suggested sheepishly when Mina commented on this.

The two of them prepared for the day and then went downstairs, where the inn's kitchen was full of activity. People were cooking their provisions in the kitchen, and Mina was able to exchange a small share of their provisions for an already cooked breakfast. The woman who made that offer seemed quite pleased to be cooking, and when Mina thanked her, she mentioned that she had unlocked the Job of Cook within the System.

Convenient, Mina thought. *I wonder what the conditions are to get it. I probably need to start cataloging these kinds of details. It could be important to figuring out both these murders and just how to live in this world now.* But the Cook Job in particular didn't seem to be a clue toward the killer, or even a very desirable Job if there were other options, so she didn't ask follow-up questions about that one.

Instead, Mina watched as people came and went in the dining area of the inn. She occasionally popped her head outside to see what people were doing and saying. But it was an uneventful morning, generally.

With no challenge set for the day, people relaxed. The inn and surrounding area came to life.

People came downstairs, sat, ate, and chatted. Maybe it was the roaring fire in the hearth or the atmosphere of general relaxation. Maybe it was the fact that the people staying in this inn all had plenty of food.

But people outside seemed more guarded than the people inside the inn whenever Mina peeked out at them. They kept to themselves or in small groups, whispering and hurrying along on whatever errands animated them before returning whence they came.

As the morning turned to afternoon, activity diminished in both the open area outside and in the common spaces of the inn. Mina lost interest in people watching, and she and Yulia returned to their room.

"Let's go over our Status sheets," Mina suggested. Though she and Yulia were both wary of going outside without others to accompany them while a killer was on the loose, Mina was very conscious that her sister could get bored if she didn't have some form of stimulation.

Now I have a more constructive activity to do with her than puzzles, at least.

"You have to promise not to laugh," Yulia insisted.

"Yes, yes, I promise," Mina replied.

It turned out that Yulia's unique Talents were Confidant, Observation, and Peacemaker. She was embarrassed that Observation apparently resulted from a tendency to watch other people interact without participating herself. But Mina couldn't help but think of the applications of the Talent to their present situation.

It comes with the Skills Trace and—

There was a harsh sound of knocking at the door: *Bap! Bap! Bap!*

Mina and Yulia both looked up, stunned.

Then Mina rose, peered through the peephole, and saw it was DaSilva.

"Detective, you scared me for a moment!" she called through the door.

"Mina, you and your sister probably need to stay in your room for the rest of the day!" DaSilva said urgently.

"What's wrong?" Mina asked, trying to keep the panic out of her voice.

"One of the two people killed was Paul. There are people who remember how he behaved toward you yesterday and think you might have had something to do with it."

CHAPTER NINETEEN

Roadkill

James took a step forward, and Anansi raised one limb in the universal gesture for "Wait just a second."

"I have one more thing to pass along before you leave, James." His long, raised limb reached out, and James saw a tiny spider resting on the tip.

"Oh, one of your children," James said, a little uncertainly. "You did mention keeping in touch."

"Yes," Anansi agreed. **"Hester is a descendant, and she carries many more of her children within her body. This should make it easy for us to remain in touch indefinitely."**

And they'll live on my body that entire time, James thought. *No, don't be a wimp. It's fine.* Something about this spider being more spider-sized than those he'd encountered in the Orientation forest made this feel slightly ickier. But he knew that was completely irrational. He'd been covered in spider viscera just, what, a few days ago? He was a little hazy on how quickly or slowly time passed in Anansi's realm, but it felt like the spider fight was very recent.

James extended his hand to touch the tip of Anansi's limb, and the little spider crawled from Anansi to James without further prompting. She quickly maneuvered up James's arm, then his shoulder, and then up his neck until she rested on the skin behind his ear. James was pleasantly surprised that he didn't feel ticklish.

When my mom used to sing "The Itsy Bitsy Spider" and run her fingers up my arm, I was much more sensitive, I guess?

"A pleasure to meet you," a tinny voice said.

James half expected it, which was the only reason the voice didn't make him jump.

"The pleasure is all mine, Hester!" James said, smiling.

"Please take good care of me and my children, James," Hester said.

How long do spiders live? James wondered. *She made sure to mention her children. Will she die soon?*

"Of course," James said. He looked at Anansi as he spoke to his new passenger. "Anything special I should know about how to take care of you?"

"Not really," Hester said. "We'll catch any insects that fly near you for food. Just try to give me a little warning if you're planning to suddenly surround yourself in flame or something. We'll find some place to hide."

Where?! James thought. If he was engulfed in flames, he'd raise the temperature of his whole body to a level that would kill any ordinary spider or insect— but maybe the spiders from Anansi's realm were different. Or maybe they could hide inside his body? Under his skin or something?

"I'll do whatever I can to keep you safe, Hester."

"They don't live long," Anansi said, as if reading his thoughts from earlier. **"Especially not on this sort of mission. But if the spiders who live on your body become integral to your legend, they will live on forever in the stories that are told of your exploits. Like the Spider Queen and her children."**

"It is our honor to live and die in your service," Hester agreed.

James shuddered slightly. The different view of mortality was the most jarring thing about Anansi he'd noticed since they met. *How concerned was he really about the risk of Mina and Yulia dying when he projected the possible risks of their Orientation? How big of a deal is death to Anansi really? What value does a mortal life, any mortal life, represent to a god?*

But he realized these questions were getting him nowhere. He wasn't going to change his decision now. He'd decided what to do based on the best possible information, and now it was action, not doubt, that was needed.

Be like the spiders, he thought. *They scurry off on a mission that guarantees an accelerated death with the equivalent of a smile. Our outlook is hopefully better than theirs.* Unless the tale Anansi expected him to weave had a sad ending.

"Thank you for your sacrifice," James said somberly. To Anansi, he said, "I'm going now, then."

The Spider God silently pointed behind James, and he saw the same portal he'd entered Anansi's realm through. He strode up to it, and with one final wave to Anansi, he hurled himself through. Into darkness. Into the void between worlds.

This time, he knew exactly how to get to where he was going. He navigated silently and swiftly, as close as he could get to where he felt the presence of his comrades.

When he reached out with his mind, he sensed them now, like flickering lights in the darkness. He didn't know which power this was, or if it was just how accustomed he'd become to navigating the void. But he pulled toward the dozens of points of light. Dozens of people who wished for his return. Who needed him.

I hope they've gotten stronger, he thought. *If they haven't, Cliff has a lot to answer for. He had one job. If they aren't more powerful than they were, I'll almost be fighting on my own.*

At last, he burst through the blackness into dim sunlight. He was at the bottom of a deep chasm, but the feel of the sun's warmth on his skin was unmistakable.

He wasn't sure if it was near sunrise, midday, or sunset, and it didn't matter for now. The first priority as he got his bearings was to grab onto something solid. He found a cliffside, and he began to climb.

Once he'd pulled his body up completely out of the inky darkness, he took a moment to look around. He could immediately tell that, as planned, he had come out of the void in a very different spot from where he'd entered. Before, he had dived from a cliff into what seemed an endless abyss. By contrast, this was a relatively small chasm. He could see cliffsides both in front of and behind him. Not close enough to be claustrophobic, but close enough that it would've been easy enough to jump from one rock face to the other.

He noticed the sunlight filter through the branches of a tree that stood on the cliff's edge, directly above him.

As he climbed, he thought about what his next priorities would be.

While I travel toward the group, I'll work on Skill Fusion. And I guess I'll find some bits of myself that can be expended to create monsters too. This last idea was one he adopted more reluctantly. Even though he had leveled up Pain Resistance over and over, chopping his arm off to gather enough flesh to make a golem had been an excruciating experience. And the regeneration was more painful than losing the arm. It almost made him feel bad for having forced such quick regeneration on Cliff after their first battle with the Corpse Eater. Almost.

But then, maybe I helped him get Pain Resistance, James thought. *I don't know what abilities anyone has except me. Important to remember all the things I don't know about the people around me.* His mind returned to the last dream he had invaded. *I'll see if I can return there too. I shouldn't have let myself get scared off so easily. I need to understand what that was about.*

Finally, James was able to grab onto the root of the tree. He easily pulled himself up onto the level surface above.

Pull-ups used to be hard. Now I only need one hand and minimal effort.

"I never thought I'd be so glad to set foot on solid ground," he said under his breath.

"I'm also relieved," Hester replied.

I'm going to have to get used to this.

"Do you have any idea which way I need to go to get back to my group?" James asked.

He looked around. The cliffside he'd come up looked to just be somewhere in the Orientation forest, but across the narrow chasm he saw what looked to be a large desert. *I didn't realize the Orientation space had such vastly different ecosystems. Probably could have gotten this information out of that Spider God with one of my questions, but then, maybe I still will.*

"Um, it depends on where they go," Hester said. "Lord Anansi says that if you want to get to the Dead Marsh, where they're probably going to end up, you should cross the Wasting Desert. Otherwise, you'll probably take longer and run into Moloch's cultists before you reunite with your people."

"Very helpful, thank you! Let's go, then." He hopped across the chasm. "Let me know if you come up with anything else about which way I should go, okay?"

Anansi is being much more helpful and straightforward than when I was in front of him, James thought approvingly.

"Or, for that matter, any tips!" James added.

"Will do!" Hester's tinny voice said. From her tone, she seemed weirdly excited to be of service, but James decided not to question it. Anansi and Hester had given him an explanation of her motivations, difficult though it was for James to understand.

He began working on Skill Fusion as he walked through the desert in a straight line, using the sun to navigate.

When he got thirsty, he conjured water with Basic Elemental Magic: Water, which he had decided he would keep unaltered. He had decided the same for Basic Elemental Magic: Earth. Those elements seemed likely to be especially useful back on Earth, since he had Water Affinity and Earth Affinity naturally, and the Earth itself was made of water and earth.

After he had finished, he reviewed his improvements. He kept walking as he did so, alternating between looking at the screen and the empty desert in front of him. *Status.*

[Status

Name: James Robard

Race: Evolver Human, Lv. 14

Class: Predator in Human Skin, Lv. 20

Job: Politician, Lv. 8

Health: 5041/5041

Mana: 6776/6776

Stamina: 4225/4225

Wrath Meter: 0%

Stats

Strength: 82
Agility: 89
Stamina: 65
Fortitude: 71
Dexterity: 62
Perception: 77
Will: 77
Intelligence: 88
Charisma: 69
Stealth: 49
Free Points: 0
Skills
Air Strike, Lv. 0
Basic Elemental Magic: Earth, Lv. 2
Basic Elemental Magic: Gravity, Lv. 2
Basic Elemental Magic: Water, Lv. 3
Basic Non-Elemental Magic, Lv. 1
Berserk Mode, Lv. 0
Blame Avoidance, Lv. 0
Compulsion, Lv. 4
Dreamwalk, Lv. 2
Empathic Projection, Lv. 9
Enhanced Stem Cell Production, Lv. 4
False Reality, Lv. 0
Fate Resistance
Hand of Glory, Lv. 1
Identify, Lv. 6
Illusion Magic, Lv. 0
Indeterminate Past, Lv. 0
Laying on Hands, Lv. 5
Lightning Strike, Lv. 0
Loyal Following, Lv. 3
Mass Pillage, Lv. 1
Meteor Strike, Lv. 0
Mind of the Predator, Lv. 0
Monster Control, Lv. 2
Monster Generation, Lv. 4
Natural Camouflage, Lv. 2
Omnivore, Lv. 0
Organization, Lv. 2
Pain Resistance, Lv. 5

Perfect Choice of Words, Lv. 0
Pillage, Lv. 9
Predator's Missile, Lv. 0
Predator's Sacred Armor, Lv. 0
Predator's Strike, Lv. 3
Predator's Venomous Armaments, Lv. 0
Rapid Recovery, Lv. 0
Self-Control, Lv. 0
Silent Spellcasting
Silk Production, Lv. 9
Skill Fusion
Skill Transfer
Spellbinding Words, Lv. 0
System Interface
Threads of Fate, Lv. 0
Universal Language Comprehension
Way of the Predator, Lv. 0
Talents
Basic Spellcraft, Lv. 4
Cannibalism, Lv. 6
Cool-Headed, Lv. 8
Earth Affinity
Efficient Magic, Lv. 4
Flame Affinity
Leadership, Lv. 5
Manipulation, Lv. 9
Mass Manipulation, Lv. 3
Monster Patriarch, Lv. 3
Selective Empathy, Lv. 5
Water Affinity
Titles
A Stitch in Time
Chosen One of Anansi
Citizen of the Dead Marsh
Deceiver
Devout Beacon
Dreamweaver
Figure of Destiny
Friend of All Spiders
Living Legend
Spider-King

Storyteller
Swiss Army Mage
System Pioneer
Trickster]

Such a lengthy list, and that was without his preferred armor and equipment. He hadn't taken out his Royal Exoarmor or Ego Antler Spear for the walk through the desert, which had been uneventful for these first few hours.

I'm looking pretty damn dangerous, James thought. *I don't even know if I really need a weapon or armor anymore.*

And then he felt a rumbling beneath him. The sand began to shake.

"I don't suppose this is just an earthquake," James said wryly.

"I don't think so either," Hester replied. "Should we run, or—"

Just ahead of James, three giant creatures that looked much like worms burst forth from the sand. It took James a second to recognize that the creatures actually had lots of limbs. The many legs were extremely scrawny and twig-like compared to their thick, long bodies.

"Better buckle up," James murmured.

"Oh no!" Hester cried quietly.

Identify. He used it on the closest one.

Monstrous Desert Centipede, Lv. 11

Hm. Looks and sounds weak. Time to test one of my new Skills.

He swung his right arm through the air and visualized the attack. *Air Strike!*

A large, thick blade of air flew from his arm and moved invisibly away. For a moment, the only sign that he had done anything was the movement of sand.

Then the three centipedes broke into pieces, each hit and bisected by the attack.

Their torn exoskeletons tumbled to the desert sand.

Brown liquid gushed out in juicy spurts, staining the sand beside their shattered bodies. It smelled a little like battery acid.

[You killed Monstrous Desert Centipede, Lv. 11! You gained 110 exp!]
[You killed Monstrous Desert Centipede, Lv. 11! You gained 110 exp!]
[You killed Monstrous Desert Centipede, Lv. 10! You gained 99 exp!]

"Blegh!" James wrinkled his nose. *Gross! They smell worse than roadkill! I guess I won't be getting any food in this desert. If the spiders from before weren't edible, I doubt these ugly things are. I still have some human meat, but hopefully I can wait to eat until I get back to the others.*

He didn't feel either tired or hungry after the exchange with the centipedes. Unlike Precision Strike, one of its originating Skills, Air Strike used a combination of Stamina and Mana, and it therefore drained James less than Precision Strike would have.

"Oh, um, those things weren't friendly with Anansi, right?" he asked sheepishly. "Just realized I probably should have asked questions before I sliced and diced."

"No, um, no. Don't"—she laughed—"don't worry about it," Hester replied. She sounded a little flustered. "Centipedes actually eat spiders, James."

"Oh, okay. Then there's no problem if I exterminate any we come across. Good to know!"

There was another quiet pronunciation in his ear, but it was so quiet, James wasn't sure if Hester had meant to say something to him.

It sounded like, "Oh dear."

CHAPTER TWENTY

Memento Mori

As Moishe rejoined the Rodriguez camp, he found them in poor order.

Moving, yes—they had packed everything up and were on the move when he caught up to them. Rightfully afraid of the cultists and Rostov's evil god, yes. None of them wanted to be sacrificed. But still, they were far slower and less organized, less certain, than they had been when he'd last seen them.

Perhaps the morale was slowly draining out of them. The hope.

Rumor had clearly spread among the family of Rostov and Moloch's powers.

Some people looked up at the sky far too often, as if wondering whether the enemy was spying on them at that very moment. Others pointedly avoided looking in the direction of the sun. Either way, they were giving the enemy more of their fear, more of their emotional energy, than they could sustain.

This is how armies lose battles, he thought as he stepped through the branches. *They need enthusiasm. Something to give them heart. Help them endure. They need . . .* His mind fumbled for the concept he was looking for until it smacked him in the face. *They need leadership.*

Rostov's camp had awful leadership. But as much as their Prophet was a horrendous monster with no sense of loyalty to anyone but himself, at least he was decisive. He gave them a clear sense of direction.

If I were to approach someone and ask who's in charge here, I wonder what they would tell me, Moishe thought. They were in a far worse state now than they had been when he and the other Moloch refugees discovered them before. *It's the absence of that man.*

Unfortunately, Moishe didn't feel that he personally was well suited to replacing James Robard. And the position of interim leader was perilous anyway. He still thought that James would return. Depending on the leader's temperament, he might not take kindly to someone occupying his place while he was gone. Some leaders would seek an opportunity to get rid of such a person. Who knew if James was the jealous type?

Therefore, instead of trying to take charge of the situation, Moishe joined the camp in marching forward. By his own example, he tried to encourage an accelerated pace.

They walked for a few hours before Moishe heard a fuss from the back part of the camp.

"Cultists getting close!" People spoke in tones of alarm.

Moishe saw Ramon standing back among them. He had to be the source of that information.

I should have known he would go back on scouting duty, he thought. *I should be doing that with him.*

"Everyone march, double time!" Chava Rodriguez called out. "Now is when it really counts! Unless you want to wind up food for an evil god, you have to move!"

Moishe approached Ramon, clasped his hand, and pulled him in for a brief hug.

"Good to see you're keeping up the good work!" Moishe said when they pulled apart. "Do you need another pair of eyes?"

Ramon smiled. "Glad to see you made it back in one piece. I don't know if we really need scouting right now, though. We just need to run."

Moishe looked up. He noticed a thin mist rolling in overhead.

That's a first, he thought. *The weather has been nothing but sunny since we entered Orientation. Maybe some god has decided to protect us from sight.*

"I think we'll manage to get away," Moishe said.

Nikolai Rostov grinned.

"So, someone saw you?" he asked Officer Ross.

"Yeah, one of the enemy spotted me and ran away."

"And you marked him with your ability?"

"Correct," Ross's expression remained unchanged as he spoke, as if he couldn't even fake a smile at the good news. Rostov's grin widened. He enjoyed it when Officer Ross wasn't enjoying himself.

"Excellent," Rostov said. "Then we'll know where they are even once they pass through into the Dead Marsh. Moloch's vision into that place is impaired, which makes it all the more important to maintain some other way of tracking them."

"You know there's a time limit for Trace?" Ross said.

"Details, details, Officer. You said it was something like three days at most that you could monitor a target, right?"

"Yes."

"Then we'll have plenty of time. There's no way people who are running from us so frantically will last long in the Dead Marsh."

"If you say so," Officer Ross replied. He looked pale, as if the hunt was getting to him.

"Why don't you get some rest, Officer?" Rostov suggested, smiling with faux benevolence. "There are others I'll send to the front now so that any scouts for the enemy can see we're still advancing. So they know that they have no choice but to flee into that bog."

Ross let out a long breath and walked away. His obvious discomfort was more enjoyable to Rostov than the good news had been.

The Prophet grabbed hold of Kassim and whispered instructions in his ear.

"Kassim, grab a bunch of our people and get out in front of the group. There's no more urgency for the bulk of us to move forward anymore, so I'll let the rest know they can camp. But I need you to walk forward with enough manpower to ensure that anyone who sees you will think you're the advance party for the group."

Kassim swallowed loudly. "Prophet, are you sure that's wise? You remember what they did to our previous scouts. They could be trying a death by a thousand cuts strategy—"

"No, Kassim, don't worry. They won't hurt you!" Rostov reassured him. "One of their scouts just ran into Officer Ross and took off in the opposite direction. They're running scared. I just want to make sure that if they have any other scouts looking around, they'll keep seeing what looks like the group advancing. We want them to rush into the Dead Marsh. The best way to guarantee that is to make sure they believe that we continue to advance."

"Will the group no longer be advancing? What are we *actually* doing?" Kassim asked with a frown.

"I'm going to let people slow down. Ease tensions a bit. People are rattled. I need you and the least rattled people you can find to go and make it look like we're still hot on their trail. In another day, after people have rested, we'll follow the enemy right to the border of the marsh. Then we'll set up a perimeter and make sure they don't escape that place once they've entered."

"Visibility is getting bad, and people at the front are finding it hard to move forward through the muck," Ramon finished.

"What do you mean, it's hard to move forward?" Cliff exclaimed. "Do you understand what's chasing us?"

"I understand perfectly well, *sir*," Ramon said. It was the sort of quasi-respectful way he was used to speaking to his uncle when Tio Chava was being unreasonable. "I'm the one who's been reporting back to everyone on who has been chasing us, if you recall."

"Yes, yes, of course," Cliff said a bit stiffly, wearing a forced smile. "We appreciate your contribution, Ramon. This is just a very stressful situation. It feels a little like the people out front don't fully appreciate the urgency or something."

"Maybe there's something we could do with magic to improve the soil?" Alan suggested.

"I'll walk over there and take a look," Mitzi said. "Maybe I can bake the ground a bit or something."

Ramon seriously doubted that would work, but he also knew that the other family members, who were trying to find ways to move forward in the swamp muck, would appreciate the effort. He smiled and nodded appreciatively to Mitzi.

Mama Camila looked worried. "If we can't move forward, we'll need to prepare to make our stand here, no?"

"No," Tio Chava replied immediately. "We should scatter in that case. They can't catch all of us if we go in different directions. We know they defeated James. A straight fight with them means death for the whole family. I'm not convinced that we won't be able to proceed further into the marsh if we try. I want to go and see what exactly is giving us so much trouble—"

"Can I go back out to the edge of the marsh?" Ramon interrupted. "We need to know if they're still chasing us or if the swampy ground is slowing them down too."

"Sure, man," Cliff said lightly before anyone else could speak. "Keep up the good work. Thanks!"

Ramon smiled and left.

As he walked away, at the edge of his range of hearing, he just barely caught Cliff swearing under his breath. Ramon was pretty sure that was directed at him. But he could only roll his eyes. He had more important things to do than swear back and forth with Cliff.

He approached Moishe to come along with him, and they set off toward the area where they expected to find the cultists.

Jeffrey Ross walked away from Rostov, tired in body and soul.

He thought he had waited for the perfect moment to kill Rostov, but it seemed destined not to happen. Instead, they would continue chasing the only sacrifices who'd had the pluck to escape from Moloch's cult since he'd been pulled into this. And something in him felt drained of life.

I'm still useful to the group, he thought sullenly, *so if Catherine's right, I might at least outlast Rostov. But is* surviving *really worth all this?*

He pictured his children's shining faces. Howie and Rena. They were even younger in his mind than in real life. He had to survive this for them, right?

But for once, the motivational tool he'd been using these last weeks turned itself on him.

What would they think if they knew what you've done? he thought. *What you plan to* continue *doing, until Catherine's moment comes?*

"Prophet!" a voice called from the edge of the camp. Excited. Good news of some kind for the Moloch cultists, which almost invariably meant bad news for someone else.

"New guests!" the same voice called. Ross recognized it now as Ted Rowan. He was in charge of the team Rostov had assigned to seek out new sacrifices while the camp moved forward. The group had one priest with them so that they couldn't lose their way.

Ross walked toward the sound of Rowan's voice. He needed to see who these potential sacrifices were.

A small group of five figures stood huddled in a group encircled by the hunting party. Their postures revealed that their hands were bound in front of them, which probably meant that they had struggled a little. Not very effectively, clearly, but enough to be treated as enemies already. This would impact how the cult would deal with them.

Ross had to walk closer to get a better view of their faces, but that only affirmed the sinking feeling in his stomach.

A bunch of teenagers, Ross thought. None of them even eighteen years old, if his eyes were any good. *How did they survive in the forest so long? Where are their parents? Did the adults die when the hunting party found them?*

But none of his questions was as pressing as the reality in front of him. They looked terrified, and he couldn't avoid thinking about what was likely to happen to them. *Are we really going to stoop so low?*

He turned away from the sight and found himself face to face with Catherine. His expression of consternation met her look of careful, studied indifference. They stared into each other's eyes for a long, pregnant moment.

Are you really thinking of letting this happen? he wanted to ask her.

Even as he had the thought, he already knew how she would answer. She would raise the practical questions. *How do you propose we stop it from happening? At what cost? Think of your own children, who could lose their father, before you think of these strangers' children.*

He had no immediate answers to those questions, but he knew that those practical considerations didn't matter so much right now. He hadn't become a policeman so he could put his own life and needs above those of others.

I have to do something.

CHAPTER TWENTY-ONE

Proof

I already told a few people that you were with me at the time that the population counter ticked down," DaSilva said. "Still. You and the girl should stay out of sight for the rest of the day. People are angry and stressed and looking for someone to blame."

"Yulia and I will stay here together, Detective." It was hard to even be annoyed at DaSilva for forgetting Yulia's name. It sounded as if he was keeping them out of some real danger. "Will we be safe if we come out for the challenge tomorrow?"

"I'm sure I can sort this out by then," he said, noticeably relieved. "I'll tell anyone I can exactly what happened."

"Yeah," Mina said. "I mean, thank you!" *I hope this doesn't interfere with his ability to continue the investigation, though.* Managing the strange, cramped politics of the Orientation at the same time as DaSilva tried to identify a completely anonymous killer or *killers* of unknown species, who might also possibly be employing a magical murder method, seemed like a tall order.

"Of course," he replied. Then Mina heard his slow, heavy footsteps tread away from their door.

Goodness, she thought. *People in this place are so combustible. We might be safer if we could find some place in the wilderness to hide out. If only the weather wasn't so dangerous!*

Even as she had this thought, she could see faint glimmers of snow falling outside the window. The stakes of this Orientation would only increase as the environment grew deadlier.

Mina and Yulia spent the rest of the day going through their various abilities and how they might help, both in the challenges and in finding the identity of this killer.

Mina's Status read as follows:

[Status
Name: Mina Danailova
Race: Base Human, Lv. 3
Class: Mage
Job: Structural Engineer (Pre-System)
Health: 49/49
Mana: 272/272
Stats
Strength: 4
Agility: 8(5)
Stamina: 6(4)
Fortitude: 7
Dexterity: 10(9)
Perception: 11
Will: 16
Intelligence: 17
Free Points: 0
Skills
Accelerated Learning, Lv. 5
Adamant Will, Lv. 0
Basic Elemental Magic: Water, Lv. 5
Basic Elemental Magic: Wind, Lv. 0
Deception Resistance, Lv. 1
Defiance, Lv. 0
Intuitive Aptitude, Lv. 2
Emotional Control, Lv. 4
Identify, Lv. 9
Prediction, Lv. 3
Situational Intelligence, Lv. 6
System Interface
Universal Language Comprehension
Talents
Cool-Headed, Lv. 5
Logic, Lv. 2
Quick Study, Lv. 3
Water Affinity
Willful, Lv. 0

Titles
Challenger]

The two sisters gradually shared their Status information with pauses for questions, clarification, and laughter.

"That Talent is so you," Yulia said, when Mina explained the Logic Talent.

"Strange that it highlights certain aspects of our personalities so strongly and not others," Mina said. "It didn't give me anything related to how nurturing I am."

Yulia bit her lip and said nothing, and Mina quickly changed the subject.

Most of Mina's abilities seemed unlikely to help the investigation. But there was Deception Resistance. That would at least make it difficult for people to lie to her directly. And there was Prediction, though Mina anticipated she would need to level it much more before she would be able to use it effectively in this context.

Yulia's Trace will be a lot more useful. If I can anticipate who the killer's most likely to target next, she can track the person's whereabouts. We could catch them red-handed.

The only problem was that Mina had no idea why the killer was targeting who they were targeting—or if the people killed were simply victims of opportunity. She still knew nothing about the first victim, and the only thing she knew about the two recent victims was that one of them was Paul, who had tried to assert a leadership role in Orientation.

I hope the murders are all by a single human as Detective DaSilva thinks. If there were in fact multiple killers, then it was possible the social order here was already beginning to break down. And if it was a monster or monsters, then Mina wasn't optimistic about their prospects for catching something that seemed to prey upon humans at will and leave no trace.

The sisters spent a little more time going over their abilities and practicing them. Mina's use of water elemental magic earlier had awakened her latent Water Affinity and helped her unlock wind elemental magic. So she spent time further refining her precise control of water. If she could develop specialized abilities around Water Affinity, perhaps it would make up for her lack of physical power and delicate condition.

It seemed to give her more experience to use fine control of the ability, such as by manipulating lots of individual droplets through the air around her, rather than just to flood it with Mana and conjure as much water as she could. This was good, since Mina still didn't have much Mana to play with.

It doesn't matter so much how deep my reserves of Mana are, Mina thought. *It's how I use it. I'll learn to use my 272 Mana like it was ten thousand!* She was grateful that she'd chosen the Mage Class. If she'd been any of the warrior Class options, she wouldn't be able to practice effectively without possibly injuring herself and her baby. And Mina desperately wanted to practice her Skills. If there was anything that she hated, it was falling behind.

The sisters discovered that Yulia did not require an injured person nearby to accrue experience for Healing Aura and Laying on Hands. So Mina encouraged her to practice those abilities and switch back and forth between them, trying to get a feel for how they felt, how they worked, and how best to use them.

After an hour or so of that, they went to bed. They'd both exhausted their Mana, and there wasn't much else to do. They didn't want to push their luck by going out, even if Mina did feel a bit restless just staying in place and waiting.

The new day dawned cold and cloudy, and the two women dragged themselves reluctantly from bed and prepared for the day, uncertain what reception they would face outside. They packed their things into their Small Bags of Deceptive Dimensions, unsure if they would be able to return to this room.

Once they were downstairs in the inn's common area, it was surprisingly quiet. As on the previous day, most of the people in the winners' quarters were relatively content. The only hints that something might be wrong were the odd sideways glances at Mina and Yulia and the generally quiet atmosphere in the dining room.

But the woman who had cooked their breakfast yesterday was still friendly and was still willing to exchange some already cooked food for provisions. This time there was less of a rush in the kitchen, so Mina was able to introduce herself without feeling she was holding people up.

"I'm Alba," the Cook replied. Mina detected a fellow foreigner from her accent, and it provided an entrée into a longer conversation. It turned out that Alba and her family were Spanish. In the pre-System world, she was a reasonably well-known Spanish poet. She and her family had been on vacation at Disney World when they were swept into the System. Tragically, due to Spanish naming conventions, she was here alone, while her husband and children were somewhere else, facing dangers unknown.

Somewhere around the time that Mina had started to understand how Spanish surnames worked, Yulia came in looking for breakfast. So Mina made another introduction.

Alba seemed very pleasant, and Mina suggested that they eat together if she was willing to take a break from her job.

They had just begun eating when the announcement rang out.

[Attention all survivors! The next challenge is about to begin. You have five minutes to prepare yourselves.]

"Well, that's rotten timing!" Alba griped in instantly translated Spanish. "Just when I was getting to know you girls."

"I'm glad we got to say hello and get some food," Yulia said, smiling.

"Thank you for your kindness," Mina agreed.

"I'm just getting experience with my new Job, you know," Alba said modestly. "I'm so glad both of you are enjoying the food. Eat quick! I'm going to go and find my group in case we need any last-minute preparations." She picked up her food and walked out the door.

With the Cook gone, Mina and Yulia were free to wolf down the rest of their meal. It was smaller than they'd had yesterday, with slightly less food available. Alba was clearly rationing a bit, and Mina couldn't blame her.

When the five minutes were up, Mina blinked and opened her eyes to find herself in a different place. Just like in the first challenge, they'd disappeared from where they were and reappeared in an outdoor location.

A look around revealed snow, trees, and a steep upward slope to one side of them and the open sky to the other. They were on a mountain, and they seemed to be at a fairly high elevation.

As Mina inhaled the air, she had to take slower, deeper breaths to get the same feeling of energy that breathing normally gave her.

This air is horribly thin. I'm not going to be able to move around very well if I have to breathe like this just standing still. I hope this isn't a physical challenge. But given that their first challenge had not been physically demanding, she anticipated that this one would be. They were probably supposed to finish climbing to the top of the mountain or something like that.

Fortunately, she noticed that their group from the first challenge had been transported to the same place as her and Yulia. And if this was like last time, they wouldn't all have to participate in whatever challenge was coming up.

"Good to see you all again!" Mina put on a big smile and waved at the other members of her group as if she was thrilled to be here.

She saw them smile back at her. They remembered her contribution from last time, she was certain. She was counting on it since she'd almost certainly need them to excuse her inability to contribute this time.

The group huddled closer together, and people exchanged quiet chatter about the setting and about what they imagined the new challenge would be. People were already looking forward to their new rations, though Mina couldn't understand how any of them could have finished what the System had given them last time. Her and Yulia's food would last another two days since the Cook had rationed what she made carefully, and the exchanges between her cooked food and their rations had been reasonable. Mina hoped the group wouldn't be disappointed.

After a couple of minutes, Cygnus's voice interrupted them.

[Everything is prepared now, and all groups are together. You find yourself on a picturesque mountainside. However, you are not there to enjoy the view. Near each group there is an opening to a cave. Within that cave, there is a Dungeon.]

Mina found herself looking around as the proctor spoke, both for the Dungeon she mentioned and for Cygnus herself. The Dungeon entrance quickly became visible. A cave dug into the mountainside began to glow gently.

[Today's Dungeon challenge is largely trap-based, though it includes some monsters as well. As with the previous challenge, it is not necessary for all members of a group to participate. If you intend to participate in the challenge for your group, please walk toward the opening of the Dungeon.]

The group as a whole began walking toward the Dungeon, though Mina hesitated.

"Of course, we don't expect you to participate in this one, young lady," the old gentleman in the group said quietly, with a gentle smile. "You contributed far more than your share last time, and I hope we can win the challenge and pay you back this time."

Others nodded in agreement and looked pleased with what he was saying.

DaSilva simply smiled, as if this was something he had hoped someone would say so he wouldn't have to bring it up himself.

[It should go without saying that there will be winners and losers in this challenge. The first half of the groups to clear the Dungeon will be the winners. The second half will be the losers. In the event that a member of a winning team happens to die in the Dungeon, his or her reward will be split among the surviving members of that team.]

Everyone grew more serious at that announcement, but they continued moving forward, leaving Mina and Yulia behind, holding hands near the cliffside.

"Sis," Yulia said, not making eye contact with Mina. "I really want to go, and I think they might need a Healer if there are traps. Can I, please?"

Mina was a little surprised, but she realized she shouldn't be. This was all an adventure to Yulia to some degree. It wasn't as though the serial killer would be murdering people in the Dungeon. Hopefully. It was an opportunity to see some more of the new world—

No, no, that isn't the right way to think about this at all! Mina corrected herself. Yulia was volunteering to go into danger because she wanted to help other people. *Like she always does.*

"You could get yourself killed trying to help them!" she hissed sternly.

"How will they feel if someone dies in there, and I could have helped them?" Yulia finally made eye contact with Mina.

Mina looked over at the group. Yulia raised a good point, actually. The proctor had made clear it was possible to change the compositions of teams. DaSilva would probably stick up for them, but that might just turn them into a team of three. The weakest team in the competition.

"No, I don't care about that!" Mina said, flustered. "I'm concerned about *your* life, sweet!" She cupped Yulia's cheek with her palm. "If someone dies in there, that just proves it was too dangerous for you to go."

"The world is dangerous," Yulia said quietly. "Especially now. Can you even promise that it's less dangerous out here? There could be wild beasts roaming around, couldn't there? And I *want* to go. No one's forcing me. I just want your permission. Can I go?"

Mina thought of comebacks. *If there are wild beasts roaming the mountain, are you really going to leave me here alone?* But she didn't really want to argue. Yulia had already given her good reasons. *I'm clinging too tightly.*

"Well, I have to let go sometime," Mina said softly, reluctantly. *You were always going to leave home eventually. And it seems the world is going to be extremely dangerous from now on. At least this time you'll be with people who seem decent enough.*

Mina released Yulia's hand.

"You can do this," Mina said with more conviction than she felt. "You're a Danailova." She paused. "I love you!" She pulled Yulia close, and Yulia returned her embrace. Mina felt a little bit of liquid gathering at the corners of her eyes. And there was a terrible pit in her stomach. She knew she might never see her sister again.

Mina blinked the tears away before Yulia could pull back from her and see them.

"I have to remind them how much the Danailova sisters contribute!" Yulia said fiercely, stepping back and staring Mina in the eyes.

There was a fire in her, Mina noticed. It was her own look, one that she had never expected to see on her baby sister's face.

Maybe this situation is forcing her to really grow up.

"You're going to be amazing," Mina said. She had never felt prouder of Yulia than in this moment when she was volunteering to go into mortal peril. It might end up being wildly foolish. The degree of danger was completely unknown except for Cygnus's mention of death, which had clearly been off the table in the previous challenge.

The sisters exchanged cheek kisses, and Mina watched Yulia sprint over to the rest of the group.

As they had spoken, the proctor had been making last announcements, which they'd both ignored. Those announcements now wrapped up.

[With everyone who wants to participate now on the starting line, we will take down the barrier sealing the Dungeon shut. Everyone at those barriers, this is your last chance to decide whether to enter. Once you walk into the Dungeon, you will not be able to leave without completing the Dungeon.]

No one on Mina's team changed their minds. She saw them all march resolutely in as soon as the light emanating from the Dungeon entrance faded and they could enter.

Mina was left alone outside. She paced back and forth, rubbing her arms together and breathing warm air into her hands. She wished she'd thought to throw a chair into her Small Bag of Deceptive Dimensions. It seemed to be able to hold fairly large objects without increasing in size or mass, based on its ability to contain all her System-provided rations and equipment as well as her bag from back on Earth. She made sure to take out her warm coat and put it on now that she was no longer in the high stakes situation of deciding what to do about the Dungeon.

And she waited.

With nothing to do, and little to distract her from the cold, Mina began Identifying random bits of plant life nearby. She'd been using Identify on humans frequently over the last few days, but she hadn't seen any non-human creatures since she had come to Orientation. She was a little surprised to find that Identify worked on plants.

[Pinus aristata, Lv. 6]

[Rosa woodsii, Lv. 2]

[Juniperus communis, Lv. 4]

I wonder if the Latin names mean these are just normal plant species from Earth. Or does the System name the things it creates in Latin too?

[Dasiphora fruticosa, Lv. 4]

[Sufficient experience accrued. Identify leveled up!]

Oh, that's nice, I guess.

[Required conditions met. Skill Investigate unlocked!]

That made her sit up. What would Investigate be? A more detailed form of Identify, maybe? Something that she could use to try to figure out the killer's identity?

Mina immediately used Investigate on one of the plants she had Identified before.

A Status screen appeared for the plant.

[Status

Name: Unnamed

Race: Pinus aristata, Lv. 6

Health: 121/121

Mana: 0/0

Stats

Fortitude: 11

Skills

Photosynthesis, Lv. 6

Solar Recovery, Lv. 0]

That could be very useful, she thought. *That could help me figure out who's kill-ing people if I can get an idea of what kind of abilities they're using.*

The more she thought about how she might apply this Skill to DaSilva's investigation, the more excited she became about this breakthrough.

She was sure she would have been one of, if not the first, to have leveled

Identify up to this point and unlocked Investigate. Quick Study ensured that her Skills increased their proficiency more quickly through practice than most people's.

That would probably give her the element of surprise relative to the killer.

And somehow or other, between Investigate and Yulia's Trace Skill, Mina was certain she could prove the killer's identity if they were human. She wasn't sure if proof would be enough. Maybe the killer would be too powerful to be stopped by the time they knew who it was.

But this was a big step toward collecting the evidence they needed.

CHAPTER TWENTY-TWO

From Childhood's Hour

Yulia Danailova felt nervous and excited at the same time as she sprinted toward the group to catch up.

The group members seemed pleased to see her, but she barely noticed.

They all looked so much more prepared than she felt. Jose Dante wore Mage robes and wielded a stave. Cara Dahlhaus wore Light Warrior armor. Detective DaSilva looked a bit like a tank in his Heavy Warrior gear. The other warriors—Adelaide's brother, Derek, and Jose's brother, Paulo—likewise bristled with armor and weapons. Even the Mages of the group, Jean and the Davidsons, and the other Healer, Adelaide, despite having no armor, just *looked* more confident and ready for action than Yulia felt.

She was dressed in her warm winter clothes and coat. She had her stave in her bag if she needed it, although Mina had suggested to her that a stick was an almost useless piece of equipment for a Mage or Healer. But she didn't *feel* like an adventurer. She wasn't sure she was quite ready to go explore this unknown place.

Going into a Dungeon is just like talking to a boy you like, she told herself. *You start out nervous and then slowly it turns out that you didn't need to be.* She thought of her sister. *Mina believes in you. You can do this.* Her teeth chattered. *And at least it will be warmer inside the Dungeon. Probably.*

She looked back to face her sister one more time. Mina gave her a smile, and Yulia returned it. *From that distance, she won't be able to tell how anxious I am. No take backsies!*

When she turned back to the group, Yulia noticed that Jose was looking at her as if he knew what was going through her mind. The way he smiled, it felt almost as if he wanted to transmit his confidence to her. They had spoken a little during the last challenge, while Mina had been shooting targets, after Yulia had caught him checking her out. He seemed sweet but a little shy. She hoped he wouldn't be distracted from the Dungeon.

Thinking more seriously about their situation, she placed a hand in her pocket where she usually kept her crucifix. She sent out a quiet prayer. *Dear Lord, please protect me as I descend into the Earth as you protected Daniel in the lion's den. Please protect Mina as she waits here alone, where I can't reach her if she needs help. I know she doesn't believe in you, but she is the best person I know. I don't know what I would do without her.* She cut the prayer short there with a quick *Amen.* She'd prayed for James before she'd fallen asleep the night before, as well as for herself, Mina, the rest of her family, and their mother's soul. But today, she felt that she and Mina needed it more than anyone else.

As the group began moving forward, she focused her mind on the cave.

Observing the group, Yulia thought that Detective DaSilva had noticed her—she was probably moving her lips while she prayed again.

But while she kept her faith private from Mina, who had a skeptical view of religion at best, she didn't think she needed to hide it from the detective. She'd seen the thin necklace he always wore, and she was pretty sure he was Catholic, like most Italian Americans.

When their eyes met, he just smiled and touched the necklace where it dropped under his shirt. Where the image of Christ must be.

She smiled back and then returned her focus to the cave.

It grew darker the deeper they walked, and quieter. The first part of the descent took place to the sounds of loudly dripping water. Then the dripping gradually became quieter and less regular. When Yulia looked back, she saw the cave entrance had become a "light at the end of the tunnel" image.

Then the cave twisted, and the entrance moved out of sight completely. The darkness swallowed them whole.

Still, they moved forward briskly. They had no choice since the proctor had mentioned they would be unable to leave without completing the Dungeon. And they were in a race.

After a minute of walking through the challenging darkness, DaSilva took a pocket flashlight out and added some extra light, though it only illuminated a tiny area right in front of his feet. At least the descent wasn't too steep. If this was the most physically demanding part of the challenge, Yulia thought Mina would have managed. The air was better at this slightly lower elevation than it had been outside.

Yulia felt something cold touch the nape of her neck, and she jumped half out of her skin.

Everyone around her started at her sudden movement, and a few suddenly drew weapons.

"Are you all right, Yulia?" DaSilva asked in his rumbling voice.

"Yes, sorry," she said meekly, looking down at her feet. "A drop of water landed on my neck."

The droplet had rolled down the back of her shirt. That was how she knew she wasn't being attacked by some slimy monster. It was just water.

Everyone relaxed a bit, though the tension didn't completely fade away.

A light appeared in the distance, and Yulia sensed that the challenge was about to really begin.

The whole group let out a collective sigh of relief, and the fear of the dark that had silently surrounded them began to dissipate.

They walked along until they were within sight of the light source. It was a brightly glowing orb—whether of Mana or something else was impossible for Yulia to say—affixed to the wall. Roughly the size of her hand. It shone the vibrant orange color of torchlight. Beside it stood a stone door with writing inscribed on it. They had arrived at what seemed to be a dead end in the cave. They would need to pass through this door.

But it had no handle, and the stone looked dense and heavy.

As they stepped closer to the door, she could see something was inscribed on it:

From childhood's hour I have not been

As others were—I have not seen

As others saw—I could not bring

My passions from a common spring—

What am I?

A riddle? Yulia thought. *Oh no! Is it too late to go back for Mina? Will we need to answer this to get through the door?*

A figure stepped forward. Yulia saw it was Jose. He glanced back—*At me?* she thought—and then moved through the group and got up close to the door. And he simply tried to push it open.

It didn't budge.

Oh. I thought maybe he knew.

Jose threw himself against the door for another few seconds, grunting with exertion, before he gave up and turned away, his face downcast.

"Don't feel bad," she said quietly as he returned. But her voice was so soft that she wasn't sure if he heard. He didn't say anything back, and she didn't want to repeat herself and embarrass him.

"Alone," DaSilva pronounced quietly. The door began sliding open.

A few people looked at DaSilva in disbelief.

"It's not a riddle," he said. "It's an Edgar Allan Poe poem. What, you guys thought I was just a pretty face?"

Yulia smiled. That lame dad joke reminded her of James. And it seemed the group was in good hands even without Mina there this time.

DaSilva led the group through the door into a hall lit by torches. It still felt like a cave, but the walls were smoothed down as if thousands of hands had felt their way along it. And there was no longer a sound of dripping water accompanying them as they trudged forward into the depths.

As they all advanced into the hallway, the door suddenly slid shut behind them, and the torches flared up, illuminating the walls.

Inscribed on the right-side wall was a message that hadn't been visible before: *Keep your heads!*

"What do you think that's supposed to mean?" the detective asked. He leaned in closer to get a better look at the wall, and there was a sudden mechanical sound. Springs released, and then a spray of projectiles flew through the darkness.

DaSilva barely had time to turn his head. Arrows struck him in multiple places. Most of them clanged off his armor. One penetrated through the chainmail over his leg. And another hit a gap in his armor, at his armpit.

A last projectile flew forward: an ax that hurled itself at DaSilva's neck.

But Jose leaped in from the side and blocked it with his stave. He couldn't stop the axe's momentum, but the axe head ricocheted and changed direction, slicing into the floor instead of DaSilva. Then everything was still.

Incredible reflexes! Yulia thought, eyes full of admiration. *He didn't hesitate at all! So brave!* Jose cut a rather dashing figure when he was saving someone's life.

She took a breath and also noted that the staves were not so useless after all. She opened her bag and quietly drew her own.

Jose's weapon had been practically chopped in half by the collision with the axe. But it only needed to save your life, or someone else's, once to justify its existence.

Everyone was nearly frozen for a few seconds.

Then DaSilva spoke.

"Looks like I triggered a trap." A few people laughed nervously at that. He gestured toward his foot, which appeared to have sunk slightly into the ground. It was some form of trigger set off by his weight. He nodded to Jose. "Thanks for saving my life, young man." Speaking to the group as a whole, he added, "Everyone stand back, without stepping on anything that's uneven with the ground like I did. I'm going to lift my foot, and I don't know if it'll trigger something else."

I don't know how he can keep so calm with two arrows sticking out of him, Yulia thought. But she hastened to follow his instructions.

The group stepped back. DaSilva took a step, and nothing happened.

They let out a collective sigh of relief.

The situation had momentarily calmed.

Yulia took a few steps forward to get a closer look at DaSilva's wounds. Then she and Adelaide pulled the arrows out—the detective barely grunted, though he looked very uncomfortable—and they began healing him with Laying on Hands. The wounds were a little deeper than they had looked at first, but under their magic, the flow of blood quickly slowed to a trickle.

As they worked, members of the group began debating what should happen next.

"Are we sure we want to continue?" Frank Davidson, by appearance the oldest member of the group, asked.

"What, we just wait this challenge out here?" Paulo asked. "Hope the other groups share?"

"Why not?" Frank replied. "Her sister already set the precedent." He gestured at Yulia as he spoke. "Lots of people have already been sharing rations! Someone will surely be receptive to sharing something with the group that started the trend."

"Frank has a point," Adelaide agreed without looking up from her work next to Yulia. "We would have lost a teammate just now if not for Jose's quick action."

"We should just wait here," Karen Davidson said, agreeing with her husband.

"As much as I'd like to avoid further axes aimed at my neck, I'm not sure that's a viable option," DaSilva said. "I think people will be less willing to share based on what you just said, Adelaide."

"Some of the teams are going to lose people," Jose affirmed quietly. "How willing to share would we be if we sacrificed one of our teammates to get this food?"

"That—I don't know," Frank admitted.

"We wouldn't," Cara said. Jean stood next to her, shaking his head, agreeing with her.

"I think we should keep going," Yulia said tentatively, looking up from DaSilva's injury. The leg wound she'd been working on had fully closed up now. She spoke with more conviction after that first sentence. "We knew there would be traps when we decided to take this challenge. We haven't even seen any monsters in here yet."

The group looked at each other for a few seconds. Then the Davidsons and Adelaide finally agreed to go on after all. Yulia thought she might have influenced the result. Who would want to give up when the scrawny little girl was still willing to move forward? She didn't like that people still saw her as a child, but there were occasional advantages.

DaSilva silently led the way down the hall until they reached another doorway. He moved more slowly this time, head moving as if he was looking out for uneven ground.

This doorway was simply an opening, and more torchlight was visible emanating from the other side.

After visually scanning the floor of the room, DaSilva moved forward.

As Yulia stepped through, she noticed that they now appeared to be in an underground building that resembled a temple. The floor was stone tile, and the walls were stone blocks stacked in a brick pattern.

The System certainly is powerful. I don't know if humans could do something like this down at the bottom of a cave, even with all our technology.

There was a mural on the right-hand wall next to the doorway, which Yulia's eyes immediately focused on once she cleared the threshold. The art depicted a man hanging upside down from the ceiling as someone cut his throat and drained his blood.

She swallowed. *I have a really bad feeling about this.*

But she moved further into the room, following her group forward.

At the front of the room, there was a mid-sized vase, which Yulia estimated was about the right size to hold a gallon and a half of liquid. Above that, there was an inscription and another mural, though it was hard to make out at first. Yulia found it interesting that there was a second mural, and she inspected the other walls curiously.

There were multiple murals, as it turned out. Ten in total, including the one at the entrance. Each depicted some person spilling blood from a different wound. She hadn't seen them at first, only vague patterns on the walls. But as her eyes grew accustomed to the faint, flickering torchlight, she saw the murals in all their graphic detail.

Creepy, she thought. *What do they mean?* Other people looking around at the murals made quiet groans or sucked in air nervously.

Then Detective DaSilva read the inscription above the vase aloud.

"'Make an offering of blood to advance beyond this room. If you fill the vessel, the path will be revealed.'"

"Jesus!" Frank Davidson exclaimed. "Is this place demanding a human sacrifice?"

DaSilva scowled fiercely back at him. "If it is, we'll be bowing out of the challenge here. The promise of a little food isn't worth sacrificing people! This probably isn't even the final task for this challenge."

The old man blanched. "Right you are, of course. I didn't mean to imply anything different by bringing it up! You'll remember I was ready for us to take a step back earlier."

The detective calmed visibly. "Sorry. I got a little heated there. We're under a lot of pressure now. I know you're just as disturbed as the rest of us that this place apparently wants blood."

Other people seemed to be looking slightly askance at DaSilva, a bit surprised at his reaction.

"A little blood from all of us," Yulia said quietly.

"What's that?" DaSilva asked, putting a hand behind his ear.

"The murals." Yulia gestured around them. "They all show different ways to get blood from the human body. Most of the injuries they're showing aren't fatal. If we each give a little blood, I think we'd have enough to get out of here. Whoever's best with a knife can make careful cuts. And Miss Adelaide and I can heal the injuries after."

This challenge had Yulia doing more public speaking than she ever had in her life. She felt an immediate urge to melt into a wall or hide behind someone as soon as the words were out of her mouth. But she didn't have any kind of camouflage Skill and Mina wasn't there.

The whole room seemed to let out a breath they'd all been holding as Yulia explained her idea.

DaSilva approached her and put a heavy hand on her shoulder. "That's a great idea, Yulia! Frank and I jumped to an incredibly dark place just because this System seems like it's trying to pit people against each other. But there's no reason this challenge should require anyone to die." He turned to Adelaide. "The human body can lose the amount of blood we need here and survive, right? Assuming that container"—he pointed at the vase—"is divided up between us?"

Adelaide nodded without hesitation. "No one here is a hemophiliac, right?"

No one said anything.

"Then we'll be all right," Adelaide said. "I'll go last so I can be in top condition to extract blood, monitor everyone else's condition, and heal, unless anyone has any objections."

"That sounds like the safest way," Mr. Davidson agreed.

One by one, they proceeded to donate blood into the vase. They opened their wounds directly above its mouth so none would go to waste.

Yulia volunteered to go first so she could get it out of the way.

It was a bit painful as Adelaide cut into her arm, but she tried to smile.

It would all be over soon.

CHAPTER TWENTY-THREE

Omnivore

*H*opefully, *we don't run into too many more of those,* James thought. *I don't want to get guts all over my clothes, and they really stink.*

He used Pillage, selected Stats, directed the new equipment into his bag, and then walked on.

Five minutes later, a half-dozen giant centipedes burst from the sand.

James threw out two Air Strikes, used Pillage again, bagged the new gear once more, and continued on his way.

This happened ten times at shorter and shorter intervals. An increasing number of Monstrous Desert Centipedes attacked each time, until finally, amidst a pile of broken centipede bodies, a squad of Superior Desert Centipedes flanking the Desert Centipede Monarch popped out.

Well, at least this has to be the last of them, he thought.

He threw out an experimental Air Strike, but unlike the previous monsters, it seemed the wind couldn't bisect these centipedes with one hit. The first attack left only thin cuts on the Superior Desert Centipedes and no visible damage to the Desert Centipede Monarch at all.

Oh? Maybe an actual challenge? James found himself smiling against his own better judgment. These centipedes were just slowing him down, and he had already killed something like a hundred of them. He needed to get across this desert and find the Dead Marsh, where his allies would be waiting. But hopefully, these last ones were actually worth slogging through all their wimpy kin. Then he'd at least get a little fun out of this.

James darted around using his remarkable Agility to dodge attacks from the

Superior Desert Centipedes. The repeated use of Air Strikes had blown the sand around until the area where they fought was basically flat, so there was nowhere to hide. But the centipedes couldn't catch him, he felt certain. Indeed, two of the giant clumsy creatures tangled themselves up in each other's legs trying to reach James with the pincer-like appendages on their heads.

He thought those pincer-like parts must be venomous fangs of some sort. He'd heard somewhere that either millipedes or centipedes were all venomous, and he didn't imagine Orientation would have spawned the non-venomous of the two species.

"Hold on tight, Hester!"

James lunged at the closer of the fallen creatures and threw a punch at the joint between the head and body. The creature tried to grab him with its forcipules, but James was much faster. His fist smashed all the way through the joint he aimed at, penetrating to the other side. The centipede's head snapped backward, and the body instantly turned limp.

The other fallen centipede that was nearby took advantage of the moment when James's arm was entangled in the first centipede's joint. It tried to grab him, but James swung the dead creature up into its path to block it.

In the next moment, James yanked his arm free and sprinted out of range.

The other two Superior Desert Centipedes appeared at his flanks.

Wow! Are they using strategy? I'm kind of impressed. But the monsters kept their distance. They seemed to be aware that he could kill them in one hit if he landed a blow in the right place. And James's Mind of the Predator and Way of the Predator were perfect for that. It was only a matter of time before they slipped up and suffered a fatal blow.

But why does it feel like they're neither trying to close the distance nor to run away?

James suddenly became aware of motion just outside the frame of his peripheral vision. *A powerful attack from the big one!*

He swiveled his head to see it directly. Between the Desert Centipede Monarch's forcipules, a ball of condensed energy had gathered. *Mana?* As James looked on, he could see more energy rising from the creature's body to fuel the attack it was charging. The energy was pure white.

I shouldn't let that hit me. No further thought was required.

James dashed toward one of the Superior Desert Centipedes, planning to use it for cover. But the Monarch's body stiffened suddenly in his peripheral vision. James knew it was about to fire its attack.

Predator's Sacred Armor! A glowing forest-green aura enveloped James's body in an instant, and he felt his skin stiffen as if he were made of iron. His body slowed with the diminished flexibility. At that moment, the Monarch's ball of energy became a large beam of light, streaking toward James at a speed he knew he couldn't dodge. He stood his ground behind the aura armor and toughened skin, arms crossed in front of himself to protect his head.

The light hit—and the aura held! There was pressure, but the aura armor remained intact beneath the attack.

Held up, even as the attack continued.

Began to falter visibly under the ray of intense energy.

Flickered slightly, a tiny bit of heat pouring through.

Cracked.

And shattered!

Searing white light fell upon James directly now, burning his arms, his clothes, his forehead—wherever it touched. But the pain wasn't so bad with Pain Resistance at its present high level. If James had to compare it to something, it was a bad sunburn happening at high speed.

Finally, the light faded. He was still standing. His shirt was torn to rags. Chest heaving, arms burned raw.

But still standing. His face below the forehead remained unburned. Beneath the rags of his shirt, his chest only looked like it was losing a few layers of skin. Bits of skin flaked and crumbled away as he stood panting, staring at the enemy.

"Is that . . . all . . . you got?"

He began Silent Spellcasting. He had underestimated the centipedes because of the weakness of the lower grades. Now he would fight with his shield of non-elemental Mana, the Skill he'd stolen from Sierra's brother David.

As he charged his Mana, the Superior Desert Centipedes attacked.

But compared to the beam he'd been forced to tank, they were relatively slow. James punched through the first one that reached him and killed it in one hit. The next one managed to grapple him with some of its legs, holding him for a few seconds. In the moments it took him to tear the legs off, the other Superior Desert Centipede managed to get a good hit in with its forcipules.

It injected the venom—and in the next moment, James was sloughing off that layer of flesh like a costume, discarding the poison and recovering from most of the damage from the Desert Centipede Monarch's blast in one move.

The discarded skin stuck onto the legs of the centipede that had grappled him.

James grabbed the other centipede's forcipules with his hands and pulled hard. They cracked and tore away from its head, and the creature twitched in obvious pain.

The centipede that had been grappling James tried to help its fellow, but as it lurched toward him, something yanked it off course, causing its forcipules to land in the sand. The monster looked back and saw that James's discarded skin was still attached to its legs. The skin was *alive*, pulling at those limbs with terrible force, and the centipede immediately lunged, trying to inject more of its venom into the skin creature.

While those two beasts grappled, James punched the centipede he was fighting, aiming for the same joint between the head and body he'd identified as a weak spot before. He again killed this one with a single punch.

As he slid his arm free of the body, he took a moment to look back over at the leader. But it seemed to be in some form of refractory period. The creature was clearly trying to charge the same big attack from before, and it seemed to stand immobile while the big attack was charging. But the energy was coming slowly.

Don't force yourself, big guy, James thought, grinning. *You could pull a muscle straining yourself like that!*

He turned back to the last remaining Superior Desert Centipede, which was now ripping James's skin creature apart with its limbs while repeatedly injecting it with venom. The damage from the venom left huge patches of the skin creature blackened and decomposed as if it had been dead for weeks. But the creature was still clinging weakly to life, trying to win James an extra few seconds.

James lunged across the short distance that separated him from the Superior Desert Centipede and slashed at its neck with his right arm. He was no longer smiling. Even though the skin creature was literally just his discarded skin animated by his Skill, he didn't like to see something that was fighting for him taking such abuse.

Predator's Strike! His whole arm became a blade. It struck the joint he had previously identified as the weak point. The head toppled to the sand.

Thank you for your help, he said to the creature telepathically. It just wriggled weakly back at him, as if to say, "Yes, yes, now go on and kill the big one."

James turned back to the last monster standing: the Desert Centipede Monarch, now probably the last of its kind. It looked like a water tower, standing strong and unmoving there. Its black head atop its reddish body stood proudly erect, energy gathering slightly more quickly between its forcipules now. Its flesh still bore no scars. The Monarch was weirdly majestic in its ugliness.

I wonder if it was born this way or if it had to fight for its place in this food chain, he thought. *And can it talk? If it can, would it try to blame me for this? Or explain why these things have been attacking me when I'm literally just trying to cross the desert?*

He walked slowly toward the big guy. His Silent Spellcasting finished conjuring, and he felt an invisible shield was now in place around him. He accelerated his pace. He knew exactly which move he wanted to try on the last centipede.

As he got closer, James sensed some degree of fear in the Monarch. Its attack charging carried a great sense of urgency now. The energy was moving more quickly and in smaller bursts. It seemed to know it would only have one more shot. James began sprinting as he closed to within thirty feet.

The creature fired its attack immediately, this time not at where James was but at where he was going to be. A familiar but slightly smaller and weaker-looking beam of white light blasted forth.

This time James was able to throw himself to the side and dodge it. The monarch moved its head so the blast shifted to follow him. James tucked and rolled, forcing the beam to chase him across the sand. He knew from the previous attack that every moment weakened it.

Finally, the centipede's attack caught up to him. It struck his shield, which became visible once hit. The beam failed to break through it. The shield didn't seem to be strained at all.

James began pushing forward through the energy beam. The centipede continued struggling to break through his defenses, slowly lowering the angle of its head to keep attacking as James drew closer and closer.

Until he was within a few feet of the centipede's body.

Then James used Meteor Strike. His flaming fist smashed through the centipede's center of mass, leaving a burned-out hole all the way through its body. The Monarch tottered from side to side but remained standing and continued its energy attack.

James pulled his arm out, and he threw another mighty Meteor Strike into its body, whipping through the same elevation of centipede flesh until his arm met the hole it had already made. Like an axe felling a chitinous tree. With more than half of the flesh from that midsection burned away, the centipede slumped to the ground.

To its credit, the creature never stopped firing that desperate ray of energy.

In its last moments, the centipede's energy attack had dropped to the lowest level of intensity James had observed in any monster attack since Orientation. But James respected the determination.

The light beam flickered and died, and he realized the fight was finally over.

[You killed Desert Centipede Monarch, Lv. 22! You gained 1300 exp!]

[Predator in Human Skin leveled up!]

[Evolver Human leveled up!]

[Required conditions met. Title obtained: Xenocide II!]

A second level from the centipedes, that's nice, James thought. He examined the Title.

[Xenocide II: As an entity responsible for causing extinction events for two species that had over a hundred members each, your nature is truly that of a monster to be feared. Your enemies will find their names erased from the history books. As such, enjoy a 15% bonus to all Stats when facing an enemy of another race. Enjoy a 25% bonus when facing an enemy who is the last or only member of their race.]

Oops, I did it again . . .

He lowered his arm and finally exhaled. He felt exhausted, and he was now fully enveloped in the awful odor of dead centipede. Also, stale sweat.

"I didn't even really want to fight any of you stupid bastards," he muttered. "There I go, reducing ecological diversity again."

"I think that after you killed the first group, they could smell the traces of their dead relatives on your body," Hester said a bit hesitantly.

Her voice surprised James slightly, but he was too exhausted to be startled.

What a bloody nuisance! he thought. *If you could smell it, you could have said something sooner. Could all this really have been avoided with a bath?*

"I tried so hard not to be covered in centipede guts," James said, slightly dispirited. "I thought I did a good job until I had to fight this last group at close range."

"Actually, you're probably right," Hester said, sounding uncertain. "Maybe you just walked deeper into centipede territory."

"Well, at least there was one enemy worth the killing," James said, looking down at the Monarch.

Pillage. While he had turned the vast majority of the Monstrous Desert Centipedes into Stat points, he stole a Talent from the Monarch.

[Desert Centipede Monarch's body processed.]

[You obtained Solar Helm, Deadly Necrotic Venom Sac, and Ego Exoshield!]

[Talent obtained: Solar Power!]

[Solar Power: Naturally harness the power of the sun wherever it touches you. It can charge your attacks or aid in your recuperation of energy. Generates Skills Solar Ray and Solar Recovery.]

Almost as if the creature had willed him to have its strongest attack, he obtained it.

Very nice, James thought, yawning slightly. He felt sleepy. But he could also feel his energy coming back a little more quickly now, and the sunlight shining directly on him was the obvious source. *Thank you, Solar Recovery.*

The Ego Exoshield seemed very pleased to become a part of James's arsenal, wiggling and jumping back and forth like a dog jumping up and down. But James just gave it a tired smile and directed it into his magic satchel with the other equipment.

From one of the Superior Desert Centipedes he obtained the Skill Necrosis. From another, the Skill Tough Skin. The others he turned into Stat points, unimpressed with the abilities he'd garnered thus far.

He walked back over to his skin creature, which was dead and half rotted away in the sand. Then he picked it up and ate some of it to recover a bit of his lost Stamina.

"Oh dear," Hester whispered quietly to herself.

He ignored both her and the disgusting flavor of the necrotic venom in the skin until he recognized that the Stamina he was recovering wasn't enough to justify consuming something that tasted so nasty. Or rather, he wasn't desperate enough.

So much for Omnivore, he thought. The Skill theoretically allowed him to consume the body of anything that had once lived and absorb the properties and energy of the material consumed, without risk. That included any threat from rot or poison. But in practice, his sense of taste was still going to be a limiting factor there.

"Well, onward through the desert, then," James said. "About how far in do you think we are?"

"Maybe halfway," Hester said doubtfully. "You walk a lot faster than most people, but you also stopped and killed everything you came across."

"All right, I'm not walking any further, then."

James used Shed Skin, infused a large quantity of Mana into the skin with Monster Generation, and created a balloon-like monster from his discarded skin this time. Then he did the same thing again. His Mana was all but used up by the end, but he now had a viable means of transportation across the desert.

One monster to grab each shoulder, he thought. *I need some sort of flight Skill. This feels silly. Maybe I'll find some birds to kill.* He'd seen nothing living in the desert so far except centipedes, but he recalled vultures always seemed to appear only when something was dead or dying.

He ripped off the remaining shreds of his shirt to make it easier for the Skin Balloons to latch onto him.

"Wow!" Hester exclaimed. "What a creative use of that Skill!"

"Thank you, Hester."

"You know, you probably could've avoided all those fights and finished crossing the desert by now if you'd used it sooner. We only saw ranged attacks from the boss, right?"

James suppressed a groan.

"I'm going to take a nap now," he said. "Please let me know if you see any monsters or other threats while we're flying."

"Sure thing!"

At a silent command, the Skin Balloons tied themselves onto one of James's shoulders each and took off.

CHAPTER TWENTY-FOUR

Alpha Male

J ames shook his head, irritated.

My dream was just getting to the good part, he thought. He hadn't been able to visit anyone else's dreams this time. It seemed everyone he knew was awake, and he'd had a problem when he tried to find Mina's dream.

Where the dreams of people he knew in this Orientation were like flickering flames in the darkness, Mina and Yulia's dreams seemed to be blocked off somewhere. Perhaps he needed Anansi's help to cross the barrier between different Orientations. Or needed to be near that void.

So he'd just been enjoying a normal nap until a tinny voice in his ear awakened him.

"What's up, Hester?" he asked groggily.

"Sorry to wake you, sir, but I thought you might want to see what we're approaching."

You don't need to call me—no, actually, I should get used to people calling me "sir."

"What is it? Giant birds?" James blinked his eyes open and shut and then saw a large plateau ahead of him. "Oh, scenery." Behind the plateau he could see some greenery on the horizon, which he guessed meant the Dead Marsh was pretty close.

"Uh, I meant down below that," Hester said.

James saw what she meant, and he immediately sent a mental command to his Skin Balloons to stop moving forward.

A couple hundred feet below James was a party of around a dozen people, as well as what appeared to be almost the same number of corpses. They were besieged by a small pack of coyotes, and James could see in the distance that more coyotes were rushing to join them.

Most interesting, though, was the identity of the lead fighter of the besieged group. Positioned in front of the body of one of his fallen comrades—perhaps not actually dead, given how forcefully the fighter was guarding him—Damien Rousseau stood, wielding a long spear.

James wouldn't have recognized him, since he wasn't covered in fur this time, but Identify had been reliable so far.

And Damien seemed almost as fierce as James remembered, despite wearing a human face this time. There was a wolfish aspect to his face. Sharp, aggressive, chiseled features. Short, scruffy facial hair.

When one of the beasts got close, he would swing the spear in a wide arc designed to force some distance. The other living members of the group huddled behind him, occasionally providing backup with their weapons when Damien's wide swings left openings.

With their backs up against the plateau, they almost had the coyotes stalemated. Almost. Except that the humans looked worn down, as if they'd already tried to stand their ground and been defeated. The coyotes looked much fresher. And reinforcements were coming quickly for the coyote side. Including a big, two-headed beast that Identify labeled as the Alpha Desert Coyote. It had attained level fourteen.

Not bad, but still not a threat, James thought. *Well, not a threat to* me. *I wouldn't want to be one of them in about two minutes.*

The only reason he felt hesitant to rush in was the memory of his last encounter with Damien Rousseau. The monstrous werewolf who had ripped a more normal-sized wolf to pieces in front of him. Why was he standing there in human form now? Surely he'd tear these creatures apart as his werewolf self.

Was he unable to transform at will? Only at night? Only with the full moon? Or maybe he was just too weakened. In any case, he looked battered. If he could change shape now, James doubted he'd still be holding it in reserve.

"Um, sir, are you going to do something or move on?" Hester asked. "I don't mean to question your decision-making, I just figured sitting still in the sky was more or less the worst of all possible options."

"Yes, I'm doing something, Hester. Thank you," James said. Hester had no way of observing what James was doing. He'd sent a mental command to the Skin Balloons to move him slowly closer to the besieged humans. They were to hover just above the humans so James would be able to face outward at all of the enemies at once.

This would need to be a quick rescue; his own people probably needed him too.

He began charging his new Skill Solar Ray. The sunlight was still bright and strong, sundown perhaps another hour away. He could feel the Skill pull in energy from the sun, gathering it impossibly quickly, as if every inch of his skin and clothing had become hyper-efficient solar paneling.

The only apparent catch was that, just like the Monarch that had wielded the technique before him, he felt his body stiffen and immobilize while he charged the attack. He couldn't move, he sensed, or the energy would dissipate.

Not a very practical ability if you're not a king with royal guards, he thought, recalling the method the final group of centipedes had used to fight him. But James was out of reach of his enemies, hovering out of likely jumping range, which was a somewhat better advantage in this case.

And he could relax a bit and let the Skill charge while he waited for the coyote reinforcements to arrive.

"Hey, uh, you up there, are you going to help us?"

It seemed one of the people below him had noticed James's shadow hovering overhead.

He ignored the speaker for the moment, though. The rest of the coyotes were almost there now, James could see, and he wasn't going to mess up the charging for Solar Ray just to answer that question.

Doo dee doo, James thought to himself, wishing he could hum. But his body was unmoving, other than the autonomic nervous system, and that included his vocal cords. *Just floating here and charging my attack . . .*

The alpha burst onto the scene. It let loose a howl, and the other coyotes moved into a fan-shaped formation around the alpha. The biggest coyote wasn't at the front but closer to the middle of the pack. But it felt to James as if the pack had become a more cohesive unit. The other coyotes were limbs, and they now moved with an enhanced coordination.

Whatever that ability is, I want it. He could just see a mass of minions all around him, moving with his mental commands like the Skin Balloons.

James caught motion out of the corner of his eye.

Damien Rousseau had collapsed to the ground. While James was admiring the smoothness of the coyote formation, several of the beasts had been wearing at Damien, biting his arms and legs, weakening him until he couldn't stand.

It was time.

James's concentrated solar energy had been focused into a ball that sat just outside his mouth. Now he let go and unleashed it as a beam of light.

James felt the light and heat peripherally, and he felt a quiet astonishment that he had endured a hit from this himself. The intensity reminded him of one of his Apophis-fueled attacks from before he switched to Anansi.

The front and center of the mass of coyotes was struck first, but James fanned the beam from side to side. He couldn't see the creatures well, because the Solar Ray was directly in his line of sight, blindingly white. But he felt the beam blasting through their bodies, leaving little in its wake. He felt where there was resistance, and he felt when that resistance melted away.

James continued killing coyotes until the power of the Solar Ray faded.

As the light died away, he looked down at what remained.

I won't want to use this Skill when I'm planning to hunt for meat, then.

Scattered pieces of coyote remained where dozens of monsters had stood. A paw here, an ear there—whatever hadn't been directly in the path of the light.

There were a few coyotes still alive. Two stragglers that had been at the edges of the blast radius at the start and had managed to run a short distance away while they waited for it to die down. One coyote half-buried in the sand, which was missing almost half its body.

Where's the alpha? He couldn't see it. *I would at least think he would leave a body that I could Pillage.* It made him uneasy. He felt as if the big guy wasn't dead yet. *I could check my alerts.*

He decided to descend instead. Even if the alpha was still alive, it was hidden somewhere out of view. He'd have some kind of warning if he was about to be attacked. He needed to finish off these last couple of coyotes and start trying to heal the surviving members of this group or this stop would just be a waste of time.

James commanded the Skin Balloons to release him and remain hovering where they were.

He dropped in front of the humans, who were staring open mouthed at the carnage in front of them. James turned.

The two able-bodied coyotes were charging him. *Foolish.* He drew a pair of Wolfbone Daggers from his magic satchel. *Predator's Missile!* He threw one blade at the closest coyote as it leaped at him. The blade pierced through the creature's heart and killed it instantly.

The other coyote saw what had happened and seemed to realize that it was outmatched. It turned to run away, but—*Predator's Missile!*—James threw the second dagger. It stabbed so deeply into the coyote's back that as the creature fell, James could see the tip of the blade poking out of its chest.

James approached. Grabbed the handle. Pulled the blade to the side, cutting through the heart that he'd somehow missed with the first throw.

I didn't have to use up any Mana. Good. The still living humans are going to need a lot of Laying on Hands—

James's train of thought was interrupted. Mind of the Predator blared a warning and indicated an appropriate course of action. He had time to leap aside while continuing to hold onto the coyote body and the dagger inside it.

James felt a weight brush past him. Something furry brushed his arm.

Something invisible.

James still couldn't tell what he'd dodged. But if he had to bet, the alpha must have some invisibility power. *How to catch an invisible beast,* he thought.

Mind racing, he began Silent Spellcasting. As he began, he felt a prickle and sense of danger from behind him. James leaped to the side again, and he felt a wind blow past him as the invisible creature leaped past.

He quickly drew the dagger from the dead coyote's body and tried to throw it where he expected the alpha's body to be. But it whizzed through empty air.

How do I find you? He already had a plan with Silent Spellcasting, but it was annoying to have to rely on magic when it took longer to work than most of his close-range combat abilities. *I need some kind of enhanced vision Skill.*

James dodged back and forth a few more times, Mind of the Predator reliably warning him of each attack, until his magic was ready.

Then he waited. The creature attacked again, apparently unconcerned or unaware of the implications of the heavy, dark-colored Mana gathered around James's body.

James felt a sense of warning from his left side this time, and rather than dodging, he planted his feet and punched at where he thought the creature might be leaping from. Impact! His fist struck fur and flesh.

It was only a glancing blow because the alpha was intelligent enough to try and jump away as soon as James tried to hit it. But James felt and heard the sound of crunching bone even so. His Strength was so far beyond this creature's that he only needed one good hit to put an end to it. If only the coyote wasn't so tricky, he'd have finished it already.

James triggered his spell as soon as his fist made contact.

Basic Elemental Magic: Gravity applied crushing weight, and suddenly, James knew exactly where the last coyote was: its body, sent flying by the force of his punch, made a big dent in the sand as it landed.

And James lunged toward the alpha before it could run away. *Lightning Strike!*

His hand penetrated through fur and flesh into hot, wet vital tissue. James felt the body convulse from the electricity wrapped around his palm. Then he grabbed the precious heart—and tore.

The coyote suddenly reappeared. It was a mess, naturally. One of its two heads had been ripped clean off, and the wound cauterized, by James's Solar Ray earlier. The rest of the body was covered in blood and sand.

[You killed Alpha Desert Coyote, Lv. 14! You gained 715 exp!]

Poor creature, James thought. *Pillage!*

He selected Talent as his target.

[Alpha Desert Coyote's body processed.]

[You obtained Shapechanger's Cloak, 3x Coyote Meat Bundle, and Trickster's Dagger!]

[Talent obtained: Alpha Presence!]

That sounds like exactly what I wanted to get from him earlier, James thought. But now he sort of wished he could have stolen whatever gave the coyote its invisibility in the second part of the fight. *Wait a minute . . .* He checked the Shapechanger's Cloak and found that it had two attached Skills, one of which was Invisibility.

He used Mass Pillage on the other coyotes and selected Stats. He'd decided he would review his new Talent and dagger later, and he directed the gear into his bag.

Then he turned to the humans. Behind him, three of the people who were still standing had already started healing a few of the more badly wounded survivors.

"Um, thank you for saving us," said a familiar voice. The same person who had wondered if James was going to save them, he realized. It was a white guy around James's age with dark hair beginning to gray at the edges.

"You're welcome," James said with a small smile and a nod. He looked down at the bodies on the ground. "Any of those people still alive and need a heal?"

"You can heal too?" exclaimed one of the Healers working on a broken body. She didn't stop using Laying on Hands, but James could see her expression morph into one of annoyance. "Fucking unfair!"

"This isn't a game," James said loudly. "Nor is it a democracy. Unfairness and imbalance are the rules here, not exceptions to them."

"Yes, of course. You're right, sir," said the man who'd spoken first. His tone was obsequious. "And if you're willing to help out, there are a few people here who could use some healing." He gestured toward another group of people. James realized they had dragged some of the wounded away from the group of bodies he'd initially noticed.

I guess they weren't just standing still behind me, he thought, gratified. *Maybe they'll be useful.*

He began Laying on Hands.

"While I'm working, why don't you tell me what brings you guys out here?" James asked.

CHAPTER TWENTY-FIVE

Keeper

Kurt Royersford held his teeth gritted in a grim smile.

He ignored the flailing resistance of the human gripped tightly in his arms.

"*Aaaaah!* Somebody help me! Guys! Where the fuck are you?" the man screamed. He was completely unaware of what had happened to the rest of his friends who had been wandering alongside him through the mist.

Although Kurt's emotions were *diminished* from what they had been as a human, he enjoyed the man's cries. He found himself wondering if James Robard would wail and panic the same way when Kurt eventually found him.

That seemed inevitable. Kurt couldn't believe Robard would get himself killed easily. And with Master Roscuro expanding the terrain of the Dead Marsh each day, sooner or later they were bound to run into him.

The human in Kurt's grip managed to tear one of his arms free of Kurt's grasp for a moment. The Ghoul wouldn't have minded that. But in his frantic clawing and attempts to get loose, the human's nails tore a small line open on the side of Kurt's face. That was annoying.

Depending on the size of the rip, it might require Master Roscuro to spend some of his precious time and energy in stitching up yet another of Kurt's injuries. They didn't close on their own as they had when Kurt was human.

He caught hold of the man's arms again, and he briefly contemplated doing something permanent to halt his resistance.

But no.

They were so close to Master Roscuro already.

Perhaps this human would be deemed worthy of the master's laborious Ghoul transformation process. If not, Kurt and his squad of Ghouls might have some fresh meat for a nice change. But he would not rob Master Roscuro of the opportunity to make another soldier for the slowly building army, in the event that this fellow was worth the effort.

As he made that resolution, Master Roscuro's voice flowed into Kurt's mind, smooth and warm and deep and rich as ever. *I see that my conquering heroes have returned victorious once again. What have you brought me this time, my dear Ghouls?*

Kurt felt the glow of Master Roscuro's attention fall on him first.

The Master's powers continue to grow, he thought. *He detected us from further away this time.*

"Master," he said aloud, "a humble offering from your most loyal of servants." He pushed the offering forward, releasing the man's arms as he did so.

The victim stumbled through the muck, taken by surprise. He fell to his knees and turned his head back and forth, as if looking for something or someone.

Master Roscuro must be speaking into his mind, Kurt thought. *It will all be over soon.*

Then the man rose from his knees and began running—right in the Master's direction, Kurt felt certain. He'd seen this pattern play itself out over and over dozens of times. Humans couldn't help but be overcome by Soul Eater Roscuro when they were in his territory. If it was otherwise, it would've been impossible for the Soul Eater and his small retinue to begin to grow the undead army that now reigned in the Dead Marsh.

Sure enough, a burst of black light struck the human, and the man froze in place.

Only then was there motion in the mist. From the same direction the blast of Soul Magic had originated from, a figure strode. The mist parted for him, responsive to his Will as if it were a part of his own body. All was exposed. Both the Ghouls and their Master.

Finally, Kurt saw Master Roscuro's face again.

Beautiful light gray skin. Gleaming golden-yellow eyes. Long, uncombed mane of gray hair. Pointed ears. That striking, sewn-shut mouth. Unmistakable.

Kurt dropped to his knees. The other Ghouls, who were now visible with the mist parted, knelt as well. They shoved their respective human charges face down into the water as they did so.

You have done well once more, Roscuro transmitted into the Ghouls' minds.

He reached out to touch the paralyzed human, standing stiff as a statue in front of him.

Interesting, most interesting. This one has been gifted with Shadow Magic. We don't have that in our arsenal yet. Such a soldier is valuable . . . Roscuro contemplated the human's value in a stream of consciousness style for the Ghouls' entertainment and enlightenment. The more they understood what Soul Eater Roscuro valued in an offering, the greater the likelihood they would continue to please him with their future contributions, after all.

Master Roscuro pronounced the man worthy of joining the army, and then he slowly went around checking the other live human offerings. Each time he shook his head.

Three Healers this time, Master Roscuro transmitted wryly. *The least useful type of human for our purposes, but at least you take them off of our future battlefields.* This was more or less verbatim what the Master said whenever they brought living Healers. The next line was the same too. *Well, kill them and enjoy your meal!*

On cue, three pairs of hands began ripping into human flesh. There were screams, but the Ghouls' efficient killing techniques quickly cut them short.

As for the others, turn them into zombies and set them loose.

These commands were also followed.

And for you, my dear Kurt, the Master added, *you continue to succeed in difficult tasks. Last time I sent you out, I asked you to bring me a form of magic that we did not yet have for our army. And you have delivered once more. Your offering was the only keeper of the lot. Today I have a mission specifically suited to your unique gifts.*

Kurt nodded eagerly. Most of his feelings were distant, hollow, artificial things—emotions preserved under glass.

His desire—no, his *need*—to please his master was something else.

"I hear and obey your every wish, my Master," Kurt groveled.

This time your mission will take you out of the Dead Marsh, the Soul Eater explained. *You know that we are not the only non-human creatures living and seeking to grow our power in this forest . . .*

Kurt joyfully accepted Master Roscuro's mission. He felt as if he had earned a sacred trust.

I knew you wouldn't let me down, Kurt, the Master transmitted. *I hope you will enjoy this reward for your hard work today.* He drew out his Small Bag of Deceptive Dimensions, which he had taken off one of their many human victims.

And he took out a whole human leg, ending in the broken off hip bone.

It was long, pale, slightly fatty, shaved hairless—a woman's limb, Kurt observed. Probably just the sort of thing he would've gone wild for back when he was human, if it were still attached to the woman's body. Those old memories, and that old identity, felt more distant with every passing day, though.

Now he felt gleeful at the thought of sinking his teeth into the meat, which Kurt knew the bag would've kept fresh.

The Soul Eater tossed the leg to Kurt and smiled with his sewn-shut mouth at the Ghoul.

Enjoy.

* * *

The next morning, Kurt led the whole body of Ghouls on their first mission outside the Dead Marsh's borders. Whether despite or because of the loss of their humanity, the Ghouls were fascinated by new sights and sounds. They would focus on one detail, zeroing in on a plant or an unfamiliar insect.

But rather than stopping and staring, they would typically continue following Kurt's orders to advance toward wolf territory. There were many collisions with trees and stumbles over shrubs over the next hour.

Finally, Kurt instructed the Ghouls to think only about reaching the destination and defending against possible enemies. That seemed to focus their minds.

And not a moment too soon.

A minute after that admonition, Kurt raised a fist to signal a halt. A group of humans were moving through the brush just ahead of them. This mission wasn't about fighting humans or collecting prisoners. Outside the Dead Marsh, Kurt was aware they might even be at a disadvantage.

"Hide!" he ordered in a guttural whisper.

The Ghouls concealed themselves in a rush. Behind trees, within bushes, in tall grass. Wherever they could.

And a few seconds later, three humans walked forward through the brush.

"The way is clear," pronounced one of them in confident tones of instantly translated Spanish.

"We have to be sure of that," said another, also in Spanish. "The whole family has to be able to march this way."

"There aren't any monsters," said the first. "That's the important thing."

Then they walked past Kurt and his Ghouls, and he did not hear any further conversation.

What he had heard was interesting, however. A whole family walking in the direction of the Dead Marsh.

I'll have to alert the Master as soon as I return, he thought. *What a delightful stroke of luck!*

The Ghouls marched forward with greater stealth now. They navigated so as to give the group the three scouts had come from a wide berth.

They marched on, deeper and deeper into the forest. The great thing about being a Ghoul was that one never tired, never weakened, never needed to sleep.

The journey was a long one, but largely quiet. With the mysterious death of the Spider Queen, a power vacuum had developed in the quadrant of the forest where she had once reigned, as Master Roscuro had explained.

There were a few species that had sought to fill that void, but only one remained as a serious contender now: the beasts that Kurt and his Ghouls were to make contact with.

Finally, the first of that race made an appearance.

As Kurt stepped through a bush, a lone Feral Forest Wolf leaped upon him, sinking its fangs into his arm.

The Ghoul scowled at the sharp pain. But his Fortitude was great enough now, after killing a dozen or so humans, that such an attack couldn't take him out of the fight. He slammed his arm against a tree repeatedly to dislodge the beast. When the wolf finally became disoriented and fell, Kurt realized that there were more wolves than he had realized. The others were engaging his subordinates behind him and to his sides.

"Peace!" Kurt hissed, activating one of his Skills. "We wish to parlay with your alpha."

A large, two-headed wolf let out a short howl and sniffed the air.

The Ghouls and the other wolves stopped fighting at the howl as the small group of wolves waited for the Command Forest Wolf to determine what should happen next.

Kurt hoped it wasn't trying to smell his pheromones to be certain if he was telling the truth or not. He was fairly certain that he no longer emitted human secretions of that kind. Only the sickly sweet odor of slow decay.

Whatever the Command Forest Wolf smelled, it seemed to decide that Kurt and his Ghouls were not enough of an immediate threat to justify siccing the smaller wolves on them again. The Command Forest Wolf made eye contact with Kurt with one head, then tilted its other head, pointing. It let out a short bark. Then it stalked off in the direction it had pointed.

Kurt didn't need a Skill to understand what was being conveyed.

Excellent. I'll follow you to your leader.

"Pursue with haste!" Kurt ordered his squadmates.

The Ghouls rushed after the wolves. The main source of Kurt's urgency was the likelihood that if they were left too far behind, they might be attacked again. This concern seemed to be borne out as the beasts led them deeper into wolf territory and more of the Feral Forest Wolves and Command Forest Wolves appeared at the edges of the trees.

They bore their fangs in snarls, but as soon as they saw that Kurt's Ghouls were escorted by some of their own, they backed down. A part of Kurt thought that this was a show, the alpha's way of showing them the strength of his pack.

They certainly have impressive numbers, he thought. Perhaps seventy or eighty in the pack if what he was seeing of the adults was indicative of overall size. The pups were not a part of this show of strength, naturally. From his past life as a veterinarian and animal lover, Kurt recalled that wolf packs were typically much smaller than this. Thirty-seven was considered an exceptional pack size. The alpha should be proud to have such a group under his control.

But individually, they were not especially impressive. They'd attained a higher average level than when they attacked the human population at the beginning of Orientation. Yet their levels were not reflective of what their strengths were. Kurt had seen these wolves' Skills, and they needed to be higher level than humans to be equally dangerous in his view.

Further, the wolves' power as a cohesive fighting force was weakened by a lack of diversity in their abilities. Most of the wolves had only their fangs and claws to fight with, nothing special to confuse an enemy or put them off balance. The higher-level wolf types had elemental attacks, but once you had seen a wolf's power, it was unimpressive and predictable. Easy enough to counter for a better-balanced force.

Kurt remained unimpressed by the pack until he saw the alpha.

Despite Kurt's undead biology, a cold dread seized his heart when he lay eyes upon the creature: a massive three-headed wolf, at least twice the size of the Command Forest Wolves, lying upon a rock atop a small hill. The creature could look over its whole pack from that position.

It rose to its feet, snarled low and long, and exhaled with each of its heads as he drew near.

Kurt realized instantly that this wolf had enough diversity of power to keep anyone on their toes. One pair of nostrils exhaled fire, one lightning, and the third a green gas that Kurt was fairly certain was poisonous.

Identify revealed that the Alpha Forest Wolf King had attained level thirty, which was quite breathtaking and especially impressive when one considered that he didn't need to do his own hunting.

In the back of Kurt's mind, he was aware that the Wolf King was trying to make an impression on him. He had to remind himself that his own Master was even more powerful, though the Soul Eater usually tried to exude a more unassuming aura.

Kurt activated his Skill and began to bargain.

"My Master, Soul Eater Roscuro, extends his greetings to the alpha of the great wolf pack of this forest!" he said in his most formal tones.

"So that is why you have come, foul thing." The Wolf King's voice emanated from the central head. It sounded like metal scraping against gravel, and Kurt struggled not to wince as the voice pierced his ears. "What does your master want? To plead with me that I should not invade his territory and take dominion over the rest of this forest?" the Wolf King taunted Kurt.

The left head let out a short howl to punctuate this last question, and the rest of the pack joined in a collective "*Awoooooo!*"

After the long howl had faded, Kurt replied, as sternly as he could, "No, Wolf King. The Soul Eater begs no one. He continues to be a more powerful ruler than you yourself, as you would learn if you ventured into his domain and attempted combat!"

The other wolves tried to howl over Kurt as he spoke, but the left head let out a bark, and the other wolves cut off their howling instantly.

"Very well, foul creature. Is your master challenging me, then?" The Wolf King sounded genuinely interested. Kurt could feel a lust for battle in the King's voice that he had never observed in his Master. For a moment he felt a flicker of doubt.

Could it be true that Master Roscuro would lose such a contest? The Wolf King exuded such a strong presence.

Then his mind snapped back to the purpose he'd come for.

"No, Your Majesty," Kurt said. "He proposes a collaboration. As you know, the System will richly reward the victors of each Orientation. For those of us who are not human, the richest rewards require that we eliminate the human presence in our ecosystem. There are humans in this forest who my Master is not able to touch on his own. They are wise enough to avoid marching into the Dead Marsh, and my Master's territory will not extend far enough to capture them before the end of Orientation. He observes that you have also avoided this particular band of humans. Together, however, your combined power could allow the elimination of every human in this Orientation. Instead of competing for dominance over this forest, there would be plenty of rewards to share."

"You raise an interesting proposal," the Wolf King admitted. "There are some humans who have been too hazardous to hunt. With each passing day, finding humans appropriate for our pack's younger members to prey upon becomes more difficult, as the surviving human groups grow stronger and more united. The idea of making a clean sweep of the remaining humans is tempting." It stepped down from its high perch and began walking toward Kurt. "On the other hand, you yourself were once human, were you not? Why should we believe that you would betray your own kind to work with us? Should we not worry that in some moment of combat, you and your fellows"—with the tilt of a head, the Wolf King gestured to the other Ghouls—"may suffer some inner conflict and choose to betray us?"

Kurt smiled. An easy question.

"Our Master enjoys our *complete* loyalty. We've killed many humans already. There is no conflict."

CHAPTER TWENTY-SIX

Miasma

The Rodriguez camp managed to forge further forward despite the marshy terrain and the unpleasant miasma that hung over it.

After Ramon returned from scouting, the camp assembled for a Rodriguez family meeting. They resolved that, rather than scattering to better evade the cultists, they would remain together and try to hide in the swamp. Almost everyone except Chava was on the same page there. Although the family members respected his pragmatic reasoning, they uniformly preferred to live or die together rather than apart.

"Thank you so much for taking us with you guys," said Charlie Roebuck, one of the escaped prisoners, almost in tears. "I feel like it's our fault that Rostov is chasing y'all!"

"Now, now, none of that!" Cliff Rogers exclaimed. "Since you've joined us, you've all contributed just like everyone else. No reasonable person would blame you for this."

That's a nice thought, Cliff, but really more something for a member of the family to say, Ramon thought. *And before, weren't you blaming our situation on the person who rescued them?*

Following that family meeting, the first night in the marsh passed peacefully enough. When Ramon came off his guard duty shift and slept, though, he had a strange dream.

The details were fuzzy when he woke up, but he remembered that James, of all people, was there. He had given a warning that the marsh was dangerous, but he'd called it something else, something more specific, like a formal name for the place, but the information was lost by the time Ramon woke up.

Ramon had had to explain to dream-James that the family had fled from the cultists into the swamp outskirts, and per his last scouting expedition, the cultists were still stalking the outskirts of the swamp. If they wanted to leave, they'd have to go through the Moloch worshippers.

James seemed to understand at that point, and Ramon's dream returned to its regularly scheduled programming. He was learning from his Tio Raimundo in his garage. Tio Raimundo was a mechanic. He was showing Ramon how to change the oil on his car. It was a soothing, peaceful memory. The System, Orientation, and James's appearance in the dream faded almost completely from Ramon's mind.

The next day dawned, but the sky remained grimly hazy, full of the same swampy miasma that had permeated the previous day. The air smelled fetid, like rot. Possibly worse than it had been the previous day.

And there was something both strange and alarming.

Are there fewer of us? It felt like one or two of the people who would normally be out walking in the morning air were either sleeping in or simply absent.

Ramon looked around. Maria and Hector were circulating through the camp, quietly talking to people with looks of concern on their faces. The couple didn't have either of their teenagers with them, which was unusual. They'd been fairly protective since the System had appeared.

When they came to Ramon, Maria asked, "Have you seen my Jessica or my Jaime, Ramon?" She tried to curl her mouth into her usual friendly smile, but the corners of her lips kept falling.

Ramon could only shake his head.

As the morning went on, it became clear that Jessica, Jaime, and Chava, plus Moishe, were all missing.

No one could precisely trace where they might have gone. The camp was on guard against the possibility of cultists entering the marsh from the forest, but no sentries were posted against people leaving. The only theory that seemed to make sense was that they had walked deeper into the swamp for some reason or other.

No one wanted to say it out loud, but the grim reality was, besides Moishe, the missing were all among the physically weaker members of the camp.

Why would they wander further into the swamp? They have to have known that they would only get themselves into some kind of trouble. There must be monsters that live here.

Only Moishe's disappearance made some kind of sense. The Assassin could take care of himself fairly well, Ramon knew, and he might have simply wanted to do more damage to the cultists.

Still, I wish he'd stuck around, Ramon thought. *The camp feels less secure without him. I can't keep them safe well myself, and I don't like relying on Cliff.* And he had hoped that Moishe, who he knew had been a Rogue before undergoing Class Evolution, might teach him a thing or two.

At lunch time, when the family gathered to eat their rations, Mama Camila suggested to everyone that the family move their tents closer together. It would be more secure. They might also want to consider posting guards on the marsh side of the camp as well as the forest-facing side.

She tried to be calm and gentle as she made her suggestions, but Ramon could hear her voice tremble as she spoke. It was clear that she feared for her family.

Jeffrey Ross dreamed.

Though his day had been stressful, the dream was soothing. He was a young teenager, still living in his parents' house. His father was showing him how to lift weights for the first time again.

"Christ on a cracker, kid, you'll hurt yourself like that!" Jackson Ross frowned and took the barbell from his son's hands.

Jeffrey suppressed a smile. Just like in real life, he messed it up on purpose. He just wanted his dad to show him how to do it again. He wanted attention, and this was one of the times he could get extra attention without any distractions. His baby brother and kid sister were too young for weightlifting, and they weren't awake now, anyway. Dad's training regimen always started before sunrise.

Jeffrey watched his dad demonstrate the proper technique once more. Then he took the weight back from him and performed a barbell curl correctly. Jeffrey's dad nodded, and then Jeffrey continued contentedly lifting the weight. Up and down. Up and down.

Until he realized that the garage around him had dissolved.

Jeffrey was still a teenager, still holding the barbell, and still standing in front of his father. But everything around him was different.

"Say, where are we?" Jackson Ross looked all around, a confused expression on his face.

They were in the Orientation forest, in the Rostov camp.

The teenagers from earlier that day were there, bound and afraid.

"Please, Officer," one of them pleaded. "You have to do something. They're going to kill us!"

And Officer Jackson Ross turned back to them. He had switched from his workout clothes to his police uniform while Jeffrey was looking at the teenagers, but that detail didn't seem strange.

"I'll cut you loose, kids!" He turned back to Jeffrey, his expression worried. "Son, you have to help me! I think something terrible is going to happen to these kids if we don't get them out of here."

Jeffrey was paralyzed. *I can't*, he thought. *It's their lives or ours! Dad, I . . .*

He tried to play out the conversation in his head but realized that no matter what combination of words he used, there would be no possible way teenaged Jeffrey could explain this to his dad.

And then he looked down at himself and saw that he was a teenager no longer. He was an adult, wearing his police uniform, armed with his pistol. His dad still stood there, looking at him beseechingly.

"Son, we have to do something! Hurry!"

"Dad," Jeffrey said softly. "I can't do anything for those teenagers. Catherine and I—my wife and I will be killed if we help them."

"Boy, I didn't raise you this way!" Jackson Ross looked and sounded more upset than angry. "What did my life even mean if you're willing to sacrifice these innocent kids to save yourself? All the time we spent together. Where did I go wrong?" His voice dropped. "What would your poor mother say?"

"Don't," Jeffrey said. "Please don't." His eyes filled with tears.

Then he felt a hand on his arm. He turned his head to the side, and there was Catherine, smiling, beautiful.

"It's all right, sweetheart. Just think about our kids and how happy they'll be to see us alive."

She pulled him into her embrace. He wrapped his arms around her tightly.

For a moment, he felt a measure of peace.

Then he noticed that his hands felt strangely moist and sticky. He pulled them away from Catherine, and he saw that they were red with fresh blood.

"*Gah!* What the hell?" he exclaimed.

He pulled away from Catherine, and he saw that she was bleeding. Streams of blood trickled down from the crown of her head, her wrists, her hands, her feet, her eyes, and the place just above her heart. She continued smiling.

"Catherine!" Jeffrey cried. "What's happened to you?"

"Don't you think the children will be happy to see me, sweetie?"

"*Ahhhhhh!*"

Jeffrey Ross sprung awake, sweat trickling down his forehead and his back. The darkness and the firelight of the camp site immediately reminded him. *It was just a dream.*

"What the hell was that dream?" he wondered aloud. He turned his head and looked at his wife. Catherine's expression was beatific, as if she was dreaming of blissful reunion with their children.

Just my conscience, I guess, Ross thought. *I wasn't cut out for this stuff. I wasn't raised to sacrifice other human beings.* He thought of his father. *You would be ashamed of me, wouldn't you?*

There was a slight commotion outside of the tent, and he perked his ears up. If it was a confrontation, he should probably involve himself. He rose to a crouch and began dressing.

Then he froze, one leg in his pants and one out.

Why should I get involved? he thought. *What the hell is wrong with me? When did I become such a good little soldier? What happened to the guy who was just looking for the first opportunity he could find to backstab Rostov?*

He turned back to his wife and smiled bittersweetly. Then he kissed her forehead. He finished putting his pants on and stepped outside.

Six figures stood in a circle, four of them kicking and punching and stabbing with swords at a figure on the ground.

"What's all this?" Ross inserted himself into the conflict confidently, loudly announcing himself.

Two of the figures bent to grab hold of the person on the ground, whose face was concealed in shadow. One of them, Hilda Rohm, turned to see Ross. She smiled tensely.

"We were very fortunate this evening, Officer," she said. Her expression looked as if she was unhappy with this good fortune. "We caught Moishe Rose. He returned to our camp to try and do some more damage, but he set off the Prophet's defensive wards this time."

"Well, then, the Prophet will want to be part of dealing with him, won't he?" Ross frowned. "Or were you all about to carry out some vigilante justice?"

A man whose face had been concealed in shadow turned to Ross. He saw it was Kassim.

"You won't hold it against us that we got a few hits in on him, will you, Jeff?" he asked. "We already know what the Prophet will do, and, of course, none of us object to making this man a sacrifice. But he killed people we knew. He deserves the lesson he's getting."

"Maybe so," Ross said. "Have you woken the Prophet?"

"I'll go ahead and do that," Kassim replied with a forced smile.

Kassim's more loyal to Rostov than anybody. Interesting that he'd do this behind his back. Rostov wouldn't even disapprove, but to not even bother waking him is . . .

It was clear the Prophet's hold on everyone's loyalty was slipping.

Maybe, despite what Catherine had said, this was the moment that Jeffrey had to seize.

As Kassim walked away, Jeffrey looked down at Moishe Rose. *Perhaps you could help me figure out how to kill Rostov and get away with it.*

Aloud, he said, "So, was it worth it coming back here again, shithead?"

Moishe looked up at him with defiant eyes.

"I already got a couple more of you," he said. "I call it worth it."

Already? It almost sounds as if he thinks he might kill more of us.

He noticed Moishe's palm tracing a pattern on his chest, and something prickled in the back of Ross's mind. The movement was too similar to the symbol he remembered Moishe tracing when he had used his ability.

With a speed that would have been impossible when he was a normal human, Ross slammed a fist down into Moishe's skull.

The Assassin collapsed instantly.

"Phew!" Ross exhaled.

Then he noticed the others were staring at him.

"He was about to use some kind of ability," Ross explained hastily.

"Sure he was," said Carl Ronson with a snicker. "You wanted to get your lick in, too, Officer. There's no reason to deny it. No one would blame you for a punch."

"Just make sure his hands are bound," Ross said contemptuously.

I don't know how I thought for a second that I might be able to work with that guy. Regardless of what kind of ability he was trying to use, he knew he'd die after he used it. He came back here fully expecting and planning to get himself killed, just to take as many of us with him as possible. Even if I can't stand how things are going right now, I'm not suicidal.

He felt certain that he had at least a few allies in the camp who would help him deal with Rostov and his loyalists. Ross would just have to choose his moment and his co-conspirators carefully.

He turned to walk away, then paused and turned around again.

"Hey, the person he attacked before was bitten by a venomous snake. Did you guys kill that thing?" Ross asked.

The five who had captured Moishe Rose looked slightly alarmed at this announcement. Then Hilda silently shook her head.

CHAPTER TWENTY-SEVEN

Safe Haven

A strange story," James said after Jeremiah Rotter finished speaking.

"But I assure you, it's completely tr—"

"I believe you." James cut him off. "It sounds like the Dead Marsh is quite dangerous."

Anansi had already told him as much, so that wasn't staggering news. Hearing more details about the threat didn't change the nature of the mission.

"Yet you still intend to go there?" Rotter asked in disbelief. "Also, where did you get that name from? It sounds appropriate, but I didn't realize these places had names."

James smiled grimly. "I have my sources," he replied vaguely. "And I can be quite dangerous myself." He tilted his head at the sand where the bodies of the coyotes had been until he had used Mass Pillage on them.

"I—I see," Rotter said. "Of course, sir. Far be it from me to question someone so powerful." He smiled weakly.

I don't love brownnosers, James thought. *Especially not ones who are so blatant about it. Things I'll have to get used to.*

"What will you and your group do?" he asked aloud.

"Oh, that—hm." Rotter's eyes noticeably darted to the unconscious Damien Rousseau before they shifted back to James.

Oh, I see. That's their real leader. Of course. James's observation thus far had been that power was the only law in the System-operated world. It was only natural that the highest-level member of the group would be in charge—especially when he was a ferocious creature.

"What happened to him, anyway?" James asked, pointing his thumb at Rousseau.

"Oh, um. Well, he tangled with a creature in that marsh that might have been just a little beyond his abilities."

James raised an eyebrow. *Rousseau was a fierce werewolf last time I saw him. A little scary even to me. What could've injured him so badly that he'd have trouble fighting off a few coyotes?*

"Are you going to give me the details, or do I have to beg?" James asked.

"Ah, I wasn't there," Rotter admitted. "But there were huge bite marks all over him when he came back, and he'd reverted back to human form. He's a Werewolf, you see. Race Evolution."

"Interesting."

Huge bite marks don't sound like an undead injury. I can't help wondering if Damien would have turned into a zombie or something if he did have bites from them. But it reminded him of the time when he'd seen Damien fighting one of the forest wolves. Maybe they were cohabitating with the undead in the Dead Marsh now. Or fighting for that territory.

If they're working together now, those are awfully strange bedfellows . . .

"Well, I'm going back toward the Dead Marsh, to kill everything inside it. Let's finish this Orientation with humans at the top of the food chain, where we belong!" James said. "You can keep trekking through the desert and try your luck with the other creatures that live here, or you can follow me."

"I, uh, I don't know—we left there because it was so dangerous—"

"Then try your luck in the desert if you want. I would stay and guard you, but there's another group of people I already promised to protect. They're either in the Dead Marsh or very near it." James smiled broadly, and for a moment he must have resembled a crocodile. "I can tell you that if you're worried about your physical safety, the safest place to be in this Orientation is right behind me, wherever I'm standing."

"Y-yes, that makes sense." Rotter looked back at his teammates. Recovering from injuries, dressed in torn clothing, or both, they seemed a motley bunch at present. "Will you wait—" He began but stopped at the look on James's face.

I've already waited too damn long! James thought. The faces of his companions ran through his mind: Alan, Mitzi, Sierra, Ramon, Camila, the other Rodriguezes—and yes, even Cliff. He owed them something, if only because he felt he'd promised them something. He also wondered what had happened to the escapees. He had nothing but admiration for those who had used the window he'd made to escape, especially since it happened despite his plan failing.

He was about to rise and tell Rotter that his group would have to take care of themselves, when he heard another voice that gave him pause.

"Of course we'll follow you. We owe you our lives. We'll provide whatever support we can." Damien Rousseau's voice came out almost as a growl, but James suspected that was just how he sounded all the time. Possibly a side effect of becoming a Werewolf. The tone of gratitude sounded sincere to him, and James currently wore the Ring of Truth, so he felt confident in his reading.

"I'm very glad to hear it, Damien," he said. "Nice to meet you, by the way." He walked a few feet and extended his hand to where Damien still lay on the sand nearby. The Werewolf shook, but his grip felt weak to James.

He still needs time to fully recover, he thought.

"Pleasure's really all mine," Damien said in his quiet growling voice. "I really thought I was going to wake up in some kind of wild fantasy afterlife there."

"Well, I'm glad you don't have to face that," James said with a smile.

"Forget about me for a minute, though. What do you need from us? How can we help you?"

"Well, I have to return to the forest as quickly as I can," James said, feeling a little bad now. "I was hoping to get some backup here, but I can see you guys need some time to recover from that attack. Do you feel able to defend the group adequately if I run ahead?"

Damien dropped his head. "Sorry, man. I think we're a burden right now. I think we're a capable group, and I know I gathered a balanced team around me." He pronounced these words in a tone of pride. "But in this open desert, we're at a disadvantage until we're fully recovered. We retreated to this plateau so we couldn't be surrounded, but that wasn't enough."

"Hm. So it's a terrain problem in your judgment?" James asked. That was something he could deal with.

Damien simply nodded.

Basic Elemental Magic: Earth! James began chanting.

After around ten minutes of chanting, while Damien and the others looked on in quiet anticipation, James unleashed his magic.

Three thick walls of condensed sandstone rose from the ground on all sides of the group. At James's further command, bits of sandstone near the tops of the walls fell away in a pattern, forming crenellations. Still wielding earth Mana, James pulled part of the plateau down to form a thin outcropping that would shield them from the sun. It didn't make contact with all of the walls, so there was a thin gap to let sunshine through. And, lastly, James made a human-sized gap between one wall and the plateau.

The walls should hold against anything short of high explosives, and the roof should be adequate as long as no flying enemies attack, he judged. *They should be able to leave through that gap, but any predators would have to find that opening to attack, and if they wanted to enter, they would have to do it in a single file. Adequate defense.*

He snuck a peek at the group's reactions. He could barely see them because he hadn't left many openings in the roof. But there were still people whose mouths hung open as they stared at James or the fortress he'd thrown up. Others looked like the surprise had passed for them, but they continued to look around with appreciative expressions. And Damien Rousseau was staring at James with the biggest grin he'd ever seen.

"Everyone feel secure?" James asked with a wink.

People began talking over each other about how much safer they were now.

"All right, recover at your leisure, and come meet me in the forest or the marsh when you can. I'll visit you in your dreams and let you know where I am."

James leaped straight up and punched a human-sized hole in the ceiling. *There, now they have a little skylight. Probably wasn't enough light before.* He landed on the roof and noted with a bit of relief that it was strong enough to hold his weight. He realized belatedly that he hadn't known it would.

That could've been bad.

"What was that he said about dreams?" someone asked from below.

James didn't wait to hear and ran across the stone fortress's roof. Then he jumped down onto the sand and kept running, a chant already working its way through his lips. He'd realized what he needed to reach the forest more quickly. *Basic Elemental Magic: Gravity.*

He had all the Stat points he needed in Agility. He just needed to decrease his weight and he would be able to clear ground more quickly than even his Skin Balloons, which he ordered to follow above him as quickly as they could.

Once James was lighter, he found that each stride carried him several yards forward. As he grew accustomed to his new, insanely light weight, he ran as fast as he'd imagined.

One hour later, the sun had almost set.

James arrived at the edge of the Dead Marsh and stopped running.

The change in terrain was immediately obvious. The ground began changing from dry sand to moist soil that supported far more vegetation. It was almost as abrupt as a line in the earth, which made James wonder if something like this would ever happen in nature, or if it was just the System skewing reality in its preferred ways. A few yards ahead, the tree line began to reassert itself. Most prominently—and this was why he stopped running—James could see a mist emanating from the marshy ground.

That feels ominous and unnatural, James decided without much thought. He wasn't sure when exactly he'd gained the ability to sense it, but he felt the presence of hostile Mana inside that mist. Some life-form was controlling it. He judged that entering the mist might provoke an immediate ambush.

And it stank of rot. Something mildewy in it, perhaps. James was no expert in swamps, but having spent much of his life in Florida, he had a healthy wariness of standing waters. Common wisdom in the Sunshine State was that any body of freshwater was likely to contain alligators.

He suspected worse predators than those lurked in these waters.

The Dead Marsh. The name almost ran a shudder through his body. But he consciously evoked Self-Control, and the normally involuntary reaction stopped immediately. Now was no time to lose his head. He tried to decide what to do. Where to go first.

I wonder where the Rodriguezes have gotten to. Are they in there? Still outside of it? Captured by Rostov and his thugs?

He just didn't have the answers he needed to make a confident decision.

"What are you going to do?" Hester asked, breaking her long silence.

I almost forgot you were there, he thought.

"I kind of missed your voice," he said. "Thank you for warning me about those humans in trouble before, by the way. I'd appreciate you doing the same in future. As for what I'm going to do, I need to figure out my strategy for taking the cultists and the Ruler of the Dead Marsh out. Still deciding the order I should fight them in, and where exactly my group is likely to be. More pressing at the moment is that I'm not sure what's up with that mist. It gives me the creeps."

"Do you think you can destroy it?" she asked.

"I was considering an attempt."

It seemed a little rash to try a frontal assault on something that was obviously infused with enemy Mana, but he doubted the mist itself was a form of attack that could reach him while he was outside the confines of the Dead Marsh.

Well, as long as I still have a little daylight, he thought. Responding to his silent command, the Skin Balloons dropped their altitude to pick him up.

They raised him back up to a height where he could get a little more sunlight. James began charging a final Solar Ray for the day. He would see if he could blast that mist away and penetrate into the Dead Marsh.

He spent longer than he had before gathering power around himself. This time there was no time pressure, after all. No coyotes about to rip people's throats out if he didn't intervene. And he was conscious that he was collecting energy much less efficiently with the sun setting already. Might as well do the best job he could.

When the sun had almost completely melted into the horizon, and he could hardly feel himself gathering any power from it anymore, James gave up and unleashed the attack, shooting it straight into the heart of the mist.

The results were disappointing.

The mist faded where the Solar Ray struck, but it only penetrated for a certain distance. Some trees and shrubbery were destroyed, and James could see he was turning small amounts of the swamp water into steam.

But even before the beam had fully discharged its energy, the mist reasserted itself. James felt the ray being pushed back, as if the foreign Mana was overpowering the beam he'd fired. Perhaps that was exactly what was happening.

He quickly ran out of power and ordered the Skin Balloons to set him down slightly further back from the Dead Marsh.

He decided not to enter the territory within the mist for now.

I have a bad feeling I'd be setting off the final boss fight a little too early. Need to figure out what the situation is with the Rodriguezes and the cultists before I decide what to do.

"Aw, man," Hester said quietly.

"Are you as disappointed as I am?" James asked wryly. The little spider was growing on him.

"Yes! That attack wiped out all those coyotes. Whatever's in there must be really strong. I'm starting to worry."

James sat down cross-legged.

"Well, don't worry too much," he said. "I'm going away for a bit. Hopefully, I'll solve some problems while I'm gone."

Dreamwalk.

CHAPTER TWENTY-EIGHT

The Thirteenth Step

As the last of the team donated blood, the vase filled up to the brim.

Creepy shit, DaSilva thought. *Like something I'd expect to see in a horror movie.*

And then the floor behind the vase opened up. A single ripple went through the surface of the blood as the floor quietly moved. DaSilva found himself strangely apprehensive that the vase might topple over and spill crimson everywhere.

DaSilva forced himself to look away from the vase and tilted his head to instead peer down into the opening.

The space looked like it became pitch black deeper down. There were apparently no lights illuminating the dark. The torchlight from the room DaSilva was currently in revealed a stone staircase leading down into the bowels of the Earth. He stepped behind the vase and looked down at the area around the opening. He expected writing of some sort. The System had given them written clues in each phase of this place thus far.

Sure enough, when he bent to look closely at the opening, he found an inscription on the floor directly in front of it, gleaming in the torchlight.

"'Fortune favors the bold,'" he read aloud, at a volume everyone could hear. "I guess it wants us to advance boldly."

But then, the last inscription had felt less than straightforward to DaSilva.

Any volunteers to go first?

He turned his head to glance back at the team, but it was as he'd expected. Everyone was waiting for him. He sighed quietly and began to descend the stairs.

Burdens of command, he thought a bit nervously. *You always have to be out front. This is why I never tested for sergeant. But here, I'm chief of police.*

As he descended, DaSilva moved slowly and counted steps. It was a way of calming himself down, and it would also help him gauge how far underground they were relative to the chamber they had just left. He found that counting, along with slow, deep breaths, was quite effective at helping him keep his cool.

One step, two steps, three, four . . .

Behind him, he could hear the rest of the team slowly and quietly taking the first stairs down as DaSilva reached the sixth step.

As he hit the ninth, he turned back just to get some reference for how deep he was, and he saw the top step was just over his head height now.

They couldn't have mounted some torches in here like they did in the previous rooms?

There had to be something up with this space. A danger they were concealing in these shadows. But at least he would be the one stepping into whatever was wrong before his team did. He reluctantly resumed the descent.

Ten, eleven, twelve, thirteen.

On the thirteenth step, DaSilva felt the stair his foot landed on shift beneath him, pressing down slightly into the ground.

Crap. Is this thing unstable, or—?

Gears within the walls audibly moved now. DaSilva tried to jump forward, but the walls began to move around him. A chunk of wall to his left detached from the rest of the structure almost silently, popping out slightly like a pouting lip. At the same time, a portion of wall to his right receded and slid out of view with a scraping sound, leaving an opening. The left chunk of wall suddenly sprang at DaSilva, shoving him into the hole on his right.

"*Aaaaaaaaahhhhhh!*" he screamed as he fell into darkness.

Where did the detective go? Yulia thought, horrified.

She was near the back of the line, out of direct view of the detective, when she heard the sound of the walls moving—and then the sound of DaSilva screaming.

"Oh my gosh!" Cara gasped from right in front of her.

"Detective!" Jose yelled from a little further forward.

"Detective DaSilva! Are you there?" Adelaide called out.

There was a moment of eerie silence, and the mood of the group began to change.

Those just in front of Yulia started to press forward to get a better look at what was happening, while Mr. Davidson tried to hold his ground at the front, arms pressed against the walls to keep himself from being pushed forward.

"Let's all stay calm!" said Mr. Davidson. He was positioned directly behind where DaSilva had been, and Yulia guessed he was nervous about being pushed toward whatever trap the detective must have activated.

"Did you see what happened to him?" Adelaide asked from a little further back.

"Yeah, the wall came open and swallowed him!" Mr. Davidson said.

"That's exactly it," Mrs. Davidson agreed. "He took a step forward, and one of the walls pushed him into an opening that appeared."

"Do you know where he stepped?" Adelaide asked.

They spent a few minutes trying to reenact Detective DaSilva's disappearance without triggering a repeat. Finally, Adelaide figured out that he had trodden on the thirteenth stair, and that was what had activated the trap.

"So, we just have to avoid the thirteenth stair," Mr. Davidson murmured. "Or maybe every thirteenth stair? I wouldn't want to test the stairs that come in multiples of thirteen to see if someone disappears each time."

"Of course not," Mrs. Davidson said. "We'll just descend very carefully, bearing in mind the lesson the detective has left us with."

"Who says it's even a bad thing?" Yulia murmured to herself.

The quiet chatter between other group members seemed to die. Yulia looked up and realized everyone was staring at her.

Oh, that was out loud. She swallowed nervously.

"What do you mean?" Adelaide asked. "About it not being a bad thing."

"Just the inscription." Yulia pointed. "The detective read it. 'Fortune favors the bold.' Thirteen is a lucky number to some people and an unlucky number to others, isn't it? I think the inscription is a hint about that. Detective DaSilva was being bold. He went first."

"You think that it must be a good thing because the person who walks down the stairs first was always going to trigger that trap?" Adelaide asked slowly. "It was unavoidable, so it must be good fortune?"

"I don't know." Yulia shrugged and lowered her eyes.

But the System hasn't outright killed anyone yet. The proctor killed someone, but that was because he was trying to get people to attack her. Then again, DaSilva had triggered a trap before that had fired arrows at him. Maybe she was putting too much faith in the System being reasonable.

"I think it does make sense that it's not a bad thing," Adelaide said thoughtfully. "The System hasn't been randomly killing people, so why would it target someone just for being the first person down the stairs?"

Yulia smiled appreciatively and nodded her agreement with Adelaide.

"Are you willing to gamble your life on it?" Mr. Davidson asked drily. "Maybe it's targeting people who don't notice traps on the ground. He got shot full of arrows before just because he stood too close to a wall."

"I think you might be right," Jose said quietly. "We should avoid touching steps in multiples of thirteen. Unless anyone has a rope we could use to lower someone down after DaSilva and maybe pull them both back up. Otherwise, there's no safe way to test this."

The group quickly came to the consensus that they wouldn't test the rigged stairs out. The first in line, now Mr. Davidson, would count steps out loud as they descended. Then he would step over the thirteenth stair, stand on the four-teenth, and give the next person a hand skipping the possible trick stair. The next person would then descend further, following the same procedure, while the rest of the party crossed the thirteenth stair.

After the discussion, they began descending the stairs in the same order they had before, employing their new strategy.

Is this really the right way? Yulia wondered as she carefully avoided the thir-teenth step. *If we really needed to avoid that step, what happened to the detective?*

Detective DaSilva dropped a short distance through open air.

Then he landed on a stone slide, and he slid downward, much less sharply, for several minutes. A much faster way to travel than walking down a staircase, and the pace was so relaxed that he didn't bother trying to slow down.

So this is what the inscription meant by "Fortune favors the bold," he thought. *Hopefully, the others figure it out somehow.*

Surely this was bringing him closer to the finish line of this race.

The only thing that gave him a slight feeling of concern was the temperature. As he slid, the air was getting warmer, and not by small degrees. It felt as if he was falling toward a desert.

Finally, he landed lightly on his feet in a small cave. He looked around cau-tiously before he moved forward. Curiously, his eyes adjusted to the near dark-ness of this cave much better than they had in the stairwell earlier. *There must be some light source in the distance,* he reckoned. And he had a guess what that might be, related to the temperature change he'd noticed.

The cave air was even hotter than the air above had been. As he scoped out his surroundings, he looked for a heat source.

But DaSilva found nothing.

Finally, having found no sign of other life or movement, he advanced. He walked away from the slide. As he moved, the heat pounded him more intensely with every step, and he began to feel apprehension about where he'd landed.

As he rounded a corner, he noticed the lighting change from a dim ambient glow to a much more vividly reflected orange radiance.

A confirmation of what he had feared.

But still, he advanced. If the others followed the same way he'd gone, or even if they took some longer route to reach the same place, he needed to know what lay at the end of this cave. As he proceeded, the air grew hotter—uncomfortably hot—before he'd reached the end of the tunnel. DaSilva finally paused, stripped off his heavy armor, and stowed it in his Small Bag of Deceptive Dimensions.

He continued to advance, sweating bullets, until he reached the mouth of the cave. There was a small semicircular landing beyond it, and a black stone bridge affixed to the landing, but neither of those captured DaSilva's attention at first.

Instead, his eyes were drawn to the glowing red river of lava that flowed slowly beneath the bridge.

No wonder it's so damn hot, he thought.

The landing felt like a tiny island in the seething, bubbling river, but DaSilva stepped out onto it. Any clue he could get would be to the group's advantage whenever they made it here.

Standing out in the open, he could see there were other bridges lining the river, attached to other landings that connected to other cave openings.

There are enough bridges for all of the other teams, he reckoned. *Everyone has to complete whatever this challenge is, then? Does that mean it's the last one?*

Then he saw the inscription.

At last, Yulia and the group finished descending the staircase.

It had comprised hundreds, if not thousands, of stairs. They had been forced to descend slowly because there was no lighting through the entire route.

But at last, they reached a landing. They emerged into what looked like a cave.

It was immediately noticeable how much warmer the air was.

"Oh, you finally made it," said a voice.

"Oh my gosh!" Cara exclaimed.

In a corner of the cave, seated with his knees pulled up to his chest and his head and arms resting on his knees, was Detective DaSilva. He'd stripped his armor off, and his sweat had soaked through his shirt in multiple places.

"I knew you survived!" Yulia said, expression bright and happy.

"So, the challenge is a bridge," DaSilva explained. "The Bridge of Faith. I'm pretty sure it's the final challenge because I've occasionally seen or heard other groups coming by and crossing their own bridges from their own caves. But they all have to do the same thing." He grimaced. "Not all of them succeeded. We have to think carefully about this."

"What do you mean, not all of them succeeded?" Frank asked guardedly.

DaSilva gave him a weary look. "Just what I said. Listen, it's okay with me if we don't do this. Sooner or later, this challenge ends. We'll get transported out once it's over, just like in every other challenge."

"What happens if you fail?" Yulia asked, looking DaSilva in the eyes.

He avoided her gaze for a moment, then sighed and slumped his shoulders.

"I saw one of the groups that failed. The first couple made it across the bridge, and then when the others were crossing, it collapsed."

"Into that?!" Frank gestured wildly at the lava river.

"Exactly," DaSilva said. "No survivors. No point in even wearing armor. You'd just get scorched before you melted, maybe."

"So, what are the rules?" Adelaide asked. "Why did they fail?"

"This inscription is probably the most straightforward of the lot," DaSilva said, shaking his head. "I still can't make heads or tails of what it really means, though. The instruction is: 'Let no one with less faith cross after one who has more.'"

"Is that religious faith, romantic fidelity, faith in the System . . . ?" Adelaide mused aloud.

"This is why I'm completely supportive of quitting now," DaSilva said. "We have no way of knowing, and we only get one shot at getting it right. More than one team has definitely tumbled to their deaths."

"'Yea, though I walk through the valley of the shadow of death, I will fear no evil: for thou art with me,'" Yulia said quietly. "I know it's insane, but I don't want to back down. This place feels like a test of faith. I have faith. I'll be okay. And we need the food."

"That's nuts!" Frank said bluntly. "Your interpretation isn't the only one. You can't—"

"It's okay to cross if you want to, Yulia," DaSilva said quietly. "But we don't know if we get any winnings if only part of the group makes it. There would be no point in you going alone."

"My faith is strong," she said, voice full of resolve. "I want to cross."

Karen Davidson spoke up. "You know, sometimes it's the kids who remind you of the things that you used to know were important. If this place wasn't some kind of a test of faith, a hallucination was the next most likely thing. But if it's either of those things—if this place is God testing us or if I've lost my marbles— either way, it makes sense to cross the bridge."

"Or this place isn't some test made by a god or a devil, and our lives are in our own hands," Paulo said.

Jose elbowed him in the ribs.

"I will fear no evil, for thou art with me," Adelaide murmured quietly.

The group discussed in hushed tones for a few minutes. Maybe the heat got to them. Maybe it was mass hysteria. Or the strength of a teenager's faith and conviction.

They all agreed to cross.

There was more discussion as the group tried to sort themselves from least to most faithful. Cara was near the front along with Frank. The Dante brothers were in the middle, with Paulo in front of Jose. Adelaide and Karen were further back.

And bringing up the rear—

"I think I'm the most faithful, so I should be last," Yulia said with a firmness she never knew she had.

"No. Full stop. No." DaSilva spoke with an absolute firmness that brooked no argument.

"But you weren't even sure if you were willing to cross—"

"And we still don't have to!" DaSilva said sharply. "This is a kind of madness we've all fallen under. If we make it, then I love that you led us to it, but it's madness all the same. I can't let you cross after me, Yulia. Do you understand? If the bridge collapsed because you tried to cross after me, that would effectively mean that *I* killed you by putting myself first. That can't happen. No fuckin' way. If you can't accept that, then we'll all fuckin' stay right here, capisce?"

"Then you—"

"Don't underestimate me," he interrupted. He was now openly rubbing the crucifix that hung around his neck. "My faith is strong too."

I would rather die a thousand times than cause you to come to harm, little girl, he thought.

Finally, she assented, a worried expression creasing her otherwise unlined face.

I've lived a long, full life, anyway, he wanted to tell her.

CHAPTER TWENTY-NINE

What Doesn't Kill Us

DaSilva led the group from the back of the cave to its mouth in relative silence.

Their faces were all set with the same look of grim, sweaty determination.

As they reached the landing that connected the cave to the bridge, DaSilva took another look at his team. People were nervous and hiding it poorly. Despite the heat, DaSilva heard at least one set of teeth chattering out of sheer anxiety.

He didn't try to identify the person. There was no way to single them out for a one-on-one chat discreetly here, and what would he say, anyway?

Don't worry, follow Joan of Arc's commands, and God will see us through this? What if they didn't believe in God?

"Well, there's no use in waiting around here," he said quietly. "Who was going first?"

Before he spoke, Yulia had bent down to look at the text DaSilva had told them about earlier, which was inscribed at the place on the ground where the bridge met their small strip of land.

Cara and Frank almost ran past her, as if competing to be first across. Given the rule the System had set for this challenge, DaSilva couldn't entirely blame them.

But he was glad when he saw Frank pull back a bit, to let Cara go first. The girl had been an avowed atheist pre-System, so even Frank's doubtful religious faith was surely stronger than hers. It was after them that the conflict and doubt would begin.

Cara vanished over the arch of the bridge, and then she became visible again as she walked a bit further away and emerged onto a landing attached to the other end of the bridge. Then Frank.

Paulo followed after, looking like his heart was in his throat. Nothing happened to him. Like the other two, he reached the landing on the other side. The trio high-fived and turned to look back at the remaining group members.

Team member after team member crossed the bridge, and it didn't budge. No hint of collapse this time.

Was it all in my head? DaSilva wondered. *Are those collapsed bridges just an illusion? Something to test our faith?*

Finally, only he and Yulia were left on the cave side of the bridge. They could see the others standing on the landing across the river, staring back at them.

"You ready to go?" he asked, looking down at her.

"I'm not going first," Yulia said quietly, not meeting his eyes.

"We already discussed this—"

"No, you *decided*!" She crossed her arms as she spoke. "We didn't discuss anything. I never agreed to go first. And you can't make me, unless you're going to push me the whole way across. Which would probably kill us both if the bridge collapsed."

DaSilva sighed. He was tempted for a moment to raise his voice, but then he saw his own Carrie's face in Yulia's expression. *She was just as stubborn at that age, wasn't she?*

He went with a different tack. "Are you really going to waste all the faith our teammates demonstrated? You were the one who wanted to go across the bridge in the first place. Everyone else risked their lives to do what you wanted. But if you don't cross, you know I'm not going to. And maybe the group doesn't get anything. I might have a hard time pushing you across in front of me, but at least it's possible. I'm two hundred eighty pounds. How are you going to get your way?"

There was a long silence from Yulia. She still wasn't looking at him. It looked like she was staring down into the lava. Her cheeks were puffed out and red, and for a second, DaSilva thought she might be holding her breath in annoyance. But that gesture was too young for her, and finally, she spoke.

"I can't get my way. You're right."

"Well, then—"

Yulia sat down cross-legged.

"What are you doing?" DaSilva asked, frowning.

"Trying to figure out what to do. I don't know how to make you cross in front of me, but I can't just let the bridge collapse under you." She replied so quickly that DaSilva's eyes widened.

Is she really that sure of herself?

He stared at the arc of the bridge once more. He hadn't wanted to cross it in the first place. Now that Yulia had gotten them to this point, maybe it was worth taking her demand to be last more seriously. Part of it was undoubtedly that he was covered in sweat, standing next to a river of lava.

But I can't . . . There was a line in his heart that he couldn't cross. He couldn't live with himself if he let someone so young and innocent die to save him. Maybe the System would agree with her that her faith was stronger than his, but maybe it wouldn't. That was a possibility he couldn't accept.

Then he noticed something.

"I have an idea," DaSilva said.

"Oh? A way you're going to force me to cross in front of you?" Yulia didn't even look up at him. She was fiddling with her shoelaces or something. DaSilva thought she had never seemed more like a moody teenager than she did at that moment. It brought a smile to his face.

"No, not a way to make you cross in front of me. A compromise."

"Compromise? What kind of compromise?" She perked up immediately, and DaSilva knew this would work.

"We cross together. I was just staring at the bridge, and I realized there's enough room for us to walk side by side. We'll have to walk pretty close, or one of us might tumble over, but it beats one of us sending the other to their death."

"Would that work?" she asked, looking up at him finally. She seemed to be studying his expression as she spoke—for any sign of deception, he imagined. "It wouldn't kill both of us?"

"The instruction is: 'Let no one with less faith cross after one who has more,'" DaSilva replied. "Nothing saying people have to line up single file. At least this way we're taking the same risk. Normally, I'd never put you in this position. But the reality is that we need to cross to get this food. So, I'll let you cross with me. But this is my best, final offer."

He stared down at Yulia for a few seconds, and at long last, she nodded, almost to herself.

Then she rose to her feet, brushed herself off, and smiled up at him.

"Let's do this."

Yulia and DaSilva walked over to the threshold of the bridge, arms linked as they took their first steps. They walked slowly, carefully, trying to remain in sync and not pass each other or put a foot in the wrong place.

DaSilva muttered quietly, "Left, right, left, right." It was partially for himself, partially trying to keep Yulia in step with him. There was over a foot of difference in height that they needed to work around.

There was barely enough room for both of them on this bridge, and as DaSilva set his foot down particularly close to the edge, he felt and heard a little piece of rock break away. He looked down and saw it sink into the liquid below them, hissing as it touched the molten lava.

Remind me to lose weight after this, he thought. This would feel much less stressful if he didn't know he could fall at any moment. Being thinner would help with that.

As they passed the midpoint of the bridge, it happened.

DaSilva felt a pressure on his ankle.

No! He looked down, and he saw it. A disembodied gray hand that seemed almost to come from the bridge itself gripped his ankle and pulled him toward the edge. It was just like earlier, when he'd triggered the trap that shot him full of arrows—at the time, he'd thought he felt something push his foot, but he'd convinced himself it was in his head. This time, he could actually see it.

An insubstantial gray hand. He could see through it slightly, but it felt completely solid grabbing him. Pulling him toward the river of death. He couldn't let it pull him over while he was linking arms with Yulia.

He tried to let go of her, but she gripped his arm tightly with both of hers. He looked at her and realized she could see what was happening too.

The two of them pulled together. After almost a minute, the hand gradually weakened and finally lost its grip.

DaSilva stumbled when it suddenly released his ankle, but Yulia was there to help him steady himself. It was good to have four legs instead of just two to balance with.

If she weren't here, he thought, *that thing would've gotten me. I'd be dead.*

There was a sound far off to DaSilva's right, in one of the areas belonging to another team. He and Yulia turned their heads to look. They saw another team emerging from a cave. The people in the front of the group started yelling while pointing at Yulia and DaSilva, but they were too far away for DaSilva to make out their specific words.

The first two in the other group started running across their bridge. Once they made it to the middle of the bridge, it suddenly collapsed.

Both men fell into the lava and caught fire instantly. Their dying screams echoed through the vast space for a few seconds.

Then there was silence.

Quietly and slowly, both their expressions hollow, DaSilva and Yulia advanced the rest of the way over the bridge.

When they set foot on solid ground again, they unhooked their arms. DaSilva kissed his crucifix. Then he pulled Yulia in for a hug, which she reciprocated. Everyone else around them seemed to let out a breath.

"You had us worried for a second there," said Frank a little uneasily.

[Congratulations! You are the final team of the first half of groups to complete the challenge! This challenge had a higher than expected attrition rate. Therefore, all survivors will be richly rewarded.]

[Heavy Warrior leveled up!]

[Heavy Warrior leveled up!]

Higher than expected attrition? What does that even mean in this context? He thought of the people he'd seen fall into the lava, both a moment ago and earlier. Apparently, enough people had burned to death to justify two level ups instead of one for completing the challenge.

Then he recalled his own experience on the bridge. He looked at his group and opened his mouth to say something about the hand that had grabbed his ankle. Then he shut his mouth again.

Assuming that hand wasn't part of the challenge, it was almost certainly an attack coming from this team. So I can't talk openly about it. Not until I have an idea of who it was. But who would try to kill me? He tried to read the faces around him, but no one showed any signs of nerves over his survival. People were hugging, cheering, and high-fiving over the System announcement.

Frank and Karen were fanning themselves. They looked about ready to pass out from the heat. DaSilva wanted to offer them some form of comfort, but he couldn't take his mind away from the fact that someone had definitely just attempted to murder him.

It would have to be the killer he was trying to catch who wanted to get him. No one else would have enough of a motive.

This murderer is on my team, then. It couldn't be the other team I just saw, because they only arrived just as the hand was disappearing.

As he tried to guess who on his team might be a serial killer, the System teleported the team back outside to the mountainside setting they'd started in. Mina was there, and when DaSilva turned his head, he saw the cave entrance again.

So, this whole challenge is really over.

"Thank goodness you all survived!" Mina exclaimed. She rushed over to her sister, pulled her into a tight embrace, and lifted her into the air.

Wow. Mina must have been very worried. It's incredible she can lift Yulia at all in her condition.

"I can't believe I let you go!" Mina was tearful. "Never again! So many people were dying, and I didn't know if you were okay!"

DaSilva checked the population counter. [2,846/3,397 **Survivors**]

Whoa. How did this happen?

He thought back to the individual components of the challenge.

There was the initial door into the mountain. That had only required discerning a verbal password. But after that there was at least one trap that unleashed a flurry of arrows. A room that seemed to encourage human sacrifice. There were the stairs down into darkness, with a benevolent and almost unavoidable trap of their own. And there was the Bridge of Faith.

I know some people failed the bridge test, but that can't account for this result, can it? Most of the groups didn't even complete the challenge. We were in the first half of people to do it . . .

He thought of various explanations for how so many people could have died, but none of them made sense.

Did other people run into more traps than we did? What the hell happened? The System mentioned there might be monsters. Maybe we got lucky and avoided them.

[Winners of the second challenge, we are aware some of you are questioning when you will be returned to your pre-challenge Orientation locations. Unfortunately, the challenge is not over for the other participants yet. Once the last of the participants complete the challenge, we will return everyone to their pre-challenge physical positions. Please enjoy your reunion, and your prizes, while you wait!]

Sacks of food dropped from the air next to each member of the party, including Mina.

DaSilva looked in her direction thoughtfully. *I need to talk to her about what happened.* Mina and Yulia were the only members of the team he could trust completely. Mina had been completely absent during the attempt on his life, while Yulia had saved him.

As he had these thoughts, other members of the group were gathering around the sisters, talking about how valuable Yulia had been In the Dungeon.

"Your girl is intense, in a good way!" Frank said. "She kept us moving forward through the Dungeon."

"She's a very strong person," Adelaide agreed, looking at Yulia and smiling as she spoke. "She has the kind of courage that makes a survivor."

She'll have to, thought DaSilva. He looked on glumly as Mina and Yulia glowed with shared pride. *She'll have to. I think this place is only getting worse and more dangerous with time.*

CHAPTER THIRTY

Seek and Destroy

What were you doing?" Hester asked once he had returned to his body.

Impressive that she noticed so quickly that I was back. He hadn't opened his eyes or even moved since returning.

"I was rigging things in our favor," James said, choosing to be mysterious. "How could you tell so quickly that I was back inside my body?"

"Oh, that's easy," she replied modestly. "Anyone could tell, especially if they were living on your body like I am. When you're using that power and you return, it's just like the difference between when you're asleep and when you're awake. There's a change in your breathing, and you're a lot more tense when you're awake."

"Hm. Thanks for the tip, there, Hester." He could actually foresee a possible circumstance where this would be relevant information. If he were to be taken prisoner and subsequently choose to use his powers while in captivity, for instance.

He rose.

"What are we doing now?" she asked.

"Now we're going to find the cultists," he replied. "I think the group is fine for now, so the best thing I can do for them is get rid of the cultists who are forcing them into the marsh."

"You're going to go and fight them all alone?" She sounded nervous.

"I am," he acknowledged, "but I'm going to find ways of getting them alone and dealing with them one by one. Or turning them on themselves. I don't want to give them another fair fight."

I already got a level in Politician from what I did to them in the dream world. What if I infiltrate them in person?

He took the Shapechanger's Cloak from his bag and put it on. It covered him from head to toe.

Invisibility.

And he began stalking toward the Rostov camp. He knew more or less where the cultists were, thanks to the Dreamwalk. He was slightly less clear on where the Rodriguezes were, but he had an idea of their location. He was now fairly certain that if he could find the flickering flames of a person's dreams, he'd be able to find them in the real world too.

It only took around fifteen minutes of brisk walking through the dense trees for James to find the camp. Fortunately, they had a roaring bonfire going at all hours, even though they'd moved camps. Perhaps it was a religious thing, but it made them very easy to spot.

He didn't need the cloak's invisibility to conceal his approach. There was a commotion ongoing. Seven people were fighting one man. As they wrestled him into the firelight, James recognized Moishe Rose from his previous encounter with the cult.

What's he doing out here? If he escaped, he should either be with the other prisoners or with the Rodriguezes, right?

For now, James just stood there and watched. Then one of the seven—a man named Kassim, James recalled—ordered another man to return to guard duty. James Identified the man.

"Come on, I want to beat the crap out of this bastard too!" Tracy Rove objected.

"None of that," Kassim replied sharply. "We already know we can get surprise attacked at night." He gestured at Moishe. "This is the proof! Once we've secured Moishe, we'll rejoin you on patrol, but for now, someone has to make sure there's no one else out there."

"Uh-huh," Rove said, giving an exaggerated eye roll. But he walked away in the direction of the tree line.

Sorry, Moishe. I'll come back to get you out of this soon, James thought. Would that technically be the third rescue or the second? Since they were recaptured after the first time he had broken them out of prison, James was inclined to think this would be the third time he'd helped Moishe escape the cult. Not that it mattered.

I like the spirit this guy shows.

For now, though, James silently followed Rove. He wanted to wait until Rove got far enough out of range that no one would be able to hear him scream.

And the guard obliged. He moved through the trees, and he kept walking, seemingly aimlessly, further from the camp. If James didn't know better, he'd have suspected some sort of trap. But he was certain enough, from his previous experience fighting the Alpha Desert Coyote, that the Invisibility Skill the Shapechanger's Cloak carried wouldn't be easily observed. Tracy Rove didn't seem like the sort of special person who would coincidentally have an ability that would let him see through James's cloak.

Sure enough, James eventually followed Rove far enough from the camp that he felt confident no one would hear them.

He waited until Rove paused for a moment. And Rove inadvertently accommodated him a second time.

He looked around, as if expecting one of the others to show up and chastise him at any moment. Then he took a pack of cigarettes from his pocket, followed by a lighter.

Still invisible, James leaped out from behind a bush at the moment Rove's lighter ignited. Rove froze, then looked up at the sound of movement. James grabbed him by the neck. Before Rove could cry out, James smashed him into a tree.

Smoking kills, he thought, smirking.

Rove's head left a visible dent in the bark, but he was unconscious in a single blow.

"Wow! That's amazing," Hester whispered.

James twisted Rove's neck until it snapped and then used Pillage.

"Thanks, Hester," he said quietly, not quite short of breath.

"I didn't know how strong you were compared to other humans. So, what are you going to do now?"

James opened his bag to store the bundles of Rove's flesh, but he grabbed Rove's armor and armaments before they could get sucked in.

"Now I'm going to be Tracy Rove," James said.

He put Rove's gear on over the Shapechanger's Cloak, and he used its other ability. *Shapechange.*

James took his smartphone out from his magic satchel just to use its screen as a black mirror. *Yep, confirmed. I'm minus three points on the ten-point attractiveness scale. I now look just like Tracy Rove.*

James used False Reality to change his name and Status to match what he imagined Tracy Rove's would show. The deceased had been a Medium Warrior at level nine, and James used imagination for the areas of the Status that he had no way of guessing.

And he began his patrol. He walked around in a circle around the camp, as he imagined Rove would have done, until Kassim came to rejoin him. There were another two people with Kassim. Identify established that their names were Carl Ronson and Catherine Ross.

Officer Ross's wife, James thought. *I remember you from his dream.*

"Glad to see you did your job, Tracy," Kassim said coldly. "We're being relieved for the evening—or, more precisely, being sent to do something else."

False Reality!

"What's that?" James asked, disguising his voice to match Tracy's.

"You know perfectly well what our other task is," Kassim said. "We're going to go relieve the warriors and priest holding down the border with the Dead Marsh. The people in there are either going to die or come running our direction sometime. We're not going to miss it." He spoke the words with no trace of enthusiasm.

"Feels like I've been up all night," James said. Tracy Rove had seemed like a whiner to him, so it seemed in-character to complain.

In fact, James was very excited to be shown where more of Rostov's security personnel were stationed.

"You'll stay awake and fulfill your duty, or the Prophet will hear about it!" Kassim replied sharply.

James simply nodded and fell in step with the others.

They walked for half an hour, before James noticed the forest soil begin softening. It was clearly about to give way to the Dead Marsh, and the group stopped. For the first time, James felt slightly nervous about his disguise. Had they noticed him somehow? Were they about to give him to the denizens of the marsh?

Kassim raised a hand and waved.

"Hey there!" he called loudly.

James turned his head and saw another man. He was dressed in the pure white garb of the priests. He had heavy bags under his eyes. As he stepped closer, James saw he had a sun-shaped pendant on a necklace.

"Oh, thank goodness!" pronounced the priest. "I thought we were never going to get any sleep tonight."

"And here we are to make your wish come true," Kassim said, smiling.

James performed some quick mental calculations. Mind of the Predator indicated a 90 percent chance of him successfully killing all four of the people around him if he started a fight right now.

But he wasn't sure if he wanted to kill Officer Ross's wife. He still had hopes for Ross and killing her seemed like a poor way of realizing them.

And this doesn't account for the possibility that reinforcements show up or one of them manages to run and get a message off to the main camp somehow. They can't know I'm here.

James decided to wait. He had an idea of how he might increase his chances of success.

Sure enough, after chatting for a few minutes, the priest walked off.

"All right," Kassim said once the man was out of sight. "The guard you're relieving will be down that way—"

As he pointed, James sprang into action. He hit Catherine Ross with a single open-handed slap, and she went down like a sack of bricks.

Carl Ronson's eyes widened. "What are you do—"

James grabbed him by the neck before he could move, and in a second fluid motion, he tore the front of the man's throat out.

"*Urk!*" Carl's neck erupted with blood, and he fell to his knees.

"You! You can't be Tracy. You must be—"

Meteor Strike!

James cut off Kassim's last words with a flaming punch to the throat. The man clutched his neck, then collapsed to the ground, dead.

Then James raced after the priest who'd left.

"What's happening?" the man asked, wide-eyed, when he saw James covered with blood.

"The enemy!" James said. "They're attacking! We need healing!" He clutched his stomach and bent his posture as if he'd suffered some painful, debilitating wound.

"Where are you hurt?" asked the priest, leaning toward James, his hands glowing golden.

"Right here!"

James struck out and knocked the priest unconscious with a single slap. Then he stomped his head into the ground. He didn't stop, even when he felt the other man's blood soaking into his socks. Not until he heard the ding.

Another fatality.

And then James returned to the border area to relieve the other guards.

Once the other three were dead, James carried Catherine Ross up into the branches of a tree and secured her there. He created a Silk Golem to hold her in place until he decided what to do with her. James took greater care with this monster, giving it more Mana than he usually poured into his creations. He also shaped it with a mouth, tongue, and vocal cords. *In case I need to talk to her. Hopefully, this is close enough to biologically correct, and maybe the System will adjust for whatever mistakes I made.*

The slaughter yielded only a single new level for Predator in Human Skin. But then, it had been all too easy. All he had to do was be patient and careful, though there had been some tension in his mind about whether he could do all of this without them alerting anyone back at the camp.

Now it was done, though. Finally, he could relax a bit and figure out what to do next.

He sat down cross-legged on the border with the Dead Marsh, and he closed his eyes.

"Are, uh, are you okay after all that?" Hester quickly interrupted his train of thought.

"After killing those guys, you mean?"

James felt rather than saw that Hester was bobbing her head in a spider approximation of a nod on the back of his ear.

"I'm just peachy," James said. "They deserved it, and they got just what was coming to 'em." He pointed up the nearby tree with his thumb. "She deserves it too, but I'm still not decided on what the best thing to do with her is. On the one hand, she definitely participated in Rostov's evil cult. She's one of his bloody priests." James spat contemptuously on the ground. "But on the other hand, she motivates Jeff Ross. And I can't help but think the officer could still be useful to me."

"Useful how?" Hester asked skeptically. "You mean you think he'll turn on the cult for her? Or do you mean useful outside of Orientation?"

"Why not both?" James asked. He resisted the urge to shrug, a gesture Hester couldn't properly see from her vantage point.

"I kind of got the impression you were going to wipe the whole cult out," she said thoughtfully. "Not that it's necessarily the best or only approach. But how would you know you could trust a guy like that?"

"I don't know if I can trust the people I've surrounded myself with already," James replied. He pictured Cliff, Sierra, and Chava as he spoke. "In Officer Ross's case, I had the distinct impression that he really didn't want to be with them. When I infiltrated his dream, I would say I confirmed that. He was willing to be ruthless to keep himself and his wife alive. To make sure they got back to their kids." He grinned mirthlessly. "I won't say I condone it, but I'd be lying if I said I didn't understand it. I know this is hard to believe, Hester, but I'm not such a nice guy myself."

The spider went silent at that. Then said, "Right. I see."

I hope she's not feeling too much regret, he thought. *Devote your life to following around a possible, maybe probable, bad guy, and you have to wonder what it's all for.*

"Is there anything I can do to help?" Hester broke into his thought process.

"With my plan to persuade Ross?" James asked, not bothering to disguise his surprise.

"Exactly!" Hester said brightly.

"Hm." A thought had occurred to him. The sun wasn't out quite yet. Maybe he could Dreamwalk once more. "For now, please watch my body. Wake me immediately if someone shows up or if Catherine starts trying to get loose from that golem."

"Roger that, sir!"

James smiled. Hester was starting to feel like a friend. And if she could apply herself to her goal of becoming part of his legend with the same energy that he intended to apply to creating that legend, they would get along famously for the rest of her life.

Dreamwalk.

CHAPTER THIRTY-ONE

The Sandman

Officer Ross checked on Leonard Robie once he was done dealing with Kassim and the others. Robie was dead, with a fresh snake bite visible on his neck.

But no snake was found nearby. Ross had decided that in the morning he would argue that they should kill Moishe right away. The snake would probably continue carrying out his wishes until the Assassin was killed. Better not to have a non-human enemy that would be so difficult to spot on the loose somewhere near the camp.

But it wasn't worth disturbing Rostov's sleep to rush this. He'd only take it out on everyone else for the rest of the day. The so-called Prophet seemed slightly less the charismatic leader he had once been with each passing day.

For now, the only thing to do was dispose of Robie's corpse, which wasn't Ross's job. After he saw to it that someone would take care of that, he debated whether to remain awake and wait for sunrise, or to go to Catherine where she was. While he was dealing with the guards, her alarm had gone off.

Then she was off with a couple of those same guards to relieve the people on border patrol. Leaving him alone. Ross decided to go back to bed and try to have a better dream this time.

He returned to his tent, and he slipped into a fitful sleep once more.

This time, as soon as he'd slipped into deep slumber, he saw a surprising face.

"What are you doing here?" he asked. He tried to make his tone demanding, but it didn't quite work. There was something hollow beneath it. Perhaps exhaustion.

"I'm here to make a deal with you," James said. "I can move through dreams now, as you can see. Among other abilities."

"Why me?" Ross asked, beginning to sweat. It was a little unnerving to have a perfectly coherent conversation with someone inside of a dream. Especially because the setting around them, he realized, was so simple. A background of pure black, stretching into infinity, with a spotlight somewhere shining down on the two of them.

"You know why, Officer." James disappeared and reappeared right beside him, then put a hand on Ross's shoulder. "I want to save you."

"Save me?" Ross choked off his laugh at James's expression, which was grim.

"I'm not joking, Officer. This cult you're with is going to be destroyed. The question is whether you're going to go down with the ship or not. That's up to you."

"Didn't we let you go before? Didn't you run away from us with your tail between your legs?" Ross asked. "You might be the Sandman now, but unless you have Freddy Krueger powers, it's not as if you could do anything about Rostov."

"Rostov is a problem anyone could solve while he's sleeping," James said. "The question is, are you the man to do it? Like you said, I'm the Sandman." He fixed Ross with a creepy stare.

"I'm not going to say I haven't thought about it," Ross acknowledged.

"But thinking isn't doing. You're sitting by while people get sacrificed. What good is Rostov even doing you and your wife now?"

"Keep my wife's name out of your mouth, James," Ross said, becoming slightly heated. "It's easy for you to sit on your high horse, but you don't know anything about us. About our motivations. We made the decisions we had to make."

James continued staring at Ross, silently, with a look of disdain.

"Who are you to judge me?" Ross practically yelled.

"Well, I'm a bad guy too," James admitted, smiling bittersweetly. Ross could feel this conversation was slightly draining for both of them, the way it was unfolding. "But we don't have to be our worst selves. The first thing is courage. The reason why I haven't killed Rostov myself is because I want to see if you're capable of it. I know you don't like him, don't believe in what he's doing. You wouldn't be the man I used to know if you didn't have doubts."

"I already said I did," Ross said. "So what? We have a plan. We know what we're doing, and when we'll get rid of Rostov." He said these last sentences listlessly, as if reciting a script.

"That's great. I'm glad you had a plan, and I'm glad you were already going to get rid of Rostov. You just have to move your plans up."

Ross looked as if he was going to object, but James raised a hand to cut him off.

"At the risk of sounding cliche, I have your wife. She's in a safe and secure place, and she's not hurt. Just unconscious. I'll let her go if Rostov dies. If not, well, I can at least cut down on his priesthood a little bit."

James watched Ross open and close his mouth several times. Finally, the policeman found his voice. "You could get us both killed, you know that? If I fail—"

"Don't fail, then," James interrupted sternly. "This is not a negotiation, Officer. This is your shot at redemption! You've been complicit in multiple deaths of innocent people now. If you don't cooperate with me, I'll kill your wife, I'll kill you, and I'll kill Rostov. In that order. And you'll all deserve it. Now go and do your work, before the sun comes up!"

Ross felt an intense pressure inside his head.

"Ahh! Oww!"

He blinked. He was suddenly wide awake. *What the fuck was that?*

James smiled. *Dreamwalk is getting easier and easier to use. Officer Ross said I don't have Freddy Krueger powers, but I figured out how to wake him up with a headache. The ability to hurt someone, or even kill them in their sleep, might not be out of reach.*

He moved on to another dream.

"Mm-hmm," Rostov said. There were two well-endowed women in his lap, wearing nothing but looks of admiration.

James saw him fondling one of their breasts and thought, *I suspect there's nothing I could really do to get him more deeply embroiled in this dream than he already is. Except conjure up more women. But no.*

He stopped to think for a moment, but there really wasn't anything else he could do. And adding more women might disrupt the flow of Rostov's dream.

Is this really what your inner life is like? he questioned. *Don't you have fond childhood memories? Goals for the future? Is it really all just lust? Embarrassing that I've had to spend this much time dealing with someone like you.*

He focused on adjusting the settings on Rostov's dream to make it as deep and soothing as possible so Rostov would hopefully sleep a bit longer than normal. Then he left.

As he returned to his body, he sent a mental command to one of his Skin Balloons, which he'd had floating around the edges of the forest.

James recalled that an aerial assault on the Rostov camp had apparently not set off any alarm bells last time. And his airborne monster could probably make the trip to the camp faster than he could.

Ross rose and prepared himself for the tasks of his day.

It was still dark outside, and he wanted to complete his most important missions before the sun rose. It was imperative, in fact. He stepped out of the tent. The personnel on guard duty weren't within sight.

He walked from tent to tent, waking a select few people. Hilda Rohm first. He shook her and put a hand over her mouth for a moment.

"I'm doing it tonight," he whispered. "Taking out Rostov. Need your help."

Over the last few days, as Rostov had shown such weakness against the masked intruder and become obsessed with the runaway prisoners, the camp had become increasingly discontented. Ross had taken advantage of the weakness of Rostov's leadership. Before he'd spoken to Catherine about killing Rostov, he'd discreetly approached others.

The five of them gathered beside the bonfire.

Ross had explained each of their roles when he woke them.

"We can make a change for the better," he said to the gathered group. "I'm going in now. Thank you all for supporting me."

The handful of people all smiled at each other.

"If we don't see each other again, it was an honor betraying this scumbag with all of you," said Chris Roach.

"At long last," said Hilda Rohm.

"It feels overdue now," agreed Ross.

Carlo Roma and Sara Rollins simply nodded. The group exchanged weary smiles. Then they went to perform their separate work.

"What are you going to do now?" Hester asked after James debriefed her on what he'd done this time.

"I want to go find the Rodriguez camp," James said. He got up and began walking away from the border with the Dead Marsh. "But if I go and find them, the cultists are probably going to kill Moishe Rose. That's even assuming that Officer Ross manages to kill their prophet. Rostov's got to have some loyalists in the cult who will keep sacrificing people even if he dies. It'll be my job to mop up and make sure that no harm comes to their prisoners, especially the one who's been doing the good work of fighting the cultists."

"Couldn't you have asked Officer Ross to set him free?" Hester asked.

"No," James replied. "I couldn't give him the idea that the cult had anyone I cared about at all. He might get the idea to treat Moishe and the others as hostages and try to exchange them for his wife. Then I'd have to convince him that I don't care as much about saving innocent people as he does about his wife. That's probably true, but there's no point in weakening my negotiating position by letting him know he has anything I want at all. Not when I can go and jailbreak the prisoners again during the hubbub while he's killing Rostov."

"I see." Hester sounded slightly confused.

James waited a moment to see if she'd voice her confusion.

"I can't help but wonder, would he really have thought that way?" Hester asked. "Are humans that callous?"

"You never know," James said. "Think about it this way. This is a man who was able to justify sacrificing other people to Moloch. We can't assume he operates according to the same strict moral standards that I apply."

"Was that last bit sarcasm?" she asked cautiously.

"Maybe a little."

Ross entered Rostov's tent, gun drawn.

Everything was squared away but this.

Rostov lay on his cot, arm half draped over his bedmate, Alice, as they both slept. Even in her sleep, Alice looked a bit uncomfortable next to Rostov. In addition to crushing her under his arm, he was also somehow hogging their blankets.

Ross thought he'd cover her up better when he'd done his bloody work. Realistically, though, she would probably wake from the sound of the gunshot, covered in blood. A detail that didn't matter.

Ross focused on the moment. Took deep breaths.

His hand shook slightly as he advanced toward the sleeping man.

Just killing a guy in his sleep, he thought. *What could be easier?*

But it was hard. Being in Rostov's tent, sneaking up on him, was closer to a nightmare than a dream. James had almost made it sound easy, but he had no way of knowing Ross's psychology in a moment like this.

Ross had killed a man since arriving in Orientation and had shot to kill in another instance, but those had been in the heat of combat. Killing a man in his sleep was something else. Even this man.

Still. It was time to steady his nerves and do what he should have done weeks ago.

He raised the pistol. Pointed it at Rostov's chest—that place just to the left of center where he knew the heart would be. Ross flicked off the safety with a practiced touch. He'd done it a thousand times on the range.

Swallowed. Took another step closer. *Can't risk hitting Alice if my hand shakes at the critical moment.* He pictured himself putting the gun right up next to Rostov's head and blowing his brains out. *Yeah, that would do it.* He adjusted his aim.

Raised his foot for a final step. Put it down on something uneven.

Alice moved, awakened by Ross's foot on her leg. She bolted upright, eyes fixed on the gun in Ross's hand.

He raised a finger to his lips—too slowly! She screamed.

Rostov's eyes burst open.

And Ross pulled the trigger.

CHAPTER THIRTY-TWO

A Beautiful Disaster

James closed his eyes.

His Skin Balloon had transmitted an audiovisual message to him. If he closed his eyes, he could see it like a movie in his mind.

There was a figure striding through the Rostov campground. It took James a moment to identify Officer Ross from the distant aerial perspective, but then he recognized the officer's profile and gait. Officer Ross ducked into the largest tent in the camp site. A few long, tense seconds passed. Then there was a gunshot.

"Well, all right, Officer Ross!" James said quietly. He hopped up a tree. The sun was only just beginning to rise now. Hopefully, that meant that Moloch was too late to see and interfere in any way.

"Good news?" Hester asked.

"Rostov should be dead," James replied.

"Hm. Wait, I'm getting something from Anansi." James felt the body of the spider on the back of his ear grow strangely *hot* for several seconds. Then it slowly returned to normal.

"What was that?" James asked, alarmed.

Silence from his tiny passenger.

"Jeez," he said quietly. He thought he knew what had just happened from previous discussion. *Anansi, are you burning through her already? I haven't been away from your realm that long. Was there a message so important that you needed to send it this way? Something about Rostov? Poor Hester . . .*

James decided to think about something other than the spider's tragically shortened lifespan. He silently communicated with his Silk Golem. First, he asked if Catherine Ross had awakened yet.

Yes, Master, the Silk Golem sent back.

Excellent, James thought. He ordered the Silk Golem to tell Catherine that her husband had killed Rostov and that Jeff might need her help keeping order back at the camp site. *Hopefully, I can keep them under control myself after all this.*

They wouldn't all be redeemable in his eyes, but the Skin Balloon had continued to transmit additional video into James's mind. Some of the activity showed that there were others who were helping Ross.

One pair were trying to keep order and prevent people from entering Rostov's tent. Another had set about freeing prisoners. All except Moishe, James couldn't help but notice. Perhaps that seemed like something other cultists would object to.

Fine. He would free Moishe himself once he arrived, and any cultist who held a grudge could take it up with James directly.

James began running through the forest toward the camp.

"Mm. Ugh." Hester quietly groaned from behind James's ear. He instantly slowed down to a walking pace.

"Glad you're still with me," he said. "Everything okay back there? Felt like you were on fire for a second."

"Oh, I'm all right," she reassured him. "Thank you for your concern, boss. I just received a divine revelation. All part of the job." She sounded exhausted and weak but determined, to James's careful ears, so he decided not to interrupt her. "The important thing is that I tell you what Lord Anansi had to say. Earlier, I transmitted your plan for dealing with Moloch's Chosen One. Lord Anansi just got back to me. He wanted you to know that Moloch probably won't give up on this guy easily. He has a lot riding on the cult's success, and if he can rig things in Rostov's favor so he doesn't die, he'll probably try to do it. He's pulled strings already. He'll pull them again. He's invested too much of his own power in Rostov to give up now."

It sounded from her tone as if she was holding something back.

"Did he say anything else?" James asked pointedly.

"Lord Anansi thinks you probably should have done this yourself," she admitted meekly.

"Hm. Well, he could've said something about that sooner," James grumbled.

"My sincerest apologies," she said. "Messages I convey have to travel through the void. There are unpredictable delays, and the way time works in the void confuses me. Sometimes he may receive my communications chronologically before I send them. Other times, Lord Anansi will not receive them in time to be of help to us. Perhaps if I had sent this information earlier—"

"There's no need to blame yourself," James interrupted softly. "We're both doing the best we can. You're a great asset to me so far, Hester. I know you'll be an important part of my legend."

He stopped walking and tilted his head sideways. He thought he heard something.

"Thank you so much!" Hester gushed. "I'll do my very best to—"

"Do you hear that?" he interrupted.

"Uh, no?" She sounded deflated, but James couldn't afford to worry about that now.

A few seconds later it was more obvious. The sounds of movement. Multiple pairs of feet. Enemies?

James opened his magic satchel and took out the Royal Exoarmor, the Solar Helm, several Wolfbone Daggers, and the Ego Antler Spear. In under a minute, James was fully kitted out in the best gear he could be for a fight. He put away the Shapechanger's Cloak. The time for hiding was over.

He stood firmly, deliberately visible, holding the spear in his right hand and preparing gravity magic with Silent Spellcasting.

And then they came through the trees: fifteen prisoners fleeing the Rostov camp. It was obvious they weren't cultists at a single glance. The cultists were all fairly clean, wearing decent clothes and sometimes armor. The cultists liked to dress in white, often in nearly pristine white robes. Many of the cultists wore sun pendants. These people were not like that.

James struggled to keep himself from covering his nose and mouth with his free hand. There was a rank smell, reeking of unwashed human body odor with notes of human waste mingled in.

"Stop!" James called out in a commanding voice.

They stopped. It might have been one of his communication Skills. It might have been that he was dressed in armor, obviously high level, and clearly ready for a fight if anyone defied him. It might have been the fact that he was surrounded with dark-colored gravity Mana, and the halo of energy around his body was still growing.

"Please!" begged a figure near the front of the pack. James noticed it was a teenage boy he hadn't seen when he tried his previous prison break. "Please let us pass. We're escaping—"

"I know what you're escaping," James interrupted. He removed his helm so that they could see his face, and then he remembered none of them had seen his face before. "You can ask some of the others here, but I'm the man who came by to try and free them a few days ago."

"Oh my God!" called someone at the back. "I recognize his voice. This is the masked man!"

There were murmurs of gratitude and relief from others in the group, and James was momentarily distracted by the feeling of their appreciation.

"Th-then why are you stopping us?" the boy asked.

"I'm not stopping you," James replied. "You can keep going. In fact, you need to get further away, quickly. I just stopped you to say that you should stop when the ground gets soft. There's a deadly swamp the way you're running, and if you enter without me, you might be eaten by monsters."

"Thank you!" Someone uttered the words in a choked off sob, and then a man stumbled toward James and pulled him into an embrace.

Others were murmuring things like, "You did this somehow, didn't you?" and, "You planned this," and, "I told you he didn't die!"

James didn't quite know what to make of these reactions. He didn't know if Officer Ross had told his co-conspirators about James's role in recent events. Even if the officer had, would those individuals have passed that information on to these prisoners when they were freeing them? It made little sense.

"If you're wondering why this is happening, it's one of your Titles," Hester said quietly.

How the hell do you know that? he wondered.

"That's Lord Anansi's theory, anyway," she continued. "He says that when you're a Living Legend, the public tends to read more into your actions than makes rational sense. It's as if you have a Stat for reputation, and it's always at the highest level possible with people whose lives you've touched. Whether you're famous or infamous, your stature is magnified. It just so happens that in this case, they're correct since you are completely responsible for freeing them. And for ending the cult's reign of terror, if the leader is really dead." Her tone took on a mixture of reverence and curiosity. "Think of all the people you've saved, both now and in the future. How does it feel? How does it feel to save the lives of so many people?"

[Required conditions met. Title obtained: Savior!]

I don't have time for this right now, James thought. *And I don't know quite how I feel. I'm glad they're alive and not dead. I'm glad they're free and not about to be sacrificed.*

"All of you, please, go to the border of the swamp and wait there!" James said, his voice loud and firm, cutting through the crowd's murmurs. He gently brushed those who were crowding him aside. "I've already killed the people Rostov sent there. I need to get to the cult and finish this."

He wove through the crowd without looking around him and then, once he was clear, began running again.

Strange feelings swelled in his chest. *What does it mean to be a Savior?*

"To answer your question, Hester, I really couldn't say," he said. "I don't understand how I feel yet myself."

This new world has already brought me some of the highest highs and the lowest lows of my life, he thought. *But this might be the first time it's tried to tell me that I'm better than I am. Better than I'm probably capable of being. Let's at least make sure those people who are worshiping me don't get recaptured this time.*

He raced forward, mind running through his next steps, deliberately pushing thoughts of his changing role away.

Ross's hand became suddenly steady and remained so, both during and after the moment of truth.

His bullet hit the target.

Rostov's eyes opened, then rolled back in his head like he was having a seizure. And then his body, too, began moving as if he was having a seizure, convulsing wildly.

I guess a bullet in the crown will do that to you. No one will say you didn't have it coming.

Ross turned his attention to Alice, who was still shrieking, albeit at a much lower volume than when she'd woken Rostov. He reached out and tried to pull her away. She was still closer to Rostov than Ross wanted her to be since he intended to put another round or two in the man's body.

Just to make sure.

Ross managed to yank her to her feet and push her out the flap of the tent. He threw a piece of cloth that looked like a dress after her, as he'd noticed she was almost naked.

Then he pointed his gun at Rostov's chest again. The headshot clearly hadn't been an instant kill here. He fired into the place where the heart should be. And waited for a few seconds.

Where's the notification?

Cold sweat formed on Ross's neck, and he pulled the trigger again—and shot nothing.

Somehow Rostov's body was gone. Not glowing and then slowly disappearing like he'd Looted it. Just suddenly gone. As if it was never there. And still no notification for the kill.

"Shit."

Numb with disbelief, he stumbled out of the tent. A scene of panic greeted him alongside the flickers of early morning light.

The dozens of remaining cult members were alternating between shouting questions and demands at Hilda, Chris, Carlo, and Sara. The four of them stood in a semicircle around the tent entrance, guarding the opening. They each had their weapons in hand. They were so focused on fending off would-be entrants that they didn't even turn their heads when Ross emerged.

At the sight of him, the questions intensified.

"Where's the Prophet?"

"What's going on?"

"What was that loud noise?"

"Out of the way! Let us through!"

People were becoming unruly, and Ross fired one of his precious remaining bullets into the sky in an effort to restore some order without killing anyone.

"Everyone, remain calm!" he yelled. "I do not want to have to use this on any of you."

"What have you done with the Prophet, you son of a bitch?" Rick rushed at Ross and grabbed him by the collar, lunging at him too quickly for Ross to point and aim his gun.

Rick was more than a little intimidating, with his towering height, reddish skin, and small horns all shoved right in Ross's face. But Ross had just faced his biggest threat, and he hadn't faltered. He wasn't about to be intimidated by this moron.

"Nothing he didn't damn well deserve, Rick, and you know it!" Ross spat. "Let go of me before I have to shoot you too!"

Then there was a slight humming sound, and Rick's face went slack.

Ross saw a hand that appeared to be wrapped in electricity pass through the front of Rick's chest. Stunned, he could only stare at the man who had impaled Rick with his bare hand.

"What the fuck?" Ross said after a long moment.

James was grinning like a madman, and Ross had to suppress the urge to retreat from him.

"What the fuck do you think you're doing?" Ross finally managed. "I had this situation under control!"

"Now *I* have it under control," James replied. As he spoke, the crowd was edging away from the smiling man with the corpse draped over his arm. "You need to understand something. I offered you the opportunity to save yourself. And I'll even extend it to your little group of helpers here." He gestured at Ross's allies. "But everyone won't be treated all the same." He shook his head. "Most of these people are accomplices to multiple murders and murder attempts on innocent people, with no mitigating factors, as far as I'm concerned. You, of all people, should know what that means."

"Death," Ross acknowledged in a low voice. "You would want death." *I really should have guessed. He was a prosecutor. A rigid sense of justice comes with the job. And it's not as if I care about them . . .* "All right." He raised his hands as if in surrender. "You're in charge. Now, what about my wife?"

"She's on her way here," James said. "I signaled for her release, and I also communicated that we might possibly need some help here."

Ross opened his mouth to reply but was cut off by the force of a tremendous explosion from behind them. All those who had gathered around Rostov's tent went flying through the air.

CHAPTER THIRTY-THREE

Psychodrama

After another half hour of waiting outside, the System teleported Mina and her teammates back to their pre-challenge locations. Mina and Yulia were back in the inn.

"Let's go back up to our room," Mina suggested almost instantly. She smiled nervously as she spoke.

"Okay," Yulia said. She wondered what Mina was worried about, exactly, but she didn't ask. If Mina thought she needed to know, she would explain. Hopefully, she was just being her usual careful self.

Mina stayed silent all the way up to the room. Yulia didn't know what to say to her. Mina was often preoccupied. When she went silent, Yulia felt bad about interrupting. Mina was probably thinking about something important.

But after several minutes of restraining herself, Yulia came up with something she thought Mina would want to consider.

"Sis, are we going to share our food with the people on the other teams like we did last time?" Yulia asked.

Mina looked surprisingly worried at that suggestion.

"I think we need to be more careful than we have been from now on," Mina replied carefully.

"*More* careful?" Yulia asked, barely restraining her impatience. She thought she might go crazy if she had to spend the next two days stuck in this room as she had after the last challenge.

Yulia resolved not to mention the shadowy hand that had popped out of nowhere and grabbed DaSilva's ankle back in the Dungeon. It hadn't seemed like part of the Dungeon to her, and she had guessed someone else must have been attacking him. But she didn't want to make Mina warier than she already was.

"Listen," Mina said quietly. "I'm not sure if we'll be all right sharing our food anymore. I'm not sure if we'll be safe if we don't, but I don't know if I want to risk it. We might lose the next challenge, and if we lose two in a row, we will run out of food before the one after that. We have to avoid that at all costs."

"I don't understand. We were sharing before. We could've lost *this* challenge. Then we'd be hoping for someone to share with us—"

"That was my plan *before*, sweet. Before this challenge. After the marksmanship competition, I hoped that the challenges this System would give us would all be athletic or intellectual competitions." Mina was talking with her hands as well as her mouth now as she sometimes did when she wanted to make a point more forcefully. "By sharing food, we were setting a positive example. If the challenges were all basically games, people wouldn't take them as life-and-death struggles. They might follow our example, and then this place wouldn't be as dangerous, because no one would be hungry and the games wouldn't kill them.

"Now we know things are different. A huge portion of the population died in that Dungeon. Do you think people will share the food they earned when people they know had to die to get it?" She took a deep breath, then continued on. "There's also the challenge of distributing the food. Before, we competed against a team. It was easy to share with the losers. Now, who would we choose from among the surviving people?"

"I don't know," Yulia admitted. "Maybe, uh, the people still living in the other living quarters?"

"If we go there to hand out food, though, there's nothing to stop people from mugging us to try and steal everything we have left. Of course, we could leave everything we don't want to give away here, but if they're desperate enough, people will attack first and ask questions later. We could end up dead just because they figured out that we had something to share. There will be some people who didn't win the first challenge or the second. Naturally, not everyone shared after the first challenge. Probably not even half the winners. The people who lost both times are going to be so desperate I can almost feel it already. And I—I can't protect you!"

She threw up her hands as if she was grappling with a problem that had no solution.

"I get it," Yulia said quietly. "We'd better be more careful, then."

I wish James was here, she thought. *Things would feel much safer, and Mina wouldn't have to worry so much.*

Detective DaSilva scribbled furiously in his notepad, trying to remember everything that had occurred that might make any of his teammates seem suspicious.

The only people he really trusted now were the Danailovas, but he'd decided to get his thoughts in order before he discussed things with them. Mina hadn't been present when someone had tried to kill him, and Yulia was the one who had saved his life.

For that matter, Jose also jumped in to protect me when I triggered the other trap. If we assume the killer's goal here was just to see me dead rather than specifically to drag me into the lava at the end, it wouldn't make sense for the killer to be Jose either. Probably can't share information with him, though, because I haven't cleared his brother from possible suspicion.

Going in alphabetical order by first name, there was Adelaide Davis, who was serving the investigation as its medical examiner. She was also one of the group's two Healers, along with Yulia. It would be strange if a Healer happened to be able to conjure a shadowy hand out of the air, but as far as DaSilva knew, no one on his team had a power like that. Someone had to be hiding their abilities. Why not Adelaide? Difficult to say what her motives would be, but that was true for everyone.

His mind balked at considering her. The person working as the medical examiner would be able to interfere with the investigation in any number of ways, that was true. But was that really a reason to suspect her? Someone who had been so consistently helpful? Could she really be working so closely with DaSilva and give off no signs of guilt? She had no alibi for the first killing, as she'd freely admitted. Her roommate from the first night had gone to bed early. Adelaide could have snuck out in the middle of the night. But even considering her as a suspect left a bad taste in DaSilva's mouth.

Set her aside for the moment, then.

There was Cara Dahlhaus. The only suspicious thing about her was that she'd discovered the coat left over from the first body. Often, the first person to find the body in a murder case turned out to be the killer. But here, the usual reasons to believe that didn't really seem to apply. Jean Davenport was with her when she found the coat. And there was no inevitability that DaSilva, or anyone else, would find that piece of evidence. Therefore, there was no obvious reason for the killer to draw people's attention to it.

If Cara was the killer, she could have just flown under the radar. Involving herself as much as she did had just resulted in DaSilva keeping a much closer eye on her and Jean than he otherwise would have. In fact, DaSilva thought that people would have probably assumed a wild animal killed the first victims if no remains had been found. DaSilva would've encouraged that narrative himself. Having people thinking about a killer running loose was a recipe for fear and distrust.

Overall, he couldn't get past one fact: going out and "discovering" the coat the first victim had worn seemed dumb. The killer had been good enough at avoiding direct attention until the moment came to try and murder DaSilva himself. *Probably not Cara.*

He moved on to Derek, Adelaide's brother. Like Adelaide, he had no real alibi for the time of the first murder. His roommate went to bed early, just like Adelaide's. A suspicious coincidence that each of them had the ability to get out of their rooms unnoticed that night? Maybe. Probably not.

Derek was tall, fit, and strong. Eminently capable in terms of the physical exertion required. DaSilva had every reason to think of him as a suspect, except that he was a Light Warrior like Cara. So, how could he have conjured that shadowy hand on the bridge? He would have needed an accomplice who was a Mage with some special magic, probably. But Adelaide was a Healer. So, for Derek to be the killer, he needed to have another team member helping him.

Frank Davidson was older and, frankly, seemed a bit too physically weak for the demanding task of brutally murdering people. The killer had managed to kill several people quite messily. Could Frank have done that without suffering any visible injuries? He was a Mage, so maybe he could've used some form of magic to make the hand that grabbed DaSilva on the bridge. But he couldn't do nearly as much physically as DaSilva himself, unless he was faking weakness. *Possible. Something to test in some way.*

That brought DaSilva to Jean Davenport, who had been present with Cara when she found the coat. He was a suspect for the same reasons as Cara. But neither had done anything to be more suspicious than the other. In short, if he suspected one, DaSilva would have to suspect both. Then again, if they were working together, they might have the complementary skills needed to commit the killings as well as the attack on DaSilva. Cara was a Light Warrior, and Jean was a Mage. If Jean had some sort of dark magic that made the hand that grabbed DaSilva, then on paper, the two of them could make one killer if added together. But they were both thin, not exactly the muscular people DaSilva pictured responsible for these killings. *Maybe. Come back to them.*

Skipping Jose . . .

Karen Davidson was as bad of a suspect as her husband for almost exactly the same reasons. If anything, she was slightly less plausible, if only because she was fairly small and slight, and Mage abilities seemed like a bad fit for someone who was committing fairly bloody murders. *Maybe once they were higher level, but the killer struck on the first night and killed someone with what we believe was a bladed weapon.* It was possible that the Davidsons brought weapons into Orientation with them, as DaSilva had. But the level of the brutality in the recent killings seemed beyond their physical capacity either way.

Paulo Dante felt like he should be a good suspect compared with most of the others. He was a fit young man, and he'd chosen the Medium Warrior Class, so he was also armed. Most killers were young men, so Paulo at least seemed to fit the bill better than Karen Davidson. *But if it was him, how did he create that shadowy hand? If someone used magic to kill me at Paulo's request, who would that be? No way it's Jose.* And if Paulo wasn't using his own brother as a co-conspirator, it would be strange if he'd found someone else he trusted more to be his co-conspirator.

DaSilva found that his head was starting to hurt.

Let me go and talk to Mina and Yulia, he thought. *Maybe they'll have a fresh perspective. Right now, it feels like I'm just picking a scab.*

"So, that's about where I'm at," DaSilva finished.

"That is very *interesting*, Detective," Mina said thoughtfully. *I'm not sure I agree with all of his reasoning, but there are some useful ideas there.*

"Do you guys have anything to add?" he asked hopefully.

"It's hard to believe anyone on the team could kill someone," Yulia said, chewing her lip. "Except that I saw that hand grabbing your foot and trying to drag you over the edge." She looked up at DaSilva. "Are we sure that it wasn't a part of the Dungeon?"

DaSilva shook his head and frowned. "We can't be sure of anything, but I don't think so. I wish it were part of the Dungeon, but the other people who the bridge killed—well, you saw what happened to them."

Yulia nodded and lapsed into a brooding silence.

"If you really want my thoughts, I would just suggest one change in your thinking so far," Mina said. She waited for him to nod before she continued. "You seemed to be ruling out people based on character traits, physical strength, and what kind of abilities people have. Abilities will definitely provide us with some clues here, but I don't think character traits do. There's an idea I think you're working with, in the back of your mind, that some people are too good or gentle to kill. I believe we're all capable of murder, Detective."

"Thank you for that grim thought, Mina." DaSilva smiled darkly.

He took his smartphone from his pocket.

"There's something I want you to see." He looked at Yulia. "Uh, not you, if you don't mind."

"I get the hint," Yulia said. She walked over to the other side of the room, took out a pair of headphones and her smartphone, and began playing music. Mina could almost tell the song she was playing, the music was so loud, and she barely managed to keep from rolling her eyes.

"One day she'll go deaf." Mina shook her head.

"It's good for now, though," DaSilva replied. "What I'm going to show you is extremely graphic. I just want you to know more of what we're dealing with. And part of why I have this implicit assumption that not just anyone could be committing these murders."

"Graphic?" Mina frowned. "When the coat was discovered on the second day, there was hardly even any blood. Are you saying the killer left bodies behind at the next crime scene?"

"Pieces of them," DaSilva said. "Most of the bodies were gone, but whatever cleanup Skill they used was imperfect. I guess if the body parts are spread far and wide enough, it doesn't get all of them."

He pulled up one of the pictures and handed the phone over.

"Swipe right to see the other pictures," he added.

Mina looked at the picture, then zoomed in for a better look. It was a lonely strand of intestine tossed onto a tree root. It would've blended in with the root if not for the slightly different color.

"Ugh," she said quietly, covering her mouth with one hand. Then she swiped right. Another bit of organ. Swiped again. Scattered blood droplets. Swiped once more. Another partially intact organ. Swiped one more time. But there was nothing. "Is that it?"

"That isn't enough?" DaSilva raised an eyebrow.

"I suppose I was expecting something incriminating. Maybe some of that psychodrama stuff you mentioned last time we spoke about this. The killer reenacting their traumatic childhood or something, or playing with the body in specific ways. Not just random bits of gore. Then again, maybe my expectations have been influenced a little too much by network television." She struggled to smile, but after a moment settled for a grimace.

"Well, there's definitely something psychologically aberrant going on," DaSilva said. "Adelaide and I looked closely at those remains. She was confident—and I agree with her just based on my naked eyes—that those bits of organ that we saw had bite marks. She wasn't sure if they were human or beast, but they looked pretty human to me. Can you imagine that one of our team members might be not just a killer, but a cannibal?"

CHAPTER THIRTY-FOUR

The Job

After DaSilva had departed, Yulia put away her headphones and smartphone.

Even though she was on low power mode and airplane mode, there was precious little battery left—36 percent—and no indication of anywhere she could charge her phone in Orientation thus far.

"What did the detective have to show you that I couldn't see?" she asked.

"Pictures of remains from the killings," Mina replied. "The killer is more *monstrous* than we realized before." Her expression was carefully composed, so Yulia couldn't tell how much the images had affected her sister.

Aren't all murderers monstrous in one way or another? Yulia questioned to herself. *And before, we were even considering that the killer might actually be a monster . . .* She stared at her sister, who seemed to be lost in thought.

"Was there anything else?" Yulia finally asked. "Do we need to do anything? Why did he come here anyway?"

"He just wanted to pick our brains," Mina said. "I have a couple of ideas for things we can do. But there's no rush to try and catch the killer. Now that we think it's someone on our team, we can afford to wait until the next challenge to do more sleuthing. If we start interacting with the team now just so we can investigate them, when we haven't shown any interest in socializing with them before, it will only make the killer suspicious. We would need some more specific reason. I think the best thing I can do for now is practice my magic. I have to make sure I'm strong enough to help the detective apprehend the criminal, after all."

She smiled. Yulia felt some tension leave her body. There was a plan. Mina knew what to do next. *I can relax.*

Yulia smiled back. "I'll just watch you practice. Maybe train my Healing Aura too."

Mina began quietly chanting to herself, and Yulia stood and looked at her until Mina stopped, about thirty seconds later. Several hundred droplets of water had materialized in the air around her. Without really looking at what she was doing, Mina began manipulating the droplets. Like a conductor directing an orchestra, she waved her hands, and the water moved almost like a living being responding to orders.

She's getting so much better at that, Yulia thought. *How can I make myself more useful?*

Yulia surrounded herself with Healing Aura. It was the only thing she could think to do. Then she put her headphones in again. Healing Aura didn't require much in terms of focus.

DaSilva stepped out into the frosty air of the public square.

Is it colder today? It had been snowing a lot. Maybe the weather was getting worse.

"Oh, Officer, I'm so glad to run into you!" Annette Danziger practically ran up to him as he turned to leave the inn. The tall blonde woman clasped her hands together, almost as if she was praying—or as if a prayer had been answered.

"The pleasure is all mine, I'm sure, ma'am." DaSilva smiled politely and waited. *I'm a detective, not an officer, but how can I help you?*

"Do you already know what's been going on?" she asked.

"I'm not sure, specifically, what you're talking about."

"Oh, you must come with me!" Mrs. Danziger declared.

DaSilva allowed her to lead him by the hand into one of the non-winners' lodging buildings. He immediately saw that there were nine people sitting in the main area, worried expressions on their faces.

A full team's worth of people, now that Mrs. Danziger is back with them. Did something happen in the challenge?

"Ahem, what's going on here?" DaSilva said, drawing himself up to his full height and putting a note of authority into his voice.

"Oh, it's good to see you, sir!" said one of the men. *Andy something?*

DaSilva smiled and nodded politely. "What seems to be the trouble?"

"We were just getting ready to move our things over to the new housing since our team was one of the winners of the last challenge," said another man.

Jamie something, DaSilva remembered.

"We realized after we got to the bottom of the stairs that we were getting hungry," Jaime continued, "so Andy went through his bag to get some of the food we got as a prize. And it was gone. I told Gwen here"—he gestured to the woman to his right—"and we started going through our bags. Our food was gone too!"

DaSilva's eyes widened. *This could be a serious problem.*

"Can I assume that this is true for everyone here?" DaSilva asked, looking around at all the faces. Everyone nodded.

"First those horrible murders, now this," Mrs. Danziger said, sniffling slightly. She stepped closer to Detective DaSilva and pressed her arms together on either side of her chest, accentuating her rather ample cleavage. "What will we do?"

Don't stand so close to me, to start, DaSilva thought, glancing over at Mr. Danziger. *Your husband's right there, lady!* Mr. Danziger, who looked around fifteen years older than his wife, was occupied talking to one of the other members of their party. DaSilva nevertheless took a step away from Mrs. Danziger.

"Ahem. Why don't you guys walk me through your movements after the challenge, step by step?"

They did. It was fairly straightforward, though.

The party had all been together prior to the challenge, so they remained together when they were transported back after the challenge. They continued with congratulations, high fives, and hugs for a short while longer before they split up to go and get their things out of their respective rooms. This involved some of the party members leaving for a different inn, while others simply walked upstairs. People in both groups were robbed of their food without being aware of it until they reconvened downstairs.

It's just like I thought, DaSilva recognized grimly. *The most likely scenario is that one member of the group robbed the others with some sort of thief Skill, without anyone being aware of it. Do I tell them that, though? What will they do to the thief? It's not like I have a cell to put them in.*

He listened to further discussion from the group. Nothing they told him added to his understanding. DaSilva finally reached a decision.

"I have to tell you all, the most likely explanation is that one of you robbed the others," he said. "That one person would be lying about their bag being empty. Are you all actually willing to definitively answer the question of who's responsible? Even if it's one of you?"

"Well, of course!" Mr. Danziger thundered indignantly. "It's find the thief or starve!"

"Does everyone else agree?" DaSilva asked a bit wearily.

I don't have time for this crap! Who's the idiot who robbed their friends?

A couple of people murmured complaints.

"Look, folks, I'm treating you all equally," DaSilva said firmly. "You know you were the only people apparently present, unless someone has an invisibility Skill or something. That makes you the first set of obvious suspects I have to eliminate before it makes any sense for me to look elsewhere."

A few individuals looked guarded, but everyone ultimately nodded or verbally indicated agreement with his reasoning.

"All right, everyone hand over their Small Bags of Deceptive Dimensions, please."

The party members slowly complied.

Once all bags were accounted for, DaSilva proceeded to open the first bag. He had noticed when using his own bag that he could find an item by thinking of it when he reached in. This was a subject of some trial and error for him on the first night, back when this place had seemed like a fantastical adventure out of one of the fantasy novels he liked to read. He'd gotten a childish glee out of storing his sidearm, then calling it back out of the bag with a quickdraw motion.

Now he attempted the grim task of using the bags' mechanics to identify a thief.

He had made sure to position each bag so it was between himself and its owner. DaSilva absolutely did not want to lose track of whose bag was whose, because he thought it plausible the thief might be murdered quietly by their teammates. What DaSilva would do if that happened, he wasn't yet sure, but he wanted to be certain it didn't befall an innocent person.

But as he searched through the bags, he slowly realized this careful planning had been pointless. None of them contained food. DaSilva tried pulling out weapons and other items that he imagined might be in the bags. That was successful. Somehow, though, he couldn't find food.

"Ugh. What kind of nutso result is this?" He shook his head irritably. "The good thing is that you guys might all be cleared. Unless we think the thief actually hid the food somewhere or consumed it all incredibly quickly. What seems more likely is that someone has a kind of Skill that lets them rob you without you having to be near them. But if that's the case, I don't know how we'll ever catch them."

"Well, shit!" Andy swore. "If I catch this son of a bitch, I'm going to string him up from—" He stopped himself and looked at DaSilva meekly.

"I'm a man of the law," DaSilva said. "If we catch the thief and definitively prove who it was, we'll find a way of punishing them. I don't know how we'll identify which food is yours, though."

I'd probably have to let them kill the person, honestly. In this setting, leaving someone free who can rob people of their food without being near them—and who we know has actually done *that!—just seems like a recipe for trouble.* Maybe he could get the System's proctor to erect a jail for their ne'er-do-well. But DaSilva doubted it. The proctor had been very hands off thus far.

"Anyone write their names on their food or something?" Mrs. Danziger asked wryly.

People either shook their heads or stared at the ground despondently.

"How will we survive?" Gwen asked. She spoke with a slight Irish lilt. "We've all had to go rather lean these last few days. I'm sure I'm not the only one who was hoping this food would get us through the next couple of days, plus more in case we lost the next challenge."

The room looked quite glum.

"You all are moving to the winners' housing, is that correct?" DaSilva asked.

Nods from the group.

"All right. I think we can ask the people living in the same buildings you're moving to whether they can share their resources. I'll explain what happened to you all. Hopefully, the people in the buildings you choose will be reasonable. If not, we'll try and take up a collection elsewhere. No one wants the other people in here with them to starve."

Murmurs of agreement and gratitude.

DaSilva accompanied half the party to the inn they had planned to move into. Then he went upstairs with them and knocked on a few doors to explain the situation. People were understanding and willing to commit to sharing some of their food, as long as they weren't expected to give up more than half.

Fortunately, the System has been generous enough this time that there's really food to spare.

As he came out of the building, another individual approached him.

"Detective," the man said, "am I glad to see you!"

DaSilva forced a smile.

"What can I do for you?"

The man answered him, and the smile slid from DaSilva's face.

A knock startled Mina and broke her concentration.

Probably for the best that something happened to stop me, she thought. Looking down at herself, she saw that she was covered in sweat. She had practiced for hours this time. She hadn't looked at a clock, but it had been mid-afternoon when she had started applying her water magic. And now the sky outside was completely black.

She checked her System alerts while she walked to the door.

Wow! I leveled up twice! And at some point, Basic Elemental Magic: Water had become simply Elemental Magic: Water.

It seemed that the post-System world was one that would reward Mina's unyielding focus.

"Hello, Detective," Mina said. "Any good news?"

She wasn't optimistic. DaSilva looked harried and exhausted.

"We have a new crime epidemic on our hands," he said. "May I come in?"

Wordlessly, she let DaSilva into the room. Yulia took out her headphones and greeted the detective. Then he dropped the bombshell.

"Someone has been stealing food from people who won the last challenge. At first, I thought it was just a handful of people who got robbed, but there have been more reports since then. Around a half-dozen teams have been relieved of their rations. I haven't figured out how they're doing it, or where they're keeping the food. But I think this could end up being a bigger problem than a killer who murders a few people every other night. If people start to go hungry—" His voice faltered.

"They'll cease to be as civilized as we've experienced," Mina finished.

"That's a nice way of putting it, yes," DaSilva agreed.

"So, we need to share our food?" Yulia put in, arms crossed.

Mina smiled at her and chuckled. DaSilva nodded and gave a weary smile of his own.

"It's either share food and carefully ration, or we have to go out and try to hunt some of those beasts the System has mentioned might live around here," DaSilva agreed. "I don't really know how much I like the hunting option. We don't know how dangerous the creatures that live around here are, and I think it's getting colder outside. Bad weather to be out in the woods, especially if the hunting party has to leave sight range of the settlement. Which I think would be necessary. Of course, if the theft continues, we'll have no choice but to go out and look for food."

"On that subject, I should mention a Skill I unlocked while the team was in the last challenge," Mina said a little reluctantly.

"It's not a theft Skill, is it?" DaSilva asked sarcastically.

"Ha! No such luck. You'll have to find your thief elsewhere. But I might be able to help with that." She explained the Investigate Skill that had evolved from her Identify.

"So you can get a person's full Status information just by looking at them?" DaSilva asked.

"It seems that way," Mina agreed. "I haven't used it a lot, but it worked on plants."

"We can Identify plants?" DaSilva asked. "Never mind, not important. Why didn't you mention this earlier?"

"I was planning on doing a little Investigating for you, but I also didn't want to go out using the Skill today. And not next to you, either. I figured that after the challenge, people would be on edge. It would be dangerous for me or Yulia to be out on our own. But if I was walking around with you, people would figure out that I was a part of your investigation. Either situation seemed dangerous. Someone has tried to kill you, after all. Therefore, I wanted to wait on trying this out until I was sure it was a good moment. So I didn't mention it."

"You're a very careful person," DaSilva said in a slightly affronted voice.

"Oh, don't be that way, Detective, it wasn't because I didn't trust you or something!"

"You already used this Skill to make sure I didn't have any suspicious Skills, though, didn't you?" he asked.

She nodded slowly.

"All right," he said. "Fair enough. When and how would you propose to use Investigate to gather more information?"

Mina already had her answer ready.

"On the morning of the next challenge," she said. "You can gather the members of our team together, and I'll use it on all of them. We'll confirm once and for all whether any of them could be the killer or the thief, or if we have to look elsewhere. And then, once we're in the challenge, I'll start using it on the other teams there with us."

DaSilva nodded slowly. "Sometimes it's good to be cautious. I'm glad you told me about this *now*, Officer Danailova. I really didn't want to make demands on you, but you've been more helpful thus far than anyone except Adelaide. Consider this to be me officially deputizing you. I have faith that together, we'll get to the bottom of both of these matters."

"Well, Detective—"

[Required conditions met. Job unlocked. Job Detective is available to you. Accept?]

DaSilva, Mina observed, looked just as surprised as she did.

"Did you just get a System message too?" she asked.

He nodded and swallowed a lump in his throat.

"The System is trying to name me chief of police," he said.

"Well, then, consider me your subordinate. It wants to make me Detective Danailova!" Her lips curled in an uneasy smile.

"Congratulations on the very quick promotion, Officer," DaSilva said with faux solemnity.

They shared a brief laugh.

"I wonder if it's because we hit on the correct means of catching these criminals," Mina said.

"Well, it can't be a bad thing."

DaSilva left, and the sisters went to bed.

Another night passed.

The snow continued slowly drifting downward through the black night sky.

A handful of people disappeared from the population counter.

[2,842/3,397 Survivors]

CHAPTER THIRTY-FIVE

The Bond

Nikolai Rostov was enjoying a wonderful dream.

The ladies were all over him, and they were not shy. Hands roamed all across the landscape of his body, and where fingers touched, lips followed. In Rostov's dreams, all massages seemed to have happy endings.

As he anticipated an intensification of pleasure, there was a sudden piercing noise in his ear.

What the fuck?!

His eyes fluttered open as his brain struggled between the sharp noise and the temptations of the dream, which seemed to grip him more forcefully than normal.

There was a shape in front of him. A man-shape that slowly moved from blurry to focused. He was at the point of being able to recognize the figure.

Then he felt a splitting pain in the front of his head, and the world of his dream began to shatter.

There was a stabbing pain in his chest next.

Then nothing. Darkness.

And a sudden burst of intense heat, spreading all around him.

"W-what's happening?" he whimpered, confused.

Rostov's eyes opened wide, and he found himself in a place of sweltering heat and encircling flames. Above him a deep blackness opened wide. He exhaled slowly.

Okay. I know this place.

"L-Lord Moloch!" Rostov called. "It's such a pleasure to be pulled into your realm again. Um, thank you for the great honor?"

Nothing for a few seconds but the movement of flickering flames.

"Is something the matter, Master?" Rostov asked hesitantly.

Finally, there was a familiar swirling of fire and smoke from all around Rostov, forming a tornado of flames in front of him. He didn't bother to shield his eyes this time. He simply stared into the flame. The brightness brought tears to his eyes, but other than the involuntary tearing, he had no further reaction.

The body of Moloch appeared once more.

A nude humanoid figure with the head and horns of a bull and the wings of an eagle, body wreathed in flame, breathing fire in and out of its nostrils.

Rostov silently knelt.

"So, Nikolai, we are reunited once again. Under most unfavorable circumstances this time, I must say," Moloch said. There was clear displeasure in his voice.

"What, if I may ask, are those circumstances, Lord? I was just sleeping, and I seem to have awakened here."

"The circumstances are such that punishing you for them would be pointless, although I would like to." Moloch spoke these words with a sadistic relish. **"You see, you somehow managed to end up receiving two fatal gunshots. One to the head, and one to the chest. Frankly, the only reason that you remain alive, in a sense, is that in the moment before you would have died, I pulled upon the bond that connects a god with his Chosen One. Out of appreciation for all your efforts on my behalf, I brought you here to give you a choice. Your final choice in this life."**

Rostov swallowed and fixed his eyes on the ground. *So, it's come to this. Well, I can't fight my fate here.*

"Am I to become food for you, Master? Is that what you mean by my final choice? Is it death or being consumed by you?"

"That is not quite what I mean, Nikolai. You are not far from the mark. Your choice is between immediate death at the hands of the one who shot you, or the possibility of revenge. If you die now, you will become food for me. However, I wanted to give you one last chance to destroy your enemies before you die. A forced Evolution to a certain specific Race would allow you to circumvent your fatal wounds. You would no longer be quite yourself, and your personhood would fade further and further away over time, but at least you could have your revenge. What do you say?"

So, a quick death or a slow one in which I take others with me, essentially? Rostov thought. *Easy choice.*

"Where do I sign?" Rostov managed a smile, though his eyes were tearing up again. He already missed his humanity.

An alert appeared.

[Divine flame detected within and around your body. A Race Evolution is available! Accept Evolution to Flame Elemental Race? Y/N]

Rostov immediately selected "Y" before he could chicken out.

The world went dark again for a moment. Then all he felt was flame, engulfing every part of his body. He felt all the pain of being incinerated alive. He tried to scream, but when he opened his mouth, the fire flowed in between his lips. It kept pushing in until it filled his insides and burned away all the oxygen in his body.

In a few seconds, all that was left of Rostov was the shape of him, the unending pain, and fire.

So, you had the situation under control, Ross? James shot the officer a dirty look as they both flew through the air.

Officer Ross didn't seem to notice. He was too busy trying to steady himself and put his feet on the ground. James didn't bother trying to steady himself or control his landing. He'd used gravity magic to cut his own weight by more than half before he'd launched his sneak attack earlier. Whatever force he landed with was unlikely to hurt him, even if he hadn't been wearing his Royal Exoarmor.

It's really my fault the situation went sideways, James thought, looking back toward the column of fire that had engulfed the tent where Rostov used to live, along with a half-dozen cultists who were standing too close.

If you want someone killed right, you have to kill them yourself.

James's eyes adjusted to the brightness of the flame the longer he stared, and he finally made out a humanoid shape in the center of the flames. Rostov didn't look like a human anymore. He was just a big outline of a man, radiating flame in all directions. He still had facial features, but they were just shadows in the region of his head. *Overall, perhaps an improvement.*

"YOU DID THIS TO ME?!" a horrendous voice bellowed in anger and pain. It took James a moment to recognize the sound as Rostov's voice it was so distorted by pain.

I guess he can still talk. Not as much of an improvement on Rostov as I thought. Still, I like that he seems to be suffering wonderfully.

A tiny projectile that James could barely see flew through the air at inhuman speed. For a moment, he braced to try and change his direction. Though he was still in midair, some of his abilities might propel him one way or another. But then he noticed that it wasn't aimed at him.

Officer Ross, who had managed to land a few feet in front of where James now was, didn't even have time to change his expression.

The tiny object struck its target—and embedded itself deep in Officer Ross's skull.

The policeman collapsed to the ground a moment later.

Son of a bitch, James thought. He found himself getting angry.

He grabbed hold of the Ego Antler Spear, which was floating in midair alongside his body. James used the haft to catch onto a tree and break his momentum as he landed.

Then he charged forward. Screaming cultists running in a panic, burning tents, and the few allies of Officer Ross who were throwing projectiles and trying to hurt Rostov—James ignored them all. He focused on the enemy and prepared to make an attack on Rostov's center of mass.

And he began Silent Spellcasting, gathering non-elemental Mana. He wanted to make a shield around himself. Though he felt wrathful, James was keenly aware of how hot the flames of Rostov's new body looked. If he was going to get close, he would need some protection.

It would have to be a quickly charged shield because he wanted to strike while Rostov was distracted with Officer Ross's allies.

Then a voice penetrated his focus.

"James! James, help!"

I recognize that voice, he thought. He dodged a fire blast that Rostov tossed off in his direction, and then he ran toward the voice.

"Thank God for you, James!" Moishe Rose breathed out a long sigh of relief as James moved into close range with him. James slashed through the stone that Moishe was chained to with a single swipe of his spear.

Moishe's chains had instantly become looser when the stone they bound him to was smashed apart. He pulled a bobby pin from his hair and immediately started picking the locks on his chains.

"What can I do to help you, man?" Moishe asked, looking at the fiery figure of Rostov that was now incinerating one of Ross's allies as he screamed for his life.

"I can't protect anyone from this thing," James said brusquely. "Whatever your Skills are, it's probably best that you run." Then he shook himself slightly and smiled. "We really have to stop meeting like this."

"Just run?" Moishe asked, a little disappointed.

"Do you think you can destroy that?" James asked, pointing a thumb at Rostov.

"No," Moishe admitted.

"Then you would be a distraction for me more than a help," James said bluntly. "Actually, you can do one thing to help me. Grab Officer Ross. I think he's still alive over there." He gestured in Ross's direction. "If you run off carrying him, it's possible we can find a way to heal him later."

"Ross," Moishe said distastefully. "Well, if you say so."

"Hey, I'm not happy with him either," James said. "But he put a bullet in the big guy's head, which is why he's in final boss mode over there. And I can sense that he's in a great deal of well-deserved pain. I think he's done all he can to earn a second chance."

Moishe smiled, then gave a slight nod.

And the two men ran off in different directions.

James's Silent Spellcasting finished a moment after he and Moishe split off from each other. An invisible shield appeared around his body, and he felt that little bit safer. He began Silent Spellcasting again, gathering water Mana this time. Just in case his spear couldn't do the job.

Then he rushed into melee range with the giant fire monster, who was fighting many of his own cult members at this point, mindlessly throwing flames everywhere.

"Stop this, Prophet!" screamed one woman before she was engulfed in flames.

"Please, no!" cried one man as he suffered the same treatment.

Then James leaped in and jabbed at Rostov's center of mass with Deep Antler Penetration. Two big holes appeared in the burning abomination—and almost instantly filled in with flames again. The antler looked very slightly darker around the edges, as if it had taken some damage from attacking Rostov.

James jumped back instantly, but at the same time Rostov threw a flaming left hook. James could feel his shield drop to around 50 percent power after that single contact.

He pushed off the ground and got another few feet of distance, then kicked his legs and threw out two Air Strikes. Just like the Deep Antler Penetration, the wind blades passed through Rostov's fiery form—and then he re-formed around the places where he'd been cut.

At least that attack seemed to slow him down a little, James thought optimistically. His rage was giving way now to simple admiration for how durable Rostov's new body seemed to be. James might almost envy him his seeming invulnerability if only he didn't display with his posture, that brief sound of his voice, and his erratic behavior that he was in horrible pain at every moment.

I only have enough juice left in my shield to endure one more close-range attack, he thought as he did a backflip to avoid a curtain of flame that Rostov had thrown his way. *And I can't re-cast the shield until after I finish with my water magic. Probably the water magic is more useful than a melee attack would be anyway since he seems to be made of fire.* There had to be a core or something somewhere that James could destroy, though. If this was a video game, there would be a weakness like that. And the System operated on video game-like logic a lot of the time.

James dodged another wall of fire and leaped in close with a Lightning Strike aimed where the equivalent of Rostov's neck was. A decapitation move would normally end a fight with anyone in his experience so far. This time his attack didn't even seem to do any damage. There was no parting of the flame, perhaps because lightning wasn't harmful to fire on some elemental level.

James bent backward at a ninety-degree angle as one of Rostov's limbs swung out at him. Then it smashed downward into him, wiping out his shield and slamming him into the ground with a single hit.

James jumped away before the next blow landed, slightly winded but otherwise unhurt.

He dodged around for a few minutes, which was increasingly difficult. Rostov was focusing all his wrath on James now, and he had burned most of the nearby trees away, so there wasn't much cover for James to hide behind. The small number of cultists remaining had almost all run for it while James was engaging Rostov up close. Only two of Officer Ross's little band of helpers remained nearby, and they had backed off beyond melee range, apparently content to watch him fight Rostov.

What the fuck do they think this is? A spectator sport? Either help me out or get the fuck out of here!

The only advantages remaining to James were his superior Stats and his sheer variety of Skills. With Empathic Projection he had started to get an idea of where Rostov was likely to strike next. He could use that to perform otherwise impossible last second dodges. And with his impossible Agility he managed to avoid any serious damage even when Rostov surprised him with a sudden wild barroom swing.

Finally, James unleashed the thick, heavy aura of blue Mana around him, conjuring a lake of water over Rostov's head. Rostov had a single moment to tilt his head up, and then the water fell straight down onto and all around him.

James had a moment of thinking he had won.

Then the center of the lake turned to steam, and he saw Rostov's fiery visage and heard his howl of frustrated anger.

"KILL YOUUUUUU!"

James used his hands to direct the water, condensing it around Rostov's body. But he was simply too hot.

Whatever water touched or drew near him Rostov boiled and turned to steam almost in an instant. Clouds of steam billowed between the two combatants, but James could see through the water vapor with his superhuman Perception. But James couldn't think of a creative solution to make the water function better as a flame retardant. And finally, he had too little water to contain Rostov anymore.

Rostov stood, uninhibited, yowling with rage, "KILL YOUUUU!"

He took a step toward James, his foot evaporating some of the puddle around him. James began to reassess his strategy.

It was gratifying to see that he had reduced Rostov slightly in size, from a fourteen-foot-tall monstrosity to perhaps an eleven-foot-tall fire monster. But conjuring up that lake had taken a large chunk of his Mana, more than one third. James was doubtful that the same tactic would be effective if repeated. And if it didn't work, his only option would probably be to run. It didn't seem wise to fight this non-physical creature without the use of Mana.

So, what do I do now?

CHAPTER THIRTY-SIX

Last Gasp

Moishe retreated into the forest. He moved as quickly as he could in the direction the former prisoners had run. Jeffrey Ross's body lay slumped over his shoulders.

Cecilia slithered through the trees above them, keeping pace quite easily with the weight of a human body slowing Moishe down.

Ross's breathing was shallow and ragged, his heart rate weak and slowly dropping, but as James had noted, he was still alive.

Seems like a head shot isn't what it used to be, Moishe thought. Both Rostov and Ross remained alive despite bullets striking them in the head. Though Rostov had only thrown the bullet from his own injury at Ross, it had moved with such speed that Moishe thought it was comparable to a gunshot. *I think my Assassin Class is only going to get harder to level up as time goes by.*

There was a sound of water moving around in the distance behind Moishe, shortly followed by the searing hiss of steam. He didn't even bother turning around. He guessed James was trying to extinguish Rostov with some sort of massive magic attack. But it was Moishe's role to avoid becoming entangled in that fight, and turning into a spectator wouldn't help him fulfill that role. And he'd made a bit of distance now, anyway. If he looked back, all he'd see would be trees and perhaps a bit of steam.

As he put his left foot forward, Moishe froze. There was rustling in the shrubbery around ten feet ahead of him. He had a choice to make: try to duck out of sight before the source of the noise stepped into view or stand his ground and prepare for a possible fight.

He decided to stand his ground. It wouldn't be easy fighting while protecting Jeff Ross, but hiding while carrying him would be nearly impossible.

A female figure stepped through the bushes. Catherine Ross, one of the Moloch priesthood.

Moishe felt instantly uneasy. *James never said whether he'd recruited both of them to his side. He only really mentioned Jeff. Is she on James's side too? Or . . .*

And Catherine looked instantly wary of Moishe.

"Hello, cultist," he said. *Let's see what she says to that.*

"Hello, Assassin," she said, giving him an unnerving smile. "I see you have my husband there. Hand him over to me now, and I won't strike you down where you stand."

So, not on the same page as James, I guess! Crap.

"Bold words," Moishe replied. He adjusted his hold on Jeff, pulling the man closer to his body. "But I think you'd have already done that if you could. I think my lifespan would probably be longer if I didn't hand over my biggest leverage."

She took a step forward, and Moishe took a corresponding step back.

"Better not move any closer," he said. "I can kill your husband at any moment if I want to."

She sucked in a long, slow breath and stopped.

I actually have an extremely valuable hostage, Moishe realized. *She doesn't know he betrayed them, or something. She really wants to get Jeff back. I can use this.*

"If you let me have him back, I'll make sure the cult never comes after you," Catherine said.

"Mighty big promise for Rostov's little apprentice," he replied dismissively. "And I don't think your little gang will be in any condition to come after anyone after today. Heh."

"Then he's not—" She looked at Moishe's face, then up to Jeff's body. Her expression was confused.

Oh. She does know something about what happened. He made a few mental leaps to figure out what he should do next.

"Rostov is still alive, but he turned into a giant fire monster," Moishe said. "I'll give your husband back to you. He's not in great shape."

She let out her breath in a slow, steady stream. "Thank you."

"Yeah," Moishe said. "I guess we're not enemies right now."

He dearly wanted to kill her. Catherine had been more instrumental in Rostov's doings than Jeff by far. But it wasn't as if he had a weapon handy. And if she used her powers, he didn't know if he could do any damage at all. He might end up getting captured again. Better to play nice with her for now.

Moishe set Jeff's body down between them.

"Sweetheart, what happened to you?" Catherine said softly, eyes widening as she looked at her husband's face. There was an ugly diamond-shaped hole just above the center of Ross's forehead, where the bullet had entered.

"After he shot Rostov, the prophet gave him the bullet back," Moishe said, trying to match Catherine's tone as he spoke.

Her eyes leaped up to meet his, as if she was inspecting his face for any sign that he was enjoying giving the news.

Apparently, she found nothing objectionable in what she saw because she turned her eyes back to her husband.

Her hands glowed with the same energy Moishe had seen her use every time she had healed someone on their trek through the forest. Ross's forehead wound closed up, but he looked as near death as he had before.

Well, of course he does, Moishe thought. *The bullet's still in the wound, isn't it? Not that we could remove it without causing more brain damage, maybe killing him in the process.*

"This is all my fault, isn't it?" she whispered.

She cradled her husband's body in her arms, and Moishe saw her body shake and shiver as she wept over him. A few minutes passed. He stood off to the side, alternately staring spitefully and forcing himself to look away.

Moishe wasn't sure what to do. These people he hated were locked in their own private tragedy. On the one hand, he felt livid. *I didn't even get to give my sister's body a proper burial, but you can moon over your fucking husband for as long as you want . . .*

On the other hand, he felt that his options were limited. He didn't want to stay near them, but he didn't think he'd be doing anything constructive by leaving them either. James had asked him to keep Jeff out of harm's way. For whatever reason, James still saw some value in Jeff's life. And Moishe felt a debt of gratitude to him that could never be fully repaid.

If something came upon Jeff and Catherine while she was in this state, they could both be killed. And Moishe would have failed at the one thing he'd been asked to do while James finished destroying the cult.

But it made his head pound and his heart ache to be so near these two people.

Jeff shuddered slightly in Catherine's arms and let out a rasping breath. It seemed almost like a last gasp.

She shook her head and pulled away from him.

"You're getting worse. I have to do something. Only one other thing I can do."

Then Catherine spoke softly into her unmoving husband's ear. Moishe's high Perception allowed him to catch all of what she said, but he looked away respectfully to try and give the woman the illusion of privacy with her husband. Even if he had a grudge against them, no one deserved to be robbed of their last moments with the one they loved. Even if these two had done exactly that to Isabelle and Moishe.

"You were always better with the kids than me, anyway. And you'll definitely do better with them than I could now. You don't have the same blood on your hands that I do. You're not a monster like me." She pronounced the words with a self-loathing that surprised Moishe.

If you thought this way, you could have behaved differently before, he thought sternly. *Look at all the harm you've done because you* chose *to, knowing that there was another way.* Not that he was some angel. But there was a difference between running with the cult for a little while and directly assisting Rostov with his sacrifices. Or so he wanted to believe.

"Moishe," Catherine said suddenly. He turned and gave her his full attention. "Please tell my husband that I love him. Tell him to be good to the kids. Tell him I said I'm sorry."

He wanted to say that she should tell him herself. But he could feel that something was about to happen. Her whole body glowed with a golden light. Moishe simply nodded.

"Goodbye," Catherine said, looking at Jeff.

She leaned in and gave him a long open-mouthed kiss.

And her body turned translucent and slowly faded away.

As James stared at Rostov's body striding toward him through the steaming mud, an idea struck him.

Then he felt a heat behind his ear. It was Hester again.

"Hester, tell Anansi I don't want help!" James said hotly.

The heat cut off almost instantly, as if James had cut off the Spider God midsentence. Perhaps he had.

"He was about to give me a solution to your problem!" Hester said softly.

"I don't need it. I came up with a solution!" James ran as he spoke, doing a loop around Rostov. It forced the Flame Elemental to remain in place, turning and looking after him. James's Agility was much higher than Rostov's, so Rostov ultimately gave up on catching him in close range and started throwing fireballs wherever he thought James would be next.

James couldn't help noticing that the attacks had gotten smaller and a bit less energetic. *So, the giant water attack really did do something to weaken Rostov. Yes.* His new plan would work.

James began Silent Spellcasting again. This time he was gathering earth Mana.

"Hey, how can we help?" a female voice asked loudly. James dodged a fireball and looked behind him. It was the woman in the white armor. James remembered she had stabbed him a few times when he had last fought Rostov's group. It was nice that at least one of the more powerful cult members had joined Officer Ross's little rebellion.

"If you want to help, distract him while I finish charging Mana!" James said.

"All right! I can do it for about five minutes. I think my friend can distract him for a minute too."

James was barely listening. He continued running away. He wouldn't need as much Mana for his planned final attack as he had to make the lake that he'd used to partially quench Rostov earlier. But five or six minutes of distraction might not be enough. Fortunately, although the fight had gone on for some time now, his Stamina was still all right.

Still, the more attacks Rostov threw, the likelier it was that James would make a mistake. If he took a severe enough attack, that might break his focus and force him to start charging his Mana all over again. Or cause him to pause, exposing him to follow-up attacks. And Rostov's fire powers seemed dangerous enough that a few follow-up attacks might roast James. In short, he could imagine a sequence of events that could lead to his defeat.

Though he was far from giving up, James felt very aware now that his decision about accepting Anansi's help had been grounded in pride. But then, it also wouldn't be very satisfying on a storytelling level if James got help from the Spider God here.

So he continued to evade Rostov, charging what he hoped would be his final move in this battle.

The woman in white armor stepped forward to prevent Rostov from pursuing James very far. Her whole body suddenly glowed and exuded a white light. She began swinging her sword at Rostov, her blade cutting through his flames. The fiery figure turned and engaged her.

James slowed down a bit just to watch the two of them fight. It was like watching two elements collide, back and forth. Her white light seemed to be able to block the curtains of flame that Rostov threw up, so she suffered no damage from any of his attacks. But no matter the damage she seemed to do to Rostov's form, he recovered almost instantly.

Rostov was an unstoppable force attacking an immovable object. Or perhaps it was the reverse. That was how it felt. Two titanic enemies colliding, unable to overcome one another.

For five minutes, the warrior in white was able to hold her own against Rostov.

Then the white light that surrounded her began to flicker and fade.

Looks like she was right about only being able to distract him for five minutes, James thought. *What an awesome ability! Such a shame it has such a short time limit.* He was ready to intervene himself now, but he needed the warrior in white out of the way.

"Hey, get out of there!" James yelled. "I'm ready to try my last move on him. If you don't move, you'll become collateral damage."

Rostov suddenly turned to look at James, as if just remembering he was there.

He's more monster than man now, James thought. *He doesn't even remember why he's fighting.*

The other surviving member of the warrior's team, a man dressed in Heavy Warrior armor, took that opening, raced in, and grabbed the warrior in white. She was staggering, as if she was about to collapse from exertion. He picked her up, threw her over his shoulder, and ran back toward the tree line.

Rostov turned back to see what had happened, but too late.

He took a step toward the fleeing enemies, but that was the moment when James unleashed all his gathered earth Mana.

The ground beneath Rostov shuddered and cracked. A great fissure opened up, stretching roughly fifty feet in diameter. James thought he could see a look of surprise dawn on the oval of fire that had replaced Rostov's face. It was the last expression James thought anyone would ever see from him, and he enjoyed it.

If you had your full intelligence, you would understand how fucked you are.

Rostov tried to take a step to one side to move away from the colossal rift that was forming.

James spread his arms and raised them in the air. The two massive slabs of earth on either side of Rostov split neatly apart. Huge plates of rock and soil turned upward, forming a ninety-degree angle with their normal positions. The gap between them opened up like a canyon, and Rostov fell straight down, like leftovers scraped from a dirty plate.

The flailing, burning man tried to find purchase in the wet soil with his fiery limbs, but James didn't give him the chance. He suddenly brought his arms together, and the two plates of rock and soil flipped to the reverse of their original orientations, closing on top of Rostov.

Burying him under tons of rock and earth.

Buried underground. Completely deprived of the oxygen that a fire needs to sustain itself. Impossible for him to lift that much rock and soil without magic or a much higher Strength Stat than me. If that doesn't end the fight, nothing will, James thought.

He let out a long breath he hadn't realized he'd been holding, and he sank into a seated position.

He could feel long rivulets of sweat running down his face, his chest, the back of his neck. Despite his helm, the flames had managed to move through the gaps in the helmet and scorch his beard at one point, and now he smelled the burned hair. His Mana was more than two-thirds gone. His Stamina was halfway gone too.

But he just smiled and shook his head.

"Okay. Yes or no answer only, Hester. Did I get the correct answer that Anansi was going to prescribe?"

Then the Earth began to shake.

CHAPTER THIRTY-SEVEN

Out of the Light

The ground quaked once more, but it was weaker the second time.

There was a third tremor, but at that point, James knew he'd won. Those were death throes as much as they were real attempts to escape.

He burned himself out trying to break free from that tomb.

"Is he dead?" the woman in white asked. She had approached slowly, cautiously, from the edge of the battlefield. She leaned on her companion to walk.

"Give it a minute," James said, shrugging. "We know he wasn't strong enough to break out."

"Riiiiight," she replied a little uneasily. Turning to her companion, she said, "Could you set me down, Chris?"

James remained seated where he had been, waiting to get the alert. Ten minutes passed in near silence; all three survivors were exhausted. James used Identify on the other two while he was waiting. Their names were Hilda Rohm and Chris Roach.

Roach, huh? Fitting name considering he survived being in the thick of all this fighting without showing any special powers. Good for him. The woman and the white aura she'd surrounded herself with during the fighting were something else, though. James was quite curious about that, but he didn't want to spook these two by prying into the details.

Finally, the crucial notifications popped up.

[You killed Flame Elemental Nikolai Rostov, Lv. 18! You gained 1400 exp, based on your contribution to the fight!]

[Predator in Human Skin leveled up!]

[Evolver Human leveled up!]

[Politician gained 1000 bonus exp, based on your destruction of a threat to the entire population of this Orientation in front of witnesses who will share the story!]

Well, that's new, James thought. *But the kill was more satisfying than the levels this time. He died alone in darkness, raging to the end. Buried alive was better than he deserved, but at least he didn't get to live to a ripe old age and die surrounded by loved ones.*

"Wow!" Hilda said. She threw James a look of respect. "You really did it."

"I did," James said. "*We* did. I appreciate your help." He looked from one to the other as he spoke, a small smile on his lips.

"We hated having to follow him, so it was only natural that we'd try to help you take him out," Chris said matter-of-factly.

It feels like he's telling the truth, but it feels like there's something else underneath it. James had been wearing the Ring of Truth for a while now, but it felt like this was the first time he was really using its functions.

"What do the two of you want to do now?" James asked. The key question. Were they going to make themselves useful, or did they want to scatter?

"I never thought that far ahead, honestly," Hilda said. "I was never sure when the next sunrise would come and one of us might be on the chopping block. But it seems impossible to survive in this forest alone. I mean, you saw how long I can use my full power for. I'm basically good for one fight in a day."

"You have a group, right?" Chris asked.

"I do," James acknowledged. "I'm imagining that you guys would be able to fit in pretty seamlessly, actually. Especially when I tell them how helpful you were in breaking up this cult." He smiled.

James's new allies followed him through the trees. He traced Moishe's footsteps, which were easier to find than he'd have expected. Maybe it was James's superhuman senses. But he guessed the footprints were also much heavier and clumsier than normal since Moishe was carrying Officer Ross.

Hilda had recovered much of her lost Stamina and was able to move at a normal walking pace, so James figured it wouldn't take long for them to catch up to Moishe.

As they moved, Hester spoke up from behind James's ear.

"To answer your question from earlier, sir, you didn't do exactly what Lord Anansi was going to suggest, but close enough. And, just my opinion, but what you actually did was more impressive than what he was going to suggest. Lord Anansi started to say that all elementals have a core somewhere in their bodies, but if you fight a semi-intelligent one, they can move the core around to pretty much anywhere in their body. He was going to tell you to crush the whole body at once, I'm fairly certain. When you cut him off, he was almost done transmitting."

"What does that feel like for you, Hester?" James asked. He spoke in a very quiet voice, trying to avoid being overheard by the two walking just a body's length behind him. "When Anansi *transmits* something."

"It's a bit like—"

As Hester was midsentence, James felt her body heat up for a moment. He recognized the familiar sensation. Anansi was transmitting something to her again.

She took a moment to recover. James waited a little nervously. What was the Spider God going to think about James refusing his advice so soon after he'd become Anansi's Chosen One? James hoped he wouldn't take too much offense, since it really would make the legend of James Robard less interesting if he was constantly receiving advice from an eons-old god.

"Lord Anansi says that he didn't have enough faith in you," Hester said brightly. "Next time you're in a battle to the death, he won't give you advice unless he thinks you'll die without it."

"That's great!" James whispered, barely moving his lips. "I think. Hm."

"Yeah," Hester said. "I think he took that well. Probably!"

"You saying something, dude?" Chris asked from behind James.

"No, man!" James replied. "I just talk to myself sometimes."

"Sorry, Hester," he whispered even more quietly than before. "I'm not going to introduce you to anyone. Your information and advice are sort of a trump card, you know?"

"Sure, of course!" She sounded pleased. "As for the way the transmissions feel, I don't want you to worry about it too much. But I think the closest analogy for a human is that it's a bit like a headache throughout my entire body."

A few minutes later they reached Moishe. He was slowly trudging forward with Officer Ross on his back. Moishe turned around as James moved into view, and James immediately noticed that Officer Ross looked different than before. The bullet wound on his forehead had completely healed over somehow.

There's a story there, James thought.

"You did it, then?" Moishe exclaimed. "You killed Rostov?"

James nodded and grinned.

"Easy peasy," he said.

"Uh, yeah, what he said," Chris agreed from behind him.

"Somehow I knew you would," Moishe said. His eyes had a look of trust in them that James recognized from the other people he'd rescued.

"Anything interesting happen since we parted ways?" James asked, gesturing at the body on Moishe's back.

"Oh, you're wondering about our dreamer here," Moishe said.

He quickly explained what had happened.

"Hm. Got it. You should set him down, I think," James said slowly.

"Uh, why?" Moishe asked.

"His pulse and breathing have changed," James said. "I think he's about to wake up."

"Sure thing, then." He put Ross down, neither gently nor carelessly, on the ground. "What next?"

"Next, I think I'd better have a chat with him," James said. "These two are joining us." He gestured at Hilda and Chris. "They helped me fight Rostov, and I think we can trust them."

"Hilda," Moishe said, nodding at the warrior in white. His eyes narrowed as he looked at Chris. "Surprised to see you here, Roach."

"And yet here I am," Chris said with a grimace and a little shrug.

"Well, I guess if James and Hilda trust you, I'll trust you," Moishe said. But he was obviously reluctant.

"I trust him," Hilda said. "He helped free the people who were going to be sacrificed, and he pulled me out of range when James launched his final attack at Rostov. If Rostov had survived what happened today, Chris would've been one of the first in line to be sacrificed."

Moishe looked mollified.

"What do you want us to do now, then?" he asked, turning back to James.

"Take these two and meet up with the prisoners," James said. "Same way you were walking. They should be waiting right on the border with the Dead Marsh."

"The Dead Marsh?!" Chris said.

"I guess you're familiar with it," James said.

"What are we going near there for?" Chris asked.

"The cult chased my group into that region, so we're going to go and pull off another rescue mission," James said. "Of course, if you're unwilling to join up with us, you're welcome to split off now and find your way on your own."

Chris frowned deeply.

"Of course we'll assist you," Hilda said, giving Chris a sharp look.

"Yeah," Chris breathed. "Yeah, that's the way, of course. That's how we work off the bad deeds. I guess this is just my karma."

"Sounds about right," Moishe said. "We can leave right away." He was looking down at Ross, whose body twitched slightly as Moishe spoke.

The others glanced down at Ross, then said their goodbyes—for now—to James and walked off, following Moishe's lead.

"Why'd you send them away?" Hester asked once the group was out of earshot.

"Still haven't quite figured out what to do with this guy," James said, voice low. "I need to talk to him alone. The situation is *complicated* by what happened to his wife."

"I see. Good thing he's not awake yet, I guess? Wouldn't want him to have overheard everything if you're trying to figure out what his reaction is going to be."

"He's not," James said. "I would be able to tell. I have Dreamwalk and superhuman Perception. I don't think anyone besides a god would be able to fake being asleep in the same room as me now. It's very shallow sleep, though."

"Oh, I guess that makes sense. Are you going to wake him up, then?"

"Yeah, just as soon as I'm confident that the others are out of earshot. This conversation might get a bit dicey."

Hester's body warmed noticeably for a split second.

"Another Anansi message?" James asked.

"This time he just sent a little mental image," Hester replied. "It's an image of a spider sitting on top of something. I'm not sure what exactly this is." Hester described what she saw.

"Oh, it's a spider eating popcorn," James said. "Great. I hope we'll provide excellent entertainment."

When Jeffrey Ross's eyes opened, the sun was high in the sky.

"Where am I?" he asked. "What happened?"

"What do you remember?" asked a familiar voice.

It took a moment for Jeff's eyes to adjust to the light, and he was also a little too dazed to easily recognize the voice. In the end, his vision and hearing confirmed almost at the same time that he was lying down in front of James Robard.

Ross shot up to a sitting position as soon as he knew who it was. The world spun for a moment. He reached a hand out and leaned on a nearby rock to steady himself.

"Whoa there, try not to make too many sudden movements," James said. He looked ill at ease, and it made Ross nervous to see it. "You should know, you took a pretty serious injury earlier, and I'm not entirely sure how well you've recovered."

"Injury?" Ross asked. His memory felt fuzzy. He remembered shooting Nikolai Rostov in the head, but the visual memory looked like an old grainy film reel in his mind. When he tried to reach forward past that, his mind went black.

"Yes, you had an injury," James said. "Like I was saying before, you should tell me what you remember, and I'll help you fill in the blanks after that."

"I remember . . ." Ross said. He let out a long breath and gathered his thoughts. Could he trust James? What were the pros and cons of telling him the truth here?

Fuck it. If he didn't tell him the truth, he wouldn't get any information about what was going on.

"I remember shooting Rostov *for you*," Ross continued. "I remember putting a bullet in his brain. That's the last thing in my memory. I think I was going to leave the tent after that, but there's just a blank where everything else should be."

"Okay," James said. "Well, the parts you're missing are painful." A moment of hesitation. He looked torn, and Ross wanted to shake him.

Out with it, man!

"You said you'd tell me what I'm missing," Ross reminded him.

"Yeah, yeah, I did. Just trying to say it in a respectful way. So, after you shot Rostov, he turned into a flaming monster. A battle ensued where he was destroying everything around him indiscriminately. He killed a lot of cult members. But his first target was you. He threw that bullet you fired at him right back at you. You took a serious, probably fatal, head injury. I asked Moishe Rose to carry you off."

"Wait, what? Fatal injury? And Moishe carried me? You've got to be shitting me! There's no way he'd do tha—"

"Let me get to the bad part, please, Jeff."

So, me taking a bullet to the head wasn't the bad part. Ross clenched his fingers around some grass and tried to control his expression.

Quietly, he said, "It's that bad, huh?"

Silence from James. Was that guilt in his expression? He had such a good poker face that it was hard to be sure.

"Tell me, then! It's about Catherine, isn't it?"

She got hurt too? But where is she?

"Yes."

"What *happened* to Catherine?"

"She sacrificed herself to save your life," James said.

What?

A flurry of emotions flashed across Ross's face. *Catherine dead? How could this—*

James spoke again before Ross could say anything. "Don't blame yourself, Jeff," he murmured. "She made her choice because she loved y—"

"I don't blame myself," Ross said hotly. "I blame you!" His face contorted in an expression of seething anger. "I never should have listened to you, you crazy bastard." Tears pooled in the corners of his eyes.

James just sat quietly across from him and let Ross continue.

"If it hadn't been for you, we would've both survived this place and rid ourselves of that maniac as soon as Orientation was over. Why the hell did you have to interfere?"

James continued to stare silently at Ross, his expression almost completely blank as the latter spoke.

"Well? What do you have to say for yourself? What do you—"

Meteor Strike.

James's fist, wrapped in flames, crashed through Ross's ribs like they were made of matchsticks. Ross's lungs started cooking as soon as the flames entered his body.

It felt to James a bit like he was touching raw chicken breasts. Ross's lungs were soft and moist, and they resisted his efforts to scorch them. James could tell that Ross must have an unusually high reserve of Health. Not high enough to withstand the destruction of his organs, but high enough to make it take a little longer to kill him.

"Ugh—you—how did you—" Ross seemed incapable of finishing a sentence.

"I wanted to let you say everything you needed to say before I did this," James said, holding eye contact with the man he was killing. "I've realized recently that I'm a little too lenient with folks. Letting people go who could become a threat in the future. At some point, I have to nip things in the bud. And you were obviously in that category." James finally allowed his emotion to show through a little bit on his face. A slightly pitying expression. He was genuinely sad to kill Ross.

I'm sorry you have to die, he thought. *I really wanted you to live through all this.* There was no point in saying any of this out loud now, of course.

"But how—*guh*—" Ross's arm flailed in the direction of the hand that impaled his chest.

"How did I smash you apart so easily even though you've been through Race Evolution?" James asked.

Ross managed a movement that resembled a nod, blood gently trickling from his mouth as he dipped his head. He seemed to lack the ability to lift his head back up after he nodded it, but James understood.

"That's a long story," James said, smiling sadly. "And despite your very impressive Fortitude, you won't be here long enough to appreciate it."

A quick death would be the most merciful. He grabbed hold of Ross's heart with his flaming hand. And squeezed. Tight, firm, pulsating muscle turned to charred putty in James's grip.

[You killed Jeffrey Ross, Lv. 11! You gained 1300 exp!]

Pillage. He chose to take one of Ross's Talents for himself.

[Talent obtained: Marksmanship!]

Hm. Hopefully, that will have some utility beyond the use of guns. I can throw most projectiles faster now than a gun can, I think. He would check it out later.

He directed everything that had belonged to Ross, including the man's pistol, into his magic satchel. Then he cast water magic and cleaned his hands off.

"Hey, boss?" Hester asked, finally breaking the silence as James picked at the flecks of blood buried under his nails.

"Yeah?"

"Um, a-are you okay?"

"Not a scratch on me," James replied. "I took him completely by surprise."

"Yeah, but—" She hesitated, then pressed on. "You knew that guy from before your world got processed into the System, I think you said at some point. Right?"

"Yes, I did."

"So, are you feeling all right, um, emotionally?" she asked.

"I did what needed to be done, Hester. You saw what his immediate reaction was. After what happened, I understand it, but I'm realizing I've been a little bit careless in the past, if not reckless. A bit too *idealistic*, maybe. Charging into fights with the odds against me. Sparing people just because I don't have the stomach to kill them. Just because I know they might have loved ones out there somewhere. Well, letting people go who have a bone to pick with me just isn't going to work out well in the long term. I have a family to protect. They come first." James's voice was stone cold.

"None of that answered my question," Hester observed.

"Heh. Right you are. Well, thank you for worrying about me. But I'll be fine." There was a hollow note in his voice as he spoke.

In the long run, it was my family or his getting destroyed, James thought. He imagined the children he'd just orphaned. *I'll do something for them when I escape this place.*

The dark voice in his mind said, *Put it behind you. You still have wars to win.*

That's right. Now it's time to reunite with my group so we can finish this Orientation.

CHAPTER THIRTY-EIGHT

Assistance Is Futile

I hope everyone enjoys their breakfast," DaSilva said, beaming at the Cook. "You should all thank Alba for cooking for us after this."

"It's really my pleasure," Alba said evenly. "Please enjoy. I have to go and find my own team."

"Well, if you ever want to ditch them, we could definitely use someone like you!" DaSilva said.

She gave the group a little smile and walked away.

"Isn't it nice, all of us getting together like this?" Karen said.

"Mm-hmm," Frank nodded in agreement, mouth full of food.

The group's rations had gotten a little tighter rather than looser since the last challenge, despite their unbroken winning streak. But today, they were eating more freely. They would need energy for the challenge they were about to face, after all.

They had just gathered for the team breakfast when the announcement rang out.

[Attention all survivors! The next challenge will begin soon. Unlike previous challenges, all survivors must participate in the upcoming event. You have thirty minutes to prepare yourselves.]

The announcement sent Cara, Paulo, and Jean into hurried speculation about what the next challenge must be. Meanwhile, others remained studiously quiet, avoiding making comments.

"I'm betting the challenge is a team sport," Cara said. "That's the only reason I can imagine why everyone would have to play. We seem to be such a strong team that it's hard to imagine us losing." She smiled with such sunny optimism that even DaSilva, despite his generally positive outlook, couldn't help envying it.

"Such a beautiful day when we walked over here," Frank said.

"I think the snow might be done for the season," Karen added. "Assuming there are seasons in this place, and it's not just endless winter."

"Or it's a no-holds-barred combat in an arena," Paulo suggested, replying to Cara. "Maybe we're not allowed to opt out because they don't want only the strongest members of each team competing."

"That sounds terrible," Jean said, paling visibly.

"I don't think they'd make us all participate in such a violent competition," Frank said, giving up on small talk and finally weighing in on his teammates' conversation.

"No, that's exactly the sort of thing they would let us opt out of," Karen agreed, speaking through her food. "Think about the last Dungeon. It was only slightly dangerous, but the System gave us a warning so that we wouldn't take anyone who didn't want to be in that situation." Her eyes cast only a flickering glance in Mina's direction, but DaSilva noticed it, and he didn't think he was the only one.

"Last time, there were parts of the Dungeon that I almost couldn't imagine us completing without Mina," Yulia said quietly. "I'm relieved she'll be with us this time. Hopefully, there are riddles or other puzzles. Then we'll have the advantage."

You have a lot of faith in your sister, don't you? DaSilva thought, looking down at Yulia affectionately. It was not the first time he'd noticed this, and he doubted it would be the last. Right now, however, Mina was straining *his* faith.

She was supposed to use her Investigate Skill on each member of the team, then signal to DaSilva which of their colleagues had tried to kill him. But so far, she hadn't given the signal. And it seemed to DaSilva that she was staring at her plate, trying not to make eye contact with him or anyone else.

She looked up for a moment at the mention of her name. "Whatever the competition is, I'll try not to slow the rest of you down." Her eyes dropped right back to her food.

Okay, what am I missing? Does her Skill not work as well as it's supposed to or something?

It was frustrating. He wanted to know who had tried to throw him from a bridge into a river of lava in the last challenge. If he went into the next challenge without narrowing the suspect pool, he'd have to watch his back around *everyone*.

Kind of makes me wish I'd switched to another team, but that would leave everyone on this team wondering why. Mina and Yulia would be left on their own, which would be irresponsible of me. And I would have only made it harder on myself trying to find the murderer.

* * *

Yes, Detective, Mina thought, *I can feel you looking at me. No, I don't know who the killer is, or I would give the signal.* She had used Investigate on every member of the team already as they had arrived at breakfast. Then she had double-checked her work.

Everyone's Status information seemed normal. Either Detective DaSilva's reckoning about who the killer might be was off, or someone on their team had a Skill to change the appearance of their Status information.

Mina finally made eye contact with DaSilva and gave him a subtle shake of her head.

He seemed to understand. He stopped giving off all his little signs of impatience. His face and body language shifted to puzzlement and concerned resignation.

"What sort of challenge do you think it's going to be, Mina?" Adelaide asked.

"If I'm lucky, it will be puzzles or riddles like Yulia said," Mina replied. "Hell, I'd settle for video games or a poetry slam!"

"Now that would be nice and relaxing," Derek said. "Video games and a poetry slam. Not exactly what they've got us used to doing so far, but I think I could manage."

"I think I'd prefer the fighting," Paulo said. Then, "Ow!"

Jose had elbowed him in the ribs.

"Whoops," he said. "Sorry." He gave Paulo a stern look. Paulo's eyes darted toward Mina. Jose's eyes shifted toward Yulia, who averted her eyes and turned slightly pink.

"Ah, yeah, it's probably not that, anyway," Paulo said.

It's a little annoying that everyone's looking at me as if I'm made of glass, Mina thought. *I can't deny that I'm vulnerable right now, but I still don't want them to think I'm a burden. And I don't want to* be *a burden either.*

"Everyone get ready!" DaSilva called out.

"Oh, right," Mina said. *The timer.*

[00:00:45]

Mina reached over and took Yulia's hand, and the sisters smiled at each other. Then Mina gave the table a last look. Everyone looked at least a bit apprehensive. She was glad it wasn't just her.

And then they were gone.

Mina blinked. She could feel, even before she opened her eyes, that her hand was empty. Yulia was gone somewhere else.

There was a moment of fear before she realized *everyone* was gone. She was alone. In front of her was a seamless stone wall. Nothing but pure gray rock. There was no veining, no colors. Just a single, perfect shade of gray. *Not like anything I've ever seen. What is this material?* It seemed to be perfectly smooth, unlike cement. Mina felt an almost irresistible urge to run her fingers across it, and before she knew it, she did. The stone felt just as smooth as it looked, more like a pane of cold glass than a dense and heavy rock. She wondered if she could take a chunk of it with her.

"Hey, Mina!" a voice called.

Mina jumped slightly and turned toward the sound.

There stood Cara Dahlhaus, looking like a fierce Valkyrie in her armor, her long blonde hair pulled back in a tight ponytail. *Thank goodness! I thought I was going to have to complete whatever challenge this is by myself.*

"Good to see you!" Mina said. *I really hope you're not a murderer.*

"Yeah, you too!" Cara said, smiling.

[You find yourselves isolated from most of your teammates, scattered within a grand maze.]

The voice of the proctor came from all directions, as if the walls, floor, and ceiling were speakers. Perhaps they were. There was only a slight echo off of the perfect stone surfaces. As Mina and Cara looked around, checking for landmarks and signs of life, the most striking detail was that the walls, floor, and ceiling were all made from the same material. The floor was slightly rougher than the walls, probably because people needed to be able to get traction when they moved across it.

The ceiling sat ten feet above the floor. As if the System had to accommodate something unreasonably large that lived in the maze.

And there was an almost imperceptible gap between the ceiling and the walls, where some form of artificial lighting came through. Cold, sterile white light. It felt like the fluorescent lighting that always made Mina feel like she looked ten years older than she was.

[Your task is a deceptively simple one. You must escape the maze within the time limit. Simple tasks are not always easy, however.]

A timer appeared in the corner of Mina's vision.

[05:00:00]

[You are not alone within the vastness of the maze. Your fellow challengers are scattered within the same structure as yourselves. Other life-forms stalk the corridors of the maze. This challenge is primarily one of navigation. Those who are among the first to complete the maze will be handsomely rewarded. The teams that have the most members complete the maze will be the winners. Naturally, anyone who dies within the maze is disqualified.]

Mina shuddered slightly at those last words. Then she felt a hand on her wrist, and she almost jumped again.

"Sorry," Cara said. Naturally, it was her hand on Mina's wrist. With her other hand, she rubbed the back of her neck, a sheepish look on her face. "Just wanted to get moving now that the announcement seems to be over."

"Yeah," Mina said. The silence had only lasted a moment before Cara approached her, but now it felt almost deafening. A creepy void hung in the air whenever neither of them were speaking. "We can get a head start if we're smart."

I need to stick close to this girl, Mina thought. Up close, it was obvious that Cara was physically more imposing than Mina. She hadn't been this muscular on the first day, Mina seemed to recall. The warrior Classes probably got some amount of physical growth when they leveled up. DaSilva was a bit bigger than he had been on the first day too, now that she thought about it. And his jawline was slightly more defined, his physique less pudgy than it had been.

But these things were only obvious now that she and Cara were standing so close. The blonde woman had once been noticeably shorter than Mina. Now they were almost eye to eye.

I could probably get that if I invested a few extra points in Strength too, Mina realized. But she had been determinedly building up her Intelligence and Will, the better to double down on her strong suit: magic.

"Where do you think we should go?" Cara asked.

Mina realized she'd been thinking silently to herself for a while. And Cara wasn't the leader type. Despite her well-muscled arms and confident pose in her Light Warrior armor, her tone betrayed a lack of confidence. She needed Mina's wits.

"Let's start out by just walking down this path to see where it goes," Mina said. "I'll keep one hand on this wall, you keep one hand on the other wall, and once we see if there are any openings on either side, we'll decide what to do next."

Cara nodded and smiled. The pair began walking.

Looking down the path a little way, it was obvious that this part of the maze was curved. Both the inner and outer walls. Mina already had thoughts on what that might mean, but the only way to test those hypotheses out was to maneuver some distance along the wall and see what they found.

"Hey, I found an opening!" Cara said after a minute of walking.

"That's great!" Mina turned to look at Cara's wall. The opening was a perfectly rectangular cutout in the stone, roughly the same height as the ceiling.

Too smooth of a cut for a human tool, Mina couldn't help but think. Just like the walls were smoother and more featureless than human-carved stone would normally be.

"Well done, Cara," Mina said after examining the opening and poking her head through. "Can you mark this opening, and we'll explore for a few minutes more?"

Cara nodded. Then she drew her sword and slashed fiercely downward at the wall.

I'd hate to be on the wrong side of her, Mina thought.

Despite the visible Strength on display, she only made a small nick in the wall. Cara frowned as if disappointed, but Mina smiled.

"Good job! I think these walls are made out of something super tough. Now we'll know which opening this is if there's more than one exit to this section of the maze."

Cara looked satisfied at that, and the two women continued walking.

Several minutes passed.

"I found another—no, wait. This is the same opening!" Cara declared.

"Hm. Well, we have to go through this one, then. We're already figuring this maze out!" Mina said. She walked on through with no hesitation.

Did I just waste the last few minutes? I could almost tell we were walking in a circle, but it was difficult with how big the loop was. How big is this maze if this is just one section? Is it more like a labyrinth, or just a maze? Labyrinths, Mina knew, typically had only one entrance and exit. If this maze was really a labyrinth, then there was only one possible route. If that was the case, then this was a race to be won rather than a puzzle to be solved.

No! Mina shook her head. *That would be so stupid! The System wouldn't waste our time like that. Right?*

She looked at Cara following behind her. Mina faked a smile and gave Cara a confident thumbs up.

"Let's keep doing the same thing we did in the last section, Cara. Could you mark this wall like you did on the other side?"

"Sure thing!" Cara swung her sword down and made a slightly bigger scratch on this wall than she had on the last one. Mina had the distinct idea that Cara was trying to show off, so she tried to look impressed.

Once again, Cara took the outside wall while Mina took the inside wall.

At first they walked in silence. Mina took advantage of the quiet and continued trying to unravel the mystery of the maze inside her own mind.

It can't be a labyrinth, Mina thought. *If it were, we would have all started in the same place. You either start on the outside of the labyrinth or in the center. Everyone knows that! Which means there are correct routes and incorrect routes, and there must be a logical way of deducing them. You can't just speedrun this maze. And if Cara's difficulty in even scratching the walls is any indication, you can't smash your way out of it either. I don't think she could chop through that stone even if her Strength was ten times what it is. This is a battle of pure wits.*

"I've realized we've never actually had a one-on-one conversation, Mina," Cara said.

"That's true," Mina said, hoping Cara would take the hint and stop talking.

Nope.

"Where are you from?" Cara asked.

"Bulgaria originally, Orange County now," Mina said. She paused for a moment, then reluctantly asked, "Where are you from?"

"Well, I was born in California, but I love to travel!" Cara gushed. "I think of myself as something of a citizen of the world. This country alone is so big, and there's still so much I haven't seen, so I don't stay anywhere long."

Please, some god or other, kill me now, Mina thought. *I'm never going to solve this maze with her going on like this!*

"Where did you go to college?" Mina asked, trying to be politely curious.

"Oh, I like to think of myself as a student of life, you know?"

Kill me. Kill me now.

"I see," Mina said, trying to fake a smile.

"I guess you went to school, though? You seem very book smart."

"Well, thank you." *I think? Or is she implying that I'm not some other kind of smart?* "I studied engineering."

"Oh, that's awesome! Totally suits you. You know, I always thought I'd go back to school, but life just has so much else to do," Cara said.

"Makes sense. A degree can take up a lot of mental energy. I'm sure you found plenty of other things to do." Mina tried not to sound condescending as that last sentence left her mouth. "Say, did you know Jean before this place?" She had just remembered that although this conversation was trying to kill her every brain cell, it was theoretically possible she might learn something of value to the investigation if she asked good questions.

"You know, I *did* find lots of other things to do." Cara launched into a description of her non-educational activities that made Mina want to cut her own ears off.

"How did you find yourself in Florida when this whole thing started?" Mina made herself ask, trying to cut off whatever rambling narrative Cara was probably about to spin out of her decision to not go to college.

"Oh, that's a crazy story!" Cara launched into a story about a friend of her cousin who won the lottery and decided to fly everyone she knew to Disney World.

"Oh, wow," Mina said halfheartedly.

In the midst of the extended story, Cara had located a door and marked it. Mina thought it would be wise to keep walking and see if there were further doors. She was now counting her footsteps between doors while trying to vaguely keep track of Cara's story.

This girl is going to kill me, Mina thought. She was good at dividing her attention, but this seemed like a waste of her willpower and patience so early in the challenge. Yet she was too polite to tell Cara to shut it. And Cara was helpful. Sort of.

"Oh, a second door!" Cara exclaimed.

"All right, mark this one too, okay?" Mina said. "But find a different way of doing it this time, if you can."

Cara nodded obediently. She swung her sword at a different angle this time, using it almost like a baseball bat. This time she left a horizontal scratch, easily distinguishable from the first one.

The two women continued walking and lapsed into silence for a little while. Long enough for Mina to decide what theory she should act on if they came upon the first outward-facing door again, as Mina began to suspect they would.

Sure enough, after a few minutes of walking, Cara burst out, "Look, I found the first door again!"

"That's perfect," Mina said. "Poke your head through and tell me if you see anything interesting."

"No problem," Cara said. She raised her sword again and held it in a ready position in front of her as she advanced through the door.

"See anything?" Mina called.

"Just a hallway like the one we were just in!" Cara replied. "Except this one has a dead end on one side."

"All right! I know just what I want us to do. Let's go back to the other door you marked."

"Sure." Cara walked back into the hall where Mina was and shook her head as if she didn't get why one door was any different from another. "Say, Mina, is there anything I can do to help you figure this place out?"

"You're already doing it, honestly," Mina said. "I couldn't ask you to do anything that's more helpful than marking doors and quietly leading the way into unsecured places."

"Oh, well, I'm glad to be helping, then," Cara said. She looked thoughtful. "Quietly, huh?"

Mina tried not to look too pleased that Cara might be taking the hint. If the other woman would be a bit quieter, that would undoubtedly be the best assistance she could give.

I'm starting to have a hypothesis about the structure of this maze, Mina thought. *Really just a wild guess based on nothing but my imagination and wishful thinking, but maybe the System has an architect somewhere who built this thing. Maybe the architect is as nerdy as I am. And maybe the maze is constructed the way I'm imagining.*

They proceeded to the other opening and walked through. It was another, almost identical, hallway. Curved like the previous hallways had been.

No dead ends in sight, Mina thought. *Not like the exit that Cara explored for a moment alone.* She considered this difference to be a good sign. *The best test of my theory is to figure out if this section has three, four, or a different number of exits.*

The two women walked until they found the first opening on the outside wall of the hallway. They stopped so that Cara could slash another mark into that wall.

Cara started walking again as soon as she'd made her mark. But Mina lingered beside that opening. It was identical to the other rectangular holes in the walls that they'd seen thus far, but there was something about it that made Mina hesitate.

It took her a minute to realize what it was that held her attention: the sound of footsteps. Something was walking toward them on the other side of that wall.

CHAPTER THIRTY-NINE

A Shade of Gray

The sound of footsteps drew closer as Mina's mind worked quickly to decide what they should do next.

"Hey, don't worry," Cara said, intruding on her thoughts. Mina turned and saw the other woman had assumed a fighting pose with her sword drawn. "If there are enemies, I'll protect you and your baby." She flashed Mina a confident grin.

To think I was so annoyed at you just a minute or so ago. Mina felt slightly guilty, but she silently stepped to the side and let Cara stand closer to the opening in the wall.

As they waited, Cara took a moment to quietly throw out a question. "Boy or girl, by the way?"

There was something about the way those words came out that rubbed Mina slightly the wrong way. As if one of the two were a wrong answer.

But maybe she was just a bit tired of suppressing her annoyance at the other woman's chatter, and she was starting to read too much into her tone.

"We wanted to be surprised," she lied. *We know, but we're not telling*, she wanted to say. But she decided to trust her initial misgivings. Mina's instincts about people were usually pretty good.

And then the footsteps they'd heard drew near and stopped.

There was a long moment of shared silence. The people on the other side of the wall didn't move. Mina and Cara didn't say anything. Cara remained poised to strike.

"Are we just going to stand here all day?" a voice finally called from the other side of the wall.

"Shut up!" another voice said, responding to the first. Both were male.

"Ugh, men," Cara muttered under her breath. She backed slightly further away from the entrance, changed her stance slightly, and pointed her sword straight at the entrance. The impression she gave was that she was ready to immediately spring at the first person to show himself.

Mina's eyes widened. *We can't afford to start a fight here!*

"Why are you two standing there in the first place?" she asked loudly.

"We could ask you the same thing!" the first voice called back immediately.

"We hoped you might be members of our group," Mina replied instantly. She had actually been worried the footsteps might be maze-dwelling monsters at first, but that concern implied that she and Cara might have been preparing an ambush, so she didn't voice it.

"Well, clearly you can tell by our voices we're not," the second voice said calmly, diplomatically.

Then Mina saw a shape move across the opening in the maze. One of these two was showing himself. Mina gestured at Cara to lower her sword, and she complied with visible reluctance.

A man appeared, standing by the far wall on the other side of the entrance. He had positioned himself cautiously, a safe distance away in case of attack. Mina noticed he looked vaguely familiar—tall, well-built, brunette with buzz-cut hair.

Cara wasn't going to hit him unless she could lunge a pretty good distance, anyway, Mina thought. As much as the other woman looked like a Viking, Mina had seen her Status information. She knew that Cara was still fairly low level.

"Oh, I recognize you!" the man said. It was the owner of the first voice, Mina noticed. The one who had seemed impatient before. "Hey, come on out, Keith!"

The second man poked his head out from alongside the near wall. He was positioned, Mina noticed, to be able to spring out and intercept any surprise attack that they might have directed at his companion.

They're careful, she noted.

She also immediately recognized the second man, who had long blond hair and reminded her of commercials for beach and surfing products. She noticed he seemed slightly sweaty—surprising considering that the maze had so far been a reasonable approximation of room temperature.

"Hey, it's you!" Keith said, smiling. "The lady who wanted to share food with the losing team."

"It's me!" Mina said, smiling with relief.

Keith stepped through the entryway and extended his hand to Mina. She gave him a firm grip and shook his hand. In her peripheral vision, she noticed Cara had backed further away.

Can't show fear, Cara, Mina thought. *That's when people get the idea that you're vulnerable. Most people aren't looking for vulnerability all the time. They only notice it when it's presented.*

"Do you guys want to go through the rest of the maze together?" Keith asked.

"You just going to make that call without even asking me?" his companion said irritably.

"Don't mind Terry, here," Keith said. "He's just like this all the time. Doesn't like making new friends for some reason."

"Humph," Terry scoffed.

Mina didn't need to turn around to observe Cara's body language. She could feel the tension coming from the edge of her peripheral vision.

I obviously need to reject this offer one way or another, she thought.

"Well, if we joined you or you joined us, we'd probably be going the wrong way," Mina said. "At least, in my mental model of the maze so far, I don't think we're supposed to take these paths that intersect with each other. We wouldn't get closer to the outside of the maze, and neither would you."

"Oh, so you think you've figured this out already?" Keith asked, curious.

"Not exactly figured it out, but I have a working theory," Mina admitted. "I don't think it would be productive for us to move together, though. Unless you're both willing to follow my lead and do whatever I suggest, when I suggest it."

Terry's body was mostly blocked from view by Keith standing in the opening, but Mina could tell he bristled at that suggestion just from the way his shoulder stiffened.

"This isn't marksmanship, lady!" Terry said. "We have no reason to follow your know-it-all ass anywhere."

"Please forgive my friend's rudeness," Keith said, turning his head to throw a glare at his companion. "We've been having a difficult time these last couple of challenges."

"My fucking rudeness!" Terry growled. "You want to follow her? It would just be the blind leading the blind."

"I think maybe we'd better go our separate ways," Mina said gently.

"Yeah," Keith agreed unhappily, turning back to face her. He stepped back into the section of the maze he'd come from.

And Mina and Cara began to walk away.

"Thanks for getting rid of those guys," Cara said once they were out of earshot of the two men. "Maybe I'm paranoid, but I just felt like they were bad news."

"Well, Keith seemed nice enough, but I wouldn't want to trust my back to Terry," Mina replied.

They walked in silence for several more minutes. Then Cara stopped suddenly. She put a finger to her lips. Mina stepped back so that she could position herself closer to Cara. If they were going to be ambushed, she didn't want to be standing alone.

"Did you hear that?" Cara whispered once Mina was close.

Mina shook her head.

"We're being followed," Cara whispered with an air of certainty. "Whoever it was stopped moving when we stopped moving. Probably humans. Those two guys." She nodded to herself.

"Okay, I trust your senses," Mina replied quietly. She looked around and spotted the next door. "When we start moving again, mark that door and then go through it." She pointed.

Cara nodded and smiled.

Then they started walking again. Mina still couldn't hear the sounds of anyone following in their footsteps, but she trusted Cara's Light Warrior senses above her own anyway. And the next few minutes would prove or disprove the idea that they were being followed.

Cara took her usual heavy swing at the wall near the opening and left a long vertical scar in the stone.

Is she getting stronger as we go along? Mina wondered. Either that, or it had taken Cara a while to figure out the precise amount of physical power she needed to use to do real damage to the rock.

She and Cara stepped through the opening. Then Mina moved counter-clockwise and pulled her through another opening. They stepped far enough away from the opening in that area that their shadows would not be visible to passersby looking through the opening. The passage had a dead end, so they stood with their backs by the wall that capped off the passageway.

And they waited.

Several minutes passed, but both women maintained a disciplined silence. Mina's heart began to beat faster as she heard distant noise. *What was that?*

The deafening quiet resumed. *Was that sound real?*

There was nothing for a few long seconds. Then another sound. A distant *clomp*. Definitely some kind of movement. A footfall? *Yes*, she thought. That was it. But was the mover walking away or getting closer?

The next sound that Mina heard was the tread of footsteps approaching, close outside the passage where she and Cara hid. Then there were two familiar voices.

"Where the fuck are they?" Terry said angrily.

"I told you we should've just apologized," Keith said.

"Where do we go now? Tell me that instead!"

"Why can't you chill out, man?" Keith asked.

"After that last challenge, you aren't in a position to scold me anymore!" Terry declared.

There was a sound of steel clanking against steel, and then Cara and Mina listened to the sounds of a struggle between the two men. The wall vibrated slightly with what Mina took to be the weight of two armored bodies slamming into it. Then there was a squelching sound, like a boot stepping into mud or a knife sinking into flesh. The sound repeated itself once, twice, a third time. There was a terrible gasp and a choking sound.

Then Mina could only hear the sound of heavy breathing and one man making small, quick, efficient movements in armor. She wished she could see what was happening.

There was the sound of footsteps again. This time they were walking away.

Mina waited for Cara to nod that it was okay to move before she walked toward the opening. Even then, she poked her head out and cautiously looked both ways before she stepped out.

She sucked in a sharp breath at what she saw.

"What is it?" Cara asked anxiously from behind her. "Are they still there?"

"No," Mina said quietly. "*They're* not."

She stepped out. Keith lay in a bloody heap on the floor, breathing ragged, shallow breaths, eyes shut. His armor looked to be intact, but his body gushed blood from at least three stab wounds. Those were just the injuries that Mina could see—one under the right shoulder, one near the right hip, and one on the left thigh. Terry had done a good job of targeting the gaps in Keith's armor.

Jesus, Mina thought. *Jesus Christ.*

She approached, knelt next to him, and began rummaging through her Small Bag of Deceptive Dimensions.

"What are you doing?" Cara hissed, stepping into the passage and looking up and down the hall anxiously. "The other guy could come back any second. We have to get out of here!"

"Then find a Health Potion if you can," Mina said evenly without looking up. "I'm not just going to leave Keith here to die. The faster we get a Health Potion in him, the sooner we can leave."

"Doesn't he have anything?" Cara asked.

"No, the other guy took his bag."

Keith's eyes flickered open and shut at the sounds next to him. Mina caught his eye for a moment and gave him a small nod. She couldn't tell whether he was even able to focus on what he was seeing, but then she saw a small smile spread over his lips.

He breathed a word out, barely audible. "Thanks."

Finally, Mina found a Health Potion, yanked out the stopper, and shoved it in his mouth. Keith drank, wasting a little when he had trouble swallowing, but ultimately, he finished most of it.

"Now we can go," Mina said quietly. Cara was hovering over her shoulder like a vulture waiting for death.

They ducked back into the opening they'd come through when they fled the sound of pursuing footsteps. Mina walked them to the next opening. This was where she'd originally planned to exit the third passage.

"Don't bother marking this one," she told Cara. "I don't want Terry to know which way we went if he retraces his steps."

"You're infuriating, you know that?" Cara said as she followed Mina through the opening. "You're clearly smarter than everyone else around us, and you seem to know your way around here well enough already. Plus, you have me to protect you." She puffed herself up as she said that last. "All of which means you and I could finish first. But we probably won't. Why did you bother stopping for that guy? He and his friend are both assholes."

"How the hell do you know that?" Mina stopped and looked Cara dead in the eye.

"How do I know?" Cara repeated.

"Yes." Mina gave her a long cold look as she spoke. "How do you *know* that Keith is an asshole with such certainty that you're comfortable leaving him to die? I understood you wanting to get out of there at the time. I was afraid that Terry would come back too. I really appreciate you being a lookout. But I don't understand why you're still talking about it."

Cara seemed to shrink a little inside herself under Mina's withering gaze.

"I just know the type," she said after a long silence. "You're a nice person, Mina, but I can tell you don't have a lot of real-world experience with bad men. People generally aren't as kind to each other as I've seen you tend to be. Most guys aren't like Jean and Detective DaSilva—"

"You know nothing about my life experiences before I came here," Mina replied, cutting her off. "You're just guessing. Poorly."

"Uh, sorry." Cara's voice grew small and quiet.

After they had walked in silence for a minute, Mina put an arm around Cara's shoulders.

"I may have been a little harsh," Mina said. "I just try not to engage in black and white thinking, and I react against it a bit forcefully when I see it in others. Most people are a shade of gray. You're a sweet girl, and I really like your protective instinct. I feel like you could be a good mother someday."

"Bleh," Cara said, grimacing and shaking her head. "I wouldn't—Oh, my gosh!" She pointed at another rectangular opening in the wall. "There's the fourth opening. That's where we're going, right?"

"No," Mina said. "We're looking for the fifth one, if it exists. I like where your head is at, though."

They kept walking until they found the fifth exit. Mina led them through it, then through the eighth exit from that passageway. In the next passageway, Mina led them through the thirteenth opening.

"Okay, I think I get it," Cara said. "There's addition involved here. You're not just counting the number of passageways and picking a number of openings based on that. The exit you choose is the number of the last two openings you passed through combined. We went through the eighth exit, and before that the fifth exit of the last passageway, so now you took us through the thirteenth exit. What I don't get is how you picked out this pattern. I guess I can understand how you know it's correct since we've been able to keep advancing over and over again."

"It's the Fibonacci sequence," Mina said. "The golden ratio. It was just a hunch at first, but it kept confirming itself based on the number of exits available. At some point we'll be in a passageway with more exits than the Fibonacci number we should be on, and then knowing that's the structure will really come in handy."

"Um, sure," Cara said. "How did you know that, though? Where did the hunch come from?"

"The shape of the maze we're in," Mina said. "It's a spiral. The more we traveled along vaguely circular paths, the clearer it became. It reminded me of the Fibonacci sequence. Some shapes in nature have a structure that corresponds to the ratios of the Fibonacci sequence."

"Okay," Cara said. "I'll take your word for it that it's this math thing. You have some really strong nerd instincts, Mina."

"Well, you have great instincts for avoiding being ambushed, Cara. Thank you for keeping me and my baby safe through this challenge. No one could have done it better." The two women smiled at each other.

After moving through a few more passageways, the next exit they took led down a long hall with no apparent exits. As they neared the end of this tunnel, Mina and Cara exchanged excited glances. They could both see a door.

[03:23:12]

Not bad. We didn't use too much of our time. I hope Yulia found her way through. She knew that no one else on the team was likely to have picked up on the pattern the maze was constructed in. Certainly not without going down a false path first.

"Hey, look!" a voice shouted from behind them.

Mina turned and saw two young men running down the hall toward them.

I guess now we've arrived at the part where it becomes a race, she thought.

Cara started jogging, trying to keep their lead.

Mina tried to run after her, but it was more of an ungainly waddle than anything else.

Cara looked back and slowed down a little so she wouldn't get further from Mina.

Their pursuers were gaining on them.

As the men approached, Mina realized she recognized these two from the first challenge too. Other members of that same team.

Then the men were beside them, trying to pass by them in the narrow hallway. Mina tried to stop and step out of their way, and she wanted to tell them they could pass, but she couldn't draw enough breath into her lungs. And there wasn't enough space to avoid them.

As they drew closer, she got a better look at the two men. One of them was the Hispanic guy with the acne scars who had asked her why she was sharing supplies. She hadn't spoken to the other guy, but she recognized his prominent chin, thick wavy brown hair, and lanky basketball-player build.

The Hispanic guy had a look of recognition on his face as they drew up beside them. He started to say something.

"Hey—"

But Mina didn't hear the rest of what he had to say. The other man shoved her—hard—out of his way.

She hit the stone wall with a heavy thud and practically bounced off.

Then she slammed into the ground, landing on her stomach.

A sharp pain lanced through her abdomen.

CHAPTER FORTY

Cradle to Grave

As if from a great distance, Mina heard Cara yelling, followed by a clash of steel.

Mina had trouble focusing on anything besides the pain radiating from her abdomen. Her eyes clenched shut as she tried to assess what was happening to her body.

My baby! Are you okay?

There was a feeling in her abdomen that reminded Mina of a more intense version of period cramps, a worse version of the contractions she had been experiencing over the last few weeks. She thought she knew what that meant. Her mother had told her what to expect years ago. A very effective way of preventing any possibility of teen pregnancy.

No, no! Please not here! Ahh! I have to get out of this maze. Now, now, now . . .

A tortured scream penetrated through Mina's mental haze. *What the hell is happening?*

As she forced her eyes open, there was a clatter of metal on the ground next to her.

Mina saw a bloodstained sword, and then Cara was there in her line of sight, reaching around her.

"I've got you," Cara said, breathing heavily. "We're going to get out of here!"

Mina rose, leaning heavily on Cara for support. The two women slowly stepped forward together. As she walked, Mina couldn't avoid seeing the smears of blood and decapitated bodies on the ground.

Wow, she thought. *God . . .*

"I'm so sorry, Mina," Cara mumbled.

"What?" Mina could barely get the word out she was breathing so erratically.

"I'm sorry I couldn't protect you," Cara said. "You guided me through the whole maze. All I had to do was keep you safe, and I couldn't even do that."

"Oh, don't beat yourself up," Mina croaked. "You're great."

"Ah, I have this!" Cara reached out to Mina with the hand that wasn't wrapped around her shoulder. It was a Health Potion.

"Thank you," Mina said, relieved. She grabbed the potion, yanked the stopper out with her teeth, and drank it almost in one gulp.

She coughed a few times, but she immediately felt a bit better. The intense cramp-like feeling in her abdomen was still there, though. And now that the pain was less than it had been, she noticed the liquid running down her legs. Her water had broken.

So, the baby's coming, and there's nothing that can stop it now. Well, I knew I couldn't hold it in until I saw James again anyway.

She gritted her teeth in a forced smile. *Welcome to the new world.*

Cara and Mina struggled the next ten meters or so together. They reached the door in the side of the maze. It looked so plain. Just hard brown wood. Out of place in a fantastical setting.

Then again, the whole maze until this had been gray stone. The knob turned, and the two women stepped through.

[Congratulations! You are among the first to complete the maze!]

"Help! Helllllp!" Yulia screamed as she ran.

Paulo stayed a few feet behind her, deliberately making himself the more tempting target of the two of them.

This is all my fault, I know it. But we just took a wrong turn or two. Why is this happening?

Behind them ran several small humanoid figures with the heads and tails of bulls.

"Jump through the next opening you see!" Paulo shouted from behind her.

Thirty seconds later, Yulia was able to throw herself through an opening in the wall into another passageway. Paulo jumped in after her. They both pressed themselves flat against the wall next to their point of entry.

There was a sound of stampeding footsteps behind them as the minotaurs ran past the doorway and further down the passageway.

"Thank fucking God!" Paulo exhaled the words in a single breath. "They're as stupid as normal bulls."

"I guess so," Yulia agreed shakily.

"Well, if they weren't, we'd be dead." He threw an accusing gaze at her. "I'm leading the way through the rest of the maze. I've had quite enough of your detours."

I didn't ask to lead the way before! Yulia wanted to say. *You asked what direction I thought was best.*

"Sure, okay," she said instead. "Which w—"

He suddenly clamped a hand over her mouth.

"Shh!" Paulo hissed.

A snorting sound came from the opening behind them. Then a snout poked its way slowly through the opening.

"Jesus," Paulo whispered.

The bull snout poked the rest of the way through the opening, and the minotaur's eyes widened in a wild, angry glare. It let out a sound like a mixture of an angry cow and a monkey. Yulia couldn't take her eyes away. She froze as the minotaur stepped all the way through the gap and turned its full body to face her.

Then Paulo swung into view. He struck a single blow with his sword and pierced through the minotaur's neck. The creature clapped its human hands over the cut to its neck. The wound gushed blood in thick, hot, highly pressurized spurts, some of which landed on Yulia's face and neck.

"Oh my God," Yulia whimpered. "Oh my God." Little tear droplets gathered in the corners of her eyes. She perceived the salty-sour metallic taste of the minotaur blood that had found its way through her slightly parted lips.

"You okay?" Paulo asked.

I thought I was about to die.

"Oh my God," she said once more. Then she realized what he'd asked. She turned to face him. Paulo was still staring at the minotaur, which had fallen to its knees and was teetering from that position as if it was about to drop.

"You'd better take a step or two back, Yulia," he said. Paulo managed to speak without inflection, despite having just been in a life-and-death situation and just killing something that looked a lot like a naked human.

"Thanks," she said quietly. She took a few steps back, and just as she did, the minotaur collapsed onto its face. The blood leaked out onto the ground where her feet had just been, and she stepped further back.

"Glad you're still with us," Paulo said. He sounded amused.

Yulia looked back at Paulo and was a little disturbed to see he was grinning slightly, as if the struggle for survival they'd both barely made it through just then was one big joke.

"Now, how does this work?" Paulo muttered to himself. "Um, Loot?"

The body of the minotaur began to gently glow with a warm, colorless light. Around thirty seconds passed, then Yulia saw the body disappear, leaving in its place a hatchet with a black metal blade and a handle that was clearly animal bone. The weapon floated into Paulo's empty left hand.

He looked at it, then looked into the air above it and smiled.

Yulia guessed he must be Identifying it.

"This is a lot better than my sword," Paulo said. He switched the hatchet to his right hand and the sword to his left.

"That's great," Yulia said emotionlessly.

Paulo looked at her flatly. She returned the empty gaze.

I must look like a maniac, she thought. Paulo certainly did. Blood had splattered all over his face and armor. The hatchet he wielded in his right hand and the bloody sword in his left did nothing to dispel that impression.

Then she saw a shape behind him.

"Paulo, look out!"

He managed to half turn, but he wasn't fast enough to move out of the way. The minotaur's horn gored him, emerging through the right side of his chest.

"*Urgh!*" He spat blood. Paulo's hatchet clattered to the ground.

Acting on instinct, Yulia dove for the weapon, and she managed to grab it despite the slick trail of blood oozing from Paulo's wound onto the handle.

"Help," he uttered. He looked faint.

Yulia looked up and saw the minotaur was trying to pull its left horn free from Paulo's right pectoral muscle. Paulo was fighting it, reaching back with his left arm and grabbing onto the beast's head. He must have known that if the minotaur pulled out of the wound, he would bleed to death.

The minotaur was smaller and shorter than Paulo, though its musculature was impressive. The result of their struggle involved the horn sliding slowly in and out of the hole, alternately allowing blood to flow more freely or stopping it up.

Paulo groaned quietly, while Yulia's mouth hung agape.

With the blood loss there was no way Paulo could win this struggle.

Yulia absorbed all of this information in only a few seconds as she was scrambling for the hatchet, looking at the minotaur and Paulo, and getting back up.

Then she buried the hatchet in the minotaur's arm.

Or she tried to. The hatchet barely grazed the minotaur. Its thick muscle and tough skin were difficult to slice. A thin trickle of blood flowed from the cut as Yulia pulled the hatchet back.

She took another swing. Another. What she lacked in strength, her toothpick-like arms made up for with persistence.

Finally, on the fifth swing, she heard a satisfying roar of pain from the minotaur. And she saw a flicker of white bone exposed through the arm wound.

The minotaur was paying attention to her now. Its eyes glared hatefully at her.

As it finally succeeded in pulling the barely conscious Paulo off of its horn, Yulia took a step back. She needed to run now, she knew.

Paulo knew it too.

"Run," he mouthed, looking up at her from the pool of his own blood.

But she couldn't just abandon him.

Yulia squared off with the minotaur. It wasn't that scary. Right?

The beast charged, swinging its head wildly to try and catch her on the point of one of its horns. Yulia managed to duck underneath the wide-sweeping horns and slash at its lower body. She swung the hatchet blade up between the minotaur's legs.

Despite how difficult it had been to cut into the minotaur before, this time the hatchet sunk in easily, as if Yulia had located a weak spot on the beast's body.

The minotaur let out a pained bovine groan and stumbled past Yulia to land on its hands and knees.

After a long moment of painful near paralysis, it released a long, hissing breath and turned its head, fixing its evil stare on Yulia again. It started to push itself off of the ground.

Yulia found that she couldn't move again. She felt weak in the knees. Somehow, she knew that if she tried to run, she would just collapse in a heap on the floor. All the adrenaline that had helped her in the last minute or so seemed burned up.

Out of nowhere, Paulo leaped in, sword raised in both hands, and launched himself, sword point first, at the minotaur. At first, his body blocked Yulia from seeing what had happened. Then Paulo fell away from the beast, and the minotaur collapsed beside him in a pool of its own blood. Paulo's sword stuck out of the place where its heart must be; with its cross guard standing so straight, it was reminiscent of a tombstone.

[Baby Minotaur, Lv. 5 killed. You gained 10 exp, based on your contribution to the fight!]

"Heh. Got him." Paulo chuckled quietly to himself. Yulia looked around and saw that Paulo seemed to have left most of his blood between where the minotaur had gored him and where he had returned the favor.

"Paulo!" She knelt beside him, tears in her eyes.

"No need for that," he said through tears of his own. "Look out for my brother, okay? He's a good kid. I hope he won't miss me too—"

Laying on Hands.

Paulo's chest wound began to seal itself back up. Yulia was very glad she had practiced this Skill following Mina's example. It seemed to work much more efficiently than when she had used it in the last Dungeon.

"Oh," Paulo said as his wound slowly closed. "I forgot you could do that."

"This is pretty awkward," she said. "But you were very sweet. And I'll look out for Jose anyway." She smiled, blushing slightly.

"Yeah," he said drily. "You and me both." He pushed himself up into a sitting position. "You know, you're good people, Yulia. I might have been a little rude before. I'll try to be nicer, for what it's worth." He looked suddenly uncomfortable, as if he'd just been caught walking around naked. "Anyway, let's get the hell out of here before more of those stupid beasts show up!"

[Healer leveled up!]

[System-Boosted Human leveled up!]

[Sufficient experience accrued. Laying on Hands leveled up!]

"Seems like you can handle them," Yulia said encouragingly, ignoring the System alerts. "But I definitely don't want to test that out more."

"I don't know whether I really can handle them," Paulo replied. "I don't know if you noticed, but when I killed that one, the System said it was a Baby Minotaur. I'm guessing the Mama and the Papa Minotaur are not so small and cuddly." He smiled weakly and shrugged. "I think if we meet those, we're fucked."

Yulia nodded. "Let's just find a place to hide for the next few hours."

Paulo looked down at the ground for a moment, as if wrestling with whether to accept that. Then he nodded too.

In a tone of self-loathing, he added, "I guess I'm too weak to do anything else."

Paulo Looted the other Baby Minotaur, and the two of them slipped through another opening into a passageway where they had not encountered any monsters. They made their way back to the starting point and waited there for the next few hours. The timer finally ticked down all the way to zero.

[00:00:00]

[Congratulations! You survived the maze, despite wandering off in the wrong direction and encountering Baby Minotaurs! Due to the success of others in your group, you are among the winners!]

A sack of food dropped next to them.

Oh, that's nice, Yulia thought, sighing with relief. *I guess Mina had a much better time than we did.*

[Our condolences to those who knew the groups that encountered the Minotaur Patriarch! Since they did not survive, the rations that would have been awarded to the winners among them will instead be distributed to their teammates, per our usual protocol.]

Oh. I hope none of our team members ran into the Minotaur Patriarch.

"You did it!" Adelaide said, holding up the baby so that Mina could see him.

"Thank you for your help," Mina croaked. She cleared her throat. "Can I have my baby?"

"Of course you can!" Adelaide exclaimed. "What should I call this little fellow, by the way?"

She reached over and held the baby out to Mina.

"Hm," Mina said. "My husband and I actually had a few different ideas for a name that we were kicking around. We didn't agree on the best one. But he's not here, and we're not going to call the baby 'you there' until I get to reunite with him. The baby's name will be James Robard Jr."

"Mm-hmm," Adelaide said with a knowing look. "You miss your hubby, so you're letting him win on the baby name?"

"No. I miss him, but he wanted to name the baby for his father. I just thought, wherever he is, my James is fighting. He's doing whatever he has to do to get back to us. I wanted to give the baby a name that would remind him what he's fighting for." She grinned sheepishly. "I know it probably doesn't make much sense to you."

"Nope! I'm not married, and when I find the right person, I'm not naming a baby 'Junior.' No judgment on your choice, though! You want some alone time with the baby?"

Mina nodded. "Could you tell Cara to come in if she's outside, though? Just for a minute. I want to thank her for everything she did."

"Sure thing," Adelaide said. She smiled and stepped outside of Mina's room, where she, Cara, and Jose had brought Mina after they had returned to their starting point at the inn.

Mina lay staring at her baby and cuddling with him for a few minutes until Adelaide poked her head back in.

"Looks like Cara's stepped out," Adelaide said. "I'll tell her you asked for her when she comes back, though, okay?"

"Please do," Mina said, eyes flickering up to Adelaide before they returned to being fixed on her son.

Adelaide smiled in Mina's peripheral vision.

"There is one other person who I thought might want to say hello, though. She just got back from the maze. Seems like we still haven't lost anyone from our team, by the way!"

Mina's eyes lit up. "Please send her in."

Yulia stepped in from behind Adelaide at the sound of Mina's response.

"The baby came early," Yulia said immediately. Her face fluctuated between ecstatic joy and sadness. Tears flowed down her cheeks, and she wiped them frantically away and stared wide-eyed at the little angel.

Finally, Yulia gently sat down on the bed next to Mina. She stroked the baby's hair and chubby cheeks, and she kissed him until he made a wriggling motion that looked like a feeble attempt to escape. Yulia slid down into a lying position.

Then she just lay there, gazing at the baby and cuddling with Mina, a mix of joy and something that looked like shell shock set on her face. Mina could tell at a glance that Yulia had much more on her mind than what little she'd said. And tomorrow they would probably have new deadly threats to worry about.

But for now, the two of them basked in the warmth of the newborn. Little James Robard. All eight pounds of him, with his big round cheeks, tightly closed eyes, and dark, curly strands of hair.

Despite all odds, Mina had successfully brought her baby safely into the world.

CHAPTER FORTY-ONE

Night Lights

The second night began much worse for the Rodriguez camp than the first had. Where before they had been assaulted by an unseen menace and a few members of the family had been kidnapped in the darkness, tonight their enemy was more brazen.

Strange dancing lights appeared in the dark mist that shrouded the night sky.

Ramon, Felicia, and Hector were on patrol together. They all saw the floating night lights.

"What are those?" Felicia asked, looking at Ramon as if he would have some explanation.

Ramon shrugged. "I've never seen anything like them before. How would I know?"

Hector walked forward, and the two younger Rodriguezes snapped to immediate attention.

"Uh, hey, Hector, where are you going?" Felicia asked.

"The lights," Hector said. He sounded drugged or drunk. "They know where our children are. The missing are with them."

Ramon and Felicia exchanged a look.

"I think it would be better if we all stayed here and reported this to the others," Ramon said carefully.

"You stay. I have to find my family."

Ramon had been afraid that he would say something like that. He took a step back and then made a sideways move, putting himself completely in Hector's blind spot. Hector continued moving forward, steadily leaving the solid ground in favor of the uneven marshy soil. Walking, no doubt, toward some entity's trap.

Ramon gave Felicia a significant look, and she nodded. Then she stepped forward and quickly moved to block Hector.

"What happened to the man who didn't trust magical fires in the darkness?" Felicia asked, her tone chiding. "You're really going to do something so crazy?"

"Move out of my way," Hector half-yelled, stepping in and getting in her face. "I'm going to find my family!"

That was when Ramon struck. He lunged and used his right fist to deliver a precision strike to the back of Hector's neck. He had only rarely had to use the special Rogue technique, but it landed perfectly. Hector crumpled into unconsciousness.

Felicia caught him and kept him from falling. She smiled at Ramon.

"Good teamwork," he said.

"I'm glad I didn't have to shoot him with an arrow," she replied.

That was when Ramon heard some movement from about ten feet to their left. He and Felicia turned to look, and there was another figure wandering toward the lights. A young woman who they recognized as Raquel Rodriguez moved through the darkness.

"Rocky, what are you doing?" Felicia called to her.

Then they heard a splash of movement to the other side of them. Ramon turned and found Javier Rodriguez also walking toward the lights.

"For the love of God," he said quietly. "How many of them . . . ?"

"I'm going toward the lights," Raquel said, her voice dull. "They know the way out of this terrible place."

In all, Ramon and Felicia had to subdue five members of the Rodriguez family who tried to wander off toward the will-o'-the-wisps. Only then could they return to the campsite for their report to the others.

"I can't believe so many of us would follow a bunch of weird glowing lights into the darkness," Ramon muttered. "They must be some powerful magic."

"You don't feel the pull at all?" Felicia asked.

"Hm?" Ramon looked at her, startled, a suspicious look spreading on his face.

"I'm in control of myself!" she said, annoyed. "But I can feel something when I look at the lights. You don't feel anything?"

Ramon turned his head back and looked at the lights for a few seconds, and he felt something. Perhaps he'd felt it already, but he'd ignored it in the heat of the moment. A warm glow about the lights that told him that everything would be all right. All his fears would turn out to be nothing if he would only go toward the lights.

He shuddered and forced himself to turn away.

"Now you feel it," Felicia said, nodding in satisfaction.

"Now I feel it," Ramon agreed. "I don't know how I missed it before. Let's get back."

Felicia nodded, and between them they managed to drag the five unconscious people back to the Rodriguez campsite.

But that was only the beginning of the evening's events.

When they returned, the whole camp was wide awake despite the fact that it was the middle of the night. They were all gathered together in a tight formation around the central tents. Some of them had weapons drawn. It felt like they were prepared to make a last stand against some terrible enemy.

"What's going on?" Ramon asked the first person he saw turned in his direction.

It was Cliff.

"Wolves spotted," Cliff said. "Higher level than what we used to see near the starting point. Coordinated. They dragged Jaime off. Everyone else who saw the wolves managed to retreat from the camp's edge. Now if they want to get us, they have to hit us all at once."

That's actually a pretty good plan, I think. If the wolves are that big of a threat this time. But . . .

"We're really running from wolves?" Ramon asked. "After all that we've been through already? Why not take the fight to them?"

Cliff's voice dropped as he replied, "On the other side of the camp, I'm told our people saw something *else*. Something less natural than fire-breathing wolves."

Ramon's mind shuffled through the different kinds of monster that he'd encountered since entering the Orientation forest. There were the spiders, of course. Forest beetles. Those boars they had run into on the way to what turned out to be the cultists' camp. But he hadn't seen anything that felt unnatural.

Then he didn't need to guess anymore. The *Night of the Living Dead* appeared in the distance.

A dozen full-blown zombies staggered out of the swamp water, through the mist, and into view. All around Ramon, he heard cries of dismay. He knew their courage had drained out of them. There was a moment when he thought that his family members might break and run.

"They're just walking corpses, everyone!" Ramon shouted. "They can't be any stronger than they were when they were human. Just look at them. They don't even outnumber us!" Ramon drew his sword and prepared himself mentally to lead by example.

A little bit of the panic seemed to subside at his yelling.

"He's right!" Cliff called out unsteadily. He raised his Ego Spidersword in the air. "We can win this!"

Then a figure stepped out from behind the zombie vanguard. This one didn't look nearly as decomposed as they did, but his skin nevertheless had a strange gray sheen that it had never had in life.

"Lay down your arms and surrender, Rodriguez family," pronounced the cold dead lips of Chava Rodriguez. "We promise that if you come peacefully, you will be spared."

The words were absurd. As absurd as the idea that those mindless creatures shambling toward them would accept, let alone understand, surrender from anyone.

Yet Ramon felt an almost irresistible urge to put down his sword.

Of course, Tio Chava would never let us get hurt, he thought.

"No, no, you guys can't give up now," Cliff whined. "Don't listen to that guy!"

The words seemed to Ramon to come from a great distance. A whisper. It should be easy to ignore. But . . .

No, I can't let my family get hurt. We can't die here. He pictured his younger siblings who hadn't made it here. *Luna and Ángel. I have to see them again. I can't die here.*

Then there was a howl of pain from behind him. It took him a moment to make sense of what he was seeing, but then the sight snapped him completely out of his reverie.

Mama Camila was screaming, struggling, writhing on the ground. A big, two-headed wolf had half of her hip clenched between one set of closed jaws.

"*Ayúdame!*" she begged.

"No!" Ramon shouted. Around him, others had similar reactions.

Some of them kept their heads and leaped on the wolves that had snuck up on them while they were distracted with the zombies. A dozen swords and knives found their target in the big two-headed beast almost at once.

Then the enemy was upon them on all sides. Wolves and zombies were everywhere, wrestling with family members or sinking their teeth into them. Occasionally Ramon could see creatures more human and less decomposed than the zombies attacking alongside them. Creatures like what his Tio Chava had become.

They were surrounded on all sides by monsters and the mingled stench of death and wolf musk.

Ramon saw, despite his family members' best efforts, that the wolf that had become a pincushion was still moving. It ripped Mama Camila in half between its two pairs of jaws.

"No," he whispered. "No."

To his left, Felicia fell, her throat crushed between a smaller wolf's jaws. Caught too much by surprise even to scream. To his right, Cliff collapsed under the weight of a half-dozen wolves. He cried out loudly, clearly in agonizing pain. In the space Cliff had left open when he fell, Ramon saw little Luna.

No, that's impossible! She's not here.

Despite the impossibility of it, the zombies were sinking their teeth into her shoulders. Positioned behind her, Chava grabbed Luna's neck, pulled, and twisted. There was a horrendous cracking sound, and Ramon realized she was no more.

He fell to his knees, vomit rising in his throat.

I can't do this. None of us can do this. Years of religious instruction that had gone in one ear and out the other rose back up and hit him like a freight train. *We're in Hell or something. These are the end times, and we're being punished for our sins.*

Then he felt a crushing weight shove him headfirst into the soil. He couldn't feel anything pressing him down. It was as if his body had just come under some invisible force that kept him from rising.

He could barely lift his head an inch or two off the ground. When he did, he opened his eyes to see a completely different reality than what he'd experienced before.

His vision blurred, and then he saw Mama Camila lying on the ground in front of him, still in one piece, her body bleeding from a massive bite wound to the hip. She was unconscious, but her chest rose and fell. She was clearly still alive.

Beside her lay the two-headed wolf that had chomped onto her, neatly bisected, two pieces split at the gap that separated the two heads. As Ramon swiveled his head slightly, he could see a dozen more wolves ripped and chopped into pieces, as if some savage monster had attacked them.

What does this mean?

"Sorry I had to do that," a familiar voice said loudly, projecting to everyone around. "I don't know what you all saw, but I have a good guess. My illusion was more *effective* than I intended. Unfortunately, I couldn't target it to just the monsters. And it doesn't seem to work as well on the undead, so there's no point in keeping it around and torturing you guys any further."

James, Ramon thought. *Thank God.*

There was a sound of bone breaking from behind Ramon. Then another sound, like flesh being ripped apart. But Ramon wasn't worried anymore. He could almost fall asleep. He was exhausted, he couldn't move, and all the tension had left his body. Tears filled his eyes.

Thank God. My family isn't all going to die . . .

"Wow," an old voice said. "Not a single casualty once we arrived. You know, I think he was telling the truth. I really believe the safest place to be in the whole Orientation is right behind wherever he's standing."

"We have to chase after the rest," James said, his voice quieter now, slightly weary. As he spoke, the weight that held Ramon in place vanished like a lie. "We can't afford to lose our advantage. They're running. They won't be as organized. We have the numbers, and against a fleeing enemy, we could win even with fewer than they have."

Hostage

Kurt tried to bury the strange cold emotion he felt. He pushed it deep beneath the thick glass that seemed to cover over almost all his emotions. Somehow, it didn't work.

He had seen James Robard again; the reunion he'd wished for these last weeks had come much earlier than he had any right or reason to expect. The enemy he'd wanted so badly to destroy.

Now that idea seemed like a childish fantasy. When James descended on the battlefield—what was supposed to be the field of slaughter—he caught two dozen wolves and most of the human camp members in his illusion. The pace of the conflict changed in an instant.

Kurt was with the Wolf King, watching the battle from a distance, and he saw everything.

Robard walked among the wolves, which ran to and fro, ignoring him. He casually slashed them open as he passed, sword in one hand and dagger in the other. It reminded Kurt of one of those European works of art from the time of the Black Death, when the Grim Reaper was depicted hovering over the soon to die.

James made such quick work of the wolves and Ghouls around him that the Wolf King actually broached the subject of a tactical withdrawal first.

Kurt was too afraid. It was difficult for him to act at all.

His second encounter with Robard reminded him of his first encounters with Master Roscuro and the Wolf King. A cold dread brewed in his stomach.

He felt some of that tension release when he and the Wolf King finally ordered their respective forces to retreat. Now that they were fleeing, much of the nervousness returned. Would Robard and the reinforcements he'd brought pursue them?

So far the combined army hadn't lost too many of their forces. Two dozen wolves, almost all on the younger and weaker side. A handful of Ghouls, including the three they had created from members of the Rodriguez camp. Things could get so much worse . . .

I sense you are returning to the center of the marsh in some haste, Kurt, Roscuro transmitted into his mind. *I can only assume that you were repelled by unexpectedly strong foes.*

Kurt nodded, though he had no way of actually answering Roscuro back since they weren't in person. The Master's telepathy was a one-way communication channel.

If the enemy is that formidable, Roscuro continued, *you shouldn't let our forces take the brunt of their destruction.* Kurt's eyes widened. He knew what the Master must be getting at. *If you can do it, find a way to leave the wolves to fight the enemy on their own. I sense that our numbers are diminished, and I believe any leader worth his salt would try to take this opportunity to destroy us completely. It's what I would do.*

Kurt kept moving numbly forward, preparing himself for what he knew he would be asked to do next. In one way or another, Roscuro was about to order him to abandon their allies.

If the enemy give chase, they will be forced to leave their wounded and dead at the site of your battle. You are to go and retrieve as many of the wounded and the dead as you can. If we're to stand a chance against this enemy, we have to rebuild. Hopefully, the wolf pack and the enemy wear each other down. Roscuro paused in his transmission, as if deep in thought.

You will understand how strategically important this moment is. If you allow the force with you to be destroyed, all I will have left to defend me are mindless, Skill-less Zombies. With my physical weakness, if you fail in your mission, it's most likely that we will be completely annihilated. I entrust you with the preservation of our kind.

Kurt wanted to kneel and bow his head, wanted to show gratitude in some way for his Master's trust. But any such gesture would be wasted since they weren't in the same place.

Still, Kurt walked a ways with his head down. *I won't let you down,* he thought. *The Ghouls will survive to protect you.* Then he prepared for his conversation with the Wolf King. He would need some explanation for why the Ghouls were separating from the wolf pack.

Finally, he approached.

The surviving members of the pack gave him low growls as he passed, but they parted for him—a testament to the effectiveness of Kurt's diplomacy with the Wolf King thus far. He was trusted. An idea he would cling to through the coming discussion.

"Your Majesty." Kurt bowed his head in a show of deference. He activated the same Skill he'd used in their previous conversations: Monstrous Affinity.

"What have you come for, Kurt?" the Wolf King growled.

Though his tone was as distrustful as ever, Kurt thought he'd made great progress by getting the Wolf King to use his name.

"The enemy are in pursuit. My master senses their movements. He believes we should make a stand against them here, if it pleases Your Majesty. If you will hold your ground here"—he gestured at the area they were approaching, which included a slightly elevated patch of earth—"I will lead my Ghouls in a flanking maneuver. We can surround the enemy and cut off their ability to retreat."

"Hm. Where will you personally be in all this?" Even under the influence of Kurt's Skill, the Wolf King seemed skeptical.

"I will be hidden in that bank of fog there, waiting for the enemy to approach," Kurt replied, gesturing at a particularly dense patch of swamp haze.

"Hmmm," the Wolf King rumbled, the sound coming from deep in one of his throats. Kurt felt that he was on the verge of rejecting the plan.

"I would be happy to leave a couple of Ghouls beside Your Majesty, as a gesture of good faith," Kurt added hastily.

Sacrificing another couple of Ghouls, after they'd lost a half-dozen in the previous engagement, would be a hefty loss, but Kurt decided he would choose Ghouls who had greater Agility. Maybe they would have some chance at getting away if the Wolf King was engaged in combat.

"That does make your suggestion more palatable," the Wolf King replied, his voice contemplative. "And you have not led us astray yet. But if the enemy engage us, and we do not see you come to our aid, know that we will use the two friends you leave behind as chew toys."

"Of course, Your Majesty," Kurt said, forcing a smile. "Since you are agreed, I will pick out a pair of suitable—"

"I will decide which Ghouls are suitable to remain with us," the Wolf King interrupted. "Do not forget, Kurt. You may not have deceived us yet, but I have no reason to trust your master. Especially considering that he remains hidden in his mist somewhere even during this pivotal exchange."

"I believe that Master will join us too," Kurt lied. "He said he would send reinforcements, but given how few reinforcements we've kept back from this fight, I believe he will also try to join us here."

"That would be something to see from one who has been so cautious," the Wolf King said, voice skeptical. "But since you cannot promise that, let us direct our attention to which of your fellows will remain here as hostages."

The Wolf King chose the Ghouls he wanted. No one essential, to Kurt's carefully hidden relief, though every Ghoul was important to the Master's undead army in one way or another.

Terrence Rockington and Katrina Rowdie looked to Kurt for confirmation that they were actually to do as the Wolf King said and stay behind. Only when Kurt gave them a slight nod of affirmation did they turn back to the Wolf King and bow their heads in acknowledgement of his authority.

If Kurt still felt emotions the way he once had, there would be something heart wrenching about his fellow Ghouls' willingness to stay behind and strictly obey orders. They were perfect soldiers. Sacrificing themselves, essentially, though he had not let them in on Master Roscuro's plan. But even if he had, they would have behaved the same way.

The Ghouls were almost like eusocial insects, and Roscuro was the queen of their hive.

Kurt and the other Ghouls set off into the mist, leaving their fellows behind to almost certain doom. Either they would be killed fighting the enemy, or they would be destroyed in reprisal for Kurt and the other Ghouls' desertion.

The Ghouls left in two separate groups to give the illusion that they were moving into the mists on either side of the wolf pack for the flanking maneuver Kurt had mentioned. In reality, he quietly explained the plan to the leader of the second group, and each body of Ghouls made a wide loop, heading in two separate gangs toward the site of the battle with the Rodriguez camp.

They moved through warm mist. It recognized them as the Master's creatures, growing slightly thicker in their wake and parting slightly to make their forward movement easier to navigate. Only natural in the Master's territory.

Kurt felt substantially more secure with every step he took now that he'd abandoned the wolf pack to their fate.

His group pushed further into the swamp, back toward the Rodriguez camp by the indirect route he had chosen.

As they drew close, Kurt derived an even stronger sense of relief from the fact that he could not sense James's presence. Since he and his group had taken some time to get near the camp again, James must have already left in pursuit of the wolf pack.

Aggressive, just as Kurt remembered him.

Kurt drew within sight of the camp. The site was still a mess. Tents torn to shreds by wolves and Ghouls blindly attacking whatever had been around them in the depth of illusions. Wounded people laying on cots with barely any additional people to help them in their recovery. There was some healing going on, including by—Sierra!

"I would've sworn she was dead," Kurt thought aloud. He ignored the funny looks the other Ghouls gave him. It was atypical for them to discuss their human lives, but his experience with these people was relevant, darn it! "For him to leave her alive is much more foolish—or merciful?—than I would expect from Robard. I wonder how we might use this."

The other Ghouls quietly groaned responses.

"Who cares?"

"When do we attack?"

"Who is the girl to us?"

"Robard has gone on to face the wolves, has he not?"

"He will surely die there. Even if the Wolf King could not face the whole group, the King should at least be able to eliminate one human, however strong."

Kurt was not so confident, but he didn't feel the need to justify himself or explain his reasoning to the others. They had been placed under his command, after all. The Dead Marsh was not a democracy.

"Make sure she's one of the ones we capture alive," he said simply. "We may be glad to have her as a hostage later. She's had plenty of time to ingratiate herself with both Robard and this group. If it comes to a showdown, we'll want all the bargaining power we can steal."

There was a collective grunt of assent.

Kurt and his Ghouls huddled together, crouched in a waiting position beneath a tree. He only needed the other group of Ghouls to get close too, and then they would descend on the camp as a group, kill who they had to, and carry off as many as they could. That was the plan.

Suddenly, the Ghoul next to Kurt dropped hard. Kurt saw two daggers growing out of the top of Christopher Royce's head before they vanished. Then there was only the Ghoul's body, writhing on the ground, his perforated brains visible.

"We're under attack!" Kurt barked. "Step away from the tree until we can see what we're dealing with."

The other Ghouls turned and backed away from the tree a bit. Kurt started to follow suit until he heard a sound from above him.

It was a long high-pitched whistle, like a bird call.

Of course the attacker was up there, Kurt thought. He raised his arms above his head to shield it from any further projectiles. Any damage to his arms would be unimportant compared to a head injury like Royce had just suffered.

Then Kurt tilted his head back at a steep angle until he could see the figure attacking them from the tree. It was a dark-haired young man. He looked wiry but strong, and he had a dagger in each hand.

"You were in the camp earlier," Kurt recalled aloud. He didn't recall this young man doing anything especially impressive before, though he had been caught right in the middle of James's illusion. "Brave of you to try and fight us alone."

"Me? Try to fight? No, man, my hand slipped," the dagger-wielding man said mockingly.

I guess you'll be the first prisoner we take, Kurt thought.

CHAPTER FORTY-THREE

The Return

James frowned. He paused for a moment amid his slaughter of the combined wolf and Ghoul force and looked at Ramon.

I know what he must be seeing, he thought. *His family is dying in front of him. So, this is what it looks like when I make an illusion that's supposed to represent the targets' fears.*

It wasn't what he'd intended when he began charging his Illusion Magic. But it seemed that False Reality juiced up any deception-related ability. Including enhancing his illusions.

So now his allies were almost all stuck in the same sort of fear-inducing illusions as the enemy. It made picking the enemy monsters off incredibly easy, and James vowed to use Illusion Magic more often when hunting. But he didn't like seeing the effect on the Rodriguezes and his other comrades caught in the spell.

I'll make those creatures pay for what they forced me to do to you all, he thought as he ripped another wolf in two. Then he walked up to a Ghoul that was engaging an imaginary enemy, and he ripped its head clean off.

"You all right?" growled Damien from the ground nearby, where he was ripping apart another Ghoul. "You slowed down a bit." Every word he said in his Werewolf form sounded like a growl to James, even more so than Damien's normal speaking voice.

"Just a little sad," James admitted. Besides himself, Damien was probably the strongest quasi-humanoid life-form left in the Orientation. He wanted to get to know the Werewolf, and sharing how he himself was feeling should be a part of that. "Let's mop up the rest of these so I can undo the illusion on the group."

"Ah, I see," Damien said. "Sure thing!"

The two of them tore through the rest of the wolves and Ghouls in a few minutes' time.

"The big one I fought before wasn't here," Damien observed, spitting out a hunk of wolf skull.

"Yeah, I sense there are more of them in the area around here. For some reason they're not approaching."

Damien gave James a wry look. "For some reason," he said.

Finally, the enemy was reduced to just a couple low-level wolves, plus the last Ghoul, which appeared to be Chava Rodriguez. James was able to pull the illusion down. He gestured for Damien to take care of the last few stragglers while James began explaining and apologizing, after his fashion, for the illusions.

"Sorry I had to do that," he began, speaking loudly enough for everyone to hear him. He didn't want to repeat himself. "I don't know what you all saw, but I have a good guess. My illusion was more *effective* than I intended. Unfortunately, I couldn't target it to just the monsters. And it doesn't seem to work as well on the undead." This last point was untrue, but James didn't know quite how to explain the way the undead behaved under his illusions to the camp. Their reaction when confronted with their fears seemed to be to fight harder. Not exactly a comforting thought. "So, there's no point in keeping it around and torturing you guys any further."

"Wow," Jeremiah Rotter said, half under his breath. "Not a single casualty once we arrived. You know, I think he was telling the truth. I really believe the safest place to be in the whole Orientation is right behind wherever he's standing."

James smiled slightly despite the obvious ass-kissing. Rotter was getting better at being slightly more subtle, praising James indirectly and for things he was genuinely proud of.

"We have to chase after the rest," James said. He realized midsentence that everyone was still held in place by his gravity magic, so he released that as he continued speaking. "We can't afford to lose our advantage. They're running. They won't be as organized. We have the numbers, and against a fleeing enemy we could win even with fewer than they have."

At least that was how a battle with human opponents worked historically. James remembered reading somewhere that most casualties in ancient warfare occurred when the losing side broke ranks and began fleeing. At that point, the victorious army took advantage of their broken morale and cut down the running enemies with much greater ease.

But here, what will that look like? Against a bunch of monsters. My side has me, so it should still be an easy enough victory, regardless of their morale. But somehow, I suspect these enemies will never give up. Never break ranks. Never run. He suppressed a shudder before it registered on a level detectable by anyone but himself. Now wasn't the time to show any doubt.

"I volunteer to go with you!" Hilda declared in a loud, clear voice.

"I will also go!" Chris Roach agreed in a much less steady tone.

James could tell Roach didn't really want to participate, but he understood the optics of the situation. The only surviving members of the Rostov cult who were joining his group needed to prove their loyalty every chance they could.

He nodded approvingly.

"Don't think you're leaving me behind!" Ramon said, smiling with what James read as false bravado. "Just as long as we can get someone over here to heal Mama Camila?"

"I've got it," Sierra said. She stepped forward from among the huddled masses and began applying Laying on Hands to Camila's injuries. "Now you can go," she added without looking up from her work. "Kill a bunch of those undead freaks for us!"

James smiled. *Good to know nothing has changed.*

"I'll naturally be joining you, sir," Cliff said. "Thanks for saving our asses earlier, by the way! And I never doubted you'd come back for us. Not for a moment!"

James resisted the impulse to roll his eyes. There would be time enough to deal with Cliff's bullshit later.

"You know you can count on me," Damien said from between bites of wolf flesh. He was eating the last of his opponents from earlier.

"I can provide some modest magical backup," Rotter added.

"Same here!" Mitzi said, rising from where she sat on the ground. Alan rose with her, still healing her arm as she spoke.

"I guess I'd better stay and finish healing the other people who are injured," he said. James saw him swallow a lump in his throat. "I—I honestly can't believe you're back, but I'm glad to see you. I trust you'll keep my wife safe, James?"

"You know it," James said. "And we're in the endgame now. I think I've almost gotten us through all of the Orientation, in terms of the physical dangers at play."

"Mm-hmm." Alan seemed to want to believe what James was saying, but perhaps he'd seen too much in the last several weeks to have firm hopes.

"We want to join y'all as well!" a man said. He appeared to be speaking for a huddled group of around a dozen people that encircled him. *Former Moloch cult prisoners,* James recognized. *Both the ones who just escaped and a few people who got away earlier. Are the two groups kind of melding together? Nice to see the ones who got away earlier doing well, in any case.*

"Glad to have you," James said. He didn't have much else to say to them. He really didn't know these prisoners at all, even the ones who had traveled through the swamp with him and Damien's group.

"I think some of us who can fight had better stay and defend the camp," Moishe said. "Just in case there's another attack while you're gone. We don't know what kinds of numbers they have." James turned to give Moishe a smile and saw Moishe was looking not at him, but at Ramon.

Hm. I guess people have really been getting to know each other while I've been gone, he thought. *There's an understanding between those two that I know absolutely nothing about.*

"Yeah, you're right," Ramon said sheepishly. He looked up at James. "I hope you can understand—"

"Of course!" James said. "Think nothing of it. I know you'll both stand by me in battles to come. Protect your family right now. Moishe is right."

[Sufficient experience accrued. Politician leveled up!]

James dismissed the notification lightly, without emotion.

But it did make him wonder. *Almost time for a Job Evolution?* What would that be like?

There were multiple additional volunteers.

Ultimately, out of a dozen former Moloch prisoners, nine agreed to go. Both of the surviving former cult members volunteered. Eight out of the twenty surviving Rodriguezes volunteered. All of the others were either injured or apologetically felt that they needed to protect the injured. And then there were the twenty-six members of Damien's group. Of these, only ten volunteered to accompany James and Damien. Of course, there were also the two members of James's original small band.

It felt like a strong crew, and the thirty-one members ought to be enough to put the fear of the gods into their opposition, but James looked at the situation with a political eye.

Every group's loyalty felt very firm except that of Damien's group. Fewer than half of them had volunteered, and James thought they were only volunteering because Damien and Rotter were going. James would need to manage them carefully in the future to tighten their ties of loyalty to him specifically.

They weren't the only people whose loyalty he'd need to carefully manage, of course. He looked over at Cliff, who was introducing himself to Rotter now with his usual glad-handing approach. Then he turned to Sierra, who was healing one of the injured Rodriguezes and perhaps deliberately paying James no mind.

Finally, James and his band set out. Two people with tracking Skills, one from the prisoners' group and one from Damien's group, led the way, though James himself could have followed the signs of the enemies' retreat. The broken twigs, footprints, and disturbed shrubbery seemed obvious to him.

Not for the first time, he wondered if everyone else was seeing the same things he saw when he looked out at the world. With well over a hundred points in Perception, he probably had a meaningful advantage that had not yet made itself glaringly obvious.

"You're really accomplishing everything Lord Anansi expected, boss," Hester said quietly.

James couldn't say anything back, surrounded as he was by people he didn't want to overhear him. But he smiled slightly. He knew she must be able to tell that he was smiling from the way his ears moved when his lips did.

"How recent do you think those tracks are?" James asked one of the trackers, a red-haired former prisoner named Harry Roark.

"Oh, minutes old, sir!" Roark replied a bit nervously.

I could get used to being "sir."

"Excellent," James said, putting his hand on the man's shoulders and giving him a gentle squeeze.

"I'll just pop on ahead and try to see how far away they are," said the other tracker, a Cuban American woman named Amalia Rosario. She'd been helpful as James and Damien were navigating to find the Rodriguezes, and she seemed determined not to let her duties be usurped here.

Harry opened his mouth as if he wanted to object, to volunteer himself, but James gave him a quick, firm shake of the head. Then the woman was gone, cutting through the brush almost at a sprint.

"Just let her go ahead, man," James said. "You didn't have the chance to get much fighting experience trapped by the cult, did you?"

"No," Harry reluctantly admitted.

"Well, Amalia has. And she was in the military before Orientation. She seems tough enough, and she has the experience edge over you. So let her go ahead and scout in front of us. One of you was going to have to stay behind to make sure the whole group doesn't wander in the wrong direction. You'll get the chance to prove your mettle in combat soon, anyway."

"Right," Harry said, exhaling sharply. "I'll just look forward to that, then."

James almost laughed at the way the other man said that. There was a fatalistic irony to Harry's tone that made the words feel wittier than they really were.

"Remember, just stick close to me in the fight," he said. "Except when I engage the boss monster, whatever it is. Then get far away."

"Sure. Close, then far away." Harry sighed and shook his head. "I'll remember."

"Hey!" James said sharply. Harry looked up at him. "The safest place to be in this whole forest is behind wherever I'm standing. You'll be safe if you follow the advice I just gave you."

The look in Harry's eyes changed slightly. Became less hopeless.

"Right you are, sir," Harry said. He nodded, and James thought his body language changed as well. Became more resolute.

As the war party continued to advance, James slowly engaged others individually who looked similarly nervous to Harry. Each time, he left them looking slightly more upbeat until the six least hopeful members of his team became six of the more apparently optimistic fighters marching alongside him.

Perfect Choice of Words is powerful, he thought.

"You're working hard to inspire the troops," Mitzi said from behind him.

"I like to think that hasn't changed," James replied, smiling.

She punched his arm lightly. "We missed you, you know."

"I know." James looked at his feet for a moment, slightly guilty.

"I knew you'd come back," she added. "Unlike some people, I don't think Alan, Sierra, or I ever doubted it."

"I always will," he replied. "You don't need to doubt. You and Alan don't ever need to worry about whether I'll return alive from a fight. I've gotten even stronger. I'm pretty close to invincible." *An exaggeration*, he thought, *but an innocent one*. "And I also won't rush into too many more fights I can't win. Defeating the cultists was a massive pain in the ass!"

"You beat them?" Mitzi said, then paused. "I don't know why I'm surprised. Of course you beat them. That's why you had so many people with you when you returned. They were *all* prisoners? Those monsters."

"The people with me when I came back weren't all prisoners, but it's a long story," James said. He proceeded to tell Mitzi everything that had transpired since they'd been separated, with a few omissions where he felt he would reveal too much about his powers.

Mitzi interjected in only a few places where she couldn't contain herself:

"There are multiple gods that really exist. My whole worldview is shattered . . ."

"So, you really did visit me in my dreams?"

"Why did you go back and fight the cult alone again? Well, at least you made some preparations in advance."

After a long chat with Mitzi, James returned to the front of the party just in time for Amalia to rush back through the bushes and stumble into his arms.

"Whoa!" he said. "Are we about to be attacked?"

"No, I don't think they saw me!" She looked very flustered as she spoke, though. James let go of her. She backed up a few steps and composed herself.

"Report, then," he said. "Tell me how many we're facing, where they are, and what the situation is."

Her posture straightened at his words, and she assumed a military bearing.

"Around fifty to sixty surviving wolves," Amalia said. "A couple of Ghouls. About twenty yards that way"—she gestured at the direction she'd run from—"they're perched on one of the bits of solid, relatively dry land in this place. A patch of high ground. Just waiting for us to catch up to them." She hesitated a moment.

"Go on," James said. "Give me all the intel. What are you thinking?"

"Sir, it almost feels like a trap."

CHAPTER FORTY-FOUR

Nanny Dearest

Mina's recovery proceeded supernaturally quickly.

Yulia and Adelaide spent time with her each day, repeatedly bathing her in Healing Aura.

On the first day, after three shifts of healing, Mina felt as if she understood something about the nature of the Mana that Yulia and Adelaide were using to heal her. She'd been watching them just because she had nothing else to do, but her interest sharpened as she noticed the effect on her own body. There was a fatigue from being healed, as if it was pulling on some of her own energy, but logically, she knew the degree of fatigue wasn't enough to explain the effectiveness of the healing.

What Mina had begun observing casually she began watching more carefully and then trying to understand analytically. At some point on the first day, she felt as if she was about to have a breakthrough. Then she fell asleep, and she only woke when baby James started crying to be fed.

After sleeping through the rest of the night, the morning brought the revelation of a System alert.

[Quick Study successfully analyzed Healing Aura. You acquired the Skill Healing Aura!]

Goodness, really? Did I learn a Skill just from watching it being used and trying to understand how it worked? Mina immediately went down a rabbit hole trying to think of ways she could use Quick Study to increase her repertoire of Skills.

She was interrupted by baby James's demand for more milk, which she happily satisfied. Mother and child enjoyed a perfect connection as the baby breastfed—something many mothers would envy.

"My beautiful baby," Mina cooed, momentarily forgetting about her Skill and its delightful potential for abuse.

Once baby James was fed, she found she could walk again, though she only walked around her and Yulia's room. It was snowing outside, and Mina suspected her surprising post-natal vigor wouldn't last very long in the cold. In any case, she didn't want to be far from her son if he started crying on his first full day outside of her body.

After Mina had tired herself out a bit, she used Healing Aura on herself. The word from her team—passed on through DaSilva and Adelaide when they visited—was that no one expected her to participate in challenges anytime soon. But she didn't want to use that excuse for any longer than was actually necessary.

By the next morning, Mina had decided she was capable of more strenuous exercise. She forced her body into doing push-ups, sit-ups, and walking more briskly around the room.

Adelaide walked in, found her exercising, and ordered her back to bed.

Mina almost argued, but then baby James started crying, so she returned to bed and fed him instead of trying to change Adelaide's mind.

There's going to be a new dogma about what women can do right after they've given birth, Mina thought. *With magical healing, we don't really need to lie around and rest for weeks.* But it seemed that those changes would take a little time to take root.

For now, she focused on feeding her baby. And she used Healing Aura on herself whenever Yulia and Adelaide were busy or low on Mana.

"I can't believe you have such a useful ability," Yulia said when Mina first explained how she had acquired a Healer Skill. "But I guess I shouldn't be surprised, since it's you." Those last words were spoken with a mixture of admiration and resignation.

That night, Mina awakened to the sound of someone throwing stones, either at the window of their room or at the window of the room next door. She got up, expecting it to be Jose trying to talk to Yulia. Mina wasn't oblivious to the way he looked at her sister.

But when she made it to the window, she saw a figure she didn't recognize. He threw another stone, and when she saw that it wasn't aimed at her window, she went back to bed.

The morning dawned on another new day. The sky was clear that morning, which Mina found notable because it had snowed the previous three days, either in the morning or the afternoon. Not for the first time, she wondered if the weather was under the System's direct control. Surely it wasn't a coincidence that as the challenges went on, and people had their food stolen, the environment seemed to actively become more hostile.

The population counter had dropped by another few people in the night, as had been the pattern recently.

[2,633/3,397 Survivors]

Mina tried to ignore that. As much as she wanted to catch the murderer—and had been interested in catching them since the beginning—the fact was that this serial killer hadn't done nearly as much damage to the population as the challenges. At this rate, no one would survive the Orientation.

That wasn't even factoring in the hunger that must be growing in some corners of the settlement. And it would be difficult and dangerous to go hunting for food in this snow, even if it might have been easy walking a week ago.

If people don't have food after this challenge, what will they do? Mina wondered uneasily. *I guess we have to double down on the strategy of sharing, but I don't know if that will be enough.*

She tried to avoid letting her mind go back over a topic she had considered repeatedly over the last two days. *Cara.* Whenever she thought about the murders, her mind went back to Cara. She'd killed two people back in the maze, Mina was fairly certain. Some of the memories were hazy from pain and stress, but she remembered a bloody sword.

Mina had told no one about this. *She did that for me. How can I use that as a reason to consider her?* But no one else was presenting themselves as a better suspect.

Yulia went downstairs to perform the first of the daily exchanges: she brought rations, and Alba traded them for cooked food and gossip. The Cook heard more of what was going on in this Orientation than any other person in the building since most residents of the inn still ate her cooking and went to the common area to eat their food and socialize.

A few minutes after Yulia left, there was a knock at the door, and Mina rose to answer it.

She's a little faster than usual, she thought. A queasy feeling crept into her stomach. Was it someone else? Had something happened to Yulia during her short walk from their room to downstairs?

She couldn't have guessed who she would actually see standing outside of their room.

The proctor stood there, dressed in the full regalia of her role. The green and red robe and Judy mask looked almost comical on the tall, thin figure.

Mina opened the door fully and just stared.

"What are you doing here?" Mina finally asked.

[It has come to our attention that the other life-form that you brought with you into Orientation has emerged from your body.]

Mina felt a surge of fear, and she fought her instinct to immediately slam the door in the proctor's face. She remembered the man who had defied the proctor outside and been gruesomely killed. Her hand shook at the thought. But she abandoned any thought of trying to run back inside the room. If the proctor wanted to harm her or her baby, a wooden door wasn't going to stop that.

"Yes," Mina said. "What about it?"

[There is a challenge scheduled for today, as you know. There are no children in this Orientation besides the child you recently birthed. Therefore, I wanted to offer to take the child off your hands. He would only be a burden during the challenge, after all.]

"What do you mean, 'take the child off my hands'?" Mina asked coldly, giving the proctor a death glare.

[We offer two options: either we can take your child from you and hold onto him throughout the duration of Orientation, or we can temporarily take custody while you complete the challenge. If you prefer the latter, this will be available during every challenge going forward.]

"What, you have a nanny service?" Mina's tone was skeptical, but the ice in it had defrosted. Inside, she felt relieved. She had been concerned about what she would do with baby James if she needed to participate in a future challenge. Now it seemed she had nothing to worry about.

[I will hold onto the boy myself if you choose the second option.]

The proctor's voice seemed softer, more straightforward all of a sudden. But perhaps Mina was just imagining it.

"And how would the first option have worked?" Mina asked, curious.

[With the first option, the child would be placed in suspended animation for the duration of your Orientation. He wouldn't age a single day. In short, you wouldn't have to miss a moment with your child.]

Mina shuddered despite her effort to keep her composure.

[But I take it by your choice of words and body language that you intend to take the second option.]

Mina nodded, her slender frame suddenly shivering with unaccountable cold.

[Then I will take the boy. The competition will begin in the next hour.]

"I—I need to feed him again," Mina protested. "You have time to leave and come back, correct?"

[Yes.] There was a hint of impatience this time. Then the proctor vanished into thin air.

Yulia rounded the corner and saw Mina staring into the hallway.

"Did I take too long?" she asked.

Mina just shook her head.

Ten minutes later, an announcement sounded.

[All survivors of the first few challenges, prepare yourselves. The next challenge begins in twenty minutes. This will be a hunting challenge, so prepare with that information in mind.]

[00:20:00]

Mina was feeding baby James at the time of the announcement. *I'm very lucky*, she thought. *Clearly, the System isn't actively trying to kill me. The proctor offered me daycare and gave me a warning that the next challenge was going to start soon. This almost feels like preferential treatment.*

Ten more minutes passed. The proctor reappeared outside of Mina's door and knocked. Wordlessly, Mina handed baby James over. Despite her slightly increased trust in the System, she still felt pangs of worry as the baby left her hands.

"You'll give him back as soon as the challenge is over?" Mina asked. "As soon as I'm back here? And not wait for everyone else to be finished?"

[Yes, Ms. Danailova. You have our word.] The proctor's tone came off as impatient again, but Mina had the smallest sense that she was trying not to be.

Then the proctor and the baby were gone.

"I can't believe it," Yulia said quietly.

"What? What are you saying?" Mina asked anxiously.

"Oh, um, I can't believe the System offers babysitting services," Yulia said. "Now I've seen everything, right?"

"Hm. Yes, I guess that is surprising. Then again, they're all about fair competition here, I think. And it wouldn't be easy to do careful magic while carrying a baby around."

Please bring back my baby when it's over, she thought a bit desperately. Even this brief separation was painful. The idea of being apart from baby James for the rest of Orientation was unthinkable. But it would keep him safe. Completely safe. If Mina died somehow, she didn't want to take her baby with her. She stewed over the idea in silence for a couple of minutes.

"You know," Mina said finally, "I forgot to ask the proctor something."

"What was that?"

"I was wondering if she could take little James to his father, in case something was to happen to me," Mina said. "*You* shouldn't have to carry a baby around the rest of the time you're here if the worst should come to pass. James probably has things well in hand—"

Yulia's face went white. "Is something wrong? Are you feeling okay?" She crossed the room in a couple of quick strides and put her hand to Mina's forehead.

"No, nothing like that," Mina said, smiling despite the pit in her stomach at the absence of her baby. "You and Adelaide did a great job healing me. I just meant that the challenges seem so dangerous, after these last couple."

"Yes," Yulia said. "After so many of us had run-ins with minotaurs. I'm just glad you, James, and Cara got out okay. A lot of people died in the last Dungeon."

Mina had gathered, once her physical condition was closer to normal, that Cara had explained the premature labor as a consequence of a minotaur run-in similar to what other group members had experienced. Mina hadn't corrected Cara's version of events. She owed the girl at least that much for saving her life. Though the lies were troubling.

Cara hadn't come to visit over the last couple of days. She had sent her congratulations through Adelaide, though, so Mina hadn't been able to confront her about any of this.

"Yes," Mina agreed. "Oh, by the way, did you hear anything interesting from Alba?"

Yulia bit her lip for a moment, then spoke. "She didn't want me to tell you. Everyone thinks you're really delicate right now." She gave a strained smile. "They don't know you like I do. You remember how you've been saying that the food situation could become a crisis soon?"

Mina nodded.

"Well, last night, a few people started going around to other inns and begging for food. Even though it was freezing cold. Some of the inns are either not sharing or they're running out of food. Alba thinks it's probably going to get worse."

"I see," Mina said. "We're probably shielded from the worst here since only challenge winners can enter this building. But it looks like a serious problem is brewing outside."

Yulia must have seen how worried Mina really was. Without any warning, she pulled Mina into a warm embrace.

The two of them had spent all their time together these last two days, but most of it had been spent thinking about the baby. Playing with the baby. Talking about the baby.

Mina hugged Yulia tightly in return, and the two of them stood together in silence. Locked in their own thoughts. Waiting for the next challenge to start.

Mina had so much that she wanted to say to Yulia, especially whenever she thought of her own mortality. Or the increasing tension in their Orientation. Or baby James and his future.

There was so much to say, she didn't know where to begin.

You're so good with the baby. That was a good place to start. And it was true. Just the thought made Mina smile. If something happened to her and James Sr., Yulia would be able to handle the baby.

She opened her mouth to speak, but suddenly, they were no longer in their room at the inn.

The System, in its characteristic way, had transported them elsewhere with no warning but the silent timer.

Mina looked around and found that she and Yulia were together this time. Thankfully. The rest of the team was there with them too. They must have been transported to a completely different region, or perhaps a different universe, from the Orientation world.

They stood in a beautiful meadow, flowers and clover in full bloom. The trees bore tempting fruit that gleamed like red and green gemstones.

CHAPTER FORTY-FIVE

Blue Angel

Yulia found herself in a vast green meadow, the big flat plain broken up by the occasional tree. The space stretched out to a distant horizon.

Her teammates stood all around her, packed closely like sardines. They had been transported into a compact space. When Yulia looked down, she saw that they all stood within a white circle marked onto the ground beneath their feet with white paint.

She opened her mouth to call out a warning as Mr. Davidson raised his foot to step outside it, but she wasn't quick enough to speak. Fortunately, nothing happened when he left the circle.

"Hey, there's a circle on the ground," he said, looking down at last.

"What was it, a target for the System to transport us to?" Mrs. Davidson asked.

[Everyone has now landed successfully in the location of the Pixie Collection Challenge, so we will begin our explanation. In your world's history, there is a long tradition of contact between humans and pixies, among other sentient creatures that now conceal themselves from you. Now that the System has imbued you with the ability to harness your naturally occurring Mana, it should be possible for you to see that which was previously hidden from your eyes. Once you spot them, your task in this challenge is simple. Acquire pixies, by whatever means necessary, and keep them in your circle through the end of the challenge.]

[Unlike your previous tasks, this challenge does not prescribe a specific methodology that must be used to complete it. There is no single right way to

find and gather pixies. There are no rules here except that you must gather as many pixies as possible, and you must keep them in your circle through the end of the challenge. And finally, your pixies must be alive. I must emphasize this. Dead pixies do not count. You will receive experience if you kill a pixie, just as you would if you killed a human, but that is one fewer pixie in your circle at the end. Every pixie you manage to acquire is worth one human portion of rations, so you ought to focus on acquiring as many as possible for yourselves rather than working to undermine your competition.]

[To anticipate some probable questions: If a pixie leaves and returns to your circle before the end of the challenge, you have still accomplished the mission of having them in your circle at the end. You are permitted to steal other people's pixies, though that will naturally come with its own hazards. Your time limit is ninety minutes.]

[01:30:00]

"Hm. Pixies," Mina said. She leaned in to whisper in Yulia's ear. "Are they like samodivas?"

"I don't think so," Yulia whispered back. "Samodivas are a kind of human-sized fairy. I think pixies are something else. Smaller maybe?"

Yulia was a little hazy on the origins of pixies, though she'd always been a fan of myths and fairy tales. She was pretty sure that if they were supposed to look for samodivas, it would be easier than pixies because samodivas were bigger. Either that, or it would be impossibly hard to do in ninety minutes because of their magic.

"Do we gather iron to bind them in place or something?" Mina murmured to herself.

"I think that's fairies still," Yulia whispered.

"Then I don't know anything about these pixies," Mina said. "I finally get to play a more active role, and it's a scavenger hunt for a bunch of creatures I've never heard of." She smiled and shook her head at what she'd just said.

As the sisters spoke, others on the team were stepping outside of the circle, stretching their legs, and looking around.

Yulia saw that they weren't far from the neighboring circles—only around ten feet to their left and right, respectively—which contained teams of people she didn't recognize. There were other circles in every direction in the meadow. But she didn't see people whose faces she knew. Most of the circles were far from her view. But it was disconcerting to think that this Orientation had so many people that even though she had made an effort to be social at the beginning, and people were dying in droves, she still hardly knew anyone.

"I'm sure you'll play a pivotal role, Mina," Detective DaSilva said in a consoling tone.

But Mina didn't seem to hear him. Yulia knew the look on her face. Her mind was elsewhere all of a sudden. Yulia looked at where her sister was staring. Her eyes were shifting back and forth among the other teams of people in their white circles.

"Say, Detective," Mina said, "could you tell me—" She cut herself off and looked at DaSilva. He took the cue and leaned in so that she could whisper something in his ear.

A confused look passed over his face, but then he nodded. "Okay. Will do. And you'll explain later?"

She nodded, and the detective shook his head and smiled. Yulia wanted to ask Mina what they were doing, but she recognized it might have something to do with the hunt for the serial killer. In that case, there might be an issue with discussing it in front of the whole team.

"So, how are we going to do this?" Paulo asked no one in particular. "Does anyone have any ideas?"

"I think the tradition is that pixies are quite tiny," Mr. Davidson said. "Perhaps small enough to sit in the palm of your hand. Maybe too small to see. I don't even know if we'll be able to spot them."

"Great," Paulo said. "We're catching tiny invisible people."

"You seem to know a lot about the mythology, Frank," DaSilva said. "What do you recommend we do to start? Assuming we might be able to see them?"

"Well, I have a little Celtic in me, if my maternal grandmother is honest. I would say we walk around. Look high and low. Keep your eyes peeled for little humanoids." He shrugged. "Get on our hands and knees if need be, I suppose." The old man rubbed his kneecaps as if they ached just thinking about it.

"Well, that's a good start," Mina said.

"Let's split up to cover more ground, then," Mrs. Davidson said. "Jose, do you want to come with me and Frank?"

Jose's eyes went immediately to Yulia, then darted away with a look of slight embarrassment. Yulia smiled. She both wanted and didn't want to walk around alone with Jose. Her heartbeat quickened at the thought. It said something good about him that Mrs. Davidson, who had been paired with Jose during the last challenge, wanted him in her group again.

But Yulia didn't want to leave Mina alone right now.

"I'm going to stick with Mina," Yulia said quietly.

"Um, oh yeah. She just gave birth, so someone should go with you guys to keep you safe," Jose began.

"I'll stick with Mina and Yulia," DaSilva said.

"Then we can go with the Davidsons," Paulo agreed, placing a hand on his brother's shoulder.

Oh, Jose, Yulia thought. *I know what it's like to have other people making decisions for you.*

"I guess that makes us the other team," Adelaide said, looking to her brother, Cara, and Jean in turn.

"Let's try to stay within shouting distance of each other," Yulia suggested.

"I agree," DaSilva said, nodding. "Never know what kind of dangers this place might pose."

Then Mina, Yulia, and DaSilva began their search. They walked toward the nearest tree, a twisted fruit-bearing tree that Yulia didn't recognize.

"So, can I ask why—" DaSilva stopped talking when Mina shot him a death glare.

"We're within shouting distance, so I assume someone can hear us with an ability or just high Perception," Mina said.

"Either of which you'd know about, though, correct?" DaSilva replied.

"Unless they have a Skill to hide their Status from my Investigate ability."

"You don't think that's maybe a little paranoid?" DaSilva sounded slightly impatient but not completely dismissive. Yulia suspected Mina had been right too often about too many things since Orientation began for the detective to assume she had given into paranoia.

While the two investigators discussed their case, Yulia kept her eyes peeled for pixies.

There was nothing that she could see in the long grass, though, besides patches of other plant life like wildflowers and clover.

But as they spoke, she kept the group moving and continued to search.

"I don't think it's paranoid when it's the only rational explanation for why we can't identify the person who tried to kill you," Mina said. "We have to figure this out before this person decides you're getting too close to catching them and tries again."

DaSilva had opened his mouth to reply when a shout came from another end of the meadow.

The trio turned to look and saw a group of ten people chasing something that was moving quickly back and forth through the air. It was so small and distant—fifty feet away—that all they could see was a glittering blur. But it was obvious this was what they were all searching for.

And then the thing did an aerial loop-the-loop and disappeared away from all its pursuers and spectators in an instant.

The group chasing it scattered in multiple directions, each following some path they imagined it might have taken, but Yulia thought they all missed the mark.

She couldn't see where the pixie had gone, because it was too quick and small, and the pursuit was too far away from where she, Mina, and DaSilva stood. But she had noticed that in a meandering way, the pixie had been leading the pursuit closer and closer to a large knotty tree. She was all but certain the pixie's flight had led it there.

"Hey, why don't we ask them what they saw?" DaSilva said. "That group got a closer look at the pixie they were chasing. They'll be able to tell us what colors we're looking for at least."

"Why would they tell us?" Mina asked. "We're competing for the same fixed quantity of pixies."

"That is a good point," DaSilva said. "I guess we don't need a physical description anyway."

"I think the one they were chasing flew into that tree there," Yulia said. She pointed to the place she thought the pixie had fled toward.

"Really?" DaSilva said. "Interesting. Maybe we can sneak over there and get it out from under their noses."

"Maybe we could try the tree close to us?" Yulia suggested.

"Yeah, all right," he said.

"I've got an idea for how we might do that," Mina said.

She began quietly chanting. From the silver glow around her, Yulia was fairly certain it was wind magic this time. Wind was the only element Mina had mentioned picking up besides water. And it made sense to use wind to capture a creature that they had seen could fly.

During the few minutes Mina was charging her Mana, Yulia and DaSilva observed the tree carefully as they walked around it. They tried to figure out if it contained anything more mystical than fruit.

But it wasn't until Mina's magic was ready that they saw anything. Yulia saw her sister moving from the corner of her eye. When she turned to see Mina properly, the Mana had vanished from around her body.

Then the tree started to rustle with the sound of wind shaking the branches and leaves back and forth. A few brilliantly colorful, almost perfectly round fruits fell at their feet.

"Well, maybe we'll at least get something to eat out of this," DaSilva said. "Even if we might not catch any pixies."

Mina gritted her teeth and closed her eyes. Yulia saw her moving her fingers and hands in minute, precise gestures, as if she were conducting an orchestra in her mind. The leaves and branches moved back and forth, up and down, almost like some small animal was moving through them, searching for prey.

The detective bent, picked up one of the red fruits, and looked like he wanted to bite into its glistening skin. Then he shook his head. Swallowed. Shook his head again, as if to say, *No, I'm not going to just bite into it.*

He pulled his pocket knife out and cut a sliver from the fruit. Then he sniffed it.

"Ugh!" He winced at the smell. Then he dropped the small chunk of fruit and skin onto the ground. It was only then that he seemed to notice Yulia was watching him. "Oh, sorry if I got your hopes up," he said, "but it smells absolutely disgusting. I don't think humans can eat these after all."

She looked down and saw the inside of the fruit, which was a bright shade of green, like a lizard's skin.

"Yeah, it doesn't look like something for humans to eat," Yulia agreed. "Maybe it's pixie food!"

"Uh, yeah, hope so," DaSilva agreed. He looked slightly unsettled, as if he couldn't imagine what sort of creature would eat the fruit.

Then the tree shook slightly again, right above their heads.

A small shape dropped down from the tree, right between Yulia and DaSilva.

The tiny figure was humanoid, just over ankle height, and had pale-blue skin with dragonfly-like wings. Long silver hair cascaded from the pixie's head down the front and back of the body, a glimmering waterfall that framed its face and made its shape harder to pin down. Beneath the hair it wore something shiny and silver that looked like—*no, it actually is*, Yulia realized—a candy wrapper.

After another moment of staring, Yulia realized it was a girl.

"She's so cute," Yulia said quietly. "Like a little blue angel or something."

Yulia reached down, almost transfixed by the creature's petite form. She curled her fingers into a scooping shape and reached underneath the pixie.

The pixie turned her head and sank sharp teeth into the unprotected web between Yulia's thumb and forefinger.

CHAPTER FORTY-SIX

Supply and Demand

O w!" Yulia exclaimed. "Darn it!"

She dropped the pixie and raised her hand to her mouth to kiss the wounded place.

From the corner of her eye, Yulia saw the little powder-blue person stand up. Then the pixie blew a raspberry at her.

"So rude!" Yulia said, immediately aware that she sounded silly.

Healing Aura.

Her little cut quickly knit itself back together. While it did, she stared the pixie down. The tiny figure didn't bother looking back at Yulia. Instead, she was pulling on and straightening out her delicate wings, which seemed to have been bent in the fall.

Suddenly, the pixie took to the air, wings vibrating at impossible speed—and a delicate hand came down and swatted her back to the ground.

Yulia looked up and saw Mina glaring down at the pixie disapprovingly. Yulia was a little surprised at Mina's reaction, and her face must have shown it.

Mina clearly caught the expression, and said, "I know they look like little humans, but remember, they're not. And we have to catch them if we want to eat." She turned to DaSilva. "Do we have any string or something to bind it?"

As Mina spoke, Yulia studied the pixie. She thought that despite what Mina was saying about its inhumanity, it seemed to understand what was going on. The tiny figure looked back and forth between the faces above it, as if trying to figure out the relations among the people who were holding it captive. Though her features weren't quite human—she was a bit toothier than any human Yulia had ever seen, now that she took a more careful look at her face, and her ears were slightly pointed—the pixie's eyes were intelligent. Feral, perhaps, but intelligent.

And would a dumb creature really make itself a makeshift jacket out of a candy wrapper?

"Can you understand me?" Yulia asked, staring at the pixie.

"Of course I can!" she replied almost instantly, voice indignant. She spoke in words that sounded like gibberish, yet they were translated immediately by some System magic. "Do you think I'm some kind of dumb animal?"

"Well, wonders never cease," Mina said quietly.

"Nice magic, bitch!" the pixie said in her tinny, wrathful voice, jabbing her finger in Mina's direction. "Wait until I get back into the air, and I'll show you some real magic."

"She can talk, which means that theoretically, she—and others of her kind—can be reasoned with," Mina said to herself.

"Why were you hiding in the tree?" Yulia asked.

"Well, if I wasn't, it wouldn't be hide and seek, would it?" the pixie replied, shrugging.

"What would it take to get you and some others of your kind to come with us voluntarily?" Mina asked.

"That depends," the pixie said dramatically, raising a tiny silver eyebrow. "What've you got?"

"That depends on what you'd value," Mina said slowly.

"You like shiny things?" Yulia asked. She stood closest to the pixie, bending over her for better eye contact. Mina and DaSilva stood just behind Yulia, keeping a little more distance from the tiny person.

"Uh, Yulia, maybe we let your sister handle the negotiation," DaSilva said.

"Actually, as it happens, I like many things humans have," the pixie said. "Shinies are among my favorites, though. Love this delicate fabric you lot make." She rustled the candy wrapper that wrapped around her neck and front.

"You know, I think Yulia kind of has this down," Mina said. She sounded a little surprised, but also almost on the verge of laughter. She looked down at the wee person. "Can we have the pleasure of knowing our new friend's name?"

Yulia looked at the pixie and waited.

"I'm Seissylt, then," the pixie said, slightly annoyed. "Sissy to my friends, but you can just call me Seissylt. I don't think we're going to be friendly."

"Oh, I don't know about that, Seissylt," Yulia said. "Do you want to tell me how you ended up here, in a game of hide and seek with us?"

"That's a long story," Seissylt said.

"We have a little time," Yulia said, smiling patiently.

"You know, I'm almost sorry I bit you," Seissylt said. She sounded a little surprised to hear herself saying it.

"Well, no harm done," Yulia replied.

"Why don't we leave the two of you alone for a few minutes to get acquainted?" Mina said.

The pixie gave her a dirty look.

"Don't think I'm going to forget the indignity you subjected me to, princess!" Seissylt said.

"I wouldn't expect you to," Mina said, "but since you seem to like my sister better than me, I thought it would only be hospitable to leave you in her care."

"Hospitable," Seissylt muttered. "Talking about being hospitable to me in my own field!"

Yulia scrunched her face up as she tried to think of the right words to break the ice again.

"So, what's your family like?" she finally asked.

"Well, I'm the sixth sister," Seissylt began.

"You know, I think Yulia might actually solve our pixie problem while we give her this space," Detective DaSilva said. He kept looking back toward Yulia. On some level, he still couldn't believe that there was a tiny person talking to Yulia. She was conducting humanity's first known diplomacy with another race of sentient humanoids.

And we're here doing what exactly?

"So, what did you want to talk about?" he asked.

"Earlier, I asked you to remember the groups we had near us. Do you remember them?" Mina asked. Her voice was lowered conspiratorially.

"Yes, I remember them."

She lowered her voice almost to a whisper, forcing him to lean in to hear her. "Were they groups that had their food stolen from them?"

"They were," he replied. "Are you going to tell me why you're asking? Or maybe I should say: how did you know that?"

"I used my Investigate Skill on the people who were around us when we landed here," Mina began.

"As you apparently do habitually," DaSilva observed.

"Yes," she said.

"You know, the civil liberties people are going to hate you when we get back to Earth."

She snickered. Then she shook her head, and her expression became serious. "There were two people, one in each of those two groups, who had alarming items in their Statuses."

"Like theft Skills or something?"

"They both had the same things in common: Talents called Cannibalism and Wendigo Contagion, and Skills named Anthropophagy, Pillage, Heart of Ice, Limitless Hunger, and Wendigo Transformation."

"None of that sounds good," DaSilva said. "What does 'anthropophagy' mean?"

"Another word for cannibalism," Mina said.

"Those are some awfully suspicious abilities." He sighed. "I guess they're probably the ones who stole the food, then."

She nodded. "And more than that, I think."

"You think they're our killers?"

"I think it's pretty suspicious that they have a Skill related to eating people, and we happen to have a fair number of people randomly dying while we're also slowly suffering more and more from a shortage of food."

"But none of them are on our team," DaSilva said. "None of them were around when Yulia and I were crossing the bridge. There was another team in a different part of the Dungeon at the time, but it wasn't one of those two. So, who tried to kill me?"

"One of two answers," Mina replied. "Either someone else has the same abilities that those two do and this is spreading like a disease through the population, or someone on our team has an ability that lets them alter their Status."

"That's where I thought you might be going. You tried Investigating everyone else on our team before but didn't come up with anything. I guess this is why."

"Okay," she said. She took a deep breath. "Now that you know what I know, what do we do next?"

"First, what's the deal with Wendigo Contagion?"

"The description said it's about their willingness to do anything to satisfy their greed in an environment of scarcity. That trait drew the interest of something called the Wendigo. And the Wendigo Contagion Talent generates the Cannibalism Talent and the Skills Heart of Ice, Limitless Hunger, and Wendigo Transformation."

DaSilva let out a low whistle. "That is a powerful ability. Too bad it's evil. I'm guessing you don't happen to know what the Wendigo is?"

She shook her head.

"Then we need to find a Native American, quick. Or someone who's familiar with their mythology. I'm pretty sure it's a Native thing."

"Must be a demon or something," Mina murmured.

"Yeah. Sounds right. Let's get back. I'll do some investigating of my own once we get back. I'm guessing it goes without saying that we keep this between ourselves?"

Mina nodded.

"That includes even Yulia," DaSilva said. "Until we have a list of everyone who has Wendigo Contagion in their Status, we can't have any possibility of leaks. At some point, I'll have to have you Investigate everyone who's still alive. I wish my Identify had leveled up as quickly as yours."

"Yeah," Mina said softly.

DaSilva thought for a moment how unfair it was that he would have to put this young mother in danger by asking her to positively identify all of the possible killers in their midst. But a lot of unfair things were happening recently. Including an increasing number of innocent people dying. They had to put a stop to it, no matter what it took. As soon as possible.

By the time Mina and DaSilva returned to where Yulia and Seissylt had been, the two were gone. It didn't take long to find them, though. They had walked over to sit inside of the team's circle. The rest of the team were already back, along with a huddled group of little blue people stationed around Seissylt. The humans stood in a loose semicircle surrounding the pixies. It looked like around a dozen of the little people, though since they were so small, and they all stood close together, it was hard to get a good count from a distance.

Yulia was the only one seated, next to the group of pixies who were quietly chattering.

"Well, I guess the team figured out the secret to attracting pixies," Mina said, looking at Yulia curiously.

"No, it was all Yulia," Jose said, answering Mina's unspoken question. "It's difficult enough for us to catch these things—uh, these little people, I mean—but holding onto them seems to be pretty impossible, unless they're willing to stay."

Mina looked down and saw Seissylt nodding along with Jose.

Good job considering the audience, Jose, Mina thought.

"So, you made some sort of deal," Mina said, looking to Yulia again.

"Yes," she said simply, smiling slightly.

"Nothing you need my help with?"

Yulia shook her head, and her smile grew slightly wider.

"Well done." Mina returned her sister's smile. "Anything else interesting happen while I was gone?"

"Just the expected," Mrs. Davidson said. "People are trying to steal—uh, kidnap—pixies from the other teams. Someone even tried to kidnap little, uh, Sea Salt, and that's why we're all gathered here. Strength in numbers!"

"People are the worst," Cara added.

Mina looked at her and gave her the slimmest of smiles.

"Her name is Seissylt," Yulia corrected gently, looking down at her apparent new friend.

Seissylt smiled up at Yulia as if thoroughly charmed by her. Then the pixie ruined it by speaking. "When do my siblings and I get our sweet reward, by the way?" Seissylt asked.

"Same as I said before, Seissylt," Yulia said. "In the last two minutes of the challenge I'll start passing out your gifts."

Ah. Bribery. Historically, a very useful tool for diplomacy . . .

"I won't ask what we're giving them, since I don't want to give the other teams any ideas," Mina said. "I'm guessing most of them don't have nearly as many pixies in their circles as we do, so if there's some sort of victory bonus, we'll get it."

"I was thinking we could give the information away, but we should wait until a little later," Yulia said. "Just give the other teams a little less time than us to make some friends."

"Okay," Mina said, nodding. "You figured this out yourself. I'm comfortable with your decision." She looked around at the other team members. "You guys are okay with this too, right?"

"Choosing to do the decent thing hasn't backfired on us yet," Mr. Davidson said. "Despite my skepticism way back when you first wanted to share food. The other teams seem to look at us just a little differently since then. Sure, there was that misunderstanding that Paul created. But once people learned the truth, and especially since some people are going hungry lately, I think they've come to respect the example that we set because of you."

Jean nodded along with him. "I think that if we hadn't decided to share when we did, a lot more people would be hungry or dead right now."

"All right," Mina said quietly. She checked the timer. **[00:42:11]**. "What do we do for forty-five minutes?"

"Maybe Seissylt could tell us more about the pixies and their lives," Yulia suggested, looking down at Seissylt with an expression of rapt interest.

She's really come out of her shell here, Mina thought. Maybe the System wasn't such a bad thing. If not for all the incentive structures that seemed designed to get people to betray or murder each other.

There was a general murmur of assent from the group in response to Yulia's suggestion.

None of them, after all, were going anywhere. So, they spent the next forty minutes learning about the ways of the pixies.

They had apparently always lived on Earth, among humans. At some difficult to define point over the last couple of centuries, humans lost the ability to see them. Some critical mass of faith in the magical world was required. Pixie lore suggested it was connected to the departure of the most prominent magical peoples from Earth, even though the elves and dwarves left over a millennium before this event.

Pixie history was ephemeral, like their lives. They were a short-lived race who typically reached maturity and died in the span of twenty years.

Fortunately, every birth by a pixie tended to produce at least two infants, if not more. Seissylt was named for the fact that she was the sixth born of their mother's twenty-seven-child brood.

Pixies liked beautiful things above all else. Trees with vibrant-colored fruits, blooming flowers, green meadows, and wild horses. Seissylt mentioned that she particularly loved braiding the manes of horses.

Their magic centered around nature. Although Seissylt had threatened to show Mina her magic, it had been a bluff; they were much stronger with benevolent magic than harmful magic. Under a pixie's friendly touch, nature bloomed and wild animals acted tame.

The narrative of pixie life reminded Mina to an extent of the noble savage myth about pre-industrial human societies. Complete with the communion with nature and the short but happy and dignified lives. She didn't know whether to pity or envy them.

And they were absolutely fascinated with humans. They didn't live long enough to hone beautiful craftsmanship themselves, so they collected discarded human objects. That was why Seissylt wore a candy wrapper. She found the beauty in what Mina would have thrown away without a second thought.

"So, I guess I know what kind of gifts we're giving them." Mina said. It was nearing the end of the challenge's time limit, and although she wanted to hear more about them, she knew that she needed to break the spell of the pixie's explanation. If Yulia really wanted to pass information to the other teams, it was now or never.

"That's right," Yulia said. "I have a bunch of pretty things that are pixie sized!" She reached into her bag and pulled out a handful of small pieces of colorful cloth.

Mina pursed her lips to keep from laughing. Yulia was planning to give the pixies a bunch of her old scrunchies.

Don't laugh! she told herself. *The pixies probably want this stuff. Supply and demand says the value of the scrunchies is whatever the market will bear. Heck, Seissylt is wearing a candy wrapper right now!*

"Well done," Mina said after a long pause. "Who wants to go tell the other teams our secret?"

There were multiple volunteers. Who wouldn't want to be the bearer of good news?

Finally, almost everyone left. Mina was left with the pixies, Yulia, and DaSilva.

"How does it feel to be the person who single-handedly won this challenge for us?" Mina asked Yulia.

Yulia beamed and opened her mouth to respond.

Then there was movement in the corner of Mina's vision. The population counter was dropping again.

[2,632/3,397 Survivors]

[2,631/3,397 Survivors]

A few seconds passed.

[2,630/3,397 Survivors]

Oh no . . .

CHAPTER FORTY-SEVEN

Mixed Signals

James stared at the wolf pack through the eyes of his Skin Balloon, faintly puzzled.

He finally opened his human eyes and met the gazes of the people all around him.

Well, don't look at me as if I have all the answers, he thought. But he also enjoyed it. The way they were all ready to move on his word, to advance or retreat according to his say-so. The power was intoxicating.

He cleared his throat. First, he focused on Amalia. "I saw the wolf pack. They really are just sitting there. It does feel a lot like an ambush." His eyes shifted to Cliff and Harry. "At the same time, though, I couldn't see any sign of other forces positioned anywhere nearby. There is a lot of mist covering some of the ground, but I had my balloon monster push through that. Still, I've seen no sign of any reserve forces or backups." He turned his eyes toward Mitzi now. "I don't know if we have some way of shifting some of the liquid in the swamp to see if there are creatures hiding underwater, but that's the only concealment I can think of that would have worked against me."

Mitzi frowned and shook her head. "I've tried using magic on the swamp before. It seems to have some Mana infused into the soil and water. It resists any attempt to alter its condition or destroy it."

"Yeah, I've noticed the same thing," James said. That was why he hadn't tried to drown the wolves that had besieged the Rodriguezes in swamp water before.

"So, what do we do, chief?" Cliff asked.

James smiled grimly. "We press forward. Once we get there, I'll hit them with the same one-two punch that took them out of the Rodriguez camp fight. While we move, we remain alert and prepared for attack by the Ghouls. We keep a tight formation in case they start to pop up from underwater. If something starts trying to pull one of us under, everyone around the victim should raise the alarm." He looked from one person to the other as he said the next words. "Pass that down to everyone, please. If a Ghoul is attacking someone as we move, we can almost certainly save that person from getting drowned, but only if the reaction is quick."

He said that with confidence, and the Ring of Lies felt warm against his fingers as he spoke. Internally, he wasn't so certain. He might be leading his people into a massacre if the Ghouls had some Skills he hadn't anticipated.

Kind of wishing I brought Sierra here, actually. I don't know if the undead condition spreads through infection or some kind of magic. Either way, if the Ghouls start popping out and trying to use some ability to make my people into undead, it would be good to have someone with a Skill that removes foreign influences.

Then again, if the Ghouls could transform people into their kind with a bite or a touch, he would have seen them do it at the Rodriguez camp before, right?

As James spoke, he saw the people all around him nodding. He'd infected them all with his faux conviction. He hoped he wasn't leading them astray. But the monsters of this swamp had to be purged, and he didn't know of anyone besides himself who could lead the effort.

Besides, it's not as though you'd trust anyone else to do this, commented his dark inner voice. *Just accept that the role of power, glory, and leadership is yours, and be happy about it. These people will follow you even if you lead them into a massacre.*

James forcefully pulled his thoughts away from this self-aggrandizement. He shifted to a practical question he'd been contemplating. He'd gained two Skills from Pillaging a pair of Ghouls he'd killed while defending the Rodriguez camp. Unfortunately, he couldn't Pillage more Ghouls, because he wanted to let his allies Loot them, and he wasn't going out of his way to tell anyone that he was using a different Skill.

But there had been few Ghouls killed at the Rodriguez camp anyway. The main course of Pillaging would come later.

The two Skills were Minor Body Modification and Autonomic Nervous System Override.

The question was, should he combine the two Skills?

Minor Body Modification allowed the Ghouls to do things like dislocate their shoulders to punch further and unhinge their jaws to viciously bite into prey.

Autonomic Nervous System Override allowed the user to do things like control their own heartbeats and manipulate their digestion speed. Even though the Ghouls were quasi-undead monsters, they still ate flesh to rebuild Stamina.

James would be able to use those Skills to great effect too, but if he combined them, he thought he might transcend the already expanded limits of his body.

The risk he envisioned was that with this hypothetical Skill, plus Berserk Mode, he might become an unstoppable, mindless monster, capable of annihilating everything in his path. Possibly at the cost of his own body being destroyed. He'd read a story like that once.

The protagonist acquired a set of enchanted armor that allowed him to fight on until he'd shed every drop of blood and broken every bone in his body. But without someone to magically pull him out of his berserk trance, the character would keep going until he died.

No, that won't happen to you, James told himself. *You have the perfect mental Skills to control that. Self-Control and Mind of the Predator should more than counter it.*

He resolved to try the Skill Fusion on a temporary basis. He set the combination to last for five hours.

Minor Body Modification and Autonomic Nervous System Override combined to form Full Body Control. A bland name, but he appreciated the description.

[Full Body Control: Consciously manipulate and direct any part of your body to alter its position, behavior, or composition according to your desire. Subject to limitations based on your Fortitude and basic physiology. Consumes Stamina.]

James could feel himself able to deliberately control muscles he'd never tried to maneuver before. The excitement of something so new made him a little giddy, and he played with it for a few minutes while the group spread the word about the plan. He inflated one lung with as much air as he could, just to try it. He adjusted the flow of blood to his extremities. He almost dropped to his knees when he accidentally stopped his own heart for a few seconds, but he managed to restart it before the world went black.

Okay, enough of that for now!

As he finished messing with the Skill, Jeremiah Rotter approached him.

"I believe everyone's been informed of your orders, sir. We're all ready to leave."

Weird that he's the one coming to tell me, James thought. Or was it? Rotter seemed very interested in ingratiating himself with James. Maybe he'd volunteered.

"Let's move out, then," James replied with a small smile. More loudly, he called out, "Move out!"

And people began to move. They formed a tight formation, just as James had ordered. It ended up being a triangular shape, with James, Amalia, and Harry leading the way to the wolf pack.

For several minutes they trudged through the swamp water toward the enemy position.

Then James could see the wolf pack with his own eyes. They were still hidden from everyone else by the mist, so he raised a fist to indicate to his squad that they should stop behind him.

There was a slight jostling as people froze, and some bumped into others, but James mostly ignored it.

He turned around and quietly requested a head count, just to make sure no one had been carried off by Ghouls from his rearguard.

And he began Silent Spellcasting, preparing his Illusion Magic.

"What are you doing, sir?" Harry asked behind him in a hushed tone.

James allowed a little part of his mind to deviate from the Mana-charging task to answer Harry.

"I'm preparing an illusion to catch the wolves in," he said. "I'm planning to hit them with Illusion Magic, then a gravity bomb, same as the last time. Should turn them into sitting ducks for the group."

"Ah, right. Of course. Um, very clever planning." There was a note of resigned envy in Harry's voice.

James made a mental note to acquire some new Skill that he wouldn't mind sharing with the scout, just so he would feel a little better about his own set of abilities. Maybe he could outfit everyone who followed him with more Skills than they currently had. That would certainly give him a kind of added legitimacy as a leader.

There was the hazard that people he bribed with power would only follow him until they had a better offer, but James was confident that he was one of the strongest people alive right now. And those who stuck with him and showed loyalty could get an ever-escalating set of powers.

This might become the foundation for an empire, now that he thought of it.

After several minutes of charging, James launched his Illusion Magic attack at the wolves. The aura of Mana around him dissipated entirely for a moment until he started charging gravity Mana.

He kept his eyes on the wolf pack as he charged his second attack. They were moving now, rising from their resting positions and attacking each other. Or at least most of them were.

Above them, in the most elevated position on the uneven patch of grassy soil, sat a three-headed beast that Identify labeled as the Alpha Forest Wolf King, level thirty. That creature looked down at everything happening below him with a contemptuous curl of its lips.

James heard it bark out an order. "Cease this foolishness at once, children! Everyone, return to your seated positions."

And the other wolves obeyed. It was as if the leader had broken the spell with his voice. Those that had started to fight each other backed off and returned to their starting points as best they could.

Interesting. James could tell by how clumsily the wolves moved that they were still caught to some degree in his illusion. They didn't know quite where things were. They expected obstacles where there were none. They were getting mixed signals from their senses and their leader.

But they're obeying the leader instead of their lying eyes. Did not see that coming. Is it a Skill? Maybe one of the Skills that Alpha Presence generates? Has to be, I'd think. Whatever he's doing, it's more powerful than I would've guessed. Will it counteract some of the effects of gravity magic?

But there was only one way to find out. He kept charging his attack.

"Human!" the Wolf King barked loudly. "I know you're out there. I can smell you and your friends. They smell like fear! Come out and fight me, human. Face to face. Like a man! Unless you're afraid too."

James smirked. Such blatant taunting. *Who would that work on?*

"Well, what are we going to do about that?" Cliff spoke up from a little bit behind James.

Oh.

"I'm going to finish charging my attack, then we rush in!" James called back. He wasn't worried about the wolves overhearing him, since he figured they couldn't do anything with the illusion still effective. Even if the leader had avoided the effects himself somehow, he wouldn't be crazy enough to charge at James's group by himself. And if he was, James welcomed that stupidity.

That was how he thought. Then there was a sound from in front of him that made all the little hairs on his arms and legs stand on end. It resembled a hundred footsteps in unison.

He turned and saw the wolf pack rise, as one, to their feet. They began marching forward, moving directly toward James and his group where they stood hidden in the mist.

Goddammit, Cliff! A sharp intake of breath. *No, this is my fault. I shouldn't have said anything back to him. I was just a little way away from charging as much power as I needed. All right. Need to launch it at the group before they scatter.*

James released the Mana and observed the impact. The whole pack of wolves slowed down slightly. But it wouldn't be enough to make this easy. The wolves would be upon them in a minute or less.

James's body tensed, and he drew the Ego Antler Spear from his magic satchel. Then he noticed that no one else was moving. It dawned on him that the others in his group still couldn't see the wolf pack. The mist was too dense, and their Perception was too far below his.

"Brace for contact!" James called. "They're coming to us!"

CHAPTER FORTY-EIGHT

Poison

The band of humans standing behind James shifted into battle stances.

Suddenly, though, the numbers they'd brought didn't seem enough. James couldn't immediately understand why, but he had a bad feeling that he was leading this team into a defeat.

He shook the feeling off. Whether his intuition was right or wrong about this, if he showed any hint of doubt, it would guarantee his force would lose confidence and run. And that would mean higher casualties regardless of the eventual outcome.

James strode forward, trying to lead by example. As he passed through the mist, he ran across one of the first wolves in the enemy formation, a low-level beast that he crushed underfoot. Then the rest of the front line crashed into him, and he was grateful for the Royal Exoarmor. Wolf after wolf tried to clamp down on his arms and legs, but their fangs could find no purchase and do no damage to the armor. James was able to fling the beasts away.

He strode forward, and the rest of the wolves seemed to scatter from around him, leaving him unable to see through the mist.

Then he heard screams from behind him.

No! He immediately sent a command to the nearest Skin Balloons to fly down and try their best to defend his allies. He could make more of those things any time he shed his skin, after all. But his human comrades were much less replaceable.

There were pained howls following the screams, but James doubted that his group could withstand the wolf pack without him in their midst. The wolves had shown, when attacking James, that they moved as a coordinated body. They should still be under the influence of his illusion, but somehow, they could even find his group through the mist.

He forced himself to think calmly about the situation and run through possible strategies he could employ now that his initial plan had failed.

Go after the big guy? I'll almost certainly kill their leader, and that would weaken the pack. But how long would that take?

Go and fight the fodder alongside my group? That would win some political points, no doubt, and I'd be keeping the weaker members safe by being near them, so maybe the casualty rate would be lower. But what if the big guy gets involved?

James decided to pull back to where his group was positioned rather than look for the leader in the mist.

As he came upon his side, he saw the wolves had them surrounded now, but the humans were holding their own. Damien had transformed and was tearing into a wolf in front of him. Cliff was dueling with a Command Forest Wolf using the Ego Spidersword. He moved back and forth with the creature in a dance of fangs, claws, and blade that looked evenly matched. The other wolves were kept at bay by a barrage of fireballs and lightning bolts from a rotating group of Mages led by Mitzi. The humans who had chosen warrior Classes were having a bit more trouble keeping up with the creatures, but the wolves couldn't follow up on attacks to land lethal bites on vulnerable areas. The magical attacks kept them from staying in the close range that they needed. The battle seemed to be locked in a stalemate.

Then two more Command Forest Wolves appeared on two less-defended flanks.

They lunged in, leaping through the mist and suddenly pulling people backward with them. *Jen Robinson and Victor Rotari*, James recalled. Not people James had spent much time with or gotten to know well. And definitely not among his squad's strongest members.

These were escapees from the Rostov camp who had been held captive for longer than most. They hadn't gotten many opportunities to level or develop their abilities.

It stung James to see people he had marched into this fight, people he was responsible for, pulled into the mist.

He jumped in after them. He heard the sound of tearing flesh, and then he was next to a Command Forest Wolf that had a young man gripped by the collarbone in one of its two sets of jaws.

James swung the Ego Antler Spear at the head that wasn't holding the man, and he heard the sound of flesh tearing as he chopped through the neck. The head dropped limp, gushing blood. The beast's other head dropped the man and began charging a breath attack. Lightning crackled between its jaws.

James simply stabbed the spear into the open mouth, and the tip embedded itself deep in the wolf's second skull.

"Thank you," croaked Rotari.

But James was already pulling the spear free and rushing toward the next wolf.

This one loomed out of the mist, its jaws bloody red.

Under its paws, James saw Robinson. She was obviously near death. Her chest rose and fell in ragged breaths.

He glared at the monster that stood above her.

"No," James hissed. "Fucking sneak attacks. Cowardly son of a bitch!"

He made an angry stab at the Command Forest Wolf's center of mass. It tried to dodge but only succeeded in moving slightly to the side.

The spear pierced through the beast's chest and out the other side, and it collapsed instantly. There was a ding.

Oh. I hit it in the heart, he realized dully.

The sound of apparent dying breaths pulled his attention to the ground. He flung the wolf corpse to the side and knelt in front of the woman. He dropped the spear at his side.

Laying on Hands.

The thick green aura surrounded both his palms, and he tried to heal Robinson in the places where she was most wounded. But her condition was even worse than he'd realized. She had wounds in multiple locations: a horrible bite halfway through her chest, claw slashes through key arteries in her neck and left thigh. She was gushing blood from a dozen places.

There were too many fatal wounds. After thirty seconds of him trying to repair her broken body, he sensed that she had passed away.

James groaned in frustration, then picked up the spear and turned around. He sensed that something big was coming, and fast.

Even through the mist, it was easy to see it once he turned. The Alpha Forest Wolf King was too large to conceal. The size of James's own car.

He charged in at great speed, then leaped into the air ten feet from the humans. James realized he would kill whoever he struck as he landed.

Time seemed to slow down. James could process what everyone else was doing. Cliff, Mitzi, Harry, Amalia, everyone—even Damien—looked terrified of the beast.

James made an instant decision, and his body moved to execute at superhuman speed.

Lightning Strike!

He hit the Wolf King with impossible momentum. It wasn't quite enough to stop the beast's forward movement. With James's size, he felt almost like a deer striking a car, completely outmatched in weight and size. But it was enough. He deflected the monstrous body a few feet to the left, so he skidded past the group harmlessly.

James was thrown back by the impact too, but Way of the Predator kicked in. He released his hold on the spear and instinctively curled into a ball to minimize any possible fall damage.

As James rolled, Mind of the Predator worked through the possibilities in an instant. If James fought alongside his group, and the Wolf King fought alongside his pack, James's group would have a 73 percent chance of victory. James personally had a 96 percent chance of survival in this scenario. The group would likely lose around five more people during the fight.

If he managed to distract the Wolf King, however, the group would have an 88 percent chance of victory, they wouldn't lose more than one other person, and the chances of James's own survival only dropped to 94 percent.

Easy choice. I need to preserve my assets. I know I can kill this thing anyway. Nothing in this forest can threaten me.

The Wolf King turned to him and growled menacingly.

James pressed his palms to the ground and frog-jumped instantly to his feet. The spear levitated back into his right hand as he landed.

"You and me," he said, staring at the Wolf King. "One on one, like you wanted earlier."

Which head do I look at when I'm talking? he thought. *I guess it doesn't matter. I'll chop them off until there's only one left.*

"Finally," the Wolf King growled from his middle head. His mouth twisted into something between a hideous snarl and a smile. Then he launched itself at James.

James threw an Air Strike at the creature as he moved in midair. Then he sidestepped where he would land and positioned himself to counterattack with the spear.

The Mana-enhanced wind blade struck the Wolf King's body but didn't seem to do much. James saw a small cut on his central maw and chest, but the cuts began closing on their own almost as soon as they opened.

Okay, he thought. *This could take a while.*

As the creature landed, he pivoted and threw itself at James. He danced back and slashed with the spear. Once. Twice. A third time, this one gouging out a long cut down the creature's neck.

It didn't seem to matter. They each began closing as soon as he'd made the injuries. The healing effect came slower the more injuries the Wolf King suffered, certainly, but the rate didn't make much difference. The cuts just weren't deep enough to do any meaningful damage.

At the same time, the Wolf King was too slow to land most of its attacks. James had dodged three out of the last four. The bite that landed left deep teeth marks in the armor but only tiny pinprick holes on James's body. Those healed just as quickly as the injuries he made on the Wolf King.

James thought he would eventually win, but this was looking like a slog. He would have to get creative.

How do I win this fast?

As he had this thought, the head on the right, which had held its jaws clenched tightly during their exchange, opened wide. Green gas began pouring out.

Poison, James realized. He danced backward, trying to get a little further from the other ongoing fight. He didn't want his people embroiled in this cloud of poison. He had no way of knowing if the wolf pack had resistances to it, but the humans certainly did not.

The Wolf King obliged James by chasing after him, spewing poison more slowly as it went.

Full Body Control!

James jumped back once more from the Wolf King and sucked in breath until his lungs were completely full. He ordered his body to make use of the air he had inside him until the fight was over, and Mind of the Predator took over management of the resource.

Finally, James could stop running and start fighting again.

He used Lightning Strike with the spear, and he left another long cut down the Wolf King's side. But the monster grinned at him, and then the central head breathed lightning over him. For a moment, he felt stunned. A tiny amount of air escaped his lips.

Then he regained complete control. He sprung backward and wished he could breathe heavily. But his body was obeying him, aside from that momentary slip when he was electrocuted.

Lightning isn't going to work, James thought. He remembered the last fight he and his original crew had been in with the wolves, back in the early days of Orientation. The Command Forest Wolf that breathed fire could consume the element of fire. *And the pelt I got from that one was flame resistant! The King's probably resistant to the fire element too, isn't it? That's what I would expect to come out of that third head.*

As he had the thought, the leftmost head spewed flames at James, and he leaped out of the way with plenty of room.

Confirmed that the element of fire will also be no use. We really are in a stalemate, eh? Probably immune to poison too.

Just in case, he drew a Wolfbone Dagger from the magic satchel at his hip. *Predator's Venomous Armaments!* A greenish-black substance oozed from his skin onto the weapon. Then he threw it.

It bounced harmlessly off the Wolf King's hide as the monster charged at James. He jumped back again, maintaining his distance.

"Was that a piece of one of my children?" the Wolf King asked, his tone mocking. "Did you think that could harm me?"

James shrugged, as if to say, *You never know until you try.*

The Wolf King lunged at him again, and James placed his foot in a bit of ground that gave way. He slipped backward as the King fell toward him. Caught slightly off guard this time, he prepared to respond to the attack with a Predator's Strike.

His spear was pointed the wrong way because he'd slipped, but he could still land a good hit with his fist. The Wolf King landed a bite on James's shoulder at the same time that his fist struck the King's rib cage.

James felt a thick pair of ribs fracture under his punch, and the Wolf King's bite weakened enough for him to pull free.

The King looked staggered for a moment from the blow. Then James saw the ribs beginning to pull themselves back together.

The spear gave off a gentle heat in his hand. *Now!* It seemed to be insisting on an aggressive attack while the beast was healing.

All right, James thought. The spear hadn't done much damage to the Wolf King so far, but maybe this moment would be different. *Just to make sure the attack lands . . .*

James opened his mouth and made eye contact with the Wolf King. *Compulsion!*

"Stay!"

The Wolf King's whole body stiffened involuntarily for a moment.

And James lunged, spear pointed at the poison-spewing right-side head of the Wolf King.

Deep Antler Penetration!

CHAPTER FORTY-NINE

The Last Word

Abattle was waged between James's Will and the Alpha Forest Wolf King's. In the arena of their minds, thousands of soldiers modeled on the two combatants fought and killed and died.

The struggle lasted for less than a second, and it was a decisive victory for James.

In the next moment, the Ego Antler Spear stabbed deep into the furthest right neck of the Wolf King. The blade pierced through to the place where the head met the neck, and James felt the spinal cord break. And the spear broke too. He felt the tip of it break off on contact with the wolf's bone.

Damn, he thought.

As James pulled the weapon from the Wolf King's dead head, the remaining two heads howled and writhed violently, but the King's four paws remained firmly planted in place.

Then James stepped back, and finally, the Wolf King broke free of the paralyzing effect he had created. The second head snapped its jaws at him, but he was slow. Stunned. Easily avoided.

For his part, James felt a strange sentimentality. He wondered if the spear had some way of recovering from this. It had been with him through the Spider Queen fight, and now it had scored a decisive blow against the Wolf King. And he knew it had personality, to some degree. Intelligence. It had moved in his defense and returned to his hand more than once.

Looking down at the broken spear tip, he felt almost as if he were about to lose a friend.

The two remaining sets of jaws snapped at James. He refocused himself and jumped backward, narrowly avoiding the gnashing teeth. The fight was the important thing. The faster he won, the better off his group would be. He had no real weapon now. He wasn't going to use the spear.

As his feet landed, he released it. It hovered indecisively beside him, looking for an opening to help, but was clearly aware that it couldn't do much without either its pointed tip or James's Strength.

But James wasn't going to rely on the weapon. He'd learned something with the last few exchanges.

Even though his elemental powers did no damage, his fists did plenty. Every one of his physical attacks was dangerous to the Wolf King. He was stronger than this monster. Stronger, faster, tougher. With at least equal healing abilities.

He didn't need to use his limited Mana for any more experimental attacks. He just needed to get his hands dirty.

The Wolf King lunged in for another bite with his left head. James threw a heavy punch and knocked the head away. It smacked into the central head, and James saw that the two heads looked disoriented. He put his hands together and made a club with his interlaced fingers.

Then he bludgeoned the leftmost head again. And again. And again.

Little spurts of blood spattered on James's face from the still bleeding dead head as well as the one he was bludgeoning, but he ignored them.

The central head tried to snap at him and stop the assault, but James kicked out. He was dimly aware that his foot striking the central head knocked one of the teeth from the wolf's jaw.

After a few more punches, the left head finally looked concussed. It dropped, as if the beast was ashamed. Its eyes became unfocused. When the head was able to rise from the slump, it snapped feebly at places where James wasn't, as if it was seeing double. Then it fell back into its slumped position.

In the few key seconds while the left head was disoriented, James balled his right hand into a fist. *Predator's Strike.*

He punched his fist down at the lowered left head once more, and it struck with terrible, brutal impact. The neck made a sickening snapping sound. Then the head twisted and slumped, lifeless.

The central head tried to snap at James, but it moved more slowly now, weakened and off-balance.

James ducked underneath it and used another Predator's Strike. His fingernails hardened, and he aimed just under the rib cage. His right hand penetrated deep into the Wolf King's body.

Hot blood and guts enveloped his arm, but James ignored them.

The Wolf King tried to charge a shot of lightning breath, but James used his left hand and squeezed its throat until the lightning dissipated. The King's claws scratched at James's armor, but they couldn't find purchase, let alone deal damage.

James pushed his right hand forward and reached further into the wolf's chest. Grabbed hold of the heart. Squeezed. Crushed it like an orange until he felt the juice pulsating through his fingers.

This feels familiar, he thought. Though the heart was bigger and tougher this time, and the individual it belonged to wasn't human, this wasn't so different from his execution of Officer Ross.

A moment later, he could tell that it was over. There wasn't a ding quite yet. But he felt all the tension leave the King's body.

"You've won," croaked the Wolf King, voice damaged from the injuries to his throat. "Congratulations." The last word was followed by several coughs and a trickle of blood from between the King's lips.

James didn't detect any hint of resentment in his tone.

Remarkable. The purity of this creature's heart. Have I ever seen something face death with such dignity?

James felt a twinge of regret. *I wish I hadn't needed to kill you. But it was inevitable, wasn't it? Yes, it must have been. Just like all the others.*

"Children!" the Wolf King barked with surprising force and volume. The fight in the other part of the swamp, which James had barely been paying attention to, seemed to quiet down suddenly. James realized he could hear the sound of charging wolf paws.

He swallowed. *I don't think I'm in good enough condition to fight the whole pack now. I'm not really injured*—he had hardly a scratch at this point since his injuries had healed throughout the fight—*but my Stamina's taken a pretty severe hit.*

"Human, you must lead my pack now," the Wolf King whispered, staring into James's eyes beseechingly.

"What?" James was stunned.

"Well, they need a leader. You're strong. Members of your Race follow you willingly. Please don't slaughter them. They're loyal and well-behaved." The Wolf King's tone turned pleading.

"We were just trying to kill each other," James said.

"I forgive you. Will you forgive us?"

Easy for you to say. You're dying!

[You have been offered the Title of Pack Leader. Accept? Y/N]

James wanted to discuss this further with the Wolf King, but then he heard a ding. He didn't need to look down to know the King was dead.

That's one way of having the last word, he thought a little sourly. But it wasn't as if this was really a bad thing. Right?

You know you want this, his dark inner voice said. *You wanted something like this even before you knew it was a possibility.*

"Yeah," James muttered to himself. *I do like power. The form it takes is less important.*

He selected "Y" without further thought.

[Required conditions met. Title obtained: Pack Leader!]

[Required conditions met. Title obtained: Usurper!]

James wanted to examine those Titles more closely, but he swiped the notifications away. He could see the wolves were gathered around him now. They sat, patiently waiting for him to acknowledge them.

James reached out with his mind and realized he now had the same telepathic connection to these creatures that he had with the monsters he generated himself.

"Hello," he said both telepathically and aloud.

The wolves stared back at him silently, waiting.

"Your, uh, father has named me the new Pack Leader," he continued.

The wolves responded to that with a long, sustained collective howl, noses pointed to the sky.

He felt an undertone of grief in the long, unbroken sound. But was there also acceptance? Resigned awareness of the natural order? A respectful acknowledgment of the previous King's decision? Or was James trying to read too much subtext into what was, after all, an animalistic sound that even non-System-altered wolves made?

"Hey, James, are you all right?" Cliff yelled.

James turned and realized the squad he'd brought with him was staring at him.

"Just fine. I'm talking to the wolves!" James shouted back.

"Oh, of course!" Harry said in a tone of bewildered resignation.

"What the fuck?" Amalia said under her breath.

"He is a *beast*," Damien commented. "Killed the Wolf King with his bare hands, and now he's taken over the pack. Damn."

"It is most impressive," Jeremiah agreed.

Mitzi was just laughing.

"Right on, sir! You keep on doing interspecies diplomacy!" Cliff shouted back.

James was fairly certain that besides Cliff, the others didn't realize he could hear them. He shifted his full attention back to the wolf pack that eagerly awaited him. They were even wagging their tails.

Well, I've always liked dogs.

"So, I'd like to lay down some ground rules for you all. The main rule is that you won't harm any humans without my permission. If one of them tries to harm one of you, I want you to report that to me immediately. The other main rule is that you will follow my commands and hunt with me. In my world, there is a long and noble history of humans and dogs, which are cousins of wolves, hunting other species together successfully. I would like to replicate that with you."

He created a mental image of a man who looked like him hunting alongside a wolf, then sent it telepathically. He followed this with an image of man and wolf eating meat together.

The wolves seemed to take well to his rules and his telepathic communications. The tail wagging increased in speed and enthusiasm. He got telepathic communications back as well, though most of the responses were fairly simple. Things like, *Hunt together, yes!* and, *Follow you to next prey!* as well as a general wave of positive emotion.

"If none of you have any problems or concerns, we should rejoin the others and return to the larger group of humans. I will explain to them that we are all working together now. If there are any wolves wounded but still alive now that the battle is over, I can heal them."

James waited a moment. Then a single wolf rose to its feet. It was distinct from the others, as it had two heads. A Command Forest Wolf, then.

As it walked out from among the others, James realized that this was a female wolf. He'd passively noticed the presence of male genitalia on a few other wolves. This was the first time he noticed its absence. He wondered for a moment if the other Command Forest Wolves were also female.

The female stepped forward and approached James. He watched without a hint of nervousness, knowing how much stronger he was than any wolf in this forest. And if she was hostile, he thought he'd be able to sense it.

Sure enough, as she approached, she lowered her heads almost to ground level. If she were a human, he would interpret it as a posture of shame or fear. When she drew close to him, she raised her heads back up and licked his hand with both.

A lot like a dog, he thought.

"Is this how you express affection?" James asked quietly.

The wolf stopped licking him with one head and looked up at his face.

"Yes," she replied in a strong, steady voice. "Affection and loyalty. You are the new leader. As the highest-level member of the pack remaining, I am conveying my submission. The rest should follow suit if they don't wish to be left behind or killed."

One of her heads turned sharply and looked at the other wolves, while the other maintained eye contact with James. Most of them were already rising, but the rest got to their feet, as if their mother had caught them doing something wrong.

James showed no reaction to the sound of her talking. He'd half-expected it because of the Wolf King. But he was quite curious about the social dynamics of the wolf pack. Perhaps something to explore later.

"I accept your submission," James said diplomatically. "Would it be inappropriate if I engaged in a physical gesture of affection as well?"

"Not at all," she said. "Please do." Her tail began to wag again after a few moments of being still, James noticed.

James did what he typically did to show affection to a dog. He scratched her behind the ears. She made an expression in response that James thought was probably enjoyment.

"Do you have a name?" he asked.

"No," she replied. "Low-level creatures such as I may have nicknames, but we must achieve a certain level to earn a true name. Either that, or we must be named by a higher-level organism that has earned its own name."

"I see," he said, not really understanding. *Did the Spider Queen have a name? Did the Wolf King?* He realized he didn't know. *How high of a level do they have to be?*

"If you want to call me something, most of the pack refers to me as Luna. Ever since my mother died."

"I'm sorry for your loss," James said reflexively.

She tilted her head slightly. James understood her body language easily this time. Confusion.

"It was some time ago," she said after a long pause. "Two dozen days. It has become much less painful."

James's expression must have registered surprise.

"Is that not a long time for a human?" she asked.

"No, it's really not," James said. He thought of his father's death. In some ways, he still wasn't quite over it two decades later.

"Fortunately for you, wolves mourn more quickly than humans. We will remember our father." She tilted one of her heads in the direction of the Wolf King. "But we will not spend years thinking of his death. Speaking of which, as you are not a wolf, you should eat his flesh. Cannibalism is taboo for us, but we know that the meat of a strong enemy will make you strong."

"Right," James said softly. He was going to get along with Luna, he could tell.

He pointed a hand at the dead Wolf King. *Pillage!*

He chose to steal a Talent from the dead.

And as the items levitated into his magic satchel, the rest of the wolves came around and began taking turns licking his hands.

CHAPTER FIFTY

Cold Comfort

Members of the team rushed back to the white circle in staggered groups of two.

First, Jose and Paulo returned. Probably because they were the closest and were young and athletic. They were barely breathing heavily despite sprinting into the circle.

Neither knew exactly what had happened. They'd just decided to retreat because they saw the population counter had dropped. They were only able to tell one other team the secret of pixie persuasion.

Then Adelaide and Derek jogged over, appearing from behind a couple of trees.

Is that blood on the hem of her pants? Mina questioned. Ever since Cara had killed two people almost before her eyes, Mina was looking at all her teammates with new suspicion. Partially because she now thought anyone could be the murderer she and DaSilva had been trying to identify. And partially because she didn't want it to be Cara.

But it wouldn't be any better if it was Adelaide, would it? The woman had helped her deliver her baby after Cara had helped her take those last laborious steps out of the maze.

She owed each of them a great debt, and Mina recognized that it was starting to affect her reasoning.

Take emotion out of this, she told herself. *See them as if they were strangers.*

Jean and Cara scrambled in, breathless and sweaty, as she was thinking that.

They'd both been running, and Cara even had her sword out, so it was obvious there was some physical threat somewhere. But Mina was relieved to see the blade didn't have any blood on it. Cara hadn't killed again.

The only time she's ever hurt someone that you know of was in your defense, commented a reproachful voice in her head.

Which means that I know she's capable of violence, she retorted. *She didn't* hurt *anybody. Those two are very dead. And only one of them did anything wrong.*

Mina shook her head. She was just retracing arguments she'd had with herself in bed over the last couple of days, whenever her mind and body weren't occupied with something else.

"What's going on out there?" she asked, looking at Cara and Jean.

Cara caught her breath first. "Fighting broke out," she said. "People are getting desperate. One group had pixies, and their neighbors didn't. It's a good thing we went and told our neighbors the secret. They're busy chasing down little blue people to try and give them clothes." She grinned as if they'd played a great trick on the other groups.

Not sure I would like her outside of this place, even though she's been very kind to me personally, Mina couldn't help but think. *There's something very cold in her.*

"We managed to avoid the fighting, but it was getting worse when we started heading back here," Jean said. "The Davidsons—"

But he stopped midsentence. As he was referring to them, the Davidsons sprinted into view. Mrs. Davidson was slightly more breathless than her husband, Mina noted. Although they were both Mages and relatively frail-looking old folks, it was notable that he seemed to be handling the physical strain of this situation better than her.

"Don't worry, fellas," Mr. Davidson said, his voice breezy. "We made it out of that in one piece."

Made it out of what, I wonder? She suddenly found herself very suspicious of Mr. Davidson. If he'd really been in the midst of a fight in which other people had died, it was strange that he didn't seem to have a scratch on him.

Acting on impulse, Mina used Investigate on both Davidsons again. Her eyes widened slightly, but otherwise she managed to contain her reaction.

This time, Mr. Davidson's Status included the same Talents and Skills she'd reported to DaSilva: Anthropophagy, Cannibalism, Heart of Ice, Limitless Hunger, Pillage, Wendigo Contagion, and Wendigo Transformation.

I need to tell the detective this right away! Wait. Why the heck is it different? I just checked them a few days ago! Either Davidson had a Skill to hide things in his Status, and he just isn't using it today, or—is it possible that he was infected with this Wendigo thing in the last couple of days?

Mina swallowed. If Wendigo Contagion was spreading like an actual disease, catching people and moving from one to the next so quickly that it would infest every team sooner or later, what would that mean? Were they hunting for one killer or many?

How does it spread? Unless she's concealing it somehow, his wife doesn't even have it. So, someone spread it to him but not her? Are some people immune? Is she just lucky? Or was he exposed to something or someone that she wasn't?

"The timer's running down," Mrs. Davidson said, breaking Mina's train of thought. "We need to make sure we're ready for the end."

"Right you are," Mr. Davidson said.

"I don't think there was anything else we needed to do," Detective DaSilva said, voice slightly uneasy. "We're undoubtedly ahead of everyone else."

"Agreed," Jean said. His face was stony as he spoke, and he seemed to be deliberately looking away from the Davidsons.

What happened out there? Mina desperately wanted more information, but there was no time, and it seemed obvious that there would be some risk in openly asking the question. Otherwise, Jean would have finished whatever he was saying.

"Great job, Yulia," Cara said, smiling down at Yulia with apparent sincerity. "You and your sister are real leadership material, you know?"

"Thanks," Yulia said, smiling back up at her.

Mina responded with a nod and a smile that probably read as much more uneasy than she'd intended. She was getting more and more nervous about her team. It felt as if there was no one she could really trust here but Yulia and DaSilva. She pictured the rest of the team suddenly turning on the three of them with weapons and magic. It wouldn't be much of a fight. The little teenage Healer, the recently postpartum Mage, and the somewhat overweight middle-aged Heavy Warrior against everyone else.

She restrained a shudder. *I need to figure out what Wendigo Contagion is right away.* She checked the timer. **[00:03:43]**. That demarcated how much more time she had to survive in this group's company before she'd get a break.

There was chatter as Mina's situational analysis turned into a paranoia spiral, but she mostly ignored it until Mr. Davidson chimed in.

"I just wanted to thank you all for having Karen and me. I know it can't have been easy to decide on taking a couple of, uh, older folks on board. Somehow the eleven of us have made a go of it, though, yeah?"

There were murmurs of approval from all sides of the circle.

"We were really worried back then about whether we'd survive this place, honestly," Mrs. Davidson said with a sniffle.

Mina looked at the old woman and was surprised to see tears in her eyes. Then the Davidsons pulled their neighbors into an embrace. Their neighbors, Cara and Paulo, pulled in the next people. And in a few seconds, the team was in a group hug.

Mina wasn't thrilled about hugging these people, most of whom were still near strangers and at least one of whom was afflicted with Wendigo Contagion, but she didn't voice any objection. She didn't want to raise any suspicions by behaving coldly toward anyone.

Finally, the oddly poignant moment was broken by a little voice from several feet below them.

"Ahem. I hate to interrupt your ritual bonding, but my siblings and I are still wondering about our reward, guys," Seissylt said.

"Right," Mina said, glad for an excuse to pull out of the huddle. She stepped back and looked at her sister. Yulia took the cue and likewise broke from the group hug. She took her scrunchies out again.

"I was trying to wait until the last minute," Yulia said, "but we're close enough, and I trust you guys."

"We pixies don't break our word," Seissylt said in a high and mighty tone.

Yulia dropped the collection of scrunchies in the midst of the little blue figures, and a scramble ensued for the best colors. Pixies apparently loved bright colors because the golden yellow, bright green, and bloodred scrunchies were the most popular.

This kept the pixies occupied until the last ten seconds. In the meantime, the group hug had broken up.

Mina only noticed what happened next because she happened to turn away from the pixies at just the right moment. As the challenge entered the last ten seconds of its countdown, she saw Mr. Davidson reach into his Small Bag of Deceptive Dimensions.

He pulled out three visibly injured pixies and simply held them in his hand, low at his side where they were unlikely to draw anyone's eyes.

She quickly averted her gaze so he wouldn't catch her looking, but her pulse amped up.

What in the world did he do? The pixies' wings looked torn, and Davidson's hands were coated with a deep blue substance that Mina guessed was pixie blood. *That violence was completely unnecessary. And where did he get those three pixies? Was he carrying them around through most of the challenge, or did he acquire them during the fighting earlier? Was Jean about to say something about the Davidsons starting a fight over pixies when they showed back up?* It would explain why he'd clammed up as soon as he saw them.

[The challenge is over!]

Cygnus gave her usual explanation, but Mina heard almost none of it. Her eyes were fixed on the ground. *We have a monster on the team. More than one monster, for all I know. Probably more than one. Dear God, I don't know what to do . . .*

Mina turned to where her sister stood at her side, and she clasped Yulia's hand. Yulia looked slightly confused but happy, as if she thought the gesture was meant to connect with the results of the challenge. And that was a good enough understanding for now, Mina thought. She would have to share more of her concerns with Yulia, as well as DaSilva, once this was over. For now, let Yulia enjoy some peace.

At least she doesn't seem to be worried. Mina tried to vicariously enjoy her sister's innocent pleasure in this happy moment. But it gave her only cold comfort. Soon she would have to shatter her sister's ability to trust the team.

Notifications popped up.

We got two more levels, yay. Mina dismissed the notifications dully. They had finished in first again. It was almost something she took for granted. They gained levels every time they passed a challenge.

And then another of her slightly impulsive ideas struck her. She turned to Cara and used Investigate again. Then she turned to Jean and did the same. Adelaide. Derek. Jose. Paulo. Mrs. Davidson. Even DaSilva.

She couldn't resist a small, victorious smile at the results. *Well, I don't know how to stop you yet. But I know who the killers on our team are.*

She blinked, and she was back with Yulia in their room at the inn.

"Yulia, I have some things to tell you," Mina began.

She was interrupted by a knock at the door.

It was Cygnus again.

[Here's your baby.]

She almost shoved baby James into Mina's arms.

"Um, thank you," Mina said. "I hope everything went well—"

[Oh, yes. Such a bundle of joy. A pity that we System staff do not reproduce.]

Mina could swear that this supernatural entity, who wielded god-like power, sounded *exhausted.* As if the duration of this challenge had been the longest ninety minutes of her life.

What, is he that much trouble? He barely cries at all! She smiled down at her son and started to push the door shut with her foot. *My little angel.*

"Wait a minute," Mina said, thinking aloud. She had almost closed the door, but she opened it back up.

[Did you have further questions?]

Mina looked back and forth indecisively between her baby and the proctor. Finally, she let out a long, pained sigh.

"Is that other option still open? You taking my baby for the remainder of Orientation?"

Cygnus's face was hidden, as always, behind the Judy mask that she wore. But Mina could see genuine surprise in her body language.

[Yes. He would be in suspended animation until the Orientation is completed.]

"That means he wouldn't age a second, right? And your process for doing that is perfect? It never screws up any children?" Mina had to control her voice, which had risen almost to a tortured moan.

[It is perfect.]

The proctor's voice rang with a cold haughtiness. *Of course our methods are perfect*, she seemed to be saying. But Mina wished she had some way of knowing beyond taking this masked woman's word for it.

"Could you also make sure that if something happens to my sister and me, you give him to my husband?" Mina asked. Her words came out in a choked whisper, her throat thick with bile.

[If that is what you want. Your husband is the human named James Robard, correct?]

Mina nodded, then said, "Yes."

[We will have no trouble finding him.]

"Then please take him," she said, her voice shaking. The proctor reached out for baby James. Mina gave him a soft kiss on the forehead, and then she let him go.

She heard the sound of Yulia rising and rushing toward the door behind her, and Mina put a hand up to stop her.

"Let her take him," Mina said quietly, almost whimpering. Tears pooled in the corners of her eyes as she stared at her baby and the woman taking him away. Hopefully, only for a matter of weeks. God willing, this wouldn't be the last she saw of baby James. It only felt like it.

The proctor turned away and disappeared into thin air, as if she'd walked through a door into a room they couldn't see.

"Why?" Yulia asked simply. Mina turned to her, and she looked almost as distraught as Mina felt.

"This place is about to become much more dangerous than it has been," Mina said. She closed the door, sat down with Yulia, and explained everything she knew about the murders at length.

"Oh my God," Yulia said. She covered her mouth. Then she spoke again. "The murderer is on our team, then. More than one murderer. Oh my God. I didn't want to believe it, despite what happened to Detective DaSilva."

"I'd rather not believe it myself," Mina said. "They're hard truths. Awful things. But I think that if we don't face them, we'll wake up and find our throats cut some night. I just—I couldn't have little James here for that. If they come for me, they'll come for you too. And if they kill both of us—"

Her voice broke off. The possibilities were too awful to contemplate.

Yulia squeezed her hand.

"You did the right thing," she said. "The only thing you could do. What do we do next?"

Mina smiled through fresh tears.

"I have a plan."

CHAPTER FIFTY-ONE

Demonology

Mina knocked on Detective DaSilva's door. The floorboards creaked where his heavy footsteps landed. Then the door opened. He looked surprised to see them.

"Ladies, what brings you here?" he asked.

"We need to talk about the murders," Mina began.

Then DaSilva moved slightly to the side so that Mina could see into the room behind him. There, on the unused bed beside DaSilva's, sat Cara. She looked poised. Confident.

But as Mina looked at her, Cara's eyes narrowed. Cara turned to look at Mina, and Mina realized that she had stopped talking midsentence at the sight of Cara.

"I didn't realize you were here, Cara," she said, just to say something. Her mind raced, searching for the right words to talk her way out of this. *James would've known just what to say*, she thought. But her brain felt frozen.

"Oh, I just wanted to ask the detective about something. Jean and I were worried that this killer might come after us at some point, since we discovered the first body. He might think we know something. I was thinking we could use some sort of protection."

Mina seized on Cara's words.

"You know, that connects with what I was thinking about. I was telling the detective earlier that I thought the violence in the last challenge might have been the killer trying to take some more of us out. By disguising it as inter-team rivalry, the murderer could kill people he meant to target while also increasing hostility among the surviving groups."

Detective DaSilva's eyes widened at Mina's lie, but his back was turned to Cara. Mina thought there was no obvious tell from his posture that would give away his reaction.

"You were just telling the detective that, eh? It's funny, he didn't mention that to me. It would have validated my fears instead of dismissing them." Cara's tone had turned icy.

DaSilva turned around to look at Cara. He replied in an even voice, "I didn't want to scare you, Cara. And I still don't believe that Mina's theory is correct. We can't blame every bit of violence that occurs in these challenges on the killer. We have no reason to assume they'd be so brazen. Killing people out in the open like that would be out of character for a murderer who was this careful up until now."

Mina suppressed a sigh of relief. *Thank goodness the detective has good control of his voice.*

"You have a point, Detective," Cara allowed. Her tone switched to playful, almost teasing. "Mina, what do you think? Should Detective DaSilva be providing Jean and me round-the-clock protection? If you believe the killer was active in the last challenge, surely you must admit that we have a valid security concern. I would just feel *so much safer* if we spent the rest of Orientation under the detective's watchful eye."

Mina found her mouth was suddenly very dry, and she took a deep breath before answering. Her mind was working double time now to lie and obfuscate.

"I think you're not wrong to be afraid. But what about me?"

"Hm? What about *you*?"

"Yes. What about me and Yulia and Adelaide? We've all been helping the detective in his investigation, so we could all reasonably be targets. There's no reason to think the killer would come after you and Jean first when he's left you alone ever since that first day. All of us are in the same pickle as you, and it's not as if we can all sleep over in Detective DaSilva's room every night."

"Well, that is true," Cara said thoughtfully. Her lips molded into a thin smile that didn't reach her eyes. "I guess your superior logic wins again, Mina." Cara rose from the bed and strode briskly toward the door where Mina and Yulia stood. Mina had to order her body not to flinch as Cara drew close.

Cara spoke her next words almost eye to eye with Mina, still smiling tightly. "I'll leave the two of you to talk to the detective, then. I hope neither of you will do anything too reckless; none of us can receive the detective's protection all the time." She put her arms around Mina and gave her a *very* firm squeeze.

It was more of a crush than a hug, with a grip that reminded Mina of how physically fragile she was compared to Cara. To DaSilva and Yulia, though, Mina imagined it just looked like a display of affection. "I'll talk to you later," Cara whispered into Mina's ear. And then she stepped past Mina into the hallway.

Mina let out her breath slowly, still trying not to give any outward sign that she was nervous. She stepped into DaSilva's room with Yulia following closely behind. DaSilva closed the door after them.

As the sisters sat down on the bed that Cara had just vacated, Mina got a look at Yulia's face. It was a hollow mask. Mina could feel that Yulia was bottling up some intense emotion. Sadness? Fear? Anger?

Mina couldn't tell, and for now, she couldn't pay it any heed. The situation was bad.

"Could one of you tell me what this is all about?" DaSilva asked quietly. "I'm getting a little freaked out here. Please just be straight with me this time."

Mina didn't respond to him, didn't even look at him. She got up and stalked over to the door she'd just come through. After a moment's hesitation, she yanked it open and stuck her head out into the hallway.

No one there.

Not satisfied with that, she walked down to the staircase and descended. No one on the stairs or in the common area of the inn. She couldn't even ask anyone if they'd seen Cara walk outside. It'd only been a few minutes, but Cara was fast.

She's gone, Mina told herself.

Then she ascended the staircase again and reentered DaSilva's room.

She found him pacing.

"You've got me going out of my mind," DaSilva said. "Please tell me what's going on."

"Cara and Frank are the killers on our team," Mina replied in a tiny voice. "I was just making sure she was gone before I told you."

"What?!" DaSilva sprang toward the door and closed it firmly behind her. "How do you know?"

"First, I know Cara has already killed two people; it was right in front of me. Back in the maze."

"Why didn't you mention this before?" he asked in a tone of flat, cold anger.

"Because she did it in defense of me," Mina replied. She could barely meet his eyes.

"I see." His voice softened. "This was related to your unplanned premature birth?"

Mina nodded, not trusting her voice.

"You said 'first,'" he said after a long pause. "What was second?"

"I used the Investigate Skill on her and Frank again. Frank's Status showed that he's a Wendigo, straightforward as that. With Cara, it was more complicated."

"How so?" DaSilva asked a bit impatiently.

"I read her Status, and it was exactly the same as the last time."

He scratched the side of his head. "What was complicated about that?"

"Her Status was the same as it was when I checked it during our team breakfast before."

"Oh. Yeah, I think I see."

"She must be using some Skill to conceal her real Status," Mina said. "It didn't reflect the levels we all got from this challenge or the maze or any other progress in any of her abilities. You got those levels too, right?" She waited for DaSilva to nod before continuing. "So, my guess is she put up a fake Status screen a while ago, in case anyone had the ability to look at them. But since we didn't mention we were using Investigate on the team's Statuses, she assumed no one had checked it, so she didn't think to update it with a natural rate of progress for her Skills."

"Jesus," DaSilva murmured.

"Also, if this makes any difference, my Job leveled up when I used Investigate on her. As if the System recognized I was having a breakthrough in the case. So, I'm ninety percent certain she's the person who tried to kill you before. More certain, even."

"All right, you've persuaded me," he said, nodding to himself. "And I know what we need to do next."

"That's a relief to hear," Mina said.

"Do you know about Wendigos, Detective?" Yulia asked.

"No, but I know the next best thing," he replied. "I know where we can find a real expert."

That was what I was hoping you'd say, Mina thought. Out of everyone she'd met since arriving here, DaSilva was the best-connected person in camp. As a policeman who everyone trusted, he ended up solving, or at least being asked to address, a lot of problems. From murdered people to missing food, from scarcity to weather issues, he was at the center of much of the group's life here.

As the sisters followed DaSilva to his expert, Mina allowed herself to contemplate life post-Orientation. In particular, she wondered where DaSilva would fit into the community as it would exist after the System's arrival. She doubted the local police department would be in any kind of position to enforce order anymore, let alone to continue employing him.

He's a bit of a de facto leader here, Mina thought, *but he'd never want any actual position of leadership*. She knew him well enough now to be certain of that. DaSilva was made to be someone's right-hand man. He was most comfortable with executing decisions, not making them. That was why he'd once tried to suggest that Paul, the self-appointed leader from the first few days, wasn't a bad sort. Even though that same person had just tried to turn the whole population's frustrations on Mina and Yulia.

DaSilva preferred to have someone in charge rather than to take charge himself, even if that other person was someone he didn't particularly like. He seemed to realize that about himself on some level, which was why he'd never sought promotion beyond the level of detective.

I wonder how he'd get along with James.

Mina knew her husband. James would seek and embrace opportunities for power. He would be on the lookout for competent people who didn't mind playing second fiddle to him. People like DaSilva. *Things to address later, when it's safer.*

The trio walked through knee-high snow, which continued to fall in thick clumps all around them. Mina supposed someone must be clearing it periodically, or the path wouldn't be navigable. Mostly, she tried to ignore the snow and the deep cold that seemed to be settling into her bones.

They moved toward another challenge winners' building. Then they climbed a set of stairs. Finally, they arrived at a particular door.

Well done, for not only knowing so many people but also knowing where they live, Mina thought. If DaSilva and Yulia weren't here, she doubted she would even talk to someone every day. Compared to her, DaSilva was a true social butterfly.

He knocked on the door.

"Hey, Professor," DaSilva said, "it's me, Detective DaSilva. I have a couple of young ladies with me. We have a question about Native American myths, and we were hoping you could help us."

The person on the other side of the door must have been quite spry because the door was flung open almost as soon as DaSilva finished talking. Mina and Yulia each took a small step back at the sudden movement. But they immediately stepped forward again.

The man who stood in front of them wasn't intimidating: a neat, well-groomed figure of average height, wearing a long-sleeved button-down shirt and a bow tie. He looked like he was getting ready to go out to dinner at a nice restaurant, or perhaps heading out to deliver a lecture. His hair was a short silver-gray, and he was ruddy complected, with slightly round cheeks. Around his early forties, Mina guessed. He had a kindly face and intelligent eyes.

His attire reminded Mina that she was still wearing a dress with a few wayward drops of baby spit and breast milk spotted along the area just under her chest. She self-consciously crossed her arms in front of herself. Then she used Investigate, which confirmed the professor was not afflicted with Wendigo Contagion, or if he was, he was concealing it somehow.

"A pleasure to meet you, young ladies," the professor said, speaking with the slightest trace of a southern accent. "My name is Adam Davies." He extended his hand to Mina.

"I'm Mina. And the pleasure is all ours, I'm sure," Mina said. She reluctantly lowered her arm from where it covered the stain on her dress so she could shake hands with him.

"I doubt that very much," he said, smiling cordially. He turned and shook Yulia's hand as well. "Nice to meet you too, young miss."

"Nice to meet you, sir," Yulia said with a seriousness of tone that surprised Mina slightly. "My name is Yulia."

I guess she's adapting to his demeanor. Or still digesting the news about Cara and Frank.

"Can we come in, Professor?" DaSilva asked.

"Oh, of course, where are my manners?" he said, pulling the door open.

His room was identical to DaSilva's and an exact mirror of Mina and Yulia's. The System was nothing if not systematic in housing construction.

Mina explained what was going on, omitting a few key details including the fact that they had identified two murderers on their own team.

"So that's why we need your help," she finished. "We need to know what to do about Wendigo Contagion. Detective DaSilva explained that you might know something about this area."

"Yes, indeed," Davies said slowly, expression troubled. "I know as much about Wendigo folklore, at least, as your average anthropologist in this area. I can't know for sure if the Wendigos we're apparently dealing with in real life follow the folklore, though."

"We need to assume that they do," Mina insisted. "Otherwise, we don't have a single clue. So how do we treat this? Is there a cure?"

"Well, I hate to be the bearer of bad news," he said, "but I'm afraid not. The traditions tend to say that *you don't* treat Wendigo Contagion. Even if you try, it's generally not successful. Historically, when people are believed to be afflicted with this ailment, you kill them."

Mina's face fell. "I was really hoping you wouldn't say that."

"Let's take a step back for a minute," DaSilva interjected gently. "Let's discuss everything Professor Davies knows about this disease."

After a moment Mina nodded. Any ray of hope would be welcome.

"Well, the tradition is that a Wendigo is an evil spirit. A bit like what the Middle Eastern religions called demons. These spirits were usually associated with cold weather and famine. Sometimes environmental destruction. The spirit would possess a particularly greedy or hungry person who was willing to consume human flesh. Usually someone desperate.

"The victim becomes possessed by the Wendigo, and they eat the flesh of man. But their unnatural hunger cannot be satisfied. Some legends stated that they would grow larger with every person they ate so that their hunger would only grow with time. Other legends would make them gigantic monsters with frozen hearts. Different folklore gives them different attributes. There's endless hunger, monstrous strength, physical emaciation, an unpleasant odor that's often compared with the smell of death, and an inhuman tolerance for pain, to list examples. It's sometimes unclear if the possessed person remains human. For instance, in one story, they chop off the Wendigo's limbs, and when they return later to see if he's still alive, he remains capable of holding a normal conversation."

"Um, cures, Professor?" Mina asked as gently as she could. She was struggling to remain patient. Davies was a little too warm to his subject. Perhaps he was excited that his anthropological knowledge was now of much more practical use than it had ever been before. But he wasn't saying much that she found useful. It was more like sharing scary campfire stories.

"Oh, yes. People have attempted to treat Wendigos in the past. Cree folklore recommends feeding them fatty meats and animal grease to keep their hunger at bay."

"Do you think that would work?" Mina asked. "If we could capture them somehow and bind them in place?"

DaSilva, she noticed, was giving her a hard look as she spoke, but she ignored it.

"Honestly, no," Davies said. "In real life, we don't know if it's ever worked, but the typical result of someone having wendigo psychosis is death. This is something that hasn't been well-studied scientifically, you understand. We're almost in the realm of demonology."

"That's a fair way of putting it, but is there another treatment?" Mina asked a bit desperately.

She really wanted to save Cara if she could, she realized, though she hadn't parsed through all the reasons for that in her own mind. Maybe it was because Mina didn't want blood on her hands. Maybe it was because the other woman had looked out for her, back in the maze. Perhaps before then as well. It was hard to say.

"No," he replied grimly. "You just have to kill them. Burn the bodies. And destroy their Heart of Ice. You mentioned that was one of the traits you observed in the Wendigo Contagion sufferers. If that's true, then failing to destroy that could lead to the Wendigo recovering. And destroying the heart might possibly free the human possessed. There are some stories where the human would some-how survive the process of the Wendigo's destruction, but that's not the norm. Those are usually the more fantastical myths."

"Thank you," Mina said, smiling slightly. It was small, but the tips were something.

"Of course," Davies said, smiling a bit woodenly. "Happy to be of service. I don't suppose you could tell me if there are any Wendigos on my team?"

"Have you had any food stolen?" DaSilva asked. "I've been thinking about it, and I suspect the teams that have had food stolen from them probably have Wendigos in their ranks. There are a total of thirteen teams who have lost food before now, and I think that's the telltale sign. The Wendigos have a trait called Limitless Hunger. I'm guessing they can't resist food, even when stealing some is a bad idea."

That's extremely sound logic, Mina thought. *He's not a detective for nothing.*

"No," Davies replied with a sigh of relief. "No, our team hasn't had that problem."

"Okay, then you're probably in the clear," DaSilva said. "You should keep this to yourself, by the way. We'll be going for now. We'll come back around once we've made a game plan."

Davies nodded. "Stay safe," he said.

Mina, Yulia, and DaSilva left the professor's room, descended the stairs, and made the cold trudge back to their inn.

"Well, what do you think we do next?" DaSilva asked as they walked, snow falling more heavily than before all around them.

"I might suggest we restrain Cara and Frank and try the animal grease cure on them," Mina said a bit hesitantly.

"Mina, really?" DaSilva's voice was incredulous.

"Yes, really!" Mina replied defensively.

"You're a practical person. I know you well enough to know that about you by now. Where did that practical person go? This is crazy! You want us to try and restrain two of the Wendigos—monsters with superhuman powers, who have been slowly killing us off one by one. Then we somehow find some animal fat we can feed them in this camp that's starving, and while we force feed them that, we just hope the rest of the monsters don't figure out what we're doing and go on a rampage. Does that about sum it up?"

Mina's cheeks colored slightly. "When you put it that way, I admit it sounds like a terrible plan."

DaSilva turned to Yulia. "Yulia, what do you think of this plan? Please. Be honest."

Yulia let out a long breath that steamed the air in front of her. Then she shook her head twice. Gentle but firm movements.

"I don't think we can save them, sis. I'm sorry. I know Cara helped you in the maze, but either she or Frank already tried to kill DaSilva before. Not to mention loads of other people." She looked at her feet.

"I know, but they're possessed or something," Mina said weakly.

"They are," DaSilva agreed. "But the professor mentioned that there was an element of consent. The person has to be willing to consume human flesh. Even if that weren't the case, we have no way to free them from that possession."

"That's true," Mina admitted. "It just feels wrong to go after someone who helped me."

"I get it," he said. "You're a loyal person. But this isn't the place for that. I wouldn't normally show anyone the same grace that you're trying to show Cara here, and this Orientation is even worse than normal circumstances."

"You're right," she said. She felt hollow as the words left her throat.

"Okay. Do you have a better plan?"

"I guess we go from building to building and identify who the Wendigos are. Do you have a list of the teams that had food stolen?"

"I do. The pad is in my pocket."

"Okay," Mina said. They had arrived at the door to the inn. "If we're going to walk around in the snow any longer, though, I need warmer clothing."

DaSilva looked down, saw the thin dress she'd been wearing thus far, and winced.

"Yeah, you do," he agreed. "I'll wait down here."

"I'm dressed warmly enough," Yulia said. She wore a long burgundy sweater that hung down to below the seat of her jeans. It was one of James's hand-me-downs that the sisters shared. "See you soon." She tried to smile, but the look froze on her face, half formed.

They all had too much on their mind for smiles just then.

The trio entered the common area, and Mina walked up the stairs and over to her room.

As she approached the door she reached into the pocket of her dress for the room key. But her hand came out empty.

That's strange, she thought. Yulia had the other key, so they certainly wouldn't get locked out. But she didn't remember if she'd actually locked the door. *Maybe not.*

She tried the handle, and it turned in her hand.

The door opened. Then Mina stepped across the threshold and froze.

There was a chill in the air, though Mina was certain she hadn't left the window open.

"Come in, come in," came Cara's voice from inside the room. "If I wanted to kill you, you'd already be dead. Come in, Mina, and close the door behind you." Her voice turned at once deep, bitter, and mocking. "I'm not going to eat you."

CHAPTER FIFTY-TWO

The Perfect Storm

Mina hovered for a long moment by the doorway, afraid and unwilling to make a decision.

She could feel the presence of the Wendigo that called itself Cara somewhere in the dark room in front of her. It was in the chilled air, in the slight odor of rotting meat, and in a strange, elongated silhouette she could make out on the other side of the room. A dark and imposing shape that loomed over her, although the figure appeared to be sitting down.

She swallowed. Took another step into the room. Then heard the door close quietly behind her. Mina didn't turn to look back at it or try to escape. Running would be futile. Cara had been stronger and faster than her even in her human form. Now, with Cara transformed into a monster, the speed differential would be even bigger than it had been when Mina was pregnant. In the unlikely event that she managed to get through the door, she would only draw Cara into an area where more people would be killed.

"When did you become one of them?" Mina asked, just to have something to say. Her words fogged the frosty air.

"Oh, Mina." The weirdly deep yet feminine voice sounded slightly exasperated. "I was the *first*. You didn't figure that out?"

Mina let out a sigh that came with another cloud of visible vapor. "No, I can't say that I did. Honestly, I barely caught you at all."

"Caught is a word," Cara replied.

"Okay, I barely figured out that you were killing and eating people, if you prefer," Mina said, voice on edge.

"Can't get around that," Cara said. She sounded tired. As if she had already played this conversation out in her head more than once, and she wasn't enjoying the repetition.

"Why did you do all this?" Mina asked. It felt like the natural question.

"I feel like I've practically told you already."

"People suck?"

The figure in the shadows nodded. The image of Cara's Wendigo form was becoming clearer to Mina with every passing second spent in the darkened room as Mina's eyes adjusted. It was terrible. But Mina couldn't look away.

Cara had sprouted to almost ten feet tall. Her hair fell down her shoulders in tangled up knots. Gray-blue skin stretched across her stretched, monstrous visage. Despite her long body and limbs, her frame was as thin as ever. Her armor still fit. But with the added height, she looked emaciated.

"So, they deserve to die?" Mina forced herself to keep talking despite feeling profoundly afraid of the figure that sat staring down at her. Despite the increasing certainty that she wouldn't leave this room alive.

"Deserve. I didn't care about deserve. When a god offered me power and introduced me to the Wendigo, I jumped at the chance. All I had to do was kill some humans. Malsumis hated humanity as much as I did." When she spoke, Cara's long sharp teeth caught the light reflecting off of the snowflakes falling outside. They glinted an unsightly yellow. "I've felt powerless my whole life. Somehow, I can't imagine you'd understand." Her voice trailed off with those words, and for a few seconds the only sound was the wind whistling outside. Then Cara resumed, "I know you don't like me assuming things about your life story, or how people have treated you in the past. But you're smart. Beautiful. Educated. I bet your husband worships the ground you walk on."

"Is that why I have to die?" Mina couldn't keep the tremble from her voice. She thought of her baby, who was about to lose his mother.

James, take care of him. Yulia, help him. I love you all.

Then Cara let out a low chuckle. "Why you have to die. You misunderstand me, Mina. I mention those assumptions about your life only because I like you. I always liked you. Ever since the beginning. When you decided to share food with the other side after the first challenge, I knew. You were the nicest person here. Probably the nicest person I've ever met. And clever too. Remember how I defended you in the maze? And before, I killed Paul. He was trying to turn everyone against you! Remember? I did that for you."

"I'd started to wonder about that," Mina said slowly. "As soon as I realized you were the killer, I remembered that. But Detective DaSilva was trying to protect me, and you tried to kill him too. Yulia saw it."

Cara shrugged. "DaSilva seems like a decent human being, but I was worried he might be getting too close. I've never had the best luck with men anyway."

"What now?" Mina asked. "You decided to confront me. I guess you don't just want to kill me."

"I want you to join us," Cara said. "You're too good to be a human. The rest of them are just food in the long term anyway."

"Even my sister?" Mina asked.

"We could turn her too," Cara said, her tone almost placating. "Even DaSilva if you're really attached to him. Your husband, of course. Humans are on their way out anyway. They were never that great to begin with. You'll be on the ground floor for the new thing. A species that hunts and eats humans. The world will be full of monsters like us. Once your baby grows up, we could turn him too."

Mina let a silence hang in the air for several seconds. "I would rather die than become a monster who preys on innocent people," she said finally, looking into the darkness where she knew Cara's eyes must be. "I understand you had your reasons, but I can't join you. And I can't condone what you've done."

Cara let out a rumbling groan. "Ugh. You're really saying no, huh? Well, I almost expected you to refuse. You're *too* nice. But why couldn't you just stay blind? You could've told yourself you didn't know for sure. I never would've come after you. Now what do you expect me to do?" Despite Cara's terrifying image and voice, Mina detected a genuine conflict.

She really doesn't want to hurt me. How can I take advantage of that?

"I had no way of knowing that you wouldn't come after me or my sister, or the detective." It was all Mina could think to say.

"Fine." Cara seemed to reach a decision. Her body shrunk down to its normal size. Her skin and hair returned to their normal color and length. Her armor resumed fitting her comfortably instead of hanging off of her Wendigo frame like an ornament on a Christmas tree. Mina had a wild thought. *Maybe now I could take her.*

But Cara didn't seem to see her as any sort of a threat. She got up, turned her back to Mina, walked to the window of the room, and opened it.

"What are you doing?" Mina asked.

"I'm leaving," Cara said. "There's nothing more to be done here. You don't want to join us. Okay. I don't want to kill you, and you're much too weak to kill me. So, I'm just leaving."

"Just like that," Mina whispered in disbelief.

"Well, there's nothing more we can do for each other. Nothing you can do *to* me or my kind."

"What about the other Wendigos?" Mina asked.

Cara was perched on the windowsill now, and the thick tufts of snow were settling lightly over her body as she sat looking in at Mina. But she clearly didn't mind the cold. She smiled.

"A storm is coming," Cara said. "I think you'll find, when it hits, that it's best if you remain safe and warm *inside*. When it's over, we'll be gone. Along with some food to go. If we need anything else, we'll come around the settlement again. Otherwise, we'll be in the wild if you need us." She opened her mouth and bared yellowed teeth that had somehow not transformed back. "I won't bother you if you don't bother me. But if I see you in my woods, I might not be so nice the next time we meet. Good luck with the rest of Orientation."

Cara leaned back and dropped off of the windowsill and out of sight.

Mina had stared, frozen in her tracks, as Cara moved across the room. But with her fall, the spell was broken. Mina rushed forward, grabbed the windowsill, and leaned out to see where Cara had gone.

There was no sign of her. Just an increasingly large volume of snow falling from the sky and the whistle of the wind.

Mina slammed the window shut and latched it. Then she ran downstairs, to where DaSilva and Yulia sat waiting for her in the common area.

"Mina, I thought you were changing," DaSilva began. Then his face took on a look of alarm. "Is everything all right?"

Yulia looked up and caught sight of Mina's face, which was twisted in a look of fear.

"Thank goodness you two are all right!" Mina exclaimed. "Cara—she was in my room, and—"

A System announcement interrupted her.

[Attention all mortals! You may have observed the slowly escalating snowfall in your environment over the last ten days. The System has not been moderating the weather since you arrived, though we have kept the paths between important locations in the human settlement navigable. Please be aware that we detect a violent snowstorm brewing in the area of the settlement right now. This snowstorm is likely to arrive in the next half hour. We recommend remaining indoors for the duration of the storm. Our data indicates that many of your fragile human bodies would be endangered by exposure to this level of cold.]

Mina tried to detect any hint of emotion in the audio of the announcement, but the System voice seemed to communicate with the same neutrality as usual.

"Wow," DaSilva said. "A snowstorm is hitting. That's pretty inconvenient."

"This seems strangely convenient—for the Wendigos," Mina said.

She explained the content of her conversation with Cara.

"So, they're getting out of Dodge," DaSilva said, rubbing his chin thoughtfully.

"You don't think the proctor is trying to help them, do you?" Yulia asked. "So far, she's always seemed like she's just trying to do her job to me."

"I tend to agree, Yulia," DaSilva said slowly, "but we don't know what the System actually wants to achieve here, do we? Maybe it's preparing the world to be conquered by monsters."

"I don't think the System is trying to hurt humans," Mina said. "The Wendigos are associated with cold, so I could easily believe producing this storm is a Wendigo power." Part of her questioned whether this was motivated reasoning on her part. She desperately wanted the System to be pro-human, or at least benevolently neutral. They had enough enemies to deal with, and Cygnus had her son.

"That would make sense," DaSilva agreed. "If the System was really trying to make more Wendigos and feed them, I don't think it would've helped us level up so far. But I'm not sure it's on our side so much either."

"What do we do?" Mina asked. "The snow is only getting worse. If we want to try and warn people about the danger, we don't have much time now."

"We might have no time," DaSilva said. He gestured to the door. "Who's to say we can even get back here if we try to leave?"

Mina found herself nodding along with him. "I don't think we can go anywhere else unless we're willing to be trapped there for the duration of the storm. And the Wendigos don't mind the cold, so we'd just be targets if we walked around outside."

"So, we're just going to sit here and let them do what they want?" Yulia asked quietly. She sounded uncomfortable.

"I don't think we have a choice unless we're willing to throw our lives away to maybe save some strangers," DaSilva said. Every word he spoke sounded painful as it passed through his lips. "I know you guys probably think I'm very brave, and I like to imagine I am too, but courage should recognize limits. The Wendigo that used to be Cara didn't think Mina was any threat to her at all. That was one on one. And I suspect that the three of us combined would not pose much more of a threat than Mina does alone with her magic. And out in that storm they have the upper hand. They would gang up on us. I think we'd just be serving ourselves as a meal. I don't think we could do any good. Whether we survived long enough to warn other people would be a matter of pure luck. And we'd be guaranteed to die. That's not a heroic choice; it's just suicidal."

Mina nodded.

Yulia let out a long breath and put a hand over her face.

Finally, she said, "Yeah, okay. I don't want to die." She got up and practically ran up the stairs back to their room.

"Yulia," Mina said softly. She thought about going after her, then decided against it. *No, I think she probably wants to be alone for a while after resigning herself to this decision. That's almost how I feel. But we've done all we could, right?*

"She'll be okay," DaSilva said quietly, gently placing a hand on Mina's shoulder. "How about I go and see if Alba's awake? I have some chocolate in the supplies I brought when we got whisked away to this place. I've been saving it. Maybe you and Yulia can sip some hot chocolate by the fire while we wait this night out. I don't think any of us are going to sleep."

Mina nodded silently. She thought she might have used up more than her quota of words for the day. More than that, she felt as if everything inside her had drained out. She had nothing left.

DaSilva got up and moved toward the stairs, and Mina turned to face him. She realized she had one thing she desperately wanted to say.

"Thank you, Detective. If you hadn't pointed out how dangerous it was out there, Yulia and I would've run to warn people without question. Then who knows if we'd have survived the storm?"

"Mina, after all the three of us have been through, you don't have to thank me for anything. Ever. You and your sister have done so much for me, even at times when I should have been protecting you. She saved me from being pulled into a river of lava. You solved the murders that I was supposed to unravel. Really, I should be thanking you." He broke into a smile. "And you can both call me Leo."

"Leo," Mina said, as if the word was in an unfamiliar tongue. "I'll have to get used to it."

She didn't point out the many times that he had looked out for her and Yulia. It wasn't a contest. But she was happy to be on a first name basis. Leo felt like he was almost family by now.

I guess little James has an uncle now, she thought.

She sat staring into the fire for a while. She barely noticed when Leo came back with Alba and a group of others. Her ears did prick up slightly when she realized that Leo was explaining what had happened with the Wendigos to the other residents of their inn.

"Mina's the hero here. She discovered the monsters, and the leader confronted her. They decided to leave after that," Leo murmured from the edges of her hearing. "They seem to have created this storm to cover their retreat."

Well, it makes sense to inform people. We don't want them to trust the people who have turned into Wendigos anymore. Laying it on a little thick calling me a hero, but I guess I won't say anything. I really don't feel much like talking.

A few more minutes passed, and she basically tuned out the hum of conversation. Leo had asked them to give her a little space, and the others in the room complied with his request.

Then there was a gentle murmur right beside her. Mina almost jumped in her seat, but when she turned her head, she saw it was just Leo.

"Sorry to startle you," he said. "Alba's serving the chocolate, and I wanted to let you know so you could get Yulia. I knocked on your door when we came down earlier, but she didn't answer, and I didn't want to be too insistent."

"Oh, sure," Mina said. She forced herself to smile. "Hot chocolate can only make things better, so I think she'll appreciate the invite."

Mina walked up the stairs and over to the room.

She knocked gently.

"Yulia, it's me!" she said.

Silence.

Mina pulled the door open. A small pile of snow had formed in front of the open window.

I thought I closed that, was the first thought that passed through Mina's mind.

Then she rushed forward into the room.

"Yulia?" she called out. She crouched to look under the beds, knowing it was futile. Her sister wasn't here.

"Yulia? Yulia!" Mina yelled her name repeatedly at the top of her lungs.

Then she strode over to the open window.

Her sister must be outside. That was the only explanation. How long had she been gone?

"It doesn't matter," Mina muttered to herself. *I have to go after her.*

She threw on her warmest coat and then thrust her head through the window. She was looking for any clue to where Yulia was. The only thing she really noticed was how much worse the storm had become while she'd been sitting by the fire downstairs. The whole world was white now. Snow came down in a never-ending torrent, like a white waterfall. The sight brought a shiver down her spine.

How would a teenager navigate through that? Survive that?

Mina never saw the chunk of ice that hit her. She felt a sudden sharp pain in the back of her head. Then she fell and knew no more.

CHAPTER FIFTY-THREE

Hopeless

In response to Moishe's whistle, fourteen figures stormed toward the position of the Ghouls threatening their camp.

These were all the fighting-fit family members the Rodriguezes could muster, plus most of the remaining personnel from Damien Rousseau's group and one of Rostov's prisoners who'd been left behind. Everyone else was either still recovering from their injuries or relatively lower level.

Sierra followed behind the fighters. She felt a tremor in her hands as she walked, but nevertheless, she made sure not to fall too far behind. And she made sure not to lose her grip on her staff.

The group had decided that their fighters should have a Healer nearby while they engaged the enemy, and she couldn't deny the logic. Her presence might save lives. Or, by keeping their warriors in the fight for longer, she might turn the tide of battle. The undead seemed to be immune to exhaustion; the humans needed some advantage to stand a chance.

Just as importantly, she didn't want to see Alan up there instead. The old man seemed to have used up nearly all his Mana earlier, healing as many people as he could.

Still, he tried to volunteer. But I rebuffed him. How fucking brave of me. She looked up the slight incline of the hill at the monsters she was willingly approaching. *Hopefully, I won't regret it.* She had one small hope that she might be of some use to the group besides healing them after they fell. But she really didn't want to become a combatant, and she was doubtful she even could.

At first, will and momentum seemed like it might carry the day for the human defenders.

Felicia Rodriguez sent a flurry of arrows up at the Ghouls, aiming to kill as many as she could and soften the rest up for the melee fighters. But the arrows weren't very effective. Only one Ghoul fell to them, killed by an arrow in the eye. Others blocked the arrows with their arms if the shaft looked to be heading for something important. And at least one Ghoul didn't bother blocking, even though an arrow was going right for his head. He simply turned sideways and let it penetrate.

The sight of a Ghoul grinning with an arrow poking out of each cheek did more to demoralize the defenders than it did to soften the Ghouls. It was a horrific image that communicated, *We are not like you. We need not avoid injury or pain. Fear us and flee.*

To their credit, the family's close-range fighters didn't run from the implacable force that confronted them. They charged the rest of the way up the slope and crashed into the Ghoul bodies. Their slightly worn weapons struck at toughened undead flesh as well as armor and shields held up by unwavering inhuman bodies.

A flurry of battle ensued. The humans were outnumbered by around two to one, Sierra observed. She mainly stood back, took in the fight, and looked for places where she could apply her healing to best effect. The defenders knocked down a Ghoul or two, but the monsters didn't have the Stamina limitations of humans. They got back up every time except for when the rare fatal blow was landed.

The humans nevertheless fought with a fury that almost seemed to equal the Ghouls' implacable determination. Ramon in particular fought with incredible rage and intensity, as if he was seeing the images of his family being slaughtered in his mind's eye. Perhaps he was.

But there were more than two Ghouls to every human, and observing the exchanges, she saw the monsters looked to be stronger on average. As the fight passed the first few minutes, and the initial adrenaline wore off, it became clearer and clearer that the Ghouls were playing with them.

They seemed to avoid inflicting fatal blows, instead trying to bludgeon the humans with their shields or the flats of their bladed weapons. They blocked attacks aimed at their vital points with very little effort, and the attacks that landed anywhere other than the head seemed to do little damage. In the back, Moishe would occasionally hurl his daggers into the Ghouls' ranks, but because they outnumbered the humans, they had a couple of Ghouls with large shields blocking the daggers from striking anything deadly.

It began to look like an exercise in futility. The humans were fighting, unsuccessfully, to protect their family from the Ghouls, who would ultimately outlast them. The Ghouls seemed uninterested in a quick fight, knowing that they would win a battle of attrition. Their defensive fighting methods were also harder to get wrong than the human group's furious attacks, so very little was happening other than the humans slowly tiring. The tempo of the fight felt like a slow death by strangulation.

Sierra's role seemed particularly useless. With no serious injuries happening on her side, she felt helpless to do anything. Rather than losing limbs or suffering serious head injuries, the fighters were wearing down, losing Stamina. Her staff wouldn't do any damage unless she could crack one of these things over the head with a degree of super-strength that she didn't have.

Damn it! she thought, and not for the first time. *Why didn't I choose a combat Class?*

Then she saw *him* in the back of the Ghouls' ranks.

Kurt! He was still alive all this time! Well, maybe not alive *per se, but he's still been in this thing the whole time. In fact, given his Skills, he probably had something to do with the pincer attack from that wolf pack and these Ghouls.*

She wondered if he was the leader of this group. He didn't seem to be doing as much of the physical work. And if he was the one who could command the wolves' assistance, it might make sense that he'd be in charge.

Then he turned his gaze on her. Their eyes met, and a cold tendril crept up her spine. She sucked in air and used all her willpower just to keep from fleeing.

What must he think, seeing her with James's crew? Probably that she was some sort of traitor, which was debatably true.

But the cold look in his eyes gave her nothing. No hint of emotion. No rage. No blame. Nothing.

The moment of terror passed, and she saw an expression pass over his face. The corner of his lip tightened and rose on one side. She recognized the contemptuous sneer that she'd seen him give other people multiple times. But never her and her brother before. They were too valuable as assets. But she knew what the look meant, nonetheless.

Her own lips tightened in impotent anger. How dare he look at her like that! She wished she could strike him down where he stood.

Then he opened his mouth and raised his voice.

"Hey, let's hurry it up, guys. We probably only have a limited window!" Kurt said.

Confirmed. He's in charge, Sierra thought.

More importantly, the tempo of the fight immediately changed.

Ghouls that had largely been defending themselves lashed out at their human opponents, who were just beginning to visibly tire.

One Ghoul grabbed Felicia, snapped her bow in two, and began choking her into unconsciousness. Sierra took a half-step toward the young woman, uncertain what she would even do if she made it to her.

But then Ramon staggered backward into Sierra, bleeding profusely from a savage blow to the head.

"Make sure you take them alive!" Kurt said. "These are probably the best humans they have. This should be enough to take to the Master."

There is someone they're all reporting to, then.

The other Ghouls were grabbing people, knocking them out, and pulling them away. But for the moment, Javier had stepped in to block the Ghoul that had knocked Ramon out from reaching him.

Sierra knew there wasn't much she could do for anyone else, but she immediately dropped her staff, knelt, and began applying Laying on Hands to Ramon's head injury.

"Capture her too," Kurt said. Sierra noticed in her peripheral vision that he was looking and pointing at her. "She's probably their last Healer. If Master Roscuro doesn't think she's good for anything, at least we can get some fresh meat!"

She shuddered but kept at her work. Slowly but surely, Ramon's head mended itself. She was doing her share.

I'll die alongside the rest of them if I have to, she thought, a thick queasiness seizing hold of her stomach. Even as she had the thought, she couldn't help darting her eyes around, looking for an escape route that wasn't there. An escape route that would somehow allow her to elude the Ghouls, which never seemed to weaken or tire.

Well, at least it seems like you're saving the rest of the camp, David's voice chimed in gently. *Kurt doesn't seem to be interested in taking too many captives. The group of defenders all chose to sacrifice themselves to protect everyone else. Maybe you've accomplished the mission.*

Sierra was trying to compose a biting response to her brother's attempted reassurance when a Ghoul suddenly broke through the handful of the humans still fighting. It got past Javier and loomed menacingly over Sierra, reaching down to drag her away with the others on the front line.

Time to see if this idea can actually work, she thought. She abandoned Laying on Hands. As the Ghoul seized hold of her, she activated Purification and grabbed onto the Ghoul's arm in turn.

Come on, remove impurities!

At first there was no apparent change. The Ghoul was grinning stupidly down at her. It made a tiny motion as if to pull her forward.

And then the whole body began to unravel. The arms came off, though the fingers continued to grip Sierra's body for a moment until they, too, twitched and fell away. The legs slid off as if the bones had turned to sand. The torso tumbled to the ground, and the head rolled away.

Then the remains of the Ghoul disintegrated.

A horrendous smell of decay filled the air.

[You killed Ghoul Simon Rooker, Lv. 18! You gained 800 exp!]

[Healer leveled up!]

[Healer leveled up!]

[System-Boosted Human leveled up!]

[A Class Evolution is available. Review? Y/N]

Sierra was dimly aware that Class Evolution was extremely important, but she swiped this away for now. It didn't seem wise to take her eyes off the battle. Where before she'd only had a couple of pairs of eyes on her, including Kurt's, now every Ghoul present was paying attention. This was only their fourth or fifth casualty of the fight.

And Ghoul Simon Rooker had died in a particularly special way.

So, whatever animates them does count as an impurity. Good to know. Probably could have used that earlier if I'd really believed it would work.

Sierra dropped back down to the ground without taking her eyes off of the Ghouls. She picked her staff back up and pushed Purification Mana into it. Now her staff glowed with the intense pale green aura of the Skill. And she had an attack with a little bit of range.

She was also the last person standing on her side, besides Moishe, who was out of the Ghouls' reach. He was high up in a nearby tree; he didn't seem to be able to help. None of his attempts to pick off Ghouls from above had worked since they came on guard.

The crowd of Ghouls inched toward Sierra, some caution slowing them. But their forward motion didn't stop. They moved with the implicit awareness that she could not get all of them.

You should run, came David's voice in her mind.

Shut up! was her response.

If you run, you can be part of the mission to go kill them later, he replied.

She didn't engage any further. Her mind was on the Ghouls, fanning out into a semicircle around her, getting closer to surrounding her.

Sierra retreated, stepping back slowly. She was getting further away from any potential help from Moishe, but she couldn't avoid that. The monsters weren't giving up, even though she'd proven she had a Skill that could destroy them on contact.

She realized dimly that she was almost out of Mana. She'd used up a lot healing the wounded—not as much as Alan, but enough. Purification wasn't a Mana-cheap power, either. With the aura around her body, she could manage another dead Ghoul or three. After that, she would be defenseless.

She took a big, clumsy swing at the closest Ghoul with her staff. The Ghoul tried to dodge, but it stumbled backward into one of its comrades, and Sierra's weapon found its unarmored neck.

The Ghoul swore quietly. "Damn it."

Then it grinned and threw itself onto Sierra's staff, grabbing it and holding it in place.

It took only a second for the Ghoul to begin to fall apart. But in that second, the others were upon her.

They didn't risk touching her with bare hands this time. One swung a heavy weapon at her head. She managed to dodge that with a step to the side, which would have been a fall if not for the Ghoul on her staff. An enemy from her other side took a swing at her with an axe.

The axe took her left arm off at the elbow, and with the searing, agonizing pain came a sharp realization.

I really should have run. Too late now.

In the final moments before she blacked out she managed to slam her staff into one more Ghoul's head.

The dying monster's scowl was the last thing she saw.

CHAPTER FIFTY-FOUR

Retaliation

As James approached the Rodriguez camp, his triumphant strut faltered slightly.

He had been bracing himself for a hero's welcome, but as the camp came into his hearing range, which was far greater than sight range in the swamp miasma, he heard a discomfiting sound. Weeping. In the area of the Rodriguez camp, a handful of people were quietly wailing and crying.

"I'm going on ahead!" James barked at those around him. Then he bolted forward at a speed no one else could equal, simply running through any brush or trees that stood in his way. He felt the presence of the wolves trailing behind him, trying to match his speed. They easily outpaced the walking humans, many of them still nursing wounds.

Remember, don't get too close to these humans until I've had time to get them used to the idea that you and they are allies now, James sent. *We don't want any unnecessary fighting. The real enemy is still out there somewhere.*

Yes, my king, Luna replied instantly. *We will have revenge on those treacherous abominations!*

He heard her barking out a few quiet orders, directing the pack's movements more precisely to keep with his general orders. He smiled briefly, satisfied. The wolf pack was going to end up being one of his greatest assets, he could already tell.

Then James rushed into the perimeter of the Rodriguez camp.

The first bad sign besides the sound of weeping was that no one intercepted him. He hadn't tried to be stealthy, since he was rejoining an allied group. But no sentries responded to his crashing, tree-branch-destroying arrival.

Then James spotted Moishe rushing toward him. From the sounds of human movement and breathing, he gathered that everyone else was in their tents. But his mental headcount of the camp felt very lopsided with what he remembered.

There are only about half of them still here! he noted with some alarm.

Moishe reached him and began speaking breathlessly.

"James, I'm sorry. I couldn't protect them. You weren't even gone a full day. I—"

"Moishe, just tell me what happened. Do you know if the missing people are dead or alive? Was it the Ghouls again?"

"I don't know, James." Moishe looked terribly guilt stricken. "They carried everyone off. I don't think they were trying to kill them. They used a lot of non-lethal blows. Yes, it was the Ghouls."

"Then they're hoping to make more of their own kind," James said. "Taking them to their master."

James had gathered a fair amount about the Ghouls from Luna on the way there. How they had deceitfully abandoned their allies to fight alone. He had thought it was because they simply knew a losing battle when they saw it, but now he understood. They wanted to replenish their numbers.

Moishe's face took on an expression of horror. "What can I do?" he asked.

"Stay here," James said. "Protect the remaining members of the group. We don't know if they'll try and come back again. I—"

He broke off and looked away from Moishe. Suddenly, there were people approaching from the tents. A dozen of them. They walked as if half asleep. It took him a moment to identify the emotions their faces showed. It was a sad mixture. They were stricken with grief, and they looked at him through eyes filled with desperate hope. A few had clearly just been crying.

"James, thank God you're here!" cried Karla Rodriguez. "Please, you have to save my husband!"

That opened the floodgates. The approaching people began excitedly talking over each other.

"You have to help—"

"The Ghouls came and—"

A few more people emerged from the tents, including Alan. He wore an expression of intense anguish and guilt.

James raised a hand, palm faced outward, for silence. The talk came to an abrupt stop instantly. "I'm going to go out and rescue anyone I can," James said. "I'm going to get the details from Moishe, who saw everything happen. The rest of the group is coming back behind me." He gestured a thumb into the miasma the fighters were still curtained behind. "If there's anything anyone needs to tell me that Moishe wouldn't know, could you please raise your hand? That way we won't talk over each other."

A hand immediately went up from the back.

"Yes, Alan," James said.

"Sierra was one of those captured, so it seems important that you know this. She has a Skill that was able to hurt the Ghouls. Her Purification killed a couple of them in one shot. They knocked her out, but if you find them, you might want to release her first. She could probably do a lot of damage."

Just like a video game, James thought. *Where healing hurts zombies.*

"You don't have that Skill yourself, right, Alan?" James asked.

He shook his head.

"Thank you for speaking up. Anyone else?"

Camila raised her hand. James saw she was leaning heavily on her staff, using it like a makeshift crutch. *We need more Healers. If the injured were more fully healed, I wonder if the Ghouls would have been able to carry off so many people.*

"What about the wolves?" she asked in a low voice. She made a broad gesture at the outskirts of camp, where James's wolf pack was gathered.

"I'm glad you asked," he said. *We had to discuss this eventually. Better to get it over with sooner rather than later.* "I defeated the leader of the wolves, and he gave me control over his pack with his dying breath. They're going to follow me now. They've agreed not to go after humans unless they're humans we've decided are a threat, so no one needs to worry about them. And now the rest of the wolves are going to help me recover our lost friends and family members."

"Well, if you say so," Camila said in a soft, slightly tremulous voice.

"I won't let any harm befall you," James replied gently, looking into her eyes.

The old woman smiled, and James mirrored her expression.

"Any other questions?" he asked. "I'm getting out of here as soon as I can. I have to catch up to the Ghouls before they have time to corrupt the people we care about."

"Take me with you!" Alan burst out.

There was another torrent of similar comments from people whose friends or family had been taken by the Ghouls.

I guess Alan is taking it quite personally that Sierra went missing, James thought. *Either that, or he's grown very close to some members of the family. Maybe both. But why would he think it's a good idea for him to go? He has to know he's slower and weaker than any of these Ghouls. If I'm waiting for people to catch up to me, I'll never be able to get to where the monsters are.*

James raised his voice to be heard over the gathering. "I'm only taking the physically fittest people, who can best keep up with me and the wolf pack! If you can't keep up with us, we need you to stay here and wait. Otherwise, we won't be able to catch the enemy!"

The crowd quieted from a low roar to disappointed murmurs. Alan said nothing, but he looked particularly dispirited.

"That means I can go, right, James?" asked Moishe a bit too eagerly from his side.

Another person who wants to avenge a perceived loss of honor? James wondered. That wasn't to say Moishe would be anything less than useful, though.

"Well—"

"There he is!" interjected Cliff. James half turned his head and saw Cliff and Damien walking out of the fog. He could sense the presence of the rest of the group close behind them.

Cliff stepped into close range with James and clapped an arm around him. "We made it back, gang!" Then he took in the mood of the camp. "Hey, what happened?"

"Ghouls came and carried people off," James explained in a hushed tone. "We have to go on a rescue mission."

"Well, count me in, sir!" Cliff whispered back intensely.

I can't trust Cliff at all, James thought. *Sure, his Stats are probably high enough to keep up with the wolf pack since he's been doing more hunting than anyone else but me. But I can't trust him. So he's the absolute worst person to bring on a mission where there will only be a skeleton crew around me.*

He thought back to when he had visited Cliff's dream what felt like weeks ago. That place full of mist and snakes and wandering naked humans. In the time since he'd gained the power to enter people's dreams, he'd never seen one so ominous. *He could betray us at any moment.*

His mind took a turn into the Machiavellian. *Then again, maybe that's a good reason to keep him close. On a mission with a skeleton crew like this, anything could happen . . .*

"Naturally, I'll want to accompany you as well," Damien said. "Now that we've avenged ourselves on the Wolf King, the natural next step is retaliation against the Ghouls, right?" His lips curled into a wolfish grin.

"I don't think you should all come with me," James said quietly. "My thinking is that Cliff and Damien should be the ones to go." He turned to Moishe. "We need at least one strong person to stay with the camp, in case we do get attacked by another enemy." Moishe opened his mouth to object, but James quickly leaned in to speak directly into his ear.

"You're the only one I can trust to lead both the Rodriguezes and the prisoners," he whispered. "Both groups like and respect you. Trust me. I'll bring back our friends if they're still alive."

Moishe swallowed hard. "Yeah. Okay. I trust you completely," he said. He seemed to convince himself of the words as he said them. Finally, he nodded, half to himself, and his expression visibly relaxed.

There's that taken care of, James thought.

He sent a telepathic message to the wolf pack. *Can you all track the Ghouls' scent?* he asked.

The answer came immediately and unanimously from over a dozen wolves. *Yes, my king.*

We could track the scent of their corruption and decay anywhere, Luna elaborated. *No one can outrun their own smell. We will bring you back their dismembered bodies if you wish.*

I'm going with you, so don't set out yet, he replied. *And I want half of you to stay behind and protect the camp. I don't want any more sneak attacks carrying people off. Luna, please work out who stays behind. And if any of those who stay back get a whiff of a Ghoul nearby, I want to know about it immediately.*

As you wish, Luna said. There was chatter between her and the other wolves through the telepathic link, but James largely ignored it. The details weren't important to him right now. He'd learn more about how each individual wolf fit into the pack later.

I love the eagerness, he thought. *They can't wait to rip into those Ghouls. Though, I suspect that if I sent them out without me, with only one Command Forest Wolf left alive and without the Wolf King, I would end up with a pile of dismembered wolves instead of dismembered Ghouls.*

"We'll set out immediately if you're both ready," James said aloud. "The wolves are able to track the Ghouls' scent and guide us."

"Uh, right-o, chief," Cliff said.

Damien just nodded.

The trio walked to the edge of the camp and rendezvoused with the wolf pack.

From there, James ordered the wolves into a tight formation that would make it harder for them to lose members in the thick swamp fog.

The pack caught the scent of the Ghouls, and they began the pursuit at a run.

James proved to have been correct that all three humans were capable of keeping pace with the wolves. Damien, of course, could have transformed into his Werewolf form, but it wasn't necessary. Cliff, despite his sixty-something years of age, had acquired an Agility and Stamina in the forest that was impossible for a man of his age in normal life.

Orientation has been very good to him, James thought. *It's a pity he's untrustworthy.*

Over the next several hours, they penetrated deeper and deeper into the dense swamp, doing their best to ignore the fetid swamp fog that seemed to grow thicker in front of them wherever they turned. It was obvious the location was hostile to their presence. James hoped the Mana that permeated the fog didn't allow the enemy to pinpoint their position, though he had every reason to expect that it would.

It doesn't matter, he thought. *Even if they can set a trap for us, there's nothing in this place I can't kill.* Hadn't he managed to destroy even Rostov's fiery final form? How could he lose to an enemy who had been unwilling to even show his face thus far? Based on the wolves' intelligence, this Soul Eater seemed cowardly.

Still, every half hour, at James's request, Luna gave him a head count of the twenty-five wolves they'd brought with them, just to make sure they were not being quietly picked off.

If I thought I was outmatched, I would try guerrilla warfare. But it seemed the enemy hadn't come up with the same plan that James would have.

Eventually, the daylight began to fade. As night began to fall, James's companions started to show some signs of fatigue.

"Are we gonna stop?" Cliff asked, obviously breathless and sweating heavily.

"I'm impressed you could keep up this long," Damien replied, also slightly short of breath, but with only a few beads of sweat on his brow.

"We can take a break," James said, breathing normally through his nose, his face bone dry. "I'll check in with the wolf pack and see if we're getting close to where the Ghouls went."

He took several strides forward toward the guard of wolves around them, while Cliff and Damien tried to relax without sitting on the swampy ground.

Are we any closer to the Ghouls? James sent. *Do we know how far we still have to go?* The pack's forward-positioned scouts were still just out of sight range, but when James reached out with his mind, he could feel their presence ahead of him.

Yes, we sense that they're very close, my king, one of the scouts responded.

I need to talk to Luna about this naming thing, James thought. *Am I a higher-level organism that could name them? Thinking of them as individuals is harder without names.*

He was about to ask how much longer they would need to run at their present pace to reach the Ghouls, when he felt, rather than saw, the lights in the sky.

The will-o'-the-wisps appeared, and they exerted a psychic pull on everyone who saw them. James felt their influence through the pack members.

The lights, several wolves thought. *Everything we want, if we just walk toward the lights . . .*

CHAPTER FIFTY-FIVE

Internal Affairs

The will-o'-the-wisps pulled at the weak Wills of several wolves.

James could sense it. He could not only tell how the wolves felt, but he could tell which wolves felt the tug of the lights most forcefully.

The scouts in the front of the group were particularly vulnerable. Where other wolves in the pack might have been investing Free Points in Will, they had consistently invested in Perception. This gave them an advantage as scouts, but it made them terribly weak against mental attacks like this. He could feel they were moments away from breaking and running toward the lights, at which point they would surely never be seen again.

As for James himself, the will-o'-the-wisps had no effect on him. They were just pretty lights.

He activated one of the Skills generated by Alpha Presence. *Zone of Influence!*

[Zone of Influence: Generate a field made from your aura (a combination of your Stamina and Mana) and insulate subordinates from being influenced by foreign energies. Scales with Charisma, Will, and your own resistance to the foreign energies. Consumes Stamina and Mana.]

James's aura spiked and spread to a wide area around his body. The field around him was invisible, but there was no mistaking what was happening. It felt like he was a teapot being slowly poured out, with the water being his Mana and Stamina.

I really need to practice this Skill, he thought. The aura field drained a surprising amount of both Stamina and Mana for a field that he thought covered a relatively small area. *If it was anyone who didn't have absurd reserves of Stamina and Mana, they wouldn't be able to use it at all.*

But at least the area covered was large enough to contain all the wolves, even those out of his sight. He could feel that the influence of the will-o'-the-wisps had been broken completely.

Scouts, report! James sent. *In the area of the will-o'-the-wisps, how many enemies are there?*

We only sense a handful, my king, reported one. *Thank you for extending your protection.* This last was pronounced with what James interpreted as a slight tone of embarrassment.

Of course, he replied. *I can't have my valuable scouts kidnapped and made into Ghouls.*

"Hey, Damien!" James called out.

"Yes?" Damien asked, looking at him.

"You're resisting that just fine, right?" James pointed at the floating lights.

"Yeah, no problem," Damien said.

"Great. The wolves think there's only a handful of enemies over there, but some of them are affected by the lights, so it's dangerous for me to leave them to go fight the Ghouls myself. Could you go kill them off for us? I'll send the toughest wolf with you."

Luna, James had observed, was more or less unaffected by the lights. She was a leader, so her Will was quite high for her level.

"Sure, no problem." Damien flashed a grin. Then he took off his clothes. For a moment, James averted his gaze, though it seemed Damien had done this so many times that he felt no particular shame about the nudity involved. It was also a surprisingly quick undressing process.

Then Damien began to transform before James's eyes. Tufts of dark gray fur began to sprout from every exposed piece of skin. Muscles bulged out of places that hadn't seemed particularly toned before. His jaw bones cracked, unhinged, and lengthened into a muzzle. He let loose a monstrous roar as the muscle and fur spread over the rest of his body. And the transformation was complete.

All right, Luna, could you please go with Damien and kill off the handful of Ghouls who are obstructing our advance? James asked. Sweat was beginning to bead on his forehead, though he could see his Mana and Stamina reserves weren't falling too quickly. He wouldn't want to keep this up too long. Just until he was in a less stressful environment.

As you wish, my king, she sent. She walked from James's left toward Damien on his right. Then James heard a sniffing sound from her.

Luna began to growl, low and deep.

Damien looked askance at the two-headed wolf.

"Uh, James, what's up with your friend there?" he asked, his voice unusually nervous.

I forgot, the last time Damien lost a real fight, it was with the Wolf King, right?

That was how he ended up wounded and unable to defend his group from the coyotes when I found them. Does being surrounded by the wolf pack make him nervous?

But James was also wondering what was going through Luna's mind. He looked at her now, and she had her hackles raised and her lips partly curled back, revealing the tips of her teeth.

Luna, what's the meaning of this? James sent.

The scent of the one who killed my mother, Luna sent. *He's covered in it.*

James recalled an incident back in the forest, just before he'd had his Race Evolution. He'd seen Damien kill and eat a Command Forest Wolf, hadn't he? *Was that Luna's mother?* He paused to wonder. *Damn it, I don't have time for this right now,* he thought.

You didn't recognize this scent before? he asked. *Are you sure it's him?*

His scent changed when he transformed, she replied firmly. *I'm almost certain. Do you think it's possible that he shares the same scent as someone else in this forest?*

That does seem unlikely. He might be the one who killed your mother, then, James replied gently. *I don't know. He would probably tell us the truth if we asked him. But if he is the one who killed your mother, are you going to fight him over it right now? You're helping me, even though I killed your father.*

That's different, she replied slightly testily.

Is it? he asked. *I think this place forces people and creatures to fight each other. I don't think it makes sense to hold a grudge. Especially not now, when we're facing a common enemy, and I don't sense any hostile intent from him toward you or the wolf pack. Even though I believe your father almost killed him.*

She was quiet for a few seconds, processing.

You make an interesting point, I suppose, she acknowledged. *I do remember hearing there was a fight between the previous Wolf King and a creature like him while I was out hunting one day. The creature had to run off with its tail between its legs—*

All right, James interrupted. *Can you work with him, then?*

There was a silence that felt interminable. Finally, Luna replied.

If it's really what you want, that's fine for now, she said. *But what about later, when we're competing with him for territory?*

It felt like she was looking for an excuse, a reason why James might order her to attack Damien, although James was fairly certain Luna couldn't beat him in a one-on-one fight at her present level of power.

You're thinking very long term, he replied wryly. *We have to get out of this place alive before we can think about claiming territory on Earth. But if Damien becomes a threat to us, I'll kill him myself. Right now, he's ready and happy to assist us in defeating one of our rivals.*

Then I'll go with him as you command, she replied. *You will remember what you said, about killing him if he becomes a threat?* There was a pleading note in her tone.

Yes. I'll put the safety of the pack and anyone else who follows me loyally above the safety of anyone else.

She let out a little satisfied whimper, and then she walked forward.

"Come with me, Werewolf!" she said aloud. Then she bounded forward without looking at Damien.

"What was that all about?" Damien asked James, not moving.

"Apparently, you killed her mother," James replied bluntly. "Once you transformed, she could smell the scent you left behind when you did it. I told her not to try and kill you."

"Oh. Shit." He looked as stricken as a wolf face could look. "I never thought of these mons—I mean, these life-forms, um, having loved ones."

"I get it," James said. "I've done some things myself that would curl the hair that grows all over your body. We're all still learning. Give her time. Perhaps she'll forgive you. I don't believe she'll harm you in any way right now. It's hard to describe, but I get this overwhelming sense from the wolves. Just—" He struggled for a moment to put a word to it. "Just this intense feeling of loyalty and devotion."

"Easy for you to say. They are loyal *to you.*"

"Take my word for it, then. I've ordered her not to harm you."

Damien looked at James for a long moment before he apparently decided to trust him.

"All right, man," Damien said. "I'm putting my life in your hands, then."

He raced off after Luna, who was almost out of sight beyond the mist.

Not that she could really kill you anyway, James thought. Although he liked Luna, he had to be objective about her capabilities at present. *Among the wolves, only the king was probably capable of that.*

James waited until the two were almost fully out of his hearing range before he turned his head and looked back to Cliff. This fighting would take at least a few minutes with just the two of them against those Ghouls.

Enough time to tie up a loose end.

"So, anything you want me to do while our allies are fighting the big bad—"

Compulsion.

"I want you to tell me the truth, the whole truth, and nothing but the truth, Cliff," James said.

A silent battle raged for a moment in their minds, until James's Will had crushed Cliff's like a cigarette under a boot.

"What would you like to know the truth about, sir?" Cliff asked in a weirdly docile voice.

"I can enter people's dreams. I visited one of your dreams once, and it was a completely bizarre place. There was mist, naked people wandering around, and the walls and floors were made of snakes. Explain that."

"You witnessed one of my visits with my patron goddess," Cliff said. "When I dream, I sometimes enter her realm."

"You have a blessing from a goddess?" James asked.

"I do," Cliff replied.

"What did you have to promise her to get it?"

"I promised to sacrifice at least fifty people to her during Orientation and to continue sacrificing as many people as I could thereafter."

A cold sweat broke out on the back of James's neck. *This might be a little worse than I'd imagined.*

"You've been sacrificing people?" James asked.

"No, no, I want to get as many as I can all at once." Cliff spoke the murderous words with the same cadence as if he was talking about the weather. "I've been waiting until near the end of Orientation."

"How were you going to do it?" James was more curious than anything about this arrangement since he obviously wasn't going to let any of what Cliff had agreed to do happen.

"The goddess helped guide me to a Great Forest Scorpion on one of my hunting outings while you were gone. It dropped a powerful venom, which I claimed as the one who struck the killing blow. I was going to mix it into the food some night."

"Wow. That's, uh, quite something. Why did you agree to do this? Just for a little more power?"

"Oh no," Cliff said mildly. "I got her to keep my family out of Orientation. As long as I succeed in my task, they skate by without risking their lives. Good deal, right?"

"Uh, excuse me a second, Cliff." He took a few steps away. "Hey, Hester? Was there some possibility Anansi could have pulled Mina and Yulia out of their Orientation for me?"

"Um, no," she said a bit nervously. "It sounds like this goddess is more powerful than Lord Anansi, honestly. The System will sometimes bend a bit to a more powerful god's wishes. It's a creation of all the gods working in conjunction, but as with most things, the more powerful you are, the more of a say you get."

"All right, thanks," he said. He believed her. At least, she was telling the truth as she understood it, per James's Ring of Truth. He turned back to Cliff, who stood staring blankly into space.

"So, you agreed to sacrifice a bunch of people to an evil goddess to get power and keep your family safe, eh?" James asked.

Cliff's voice changed for the first time since James had used Compulsion. He became defensive. "You accepted a god's blessing too, didn't you? You were probably thinking the same thing as me, right? Look out for your family, to hell with anyone else?"

"If Anansi ever asked me to betray humanity, I would tell him to *fuck off and die*," James said furiously. He quietly added, "No offense."

"None taken," Hester replied mildly. "And Lord Anansi wouldn't do that."

"I only agreed to accept his support because he said he was a friend of humanity, and I choose to believe him. You forgot which side you were on and became no better than the Moloch cultists. Give me back my sword."

Cliff's body moved a bit clumsily, as if he was sedated or drunk. He reached into his bag and pulled out the Ego Spidersword. Then he handed it back to James. The eye in the pommel seemed to stare intensely at the blade's owner.

I've been missing having a weapon that wasn't broken, he thought. *I'll probably need something better than my bare hands to finish this if the Soul Eater is as tough as the Wolf King.*

Though he had ultimately beaten one of the Wolf King's heads to death and then crushed its heart with his bare hands, James was still more confident with a weapon in his hands.

"All right, Cliff, what's the name of this goddess who blessed you?"

James gave the sword a few practice swings as he spoke.

"Hel, the Goddess of Death."

"Why did you ask that?" Hester whispered. "You might get her attention, with one of the people she's blessed speaking her name like that. You don't want a death goddess watching you."

"I need to know who's a threat to me," James replied under his breath. Then he deliberately raised his voice. "If there's a goddess who's happy to see me and my people get sacrificed, I'm not concerned about being friendly with her. Like Anansi said, death gods and goddesses don't really negotiate to let people come back from the dead anyway. So there's no reason for me to pretend to be nice."

Cliff simply stood silently, waiting for the next command.

"On your knees, please, Cliff," James said.

His former boss obediently knelt.

"Bend your neck forward a little bit. This isn't so much personal as it is just dealing with a future problem, so I want to make it quick."

Cliff bent his head forward.

"How could this possibly not be personal?" Hester asked incredulously.

"Because I kind of always thought Cliff was willing to do this to anyone," James said. "I just never thought he had actually signed up to make that choice. He was probably going to fire me too, I'd imagine. Ironically, now I'm terminating him. So, I can put it all behind me and just see him as another problem I'm about to put an end to." He smiled slightly and added, "You know, I like solving problems."

James swung the sword down until it struck an object that stopped it.

CHAPTER FIFTY-SIX

Lockdown

"Mina! Mina!"

She heard the voice as if from a great distance.

Not now. I have a headache, Mina thought. She wanted to say it out loud, but the words felt very far away from her lips, and her mouth seemed to be full of cotton or something.

Water splashed on her face, and a bright light shone in her eyes.

"Mina, are you with us? Are you all right?" It was Leo DaSilva's voice, she realized. A female figure stood beside him.

Mina blinked unsteadily, and she realized that it was Alba next to Leo, holding a dripping wet cloth.

I guess I have her to thank for the water in my face, she thought. *Wait, why am I on the floor?*

In an instant, everything came back to her. She jerked to an upright position, and a sharp pain surged through her head.

"Oh, ow," she said quietly, putting a palm to her forehead.

"Are you all right?" Leo asked. "Where's Yulia?"

"That's what I was just wondering," she replied. "I think she's out there." She pointed at the window, which someone had closed.

"That *was* open when I came in," Leo said, his voice grave. "You think Cara or one of her creatures got her?"

"No, I don't believe Cara would have gone after her or let the other Wendigos target Yulia either. She spared me. Why go after someone important to me?"

"You think Yulia left on her own?" A pause. "To go and warn people?"

Mina nodded.

"Did you see this happen?" Leo asked.

"No, it's just a theory," Mina said. "I have to go get her now."

She tried to push herself up, but Leo held her by the shoulder.

"Are you out of your mind?" he asked. "You're not going anywhere. We're on full lockdown here. Have you seen what it's like outside?"

As if to punctuate his words, a huge chunk of hail struck Mina's window and stuck there for a moment before it fell away. It stayed long enough for her to see it was the size of a softball.

"I guess one of those hit me," she said, remembering the sharp pain in the back of her head before she tumbled backward into the room.

"You're lucky it didn't kill you," Leo said.

"Do you need a Healer?" Alba asked. "We have a few—"

"I'm fine," Mina snapped. She activated Healing Aura, and the pain in her head immediately began to subside. There was an awkward silence for a few moments. "I'm sorry to be impatient," she added, her voice full of sorrow. "I just don't know if I could forgive myself if something happened to Yulia. She's my responsibility. I promised my mother on her deathbed that I would protect her. And we've been through so much together now."

"Still, you can't go after her," Leo said firmly. "You'd die, and you wouldn't rescue anybody. One of the ladies down the hall is a meteorologist. She's comparing the weather outside to that big winter storm back in 2037. You remember the one they called the 'Storm of the Century'?"

Mina nodded vaguely, but her eyes were focused on the window.

Leo noticed and sighed. "Your sister probably left a while ago," he said. "She probably made it to one of the other inns and had to hunker down there. Brave girl. Don't you think? And you were downstairs for a while. I hate to say this, but if she left and didn't make it to shelter, she's dead already."

Mina's eyes darted to Leo's, but the wrath that boiled in them cooled when she saw his expression. He looked worried.

"All right," she said slowly. Wearily. "I'll come downstairs. You still have any of that hot chocolate?"

Alba nodded wordlessly.

The three of them returned downstairs.

The entire population of the inn had gathered in the common area. They seemed to be in high spirits when Mina saw them. She had forgotten this inn was mostly women. There were a few married women who'd brought their husbands, but other than them, it was only Leo.

Some people quietly offered greetings or words of thanks as Mina stepped into the room. Leo had made her the woman of the hour with his version of events. How she had outed the killers and more or less driven them off. She tried to nod politely, smile, and accept compliments gracefully, but her mind was in the storm.

Ugh, Yulia! I'm going to strangle you when I see you. What were you think—

That thought was interrupted by the sound of screaming. The group had quieted for a moment when the wind carried it over.

Multiple people, Mina thought numbly. *It couldn't be that loud with just one person screaming.* And it sounded like more than one voice. The Wendigos had begun their bloody work. But Cara had kept her word. Wherever they were feeding, the inn where Mina was staying seemed to be safe.

The group of grateful survivors seemed to gravitate to the area around where she rested, Mina couldn't help but notice. She tried not to resent them. They were afraid for their safety, and Leo had given them the idea that the Wendigos would avoid her, which was actually true. They didn't need to be so close, but she succeeded in mostly ignoring them.

The wind carried over the sound of more distant screams, but the flow of conversation around Mina picked back up and began to drown them out.

Human beings are remarkable, she thought. *I don't know how people can talk at a time like this. Does this make us the most foolish race, the most resilient, or what?*

For most of that long night, she sat in a self-imposed bubble of silence and she worried, her hot chocolate growing colder beside her by the minute. She burrowed into herself and her memories. Remembered her mother's quiet wisdom and her laughing sisters. Thought of her happy household with Yulia, James, and now the baby. *Yulia! Why are you doing this to me?* She wanted alternately to strangle her and just hold her close. *I can't let you out of my sight for the rest of—* she suddenly remembered that it was actually open-ended. They might never be truly safe again. Orientation's purpose, if she took the System at its word, had been simply to *prepare* them for the new world.

She went down a rabbit hole imagining what the new world might look like before she returned to worrying specifically about Yulia.

The hours passed with agonizing slowness.

As dawn broke, it became obvious the storm still wasn't letting up. Mina began to visualize images of her sister's dead body. Sometimes she saw Yulia mangled and partially eaten by monsters that Cara had failed to restrain. Sometimes she imagined her frozen to death, covered in ice and frostbitten all over.

That death would be better, she thought. *People in Bulgaria used to say that when you die of cold, your body gets a sudden surge of warmth from within near the end. Sometimes people get so hot they start taking their clothes off in the freezing cold. If Yulia has to die, I want her not to really understand what is going on at the end. Like slipping into a dream forever . . .*

Mina slapped herself. Now was no time to entertain those thoughts. She got up and went to her room. The crowd in the common area had dwindled over the last few hours, so only a few women bid her a belated, "Good night—uh, morning!"

Mina managed to force herself to acknowledge the words with grunted responses.

Then she went to be by herself. She withdrew into magic. This was all her fault in a roundabout way, wasn't it? Yulia left because she was worried about what Cara and her Wendigos would do. Cara got away because Mina was too weak to stop her. It was only through Cara's twisted mercy that Mina remained alive at all.

Never again, she thought. *I'm so weak. I have to become strong so no one can threaten the people I love.*

Tears welled up in her eyes before she banished them to focus on magic.

She tunneled into her elemental magic to a degree she had only matched a couple of times before. She spoke the chants, and she focused on the way that Mana felt moving through her body. When Cara had confronted her earlier, part of why Mina hadn't tried to stop her from leaving was that her magic was too slow. How could she make it faster?

Zeroing in on how the energy felt moving around her body, she tried to rush it, to make the spell charge faster. Chanting faster didn't help, but she could accelerate the flow of energy with her mind. It was like controlling how much force she exerted with a push: use the amount of strength she would use to open a door and she wouldn't knock anyone over; use the level of force that she would use if she was trying to stop a cyclist from crashing into Yulia, though, and she could injure someone. It was hard to moderate this. The first several times she tried to control the movement of Mana within her body, she failed and lost control.

Fortunately, she was just using water Mana, which she had the most familiarity with. If someone entered the room, though, they would think she had gone swimming. She dowsed herself with water five times before she started to make some progress.

First, she figured out that the chant was completely unnecessary. Once she knew the feeling of casting a particular kind of magic well enough, she could do it without the chant.

[Required conditions met. Skill Silent Spellcasting unlocked!]

Yes, yes, I know I figured that out, she thought, waving the announcement away. *I need faster spellcasting, not quieter spellcasting!*

A few hours later, she made the desired breakthrough. It was purely a matter of regulating the speed of energy movement through her body—probably through some organ she didn't know she had, like arteries or veins. In any case, all it took was disciplined, conscious practice. The energy flowed smoothly and at a faster pace than it had before. Suddenly, she found that she could cast spells almost instantly. The only downside was that casting so much faster wasted substantially more Mana. But she could feel that she would be able to increase her efficiency with further practice.

[Required conditions met. Skill Quickened Spellcasting unlocked!]
Finally!
[Mage leveled up!]
[System-Boosted Human leveled up!]
[A Class Evolution is available. Review? Y/N]

That sounds like it would make me a lot more powerful, she thought. She was about to select "Y" when she heard her stomach growl. As soon as she noticed that, she realized that she was famished.

Practicing magic had the dual effects of making her stronger and drawing her full focus, which was considerable. For hours, the problems of the world had fallen away. Even Yulia had shifted to the back of her mind; perhaps that was the main reason she did this. But apparently, she had also forgotten to eat. It wouldn't be the first time.

She rose unsteadily to her feet. She was genuinely quite weak, she realized.

When was the last time she had consumed something more substantial than hot chocolate? Yesterday morning? What time was it now?

She glanced out the window, but all it told her was that it was extremely bright outside. Definitely still the same day, then.

Whatever, the time doesn't matter.

She went downstairs and walked over to the kitchen. Alba was there, turning System-issued rations into real food, and she took one look at Mina and demanded that she eat something. Mina refused until she had compensated Alba with a portion of her own rations big enough to justify the Cook's hard work.

But it's a little nice to have someone worrying over me, she thought as she sat and began to tuck into the food. She had wanted to get back to her normal activities as quickly as possible after having her baby, and physically, she was in perfect condition again. But she felt a tiredness in her bones, a fatigue that seemed to be catching up with her. Maybe that was from the absence of a break in the normal routine of life.

Or maybe I just didn't sleep last night, she realized. *I guess I'll have to rest if the storm continues as it has. I just really hoped that I would get to see Yulia again before I slept.*

She no longer imagined Yulia dead. That had been her fear talking. No, she would find Yulia in a warm, secure state as soon as the storm ended. Maybe she would have found someone to make her hot chocolate and a meal too.

Must stay positive, she thought, forcing herself to suppress the spiraling thoughts of worst-case scenarios.

She finished her meal, brought her plate back to the kitchen, and had a quiet conversation with Alba, who was a comfort.

In the middle of talking, though, Mina's ears perked up. There was a strange sound in the background. She asked Alba as politely as she could to be quiet for a moment and just listened. Mina heard almost nothing.

But after a few seconds, she realized that was odd in itself. All night, along with the chatter of the inn's residents, she'd heard the sound of the storm. Wind buffeting the building. Hail striking hard surfaces.

"I think the storm might be over," Mina said quietly.

She and Alba parted quickly after that. Alba wished her good luck with Yulia, and Mina thanked her.

Then she dashed upstairs and changed into warm clothes before she rushed back downstairs.

As she stepped back into the common area, the System made another announcement.

[Attention all mortals! The worst of the snowstorm from yesterday appears to be over. We spent the last several minutes clearing the snow that landed in your walkways. We would still recommend exercising caution outdoors, as your fragile human bodies might still be endangered by the level of cold that remains present in some areas of the Orientation.]

Some areas, Mina thought. *I wonder what that means. Did the Wendigos leave and take their storm with them wherever they went?*

But that didn't matter for now. She had confirmation that it was safe to go outside.

She was about to walk out the front door when she heard a set of footsteps she recognized coming toward her.

She turned around. Leo smiled at her.

"I hear we can go outside and see, uh, what happened," he said. His smile faltered a little as he seemed to realize what that meant.

"Don't worry," Mina said. "Yulia's going to be fine." The words were a reassurance and almost a prayer.

As they stepped out into the world, there were a handful of others stepping out into the light of day alongside them. People looked relieved that the storm was over, but Mina barely noticed their expressions. Right now, she was only scanning their faces so she could find the one person she really cared about.

She had almost given up and decided to go searching for Yulia building by building when she saw her: Yulia, Paulo, and Jose stepped out of one of the other winners' inns.

I should have known who Yulia would want to go warn first, Mina thought. Mostly, though, she was just happy to see her sister alive and in one piece.

Yulia saw her at almost the same moment, and the sisters ran to each other and embraced.

"I'm sorry," were the first words Yulia said once Mina finally released her from her death grip. "I know I must have made you worry."

"You did, and I'm never letting you out of my sight again!" Mina said, barely keeping her voice below a yell. Tears ran down both sisters' cheeks. "That was the worst night of my life!"

"Well, Jose and Paulo kept me safe," Yulia said. "Otherwise, I might have tried to go on to the next inn . . ."

Leo stood at a polite distance throughout the sisters' exchange. Near enough that Mina remembered he was there, but not close enough to disturb the sisters' reunion.

After they'd held each other for a while longer, they walked back over to him. His expression was one of mingled joy and sorrow.

"So glad to see you're okay, Yulia," he said. "Of course, I told this one that you'd be fine." He gestured to Mina. "That you'd hole up somewhere in the storm and not freeze to death or get eaten. But we were still both pretty worried."

"I'm so sorry about that," Yulia said. She looked just as regretful as she had when she'd apologized to her sister. "I really wish I hadn't been so impulsive. I didn't even help anyone." Her eyes seemed to narrow slightly, as if she was noticing something in Leo's face. "Wait. Is there something still worrying you, Detective?"

"To be honest, there is," he said. He gave Mina a meaningful look.

"I think the detective wants to talk to me by myself, sweet," Mina said softly. "I hate to leave you alone, but would you please go back to the inn? Not even back to the room—I think Cara stole my key—just back to the common area, and I'll be back as soon as I can."

Yulia nodded. "Yeah, whatever you say, sis." She looked guilty, and Mina was glad she hadn't chastised her for running off. Her sister already had a strong sense of right and wrong, so she didn't need much guidance. But sometimes she was so headstrong. They could both be stubborn, but Mina thought Yulia might give her premature gray hairs soon.

"What has you so worried, Leo?" Mina asked, watching her sister walk away.

"Did you notice anything peculiar when everyone was leaving their inns?"

I'm too tired for rhetorical questions right now, she wanted to say. But being tired was no excuse to be rude.

"I didn't notice anything. What did you see?" She waited.

"People were only leaving the winners' quarters," he finally replied.

Her heart sank.

"Really?"

"As far as I could see," he said.

"I'm glad you had me send Yulia back," she said. "I'm guessing you want to check out the crime scenes and see what happened?"

He nodded. "You don't have to come. I just wanted you to be aware."

"No." She swallowed, then gritted her teeth. "I'm going." *These deaths are partly on my head, after all. If only I could have stopped Cara* . . . "Do you want to bring Adelaide too?"

He shook his head. "No point. We know who the killers are. This isn't crime scene investigation anymore, though frankly that was pretty fruitless this whole time anyway. Not due to any defect in Adelaide's efforts, but there was no forensic facility and barely any evidence left. I think law enforcement could end up being very different in this new world." He looked profoundly worried about that.

"No point in worrying her, then," Mina agreed.

"Yeah, I'll check on her after we're done here."

They walked to the first of the original inns the System had provided, before the challenges had produced the System's version of class divisions.

Neither was prepared for the scene that greeted them. Somehow, Mina had optimistically imagined that the missing would just be gone. Vanished into thin air.

Or, more honestly, just swallowed whole by the Wendigos.

Instead, there was dried blood and bone and bits of bodies scattered through the common areas. The floor was so bloody that much of it had been dyed a crusty brown. It was only obvious at the edges that the flooring had been another color once. Mina covered her mouth with a handkerchief to provide some protection from the awful smell of organs and human remains. Despite the slight protection, she barely restrained herself from vomiting. Fortunately, with the cold and the recency of the deaths, rot hadn't set in yet.

She and Leo ascended the stairs in silence, looking for any survivors. They found rooms and possessions, but no people. There was less gore than there had been downstairs, but some people had clearly been forcibly taken from their rooms. The doors had been ripped from their hinges in most rooms. In one room, there were human nail gouges dug out of the wall by the door, complete with a broken off piece of nail embedded in one of the grooves.

In one bedroom, Mina found a teenage girl's diary embossed with an image of a purple unicorn and instinctively shuddered. There was a blood stain in the corner of the cover, and the images of Yulia, dead, returned to her mind, accompanied by the smell of carnage wafting from downstairs. She threw open the window and retched.

She cleaned herself off in the adjoining bathroom before she rejoined Leo.

They entered the next inn.

It was a pointless search, but one they replicated over and over.

Every one of the starting inns was empty of living humans.

By day's end, they took a full reckoning of how many people the Wendigos' murder spree had cost them.

In order to do this, they got nearly every living human to line up outside and be counted. Leo used his saved-up goodwill and political capital to secure universal compliance, along with the same story he'd fed the people from their inn about how Mina had saved everyone from the Wendigos.

Everyone but those poor souls still in the starting quarters, Mina thought, listening to him give his version of events yet another time.

The few people who couldn't be summoned outside due to illness or infirmity, they visited in their rooms.

And Mina used Investigate on every living human. She made certain that no Wendigos remained in their ranks.

But Cara could hide her Status, Mina reminded herself. The only way to be truly secure against this threat was to be too strong to be considered prey.

All told, Leo and Mina estimated that roughly 250 people had vanished. They had to estimate. As they had realized early on, the population count clearly didn't reflect the full losses, or anywhere close to them, which meant that most of the missing had been taken alive.

[2,576/3,397 Survivors]

Poor souls, Mina thought again.

"Maybe we'll mount a rescue operation once we've developed our strength as a group a bit more," Leo said as they stood outside their inn once again.

But his heart wasn't in the words at all, and Mina just shook her head.

"We still outnumber them," Leo insisted weakly.

"We need to drop it," Mina replied, "or there'll be far more dead the next time."

She stared off into the distance and tried to harden her heart to the plight of those missing—those taken prisoner, surely, to be killed and eaten by the monsters in the future.

Hopefully, they took enough prisoners that they don't come back here, she thought.

It was an ugly thing to think, but it had been an ugly day.

CHAPTER FIFTY-SEVEN

To Hell . . .

Proctor!" Mina called out. "Cygnus!"

Leo looked at her, surprised and weary. "What do you think that's going to do?" he asked.

Then a figure appeared behind him.

Mina was no longer surprised to see the colorful image of the proctor step out of thin air. She felt angry, tired, and impatient.

[You summoned me?]

Cygnus's tone conveyed a hint of pique. A reminder to Mina that there were still things to be afraid of here, even if the Wendigos never came back. There was the proctor, and there were Mina's fellow humans, who she had never trusted very much anyway—and much less now that some of them had literally turned into monsters.

"I did," Mina said. "I have questions that only you can answer, a request or two, and a demand."

[A demand? Well, go ahead and say what you must. I have the sense that it was a long night for the human population.]

She sounded more amused than annoyed now, which pissed Mina off. But she kept her anger in hand.

"Did you know that our team contained Wendigos?" Mina asked.

[I keep track of all life-forms in this Orientation. I know what everyone and everything is.]

"You didn't tell us about them, even when people directly questioned you about the murders earlier. Is the System hostile to human life? Were you trying to feed us to the monsters?"

Leo looked alarmed at this question. He put a hand on her shoulder and tried to whisper in Mina's ear. "Hey, do we really want to upset the proc—"

But Mina shook him off. She wouldn't be silent. Even if Cygnus could squash her like a bug.

[The System has a role to play in your universe. It is indifferent to the survival of human life in particular, but it operates to the benefit of all sentient species. There are rules that constrain even the behavior of System administrators. I could not acknowledge the presence of Wendigos until you discovered it for yourself and identified their leader. Congratulations on accomplishing that objective. It will be taken into account in scoring your results in this Orientation.]

The proctor seemed to think this should satisfy her. A confirmation, if Mina needed one, that the System's representatives were not human, had no affinity for humanity, and enjoyed little understanding of their species.

"Now that we've discovered them, can you tell me if there are any Wendigos remaining in the settlement?" This was Mina's most important question. The one that would let her sleep easy at night, or possibly force her to take some form of extreme action.

[There are no Wendigos remaining in the human-populated region. They departed just before the storm began to let up.]

Mina allowed herself to sigh in relief. Then she resumed her questions.

"There are apparently rules we don't know about in this Orientation. What do we have to do to get out of this place? Are there hidden conditions? Some way to end this early?"

Cygnus looked at her with what Mina took to be a curious posture for a few long moments. It was frustratingly hard to read her mood with the mask covering her face. Finally, she answered. Her voice was surprisingly soft.

[You have already accomplished half of the objective. Malsumis, one of the deities sponsoring this Orientation, is satisfied that his goals have been accomplished. One of the other deities has accepted that her goals will not be achieved here. If someone satisfies the wishes of the third deity sponsoring this Orientation, it will likely end early. This could be the "hidden condition" you are alluding to.]

"What wishes? Which deity?" Mina asked.

But the proctor only shook her head.

[Were those all your questions?]

"I still have requests and a demand," Mina replied. "First, given that the Wendigos prey upon humans, I request that they be disallowed from entering the human settlement in future."

[I must convey this request to Lord Malsumis.]

Cygnus stood perfectly still for a few seconds, and it felt as if Mina had just witnessed the figure's soul leave her body. Mina and Leo just stared at her for a moment. Then they glanced around at the open space surrounding them. With the proctor no longer responding conversationally, Mina finally noticed that a number of people had stopped to gawk openly. Some of them had drawn fairly close and could certainly hear the substance of the conversation. The surrounding area was quiet as people waited for answers from the proctor.

I guess I didn't notice them because I'm tired, she thought. *I need to sleep so badly, but I still have a few more things to do . . .*

Cygnus suddenly resumed moving in the corner of Mina's vision, and Mina turned back to face her.

[Lord Malsumis has given his word that his creatures will not enter the human settlement again. He further adds that his Chosen One does not wish to return to the settlement, and he wanted you personally to know that this Orientation has exceeded his expectations.]

Malsumis is an awfully nasty god, Mina thought. *What kind of an ugly soul could be happy with this result?* Not for the first time, she considered the possibility that the gods of this universe were all evil. If that was true, then what would be required to satisfy the third sponsor? For that matter, what would have pleased the second?

"Related to that, I would like the Wendigos removed from our teams for the forthcoming challenges," Mina said.

Have to deal with every detail. Have to prevent the threat from resurfacing before I'm strong enough to face it. Even with her newly unlocked Skills, she still didn't feel confident that she could survive another encounter with Cara or her minions.

[The Wendigos have already voluntarily removed themselves.]

"Oh." That was a surprise. *I guess Cara really meant what she said earlier.* It made it that much more frustrating that the warrior had allowed herself to become this monster in the first place. "Then I have another question and my demand. The question: is it possible for everyone to be on one team for the remainder of the Orientation?"

The proctor's body language shifted subtly. Mina thought she could almost see the figure smiling behind her mask.

[That is permitted at this point. The purpose of the division has vanished. If all of the humans agree to it, the remaining challenges can be configured so that you succeed or fail as a group.]

Mina turned to Leo. "I'll have to ask you to take care of that," she said. "You're better with people than me, anyway. I hope you slept a little last night."

He nodded.

"I think that would prevent any future infighting," she said. She raised her voice slightly so that the people still gathered around could hear. "We live or die together. That's how human beings should behave in a place like this. We're a social species. There's no reason we should let an outside force pit us against each other."

[Was there anything further?]

She turned back to Cygnus. "Yes. I want my baby back."

Mina's reason, common sense, and instincts were all singing one tune. The major danger of this place had passed. It was time that she reunited with her baby.

When the proctor reached into thin air, pulled little James out of nowhere, and returned him to Mina's waiting arms, a little cheer went up. Mina turned her head and realized a small crowd had gathered, significantly more people than she'd noticed before.

Word of the conversation she'd had with the proctor would spread, then. And people would discuss among themselves whether they were willing to be part of an all-human team. Mina was glad to think that she wouldn't have to tell the story of what had happened herself.

Her eyes fixed on baby James. All she wanted now was to feed him and sleep.

There would be time to solve the other mysteries of this place later.

[Farewell, then.]

The proctor departed with no emotion in her voice.

Mina excused herself from the unexpected gathering of people and took James inside. Leo remained to deal with the crowd and, he said, to try to achieve the goal Mina had just set of putting all the remaining humans of the settlement on a single team.

Mina, Yulia, and baby James went upstairs. Mina fed James. She chewed Yulia out a little bit for her disappearance the previous night, though not nearly as harshly as Mina had imagined herself doing. Then the three of them collapsed into bed together and slept the sleep of the just.

Mina had been in bed for hours, dead to the world, when she felt a sudden jolt of motion.

The movement immediately woke her up. Just in time to catch herself before her body fell to the ground. She found herself on a rough surface, with plant roots and hard-packed earth under her hands and knees. A forest floor? Definitely outdoors, but it was hard to make out because it was quite dark.

Even the night sky offered no illumination; it was apparently a new moon.

"Congratulations on surviving thus far," an unfamiliar voice nearby barked out.

Mina looked around her on the ground, resisting the urge to glance up at the source of the voice. Where was her baby?

She stopped searching when she realized that Yulia wasn't next to her either. Something strange had happened, and she had one good guess as to what it was.

"As you humans have now formed a single team, you will all share a single fate in this final challenge," the gruff voice continued.

So, we're in the final *challenge?*

She looked up and looked around. Even in the darkness, she could see that there were a number of human beings on the ground, scattered across a large area. Some of them were blocked from view by trees. They appeared to be in a dark forest. It was hard to get a good estimate of the number of people with the darkness and the trees, but she could see enough dark shapes that she guessed there were at least hundreds of humanoid figures in the darkness.

It's the whole population, isn't it?

"Do you have a name?" called Leo's voice some distance away in the dark. It was clearly aimed at the entity speaking.

"I certainly do," the voice replied.

"We'd like to get your name and see you, then!" Leo replied. "Where are we?"

"Very well," the voice replied.

Mina heard it mutter a phrase to itself, and then she saw a strange pattern of light appear in the darkness where her hearing had approximated the speaker was. The lights were shaped like letters in a foreign alphabet. Not the Cyrillic alphabet, or she would recognize it. Maybe something older.

Then the forest burst into sudden flames all around them.

People began to scream.

"Run!"

"Everything's on fire!"

"Someone help!"

Mina turned her head. Every tree as far as the eye could see was ablaze, slowly burning from the treetops down. People began to panic and run away.

"I hope the visibility is more to your liking now," the voice said in an ironic tone. Mina turned her head back and finally saw the speaker, who was so close to her that she had to resist the urge to distance herself. The forest was quite bright now, lit as it was with orange flames. The voice had come from a large black hound, roughly the size of a horse. Curved horns adorned the proud head. Its body was covered in the glowing orange letters she'd noticed before, though the lights began to fade as she looked at it. "To answer your questions, I am called Charon, and you have come to the in-between space. The land between the living world and the underworld."

Mina instinctively used Investigate on the hound, but she almost regretted it.

[Charon, Mystic Chthonic Hound, Lv. 80]

The hound was apparently sickeningly powerful. Lighting the forest on fire was clearly just a parlor trick it engaged in to amuse itself. If it wanted to just burn them all to death, it could do so. Beside it were two much smaller hounds. It was hard to tell how old they were in the firelight, but they didn't come up to Charon's kneecaps.

She Investigated them as well and breathed a sigh of relief.

[Baby Chthonic Hound, Lv. 3]

[Baby Chthonic Hound, Lv. 3]

The other two hounds were apparently just there for appearances. Or to get experience from killing off people the Mystic Chthonic Hound didn't finish itself, assuming these creatures were there to kill them. Or for some symbolic purpose.

Three is a magic number. Was this a magic-based challenge? Was the trio of dogs, two of which were level three, a coincidence? Did it have some other meaning?

She didn't have much time to contemplate the questions running through her mind.

As she looked around, she saw that some of the flames were surrounding the humans in a large circle and were drawing closer as she watched. Those who had tried to run hadn't gotten far, but a few of them had made it to the edges of the ring of fire. They were the first to be touched by fire as the flames crept in tighter. Mina smelled the odor of burning hair and skin.

"Are you going to burn people to death before we even begin the challenge?" she demanded loudly, glaring up at Charon.

The hound looked down at her. His eyes gleamed a brilliant yellow, flames streaking from their corners like tears.

"You have a point, dear girl," he murmured. The symbols on his sides glowed once more, a gentler yellow this time, and the flames began to subside. Where the trees burned, the flames remained in place like they were growing from the branches. The ring of fire stopped moving in closer, and the people who had begun to burn were able to retreat further back. Mina saw green healing being used out of the corners of her eyes, but she remained focused on Charon.

"Whether they live or die," he said softly, "may come down to you."

CHAPTER FIFTY-EIGHT

Gatekeeper

"Are you ready for the challenge, then?" Charon asked, voice slightly brusque. "No more foolish questions?"

He seemed to cast a sidelong glance in Leo's direction as he spoke the second question.

"Just one question right now, if I may!" Mina called up to him. The hound seemed impatient and easily offended, but the answer to this question might mean the difference between surviving the challenge and becoming dog food.

"Go on," the hound prompted.

"Which deity do you serve?" she asked.

"We serve the Gatekeeper," Charon replied, his voice suddenly surprisingly tender and respectful. He locked eyes with Mina. "She sees in you the raw, unshaped material of which greatness is made. We have watched you for some time now."

Her heart sank a little. *He won't even name the goddess*, she realized. *Maybe he thinks it would be disrespectful, or perhaps he's just conscious that it might give away some sort of clue.*

She simply nodded in response, mind whirling.

I need more information, but I know so little. I don't even know what to ask.

"Follow me, then," Charon said.

The hound bent so his two young companions—his offspring?—could climb onto his back. Then he ran forward, leading the way through the burning forest. Wherever he stepped, the flames pressed themselves back, clearing a path. Mina, Leo, and the other humans did their best to follow close behind him because everywhere else was on fire. As she ran, Mina spotted Yulia and worked her way over to her. When they met, the sisters linked arms.

"We're staying together for the rest of this no matter what," Mina whispered urgently in her ear.

Yulia nodded fervently in agreement.

The two returned to their running pace, trying to keep up with the other humans chasing after the hound that galloped like a horse.

They must have run for nearly a mile when the stadium came into view.

Mina's first view of it was from a great distance, which was perhaps the best way to get a good initial impression of the structure: a massive oval arena made entirely of a pale stone. It reminded Mina of ancient Greek stadiums. *What was the name of that old stadium they used again for the 2040 Olympics? Panathema? No, that wasn't it.* But she remembered that it had been touted by the newscasters as the world's only stadium built entirely out of marble.

This stadium was much like that one, she decided. Probably also marble. And it should be able to fit tens of thousands of people like the Greek stadium had. They were a comparatively modest crowd for this place. Then again, maybe there would be other spectators while the humans competed for their amusement.

Did the System—or this goddess—build an entire stadium just for this challenge? No, why am I thinking like that? They already built a maze for the challenge before last. It didn't help her thought process that she was still a little groggy from having been woken up so unceremoniously.

More importantly, the appearance of the stadium gave Mina a sense of which culture this goddess might hail from. *Greco-Roman, almost certainly.*

Her eyes panned over the stadium as Charon drew them closer to it, trying to capture any details that might be relevant in the challenge. It was ringed with countless torches that lit the whole open-air structure fairly well despite the darkness of the night. They gave the area on the ground where everyone was arriving a dusk-like level of lighting during the day.

There was a long reflecting pool in the center, around ten feet by twenty-five, which seemed noteworthy since the only thing that it would reflect was torchlight. Around the pool there was only grass.

Wait, there's something else, Mina noticed. She caught a flicker of movement in the pond, and she instinctively looked up above it. There was something there. Something moving, just hovering gently up and down. It looked like nothing more than a short, thin white line segment in the air.

"We have arrived!" Charon barked at the closest humans. Then, with huge bounds that the mortals couldn't hope to match, he leaped into the stands and took off toward the upper levels.

Mina, some distance back, finally allowed herself to slow to a walk. She had a stitch in her side from the run, and she sucked in deep, heaving gulps of air as she tried to catch her breath. Beside her, Yulia was likewise breathless; neither sister had been especially athletic before the System.

As the two sisters closed in on the stadium and Mina tried to think about what sort of challenge they might have based on the physical cues, Mina realized she hadn't used her Class Evolution.

Darn, she thought. She didn't think it was an opportunity that was likely to disappear, as the System hadn't indicated a time limit. But maybe it would have helped with whatever challenge was to come. And who knew if it was a time-consuming process? If she had wanted to ask whether she had time or not, Charon had already gotten too far away for her to raise the question without yelling and getting everyone's attention.

Slower people began catching up to the early arrivals, who had decelerated once the hound had announced that they had arrived. The mass of humans gradually clumped together into a crowd.

"All non-magic users may take a seat in the stands," Charon announced in a booming voice that projected across the whole space. "This is an individual challenge, and the particular difficulties of it are suited only to Mages."

There was a grumble of protest at that.

"Why did the rest of us come all this way?"

"Isn't this the final challenge? But only the Mages get to participate?"

Charon howled his response. "Be grateful that you did not burn to death in the forest! You are permitted to watch this competition because the goddess has allowed it and because all of your lives are at stake. If none of the Mages are capable of completing the challenge, you will all die!"

The voice was so loud and piercing that Mina and Yulia both winced and covered their ears. Mina didn't know how the baby hounds were enduring it, though she couldn't even see if they were sitting on Charon's back anymore. Perhaps they had gone somewhere else, like a soundproofed room under the stadium. Mina had observed a covered opening and a staircase descending underground. The opening was blocked off by some sort of Mana barrier, translucent but likely formidable, considering that this place belonged to a goddess.

The little hounds were probably just covering their ears with their paws. Mina hadn't seen them drop off before Charon climbed up to the top of the stands, and the big hound was now so far away that it wouldn't be strange if they were just laying on his back, blending in, invisible to her eyes.

More objections.

"My life is my own!"

"Why is our fate in a tiny minority's hands?"

"I want to participate myself! I can take you, beast!" shouted one particularly aggressive voice. Mina saw the man, a burly fellow with thick dark hair on his head and lots of visible body hair, and she had to resist the urge to roll her eyes.

Hadn't he noticed how powerful Charon was? Even if he hadn't used Identify to check the hound's level, Charon had set *a forest* on fire in an instant with little more than a thought. Did this man really believe that he could win that fight? Mina had no confidence that the whole body of her Orientation could defeat Charon together, let alone a single warrior. She was sincerely hoping the challenge was something else.

"Very well," Charon replied. Mina could hear malice in his voice. She swallowed nervously. "This is an individual challenge, however. Everyone who will not be participating should make their way into the stands, and then we can begin taking individual volunteers from among our brave competitors. If you remain in the field, I will assume that you wish to be considered for the challenge."

Mina had intended to participate, given that this was a Mage challenge, but Charon's tone of voice made her doubt herself. This challenge would surely be murderously difficult.

You can do this, she thought. *You're probably the strongest Mage in this place. Or at least the most precise with your Skills.*

Unless the challenge calls for fire elemental magic, or literally anything besides your two elements, she argued with herself. She had seen a couple of fireballs used in the first challenge but only in her peripheral vision, so she hadn't learned the Skill with Quick Study the way she had acquired Healing Aura. At present, Mina only had Elemental Magic: Water and Basic Elemental Magic: Wind to work with. If she needed something offensive, those didn't leave her a lot of options.

Then again, other Mages likely wouldn't have been practicing as much as she had. Very few challenges had actually required the use of magic, and it was only Mina's personal drive that had caused her to cast so many spells that she had acquired a second element so quickly. Couple that with the fact that she'd likely learned wind magic more quickly thanks to Quick Study, and two elements were probably more than most of the other Mages had. So perhaps she should volunteer first. At least there was water in the stadium.

This would undoubtedly be dangerous. If it was a magic challenge, and they would all live if any one challenger succeeded, then perhaps it was best to put their best foot forward.

"Yulia, go up into the stands," Mina said quietly.

"Are you participating?" Yulia asked.

"I am," Mina said, her voice hollow.

Yulia squeezed her hand tightly and stood there in silence for a moment.

Mina spoke again, looking down at Yulia as she did. "I'm participating because I'm a Mage, and probably the strongest one we have. I've practiced magic night and day here. You know that. If anyone can beat this thing, it's me." She tried to make herself believe the words as she said them so Yulia would believe them. Mina could imbue her words with great conviction at times, but only when she said what she truly believed.

It seemed to work. Yulia hugged her tightly and smiled. She seemed to believe in Mina. Now it was time for her to believe in herself. She pulled Yulia into a hug that lasted a few long seconds, giving her a little squeeze before finally releasing her.

"All right, sweet. I love you. Since you're a Healer and not a participant, you should go sit with Leo in the stands."

Most of the people who were non-Mages were already seated in the stands. Even those in the competition who had physical handicaps had been helped up by friends or family members and now sat on the long stadium seats. Only a handful of non-Mages lingered with the hundreds of Mages on the ground level. Leo, being a sensible man, had not taken Charon's bait. He was seated in the third row, looking down at them with a smile. When he saw Mina looking up at him, he waved and mouthed the words, "You can do this."

Yulia reluctantly released Mina from her grip.

She surprised Mina by walking away from her toward the other competitors rather than into the stands.

What is she doing? But then it became obvious.

Yulia approached Jose, who Mina had forgotten was also a Mage. He looked nervous as she drew closer. She leaned in, kissed him on the cheek, and muttered, "Good luck."

Then she turned, cheeks glowing bright red, and climbed the stairs.

"Th-thank you for your confidence!" Jose called after her. "I'll make sure we win!"

"You go, kid!" an unfamiliar voice shouted from up in the stands.

Mina couldn't help but laugh a little to herself despite the circumstances.

Puppy love, she thought. Jose looked as embarrassed as Yulia following the exchange. His cheeks weren't burning, but his eyes conspicuously focused on the ground.

Mina would ordinarily be trying to assess whether this boy was really good enough for her Yulia, but she had to shelve that for now.

She was left standing in the field with a couple hundred Mages and a half-dozen *very stupid* non-Mages. All of them were men, she couldn't help observing.

"Is everyone in the field a participant?" Charon barked down at the silent crowd. "If you remain in the field for some reason but are a non-participant, please raise your hand."

No hands went up.

"Very well. Then I will explain the challenge. You must simply light, and keep lit, three candles. Not for a fixed period of time. If there is a moment when all three are burning, then you will have accomplished the challenge." The hound's mystical body letters glowed orange again, and three flames appeared in three different places.

One flame moved to light a candle that Mina now spied lying next to the hound itself. Another flame flew down and lit a candle that sat on a lily pad in the middle of the reflecting pool. And the third floated over and lit a candle that hovered in the air six feet above the reflecting pool.

That was the thin white line I saw, she thought. *Those candles are the challenge.* Of course, it seemed too simple, and she waited for the rest. Perhaps they would go out if you didn't light them quickly enough or in the correct order, or they could only be lit by a certain temperature of flame.

"The only problem you will have," Charon went on, "is an opponent that will seek to stop you, by any means necessary, and put the candle flames out." As he spoke, all of the candles instantly went out.

"I'm ready to take you!" shouted the same brave idiot from earlier. Mina wished for a moment that she could slap him.

Shut up! she thought.

"Oh no!" Charon began to make a strange snuffling sound, and to slap one paw repeatedly on the stadium seating directly in front of him. It took Mina a few seconds to realize the hound was laughing uncontrollably. Once he'd caught his breath, Charon resumed talking. "Not me, you fool! If you had to fight me, you would all die horribly. Even demanding that you all fight me at once would hardly be fair to you, let alone the idea of you each fighting me individually. No, I am summoning you a much more suitable opponent." The strange lettering on his body glowed brightly again, though this time it was a royal blue rather than orange.

Mina saw motion in the corner of her eye and turned to see that an elephant-sized hole in space had opened in the air just above the field. Through the gap, she could see a massive creature's head and a mountainous backdrop. At first, the beast looked like a lion. Then it stepped through the portal, and she saw a second head sprouting from the middle of its body. The middle portion of the body and the head attached to it looked like they belonged to a goat. The creature's rear had the legs of a lion, but in place of a tail, there writhed the long body of a snake.

A chimera, Mina thought. It was sort of breathtaking. Horribly ugly but impossible to look away from. Somehow it appeared to be functional. Once it was through the portal, it gamboled about the field, testing the ground and roaring. It barely seemed to notice the humans or the fact that the portal had closed behind it. Finally, it walked over to the reflecting pool, lapped a small amount of water up, and then laid down beside the pool and seemed to go to sleep.

Not very smart? Mina hoped. If it was just a dumb beast, that wouldn't be so hard to overcome. *Let's see what its powers are . . . Investigate!*

[The use of this Skill has been blocked.]

Mina looked up at Charon, who she thought was frowning down at her from above. The letters on his body were fading away again, but she realized they had been glowing white rather than royal blue the moment before, which she guessed meant he had just used a different type of magic.

"As stated earlier, this will be an individual competition," the hound said drily. "Please do not attempt to use any Skills or interact with the chimera or the challenge in any way unless it is your turn to participate. Humans who are not in the midst of participating, please keep to the group of prospective challengers or to the stands, respectively. Any future violations of these rules will be punished severely."

"I'm ready!" the same man from before declared. "Just as soon as I get my armor on." He had more or less donned his full armor while the more sensible men were leaving the field, but Mina saw he was putting on a helmet as well now and strapping a small shield to his arm.

Charon waited until the man had fully prepared.

"Are you ready now?" he asked.

The man nodded.

"Then you may begin."

The armored man rushed over to the wall nearest to him, where two torches sat in sconces. He yanked one free. Then he circled behind the other competitors and ran up the arena steps toward Charon.

He's not still going to try to fight Charon, is he? Mina couldn't help wondering. *He couldn't be that stupid, right?*

The man lit the candle next to Charon, and the big hound didn't move an inch. His eyes watched the man, and the man looked back at the hound, nervous from his body language to be so close, but finally, the man descended the arena steps once more.

A few in the crowd began oohing and aahing at his quick progress. Mina thought this was the moment to begin worrying.

In theory, the challenge was one-third complete now, but the warrior hadn't engaged at all with the actually challenging parts: dealing with the chimera and reaching the candle that was floating six feet in the air. It wasn't even clear whether the armored man could jump that high, let alone jump that high and precisely aim a torch to light a tiny candle wick.

But they didn't get to that point.

The warrior stepped off of the stands and into the arena, and the chimera opened its eyes.

Then it rose to its feet.

The man seemed to become petrified with fear. He looked behind him for a moment, as if considering retreat.

In that moment, the chimera leaped forward and reached him in a single bound.

The lion's jaw opened wide. Mina saw saliva dripping as it eyed the man.

The warrior turned to face the monster, but much too slowly to do anything.

The lion's head bit down on the man's head, and the goat's head sunk its teeth into the body armor, holding him still for the lion. Together, they ripped him in two.

Screams of horror shot through the crowd.

CHAPTER FIFTY-NINE

The Fallen

Well, that's annoying," James said mildly.

The sword had been stopped from chopping through Cliff's neck by a black shield that had levitated out from Cliff's bag to defend him.

"Another sentient weapon," Hester said. "I was starting to think only you had them here."

"Cliff just got lucky," James replied dismissively.

And I don't have time for this, he thought. If the others had an easy time fighting the Ghouls, they could return at any moment. *I really don't want to have to explain to Damien why I'm executing Cliff.*

He let go of the Ego Spidersword, then reached out and grabbed the shield. It resisted his grip, but he was much stronger.

"It's a shame you belonged to Cliff," James said to the shield. He had considered smashing it over his knee, though he wasn't sure he was strong enough to break it so easily. But now he rejected that idea. Once Cliff was gone, he would give it to some other, worthier wielder. Breaking a sentient weapon like this was just wasteful. He still felt a twinge of regret that he'd broken his spear in the process of killing the Wolf King, though at least he'd obtained what he was sure was some pretty good loot as a result of that. He hadn't taken the time to analyze the materials yet, but there was a big fur coat and a wicked looking sentient dagger sitting in his bag, awaiting his consideration for future use.

"Kill him," he ordered the sword. He noticed the lights floating in the distant air had disappeared. That could only mean the Ghouls had been dealt with, so Damien and Luna would surely return shortly.

The Ego Spidersword swung down under its own power, and this time, it severed Cliff's neck. The blade was so sharp, it barely made a sound as it decapitated him. The head thumped lightly to the ground. A surprisingly light impact. *I'm sure anyone who ever met Cliff would agree he had a big head on him, but it turns out that was mostly hot air.*

[You killed Cliffton Rogers, Lv. 9! You gained 360 exp!]

Damn it, Cliff. You weren't even worth a level? Actually, not even close . . . He shook his head. *Pillage. There, that should get rid of the evidence.*

James decided to steal Stat points because he suspected Cliff's Talents and Skills would be redundant to his own, and he didn't want the kinds of Titles he imagined Cliff would have acquired, like Traitor to Humanity or Chosen One of Hel, maybe.

Two more in Charisma, he thought. *That's always useful.*

After Cliff's body had disappeared, he turned his attention to the wolf pack. The wolves were milling about, relaxed. A few were play-wrestling, which made James raise an eyebrow. They didn't seem to care about what had happened to Cliff at all.

But just in case . . . He sent out a non-verbal mental command just calling for their attention. The wolves all suddenly stopped what they were doing, turned, and looked at him. James had to fight a grin from spreading across his face. *I could get used to this.*

Cliff, one of the humans who came with us, is dead, James sent. *If any of you happen to be asked what happened to him by anyone in the future, you will recall that he was killed by a Ghoul surprise attack.* Sure, none of the wolves but Luna could talk right now, but James knew that was just a matter of time and experience. And he intended to bury the truth about Cliff forever.

Then he had another idea to better cover up the crime.

Also, here's some food! He took the Cliff meat out of his bag, opened the System-wrapped parcels up, threw the chunks of meat to the wolves, and watched as they tore into them. Then he turned back to face the direction Damien and Luna had run off in. It was fortunate they were taking their time getting back.

Wait, shouldn't they be back now? Maybe the Ghouls were giving them more trouble than he'd realized. It had been a small group of them, though. Or maybe Damien and Luna were fighting each other? But he couldn't hear any sounds of combat, despite his superior senses.

The wolves finished their snack quickly, and James led them off to find the missing wolf and Werewolf. As he and the pack drew close, James could hear the sounds of ragged breathing. *At least they're still alive.* As he pushed through the mist, Damien and Luna came into view.

They were both lying on their backs on a little island that stood a foot above the swamp muck. Luna was unconscious, while Damien barely maintained alertness. His eyes opened and closed woozily. He'd positioned himself beside her, one of his limbs protectively draped over the female wolf.

All around them lay pieces of dismembered Ghouls, around a half dozen by the looks of them. James ordered one of the wolves to take a headcount to make sure.

"James!" Damien groaned. "So glad you made it here." His body instantly began reverting to human form. "Now I can finally relax."

"What happened?" James asked. He had been vaguely listening to the conduct of the battle in the distance, hoping it would last long enough for him to deal with Cliff. But he hadn't heard anything that alarmed him. The fight had sounded like a fairly one-sided affair.

Witnessing the aftermath in person gave a slightly different impression.

Looking carefully, he could see that both Damien and Luna were wounded, though none of their injuries seemed especially serious. The two were covered in shallow cuts. A lot of them. Still, they shouldn't have been enough to put a Command Forest Wolf and a Werewolf out of commission.

But even before Damien began to explain, James's other senses told a fuller story than his sight. Luna and Damien's heartbeats were erratic. And there was a smell coming from their bodies, something like corruption. Not the same as what he'd observed when Camila was poisoned—their wounds didn't look or smell particularly foul—but something wasn't right.

"I think we were poisoned or something," Damien said. "We killed the Ghouls easily enough. There were some other things, dead things, in the water"—he gestured weakly at the marsh all around them—"and that was where we had the trouble. It was like *Night of the Living Dead*. They were all trying to bite us, claw us, make whatever little wound they could. They were a lot weaker than the Ghouls, but there were at least a dozen of them hiding. By the time we'd killed them, we had taken a lot of cuts." He looked anxious for a moment. "James, if I turn into a Zombie, you have to kill me, okay? I don't want to go on a rampage, trying to infect people. That was what I was scared becoming a Werewolf would mean—"

"Save your energy," James said, placing a hand on Damien's shoulder. "I won't let that happen."

I really don't want to have to kill him. How he could prevent some kind of involuntary transformation, he wasn't sure. He tried Laying on Hands first, and though it quickly closed their wounds, he could tell that their bodies remained contaminated. Luna and Damien's heart rates remained high, and their body temperatures were noticeably elevated. Damien's forehead glistened with a sweat that smelled sickly sweet.

"It didn't work, huh?" Damien asked.

James thought he'd controlled his expression, but it seemed Damien could tell from his own body that James hadn't fixed him.

"It'll be fine," James promised. "Sierra has a Skill for expelling foreign con-taminants. I just have to rescue her and the other people the Ghouls captured, and we'll get you guys healed in a jiffy."

"Mm-hmm," Damien said, closing his eyes. "Don't let them get you, man. Keep your armor on. I'm just going to take a quick nap."

James didn't try to keep him awake. Damien needed his energy to fight this.

"I'll come back for you, man. You and my wolf here."

"Yeah, I believe it." Damien spoke the words groggily but with no trace of doubt or irony. James felt a surge of pride at realizing that he had genuinely *earned* Damien's trust over the last few days. There had been no Skills involved, no lying. Just good, honest leadership and fighting. Plenty of fighting. He could get used to this.

And, of course, Damien would be a valuable asset moving forward. If James could cure him. If he wasn't forced to slay the Werewolf. But he would burn that bridge when he came to it, as Mina sometimes said.

The wolf that had taken the headcount of the dead reported back to James. *A half-dozen Ghouls' heads present.*

James used Mass Pillage to acquire Stat points from every dead thing within range. He didn't bother putting the meat from the dead bodies into his bag. The wolves weren't going to want a bunch of undead meat, and he didn't intend to eat it either.

I want six of you to stay back here and guard Luna and Damien, James sent to the wolfpack. *Whoever is the strongest of you besides Luna should be among them. The rest of us will go on and find the people who were captured by the Ghouls earlier.*

The wolves sent back a chorus of, *Yes, my king.* He let them sort themselves out.

Then he ordered the tracker wolves to lead him to where the human prisoners were being kept as quickly as possible.

"Hester, do you or Anansi have any idea what this health issue might be?" James asked quietly as the wolves looked for the scent.

"Sorry," she replied in a subdued tone. "If I knew, I would have said something." Suddenly, her body grew hot against his skin, and James recognized that she was receiving a divine transmission.

She was quiet for a few long seconds after it arrived, and James began follow-ing the wolves, who had picked up the trail of the kidnapped humans.

"I'm guessing Anansi didn't have any useful information about this prob-lem?" James murmured.

"He didn't have an immediate solution, no," Hester replied. "He did say that undead infections are the product of a Skill, though. If you destroy the one con-trolling or creating the undead that infected them, that will probably cure them."

"Well, that is useful," James replied. "Thanks, Hester! Please extend my thanks to Anansi." *Maybe I won't need Sierra's help after all.*

"It's my pleasure to be of service, sir," she replied. She sounded very gratified at being thanked. James wondered, not for the first time, what her life had been like before Anansi gave her to him. A question for another day.

He followed close on the heels of the tightly packed wolves and kept his eyes peeled. He'd instructed them to move in a close formation to make ambush more difficult, but when it came to Luna and the other Command Forest Wolves, he knew that realistically, with the Wolf King dead, he was the only one who could adequately defend them against a forceful surprise attack.

For half an hour, he followed silently, wondering when and if he would see his captured comrades again, contemplating whether he would actually be able to do something for Damien and Luna.

He was only half aware of it when he crossed an invisible line somewhere in the swamp. There was a different feeling in the air. The Mana was denser all around him.

We're in the inner sanctum, aren't we? he thought.

As the idea percolated in the back of James's mind, the swamp water around five feet away to either side of him began to bubble slightly. He pretended not to notice the water, but he sent a message to the wolves.

Scouts, I need you to give me the direction I need to head in to get to my lost allies. Once that's done, I want the rest of you to return to where we left Luna and Damien. I intended for you to accompany me the rest of the way to the enemy stronghold, but it looks like there will be a lot of sneak attacks. I don't think it would be as effective for us to fight together in this water, and I can travel more quickly alone.

This was his polite way of saying, *I don't want any more of you getting injured like Luna, or worse, when I know you won't be much use in this fight.*

He kept moving forward with the wolf pack until the scouts gave him the directions he'd asked for. Then the pack changed directions and ran back the way they'd come.

There, I'm all alone. James stared at the places in the water where there was bubbling. The swamp bottom felt like a lake bed, soft and uneven with squishy mud and reeds. He was knee deep in the swamp, but he was ready to leap out and into a nearby tree at any moment. Mostly, he wanted to see exactly what he was dealing with: the creatures that had probably gotten Damien and Luna.

The bubbles, he thought, were probably from decomposition. He was fighting undead, after all. He remembered from the Central Florida Prosecutor Training Program that corpses released gasses as they decomposed, which traditionally made them bob up to the surface. In this case, the corpses were still animated, so they were probably holding onto reeds on the marsh floor.

But some corpses wouldn't be at the same stage of decomposition and wouldn't release any gasses at all. It was tricky to know just when to strike. If he attacked now and destroyed the undead that were producing bubbles, he'd eliminate some of the enemy but probably not all. And he'd have no way of tracking the enemies that remained.

He moved cautiously, placing his feet carefully, while he considered a plan.

After a few minutes of thought, he began Silent Spellcasting, gathering water Mana around his body.

He advanced another few yards, drawing close to where his scouts had indicated the humans should be. He wanted to avoid fighting around them as much as he could. The more enemies James faced when he rescued the kidnapped humans, the more likely one of them would start using his allies as hostages. So best to get rid of these enemies now if he could.

With that in mind, he unleashed the gathered water Mana, willing the water to move aside and reveal the hidden enemies.

To James's slight surprise, the water actively resisted him. It felt like he was pushing a boulder uphill. The water seemed to simply absorb his Mana and almost fully ignore his directions until he stopped pouring Mana in.

Not worth whatever it would cost me to make the water move, he thought, panting slightly. He'd only used up around 5 percent of his total Mana reserves, but that would have been a staggering quantity for anyone else.

So, the swamp is under the boss monster's control? It was the only explanation he could come up with. *Given that . . .*

He leaped into the nearest tree.

Then he began Silent Spellcasting again, gathering gravity Mana this time.

As he did so, he looked around for the thickest and heaviest tree branches he could find. There was more than one way to deal with zombies.

"It's the strangest thing," Roscuro muttered, more to himself than to his eager listeners.

His Ghouls knew better than to ask for clarification. If he wanted Kurt and the others to know why he was talking to himself or what he meant, he'd come right out and tell them.

The strange thing wasn't that Robard had tried to use his Mana to move the swamp water and check for nearby enemies. That was clever, but within expectations, and it was kind of him to contribute so much Mana to Roscuro's dominion. The strange thing wasn't that he disappeared from the area in which Roscuro could sense his presence. That too was a wise move. And perhaps this human could fly; wind magic was just as common as water magic in Mages, Roscuro had observed.

No, what surprised him was what happened next. Roscuro lost all contact with the Zombies pursuing James through the swamp. Over a dozen of them disappeared in an instant. *Snuffed out like candles. How did he do it?*

Zombies weren't the hardiest of his minions, far from it, but they were more durable than Skeleton Soldiers. Their destruction, so quick and without any apparent explanation, gave him pause.

Roscuro had believed he had ample forces with which to face this enemy. He had staked his life on this belief by choosing to stay where he was and fight, albeit from the rear rather than beside his troops.

But what if I'm wrong? Should I leave? There's probably still time if I use the Ghouls as sacrificial lambs and the humans as distractions. The human clearly cared a great deal for these companions of his who Roscuro had ordered tied to trees behind him. *Maybe he cares enough to make a mistake.*

Suddenly he sensed Robard moving through the water again. *He's so close!*

Roscuro decided to run. He began considering which supplies and Ghouls, if any, he needed to take with him.

It was then that he noticed the way his Ghouls were looking at him. Their expressions, quite worshipful in better times, had taken on his own worried cast. And the sight of it made him irrationally angry.

I used to be a brave man, he thought. *Before I was a monster. What happened to that man? Did he really become the sort of creature that skitters away from an enemy like a cockroach running from a light?*

He began reconsidering. Did he want to stand and fight? Was it worth possible death to uphold his pride? He thought a moment. *No. Of course not. I need to get out of here.*

Then he heard Robard's footsteps crashing through nearby tree roots. He could certainly run with great force. *Wait, why do I still sense him elsewhere in the marsh?*

But then the man himself emerged from the trees not twenty feet from Roscuro. The time for second thoughts was over.

All Ghouls, kill this intruder! Roscuro transmitted, quickly deciding that he shouldn't bother sending the Zombies or Skeleton Soldiers after this enemy. At least not yet. They wouldn't slow Robard down as much by charging him as they would by going after the other humans and serving as a distraction. *All non-Ghouls who are not committed to other roles already, go and consume the humans we bound to those trees. First come, first served. All you can eat!*

Then he activated Territorial Control and began pulling at Robard's legs with his hold over the swamp water. Roscuro hadn't used it before, because he'd never been in such desperate straits, but now that he was cornered, he would use everything at his disposal.

This would be the anti-Robard strategy: bind his legs, distract him with attacks on his friends, and let the Ghouls tear into him while he's immobilized. Some of the Ghouls were bound to die in the attack, but the man only had two arms. The ones who didn't die were certain to land blows to vital areas. And in the meantime, Roscuro would gather his Mana and prepare his strongest offensive Skill.

He began chanting quietly.

The Ghouls reached Robard's body, and he made first contact with them, landing attacks on the nearest Ghouls' head and neck regions. But his flailing arms did surprisingly little damage. As far as Roscuro could see, he'd landed glancing blows on the Ghouls at best. This was perfect. Robard was panicking, failing to properly use his power!

Perhaps the Soul Eater wouldn't need to use Soul Magic after all. He kept chanting just in case.

In the next moment, he saw something that astonished him.

The Ghouls placed hands and weapons, respectively, on Robard's body and ripped into him. That would have been ideal—except that they'd literally ripped him apart with their attacks, and Roscuro didn't think human bodies typically contained leaves and sticks. But this one did.

An illusion?

There was a sudden breeze from behind Roscuro. He turned and looked and saw half of the undead behind him fall into the swamp, bisected by some form of wind attack. The other half of the lesser undead collapsed in another identical strike. Roscuro ignored those losses, searching the tree canopy with his eyes for any sign of Robard.

From the trajectory of the attack, he'd realized the human had to be in the trees somewhere. *Clever of him to avoid the direct approach. I should have known someone who's survived this long, become this strong, wouldn't come charging in like that. Now, where is he?*

After a moment, Roscuro realized it didn't matter. He didn't need to pinpoint Robard's location; he would simply flush him out.

Kurt, go over and kill a few humans! he commanded.

Face Off

James stared down through the trees as the Kurt Ghoul shambled toward the Rodriguez camp members.

He wanted to swoop down and smash Kurt in a single motion. He would've wanted to destroy the Kurt abomination even if there was no pressing danger to his allies. James was beginning to find the undead rather abhorrent. It was some combination of their grotesque appearances, the fact that they preyed upon the living of their species, and their use of poisonous or infectious agents.

What gave him pause was the Mana gathering around the creature that Identify had determined was Soul Eater Roscuro. It was a color different from any Mana he'd seen before: black and orange and yellow, all mixed, though the black was closer to the center of the aura than the orange and yellow. Mana with the color palette of a burning photograph.

And it gave off an odor. A smell of ozone, like the smell that preceded a storm or an electrical fire. But this clearly wasn't fire Mana or lightning Mana; James would have recognized those.

His whole body was screaming at him to stay away from that aura. *Don't touch it!* would be the sentiment if he were to verbalize his instinctive response. *So, that's quite dangerous.* He ordered his body to control this response, and the tension immediately alleviated itself.

But the problem remained as Kurt reached the humans. *What do I do?*

Kurt stood nervously between Roscuro and the humans. *Well, this is it.*

He knew he was bait, and he didn't resent it. Perhaps he didn't have that capacity anymore. Instinctively, he wished to obey the Master's commands, and his brain invented reasons why he should be happy to do so.

At least when I die, I'll take James Robard with me, he thought. He looked over the fresh humans in front of him. *And perhaps I'll die with the taste of fresh meat on my lips.* The appetite of a Ghoul for human flesh was almost lustful. Unconsciously, he licked his lips as he looked from person to person.

They were awake but helpless. Patricia, one of the still-living Ghouls, had bound them to the trees with her Skill. She had earned what seemed to be a unique Job before joining the ranks of the undead: Jailer.

Kurt saw Sierra's weary, terrified eyes peeking out from the side of the tree, and he smiled. It was fortunate that one of the other Ghouls had stopped her bleeding. Otherwise, she'd be dead or unconscious already. But he wanted her to see this. To watch them kill James Robard and the rest of her companions.

Don't worry. If I survive long enough, I'll get you later, he thought. For now, he wanted her to watch him eat one of her companions. That would put her in the right frame of mind.

Finally, he reached out to grab hold of the archer. The one who'd shot all those annoying arrows at them back outside the enemy camp. He took her quivering head in his hands, easily overcoming her feeble resistance, and brought his mouth up to her neck.

Kurt barely sensed the blow before it struck him.

How? he thought. His view of the world turned upside down, tumbled, and rolled as his body and his head fell in separate directions. He was vaguely aware that he was rolling in the Master's direction as his brain shut down. But the last sight his eyes fixed on was the image of James Robard, standing impassively beside the prisoners. And the last thought he had was, *How?*

Roscuro blinked and missed the movement.

Robard had struck so quickly that Roscuro was only dimly aware that he was down a Ghoul. Kurt's head rolled unevenly across the ground between the Soul Eater and Robard, teetering back and forth at the end of its arc until it stopped moving, eyes pointed up at Roscuro.

All Roscuro could stare at was his human opponent.

He'd finished chanting, though. It was time to make Robard regret revealing himself. The human kept one eye on him, but he was using the same dagger he'd decapitated Kurt with to hack at the bindings around the humans. It would do him no good.

Patricia stood to Roscuro's right, her body shuddering slightly with every blow Robard inflicted on the bindings. Each cut he attempted inflicted a corresponding cut on her body, but by the time Robard inflicted enough damage to destroy her, he would be dead.

Roscuro flung some of his magic at Robard. The Soul Eater had trained to be faster than most Mages, once he had reawakened in this body. He wasn't as powerful as he wanted to be. Not as powerful as he would need to be to pursue his revenge. But hopefully, it would be enough to exterminate this human.

Robard clearly saw the attack coming from the corner of his eye, and he had a long moment of hesitation. Roscuro saw the uncertainty not in his expression, which was perfectly disciplined, but in his posture. Roscuro had lived the life of a warrior once. He remembered those moments when it felt as if time had slowed down, and the world just *stopped*. Robard was having such a moment now, undoubtedly.

What will it be? Try to deflect my attack with your body, or let it strike and surely kill a human?

Robard's split-second reaction was too quick for Roscuro to perceive. He only saw the aftermath. An object that Robard had flung out collided with the burst of Mana.

That won't stop it all, Roscuro thought at first, excitedly. *He made the wrong decision!*

Then he saw how the Mana stopped moving and how it concentrated around the thrown object until the object shattered, then disintegrated into nothingness.

That's not possible, Roscuro thought desperately. *Unless—*

[You destroyed Ego Scorpion Shield! You gained 200 exp!]

Damn it!

And in the moment when his eyes had focused on the dead shield, the human had gone from his line of sight.

Roscuro still had Mana gathered around his body to fire more bursts of Soul Magic, but he wasn't fast enough to turn his head as James reappeared beside him.

In his peripheral vision, the Soul Eater saw James decapitate Patricia with that vicious-looking dagger. Then, as Roscuro's body finally moved, James vanished again.

As soon as he gets within touch range, you have to grab him, Roscuro transmitted to every undead under his command. Most of the Zombies and Skeleton Soldiers had been destroyed by James's earlier wind-based attacks, but there was still a scattering around him, as well as three Zombies that Roscuro had hiding in the water around his feet. These ambush attacks were, he had learned with experience, the slow undead's best way of dealing with someone who moved at greater speed.

He just has to make one mistake—they just have to grab him once!

But there didn't seem to be any openings forthcoming. All around Roscuro, Robard flashed from place to place. Wherever he stepped, Zombies or Skeleton Soldiers fell. Occasionally Ghouls too. None of them were fast enough to respond to him properly.

There was a moment when Roscuro sensed an opening. A Ghoul managed to grab Robard, and Roscuro fired another burst of Soul Magic at him. But Robard managed a twirl that placed the Ghoul in the path of the attack, and that Ghoul took the attack instead of Robard.

A hideous yowl filled the air. *"Eaaarggghhh!"*

Then the undead body disintegrated completely.

Roscuro angrily swiped away the System alert telling him he'd killed his Ghoul, and he looked for Robard.

Another pair of Ghouls fell—bisected head to toe and decapitated, respectively—and Roscuro scowled.

I spent so much time creating this fighting force. We were ready to take the whole region by storm, yet now it's reduced to a mere handful at his hands. But he has to be running out of Stamina, right?

Robard appeared in midair ten feet in front of him, and Roscuro fired another burst of Soul Magic. But Robard had apparently charged a spell of his own. A Ghoul suddenly levitated and flew from where it had stood into position to intercept the attack.

The poor creature screamed the whole way. "No! Master, save me!"

Roscuro tried to guide the Mana around the Ghoul's body, but Robard simply accelerated the Ghoul's movement and forced the collision.

Then he darted away and vanished. Roscuro sensed that he'd moved into the trees.

I only have one more shot before I have to chant again! And it didn't seem likely that Robard would actually run out of Stamina before Roscuro was defenseless. *I need some way to deal with him once the Ghouls are gone and he can get into close range. If I've fired my last burst of Mana when he closes the distance, what then?*

Roscuro desperately looked to his left and right. *There!*

He found the remains of a Skeleton Soldier just sitting in the water. The remains of all of the undead around him began to glow—Robard must have used some version of the Looting Skill that struck multiple targets at once—but Roscuro was able to get hold of the Skeleton Soldier's body before it disappeared.

Scrimshaw! It was Roscuro's most basic Skill, but it was also his most useful close combat ability. It instantly fashioned the skeletal remains into a weapon— in this case, a sword. Roscuro still remembered how to use a sword from his previous life, though this body was far too clumsy to do it gracefully.

As the rest of the Skeleton Soldier's body vanished, the spinal column shaped itself into Roscuro's makeshift blade. In his peripheral vision, another Ghoul fell. Robard was taking advantage of his momentary distraction.

I should have run, Roscuro thought. *I can't win.*

Robard suddenly appeared, charging at him from out of the tree canopy.

Grab him! Roscuro transmitted to his underwater undead. They were somehow unresponsive. Uncomprehending, Roscuro decided to take matters into his own hands. He fired his last burst of Mana at Robard, who neither slowed nor changed direction—and it passed right through him.

Impossible. What?

Then the figure of Robard vanished in a haze.

Another illusion, he realized.

Behind him, he heard a sickening crunch. He half turned and saw Robard holding the head of the last Ghoul in his hands as the body dropped to the ground. Roscuro unconsciously gripped his Spinal-Column Sword more firmly.

"Well, they could've been some trouble, eh?" the human said, smiling broadly.

Now, wait just a minute, human, Roscuro transmitted to Robard. *You don't want to be too hasty. You have me at a disadvantage now, it's true. But I could do a great deal to help you. You desire power, yes? We have that in common. You're clearly a skillful magic user too. Well, I could teach you powerful magic and help you raise a tireless army that would fight for you day and night.*

"I appreciate the offer. Truly," Robard replied thoughtfully. He cast a glance at the humans tied to the trees off to the side. "But I think you're fundamentally a pretty serious enemy of humanity. If I kept you alive, I'd always be waiting for the moment when you'd inevitably try to turn on me and plant a dagger in my back. You're a great threat to my species, for what it's worth." The human turned his lips up as he said what he must have regarded as a genuine compliment.

Fine. Die, then! Roscuro transmitted the words, held his sword at the ready, and began chanting, aware that his underwater undead were still primed to grab Robard and hold him still if he got close. If Robard chose to keep his distance, Roscuro would finish charging his magic and be ready for another round of fighting. If he charged in, Roscuro's creatures would hold him still so Roscuro could end him with the sword.

And Robard charged. Roscuro could barely see him, but he saw the blur and recognized its direction of travel.

The Soul Eater raised his sword, aiming for that most vital of all human organs: the heart.

Everything happened as he'd imagined. Robard closed the distance insanely fast, apparently ignoring the blade aimed at his heart, confident he could sidestep at the last second. And the underwater Zombies and Skeleton Soldiers grabbed him by the legs and stopped him, inches from landing his attack on Roscuro.

Roscuro plunged the sword forward, into the heart. Blood trickled from between Robard's lips.

Yes! Yes! I won! Roscuro experienced a rush of elation. He had done the impossible. Robard would die at any moment now.

Then he felt a surge of electricity course through his body, paralyzing him.

"I win," Robard breathed. He stepped forward, employing more force than the undead holding him could restrain. And in a movement so quick that Roscuro couldn't react, he slashed at the Soul Eater's throat with that vicious-looking dagger he'd used earlier.

Roscuro collapsed to the ground, clutching his neck, barely able to think. As his blood gushed out, and he fought to remain conscious for a few more seconds, he transmitted a final message to Robard.

Well done, he sent. *I had so much to live for, so much to accomplish, but your superior power and skill took it all away. How exactly are you still alive?*

CHAPTER SIXTY-ONE

Dead End

James struck out with both hands and decapitated the four undead that still clutched at his legs, directionless now that their leader was dying. Bits of skull went flying in either direction, and the bodies slowly began to sink into the swamp.

He used Mass Pillage on them before they could sink too far. There was no reason to miss out on free Stat points.

Then he looked down at the dying Soul Eater, mingled pity and distaste competing for primacy in his mind.

Ultimately, pity won out, and he answered the monster's final question. He spoke in a hushed voice, in case any of the humans by the tree were listening.

"I have conscious control over every part of my body. It's a Skill I took from one of your Ghouls, actually. I saw where you were aiming your sword, and I recognized that if I took your attack, I could get you to stand in one place while you tried to land it. The monsters around you could have slowed me down and kept me from reaching you if you had tried to dodge, and then maybe you would have finished your chant. I could tell that magic you were using earlier was some kind of one-hit kill. So, I decided to just take the sword strike and move my heart out of the way. I even ran lightning Mana through my body to try and electrocute you the moment you landed your attack." He wiped blood away from his mouth with the back of his hand and began using Laying on Hands to heal his chest wound. "It does seem you nicked one of my lungs, though. Maybe you were a swordsman in another life, eh?"

Indeed, I was, Roscuro replied. His body went still.

I hope you're happy, James thought, looking down at the Ego Wolf Fang. He had sensed the Wolf King ego weapon's strong desire to be used against Roscuro as soon as he had taken it from his satchel. Maybe the weapon still contained a shadow of the Wolf King's own grudges. The undead had betrayed the wolf pack when he was alive, after all.

The dagger seemed to exude a warmth in his hands. *I think it* is *happy.* He also noticed that the Soul Eater blood he'd gotten on the fang had vanished, absorbed into the blade as if it were thirsty for blood.

Things to explore later, when he had more time to examine all of his new equipment.

He put the dagger away, turned, and began walking toward where his allies were still tied up.

As he moved, the notifications he'd suppressed began to flow in.

[Predator in Human Skin leveled up!]

[You killed Soul Eater Roscuro, Lv. 32. You gained 2500 exp!]

[Evolver Human leveled up!]

[Predator in Human Skin leveled up!]

"Way to go, James!" Hester shouted. "I mean, congratulations, sir!"

"Thanks, Hester!" James beamed.

The notifications continued as he stepped to almost within reach of Felicia and Ramon Rodriguez.

[You have slain the Ruler of the Dead Marsh! Required conditions met. Title obtained: Ruler of the Dead Marsh!]

Um . . . Hm. Am I just the ruler of some Orientation setting? Will this place still exist back on Earth?

[Title adapting to you . . .]

It was almost as if it had heard him.

[Title obtained: Ruler of the Dark Waters!]

That sounds pretty good.

As he finished reading, James felt a surge of power through his whole body. *What the fuck does this Title do?*

The increased power began to feel uncomfortable. Then several System messages appeared in quick succession.

[Human vessel Skill power limit exceeded.]

[Human vessel Skill power limit exceeded.]

[Human vessel Skill power limit exceeded.]

[You must discard a Skill, or your body will be destroyed.]

"Excuse me, boss, but are you okay?" Hester asked nervously.

James didn't immediately answer. He could now feel the truth of the System's message. *My whole body's on fire!* Every part of him throbbed with pain, as if his body wanted to tear itself apart and rebuild again. But he wasn't going through

Race Evolution now. He was just suffering from the backlash of getting too powerful it seemed, and his "vessel" was going to shatter from exceeding its limits.

"James! Are you all right? James? James!" Hester screamed from behind his ear, but James could barely hear her. His body felt extremely unstable, and he wanted to keep all his focus on holding it together. Remaining in one piece. His cells were trying to split apart or explode or something, and he felt a mixture of extreme pain and indignance.

It's not fair, damn it! I worked so hard to get this power. Killed so many enemies . . . but you're telling me that now I have to give some of it up or die?

He suddenly remembered Skill Transfer. He opened his Status sheet, quickly selected one of the two Skills his new Title had imbued him with, and selected it to transfer away. He threw it into the first item he saw—his wedding band.

[Skill Transfer attempted to non-magical item. Attempt at System-assisted reforging in progress. Assessing significance of chosen item . . .]

The turbulence in James's body immediately began to subside, only to be replaced by a new source of agony.

The ring flared into red-hot heat on James's finger, as if it had genuinely been thrust into a fire to be forged anew. He suppressed the pain as best he could, but the ring only grew hotter as he stared at it. James tasted blood and realized he'd bitten right through his lower lip. He kept his teeth gritted because otherwise he might have screamed.

Fighting the pain was easier than when his body had been threatening to fall apart, but it was still hard to ignore the smell of his own cooking flesh. He turned his face away from the sight and focused on his breathing. With no enemy to fight, it seemed that the pain was more severe than it would have been if he'd had some distraction.

It was only the System announcements that told him the process was over. The area he had turned his face away from was still smoking and sizzling quietly when he turned to look back at it.

[Skill Transfer successful!]

[James Robard's Wedding Ring became the Ring of the Sovereign!]

[Required conditions met. Title obtained: Sublime Creator!]

Oh, well, that's great, James thought blankly, starting at the blackened stump of his hand. *Hopefully, Mina won't be upset . . .* His mind was numb, in disbelief at everything that had just happened—but especially at what had happened around the ring as it had scathed him. He had lost all feeling in his ring finger, and the entire half of his left hand surrounding the ring was a blackened stump. Three stubby charred bits of crispy, scorched finger, with one brightly glowing object suspended in between them.

"Ugh." James coughed up a trickle of blood and remembered he hadn't finished healing his chest wound. But that felt like a minor concern now; he had another lung. Right now, he couldn't stop staring at his hand . . .

It hurt horrifically, to the point that he almost wanted to chop off his own arm and regrow it from the elbow. He still had a bit of Mana; he could do it. But more important than the injury, which he felt sure he would be able to heal, he could feel a tremendous amount of power in his newly refurbished ring.

The Ring of the Sovereign still glowed slightly orange on what remained of his finger, but as he looked at his mangled hand, the metal gradually faded to its previous yellow-gold color. There was a newly inscribed design on the ring, which had previously been featureless metal. It was shaped like a crown.

Well, let's at least see what it does before I worry about these minor injuries—

But another System notification interrupted him before he could Identify the item's features.

[Hidden victory conditions met! Orientation participant James Robard has defeated the final major threat contained within this Orientation! Due to above-normal performance, the remaining Orientation population is permitted to survive. Prepare to be returned to Earth.]

[00:03:00]

[00:02:59]

[00:02:58]

Wow. That was short notice. Not that I'm complaining about getting out of this place. I guess I'll check the ring out later . . . He tore through his allies' bonds, cutting with his right hand only, and he just nodded in response to their thanks. There were questions asked about his physical condition, but he couldn't afford to assess it too closely right now.

He turned and ran back to where he'd killed Roscuro. He wasn't going to miss the opportunity to Pillage that body before he left; the Soul Eater had shown some impressive Skills. *Yes, my body almost destroyed itself last time I tried to absorb a Skill that came from him—or from one of his Titles, at least—but I'm sure that was the strongest one. I bet I can handle whatever else he's got.*

There was an irresistible feeling of greed as he contemplated Roscuro's body—the strongest monster in this Orientation, he felt certain, having killed the other strongest monsters of every species he'd seen.

"Pillage." He spoke the word with great relish.

"Oh. Shit. Boss, I—I think I was supposed to warn you to be careful about this. That, uh, Soul Eater thing might still be dangerous. Lord Anansi said the results of Looting or Pillaging the body of a creature that's the only one of its kind can have unpredictable results. You might get stuck with something dangerous—"

"Now you tell me," James said, laughing to himself. He didn't feel worried. There was a lightheartedness in his tone. *I know this story. Dangerous forbidden powers, right?*

He selected Talent for the target of Pillage.

[Soul Eater Roscuro's body processed.]

[You obtained Eye of Roscuro and Soul Eater Orb!]

[Talent obtained: Soul Eater!]

That sounds creepy in a good way. Does that mean I'll have the same ominous powers that monster had?

His body shuddered slightly. He felt a similar sense of discomfort to when he'd acquired Ruler of the Dark Waters. But he stood as firmly as he could, breathing calmly. As his body ached, as his cells vibrated with energy, he waited to see if he would receive the same System alerts from before.

There was a tense silence in the air. Then a stillness reverberated throughout his body. And finally, a different System alert than he'd expected appeared.

[Sufficient experience accrued. Politician leveled up!]

[A Job Evolution is available. Review? Y/N]

I guess being recklessly power-hungry counts as experience for a Politician. And maybe he'd gotten some experience from working to free his allies.

He would have to check the Job Evolution out later, though.

Right now, the Soul Eater Orb was hovering in front of him. It was a jet-black sphere, roughly the size of a football. Unlike the Eye of Roscuro, which had floated into his magic satchel as normal, it almost seemed to *expect* something from him first.

Is it an ego weapon? That wouldn't surprise him, considering the name of the weapon and the fact that this monster had been so powerful. But if so, why was it floating there? Did it mean there was an enemy nearby?

"I wonder what it wants," Hester said, voicing his thoughts.

"Only one way to find out," James replied. He reached out and grabbed the black orb.

Immediately, the orb turned to a gas in his hand and enveloped him.

James simply inhaled; the black gas didn't intimidate him in the slightest.

[Soul Eater Orb is now Soulbound!]

Huh.

Now I have you, human! Soul Eater Roscuro's voice rang out through James's mind. *That powerful body belongs to me now.*

I don't think so. A battle of Wills began in the arena of their shared mental space. An army of James-shaped soldiers engaged an army of Roscuro's soldiers. Curiously, James noted that they didn't look like the Soul Eater he'd fought. His soldiers appeared to be a human version of the Soul Eater.

Regardless of the enemies' species, the struggle was quick and crushing.

James's soldiers easily smashed the Roscuro army, tearing through his fighters like they were made of tissue paper.

Very well, then, the Soul Eater conceded. *I see it was far from a fluke that I lost. I will be content in service to one as powerful as you. I will put aside my wish for vengeance and work to achieve your goals.*

Why did you want vengeance against me so badly? James replied, surprised. *I know I killed you, but you've killed a fair number of people yourself, I assume—*

Not vengeance against you, Roscuro interrupted. *Against the witch who turned me into the creature you fought.*

Well, if we have the opportunity, I am entirely open to killing someone who'd create a monster like the creature you were, James offered.

After a bit more dialogue with the Soul Eater, all conducted at the speed of thought, James returned to himself. The Soul Eater Orb remained in his hand, as if it had never dissolved into its insubstantial form. Perhaps it had all been in his mind.

"Well, I think I have everything I wanted to get from this place," James said quietly.

He sent a mental command to the Soul Eater Orb, and it shapeshifted into a pure black armband that wrapped itself around his right arm.

"I think you won every prize this place had to offer, sir," Hester replied.

"Well, let's go talk to our friends over there," James said, looking at the other people, who were looking at him curiously and tending to each other's injuries. They were still standing in a nearly circular formation around the trees they'd been bound to, as if they thought something might come from the woods and attack them at any moment. In fairness, it was a reasonable suspicion, despite the notification they'd all received.

James began walking back over. He thought he would see how people were doing, maybe find a way to keep in touch with some of them post-Orientation. And perhaps one of the Healers could take a look at his hand. He felt almost faint with pain. The battle of Wills, following the literal battle and the creation of the Ring of the Sovereign, had nearly exhausted him mentally.

He let out a long sigh. At least it was about to be over.

I wonder how Mina's doing, he thought. *I hope she and Yulia had an easier time than this.*

CHAPTER SIXTY-TWO

The Performer

Blood splatter from the warrior's sundered body sprayed everywhere, though none landed on Mina or the other competitors.

A translucent, previously invisible shield popped into existence in front of them and blocked the liquid.

Well, at least when we die, we won't make too much of a mess, Mina thought grimly.

"Well, who's the next volunteer?" Charon asked. He sounded mildly amused. "So many brave humans. I wonder how our poor chimera will endure." As the hound spoke, the flame of the candle beside him died.

That poor man, Mina thought despite herself. *The way Charon's talking, it feels a lot like he died for that monster's entertainment. He was an idiot, but no one deserves that.* She also noted that with all of the candles out, the challenge had reset for its next challenger. The only thing that didn't reset was the chimera itself.

She looked around at the people who surrounded her. Not a single one looked eager to step in where the warrior had failed so violently.

Mina considered volunteering, but she didn't want to sacrifice herself either. Certainly not just to try and improve the group's morale or something.

There was a long, uncomfortable silence. More than one person seemed to cast an eye in Mina's direction.

Surely they aren't expecting me to step forward, right? After that big guy got ripped in half?

Then she remembered how Leo had built her up in people's eyes in a very short period of time. Maybe they actually imagined she was some sort of heroine.

What would James do here? The answer was obvious. She knew what James would say. *Don't sacrifice yourself for strangers, no matter how they look at you. Be ruthless about this. Look out for yourself.* She decided not to volunteer just yet. She would watch and look for weaknesses. If other people had to die so that she could gather intel, that was that.

"If no one volunteers themselves, some individuals will be *volunteered* for the task," Charon said. "After all, the entire population of this Orientation will die if you fail to complete the mission."

Mina spied movement at the edge of her peripheral vision. It was Jose. He was starting to step out from the midst of the packed crowd, as if he wanted to volunteer.

She strode over to him quickly, just as he broke free of the group, and she grabbed him by the wrist. He looked a little alarmed.

"Jose, how old are you?" she asked in a whisper.

"Eighteen, uh, ma'am," he said politely.

"You're not volunteering," she said bluntly. "Not yet, anyway. Let some of these older people volunteer first. You haven't lived your life yet. And I don't want Yulia to see you receive the same treatment that guy got." She tilted her head at the steaming remains of the warrior the chimera had bisected.

Jose swallowed, then protested, "I'm not afraid to die. I—"

"Be a little more afraid, then," she interrupted. "That guy probably wasn't afraid either, until he was cornered by the monster. Be smarter than him. You have *so much* to live for. You don't know anything about this monster yet, and dying is forever. And very painful."

Jose's eyes had dropped to the ground as Mina spoke. There was an awkward silence while he seemed to process what she'd said.

"Yes," he said finally. "You're right. I'll wait."

"Well, it seems we have no further volunteers," Charon said. "I choose that one!"

A short balding man in Mage's robes began levitating from within the crowd of contestants, flailing his body as he was lifted over their heads and moved to the front of the group.

"Me?" he managed to choke out. "Why me?"

Finally, the invisible force that had lifted the man dropped him on all fours. The hood of his robe fell over his eyes, and he hurriedly rushed to his feet as the hound responded to his question.

"Everyone in the competitors' group identified themselves as being volunteers, as far as this challenge is concerned, Mr. Dabbs," Charon replied. "The stakes are high for all of you and no higher for you than they are for all those you fight for. Now go and do your best!"

Despite being a Mage, the man began by employing a similar strategy to the warrior's earlier. He ascended the stadium and started by lighting the candle beside Charon. Then he descended to deal with the chimera.

Here was where the Mage and the warrior differed.

While the warrior had been afraid to approach the chimera and hadn't gotten near the other two candles as a result, the Mage began quietly chanting until he had gathered fire Mana around his body.

This was exactly what I needed to see, Mina thought. Her eyes tracked the movement of Mana from Dabbs's core through the rest of his body, and she tried to break down the differences between fire Mana and the wind and water elemental Mana that she already had access to. If she could acquire Basic Elemental Magic: Fire through Quick Study, then she might have a chance of completing the challenge if Dabbs failed.

He tossed several fireballs at the candle floating on the lily pad before one actually hit. The others bounced like balls until they ended up landing harmlessly in the stands.

But when Dabbs set the lily pad candle ablaze, the chimera took notice.

As Dabbs aimed at the candle levitating above the pool, the goat head of the chimera drew in a visibly deep breath, and then it exhaled and blew the lily pad candle out.

The chimera began walking toward Dabbs, setting its body between Dabbs and the lily pad.

Keep using that fire magic, Dabbs! Mina found herself thinking. *I just need to see a little more . . .*

But at the sight of the advancing monster, Dabbs broke into a panic. He lost his focus completely, and the fire Mana vanished in a disordered rush, like mist breaking under strong sunlight. He turned, tried to run, and then the beast was upon him.

Dabbs met the same gruesome end as the first man. The crowd let out a collective gasp. Mina couldn't be shocked herself; she was focused on problem-solving.

I need someone to go in there and last a little longer so I can figure out what the monster's abilities are, Mina thought. She felt immediately guilty at where her mind had gone, but then she reminded herself, *Guilt won't help right now. I need to survive. That requires more information about this thing.*

After Dabbs's death, Mina was surprised when another Mage volunteered almost immediately.

"I think I know what to do," he said in a shaky voice as he separated himself from the crowd.

Investigate! Mina learned that the man was named Eugene Daltry, but not much else. His Status sheet seemed basically unexceptional. He was a Mage, lower in level than Mina, he had raised Basic Elemental Magic: Fire up to level three, and he had a couple of music-related Skills and Talents.

Wait, what's that? There was a Skill called Soothing the Beast. Mina read the description. *Oh . . . I can see why he would think he's the right person to handle this.* Hopefully, he was right.

Daltry started off the same way the first two had. He walked up to the candle that was positioned near Charon, lit it, then proceeded down the stadium toward the beast, though he stopped much further away than either of his predecessors had.

As he walked, Daltry drew a flute from the Small Bag of Deceptive Dimensions at his side, put the instrument to his lips, and began to play a few notes, as if he was testing it. Mina guessed he was either trying to remember a certain melody or, more likely, trying to gauge the beast's reaction to different tunes.

As she watched, Daltry switched tunes, moving to something deeper and smoother. At that point, the chimera clearly took notice. It took a few steps toward Daltry, but then something strange happened. The flutist's tune had reached a very compelling point—most of the humans in the stadium had their eyes fixed on him; he was playing beautifully—and the chimera began to sway and move gently with the music. Instead of walking forward, it almost danced.

The tune progressed, and the mood of the music began to change slightly. It became relaxing; calm, peaceful music that was nevertheless absorbing.

The chimera stopped dancing, sat down again, and the great lion threw back its head in a yawn. The goat's head shortly followed suit. Mina tried to keep her eyes fixed on the flutist. This seemed like such a useful Skill that she wanted to try and understand it with Quick Study.

Fortunately for her, Daltry kept at the flute-playing for several more minutes as the chimera's body became more and more relaxed. Mina couldn't see the snake's head at the tail of the beast, but the other two were definitely falling asleep. Their respective postures were drooping more with each passing minute. Finally, the chimera's great body lay, relaxed and slumbering, beside the reflecting pool.

He did it! Mina thought. *All he has to do now is light the last two candles!*

She kept watching, though. Daltry was still playing the flute, instead of putting it down and starting to chant, as he approached the chimera and the other two candles. Maybe he had to keep playing the flute to keep the creature sleeping.

Someone in the audience threw out a "Woo!"

Daltry turned back, without taking his lips away from the flute, and shook his head sharply at the crowd. Clearly, he needed silence or near silence for his magic to work. And it was magic, Mina had realized. It had taken her time to recognize the flow of Mana from Daltry's body into the flute, but she finally saw it now.

It was a different color than any Mana she'd seen before, a brilliant shade of turquoise, and he was using much smaller quantities than she typically saw other people use, which had made it harder to see.

He projects Mana into the flute while playing. The Mana infuses the sound waves, which forms an invisible attack since people can't see sound. But what's the nature of this Mana? Does it actually soothe the beast, as the name suggests, or is it like a drug that puts the beast to sleep the way a tranquilizer would?

Daltry was approaching the beast now, and Mina continued watching, hoping to understand. He drew a torch from a sconce just like the warrior had, and Mina realized he wasn't planning to use magic at all, aside from what he was doing with the flute. He was going to set the candles burning manually.

But how will he reach the candle that's hovering in midair, then?

The flutist seemed not to have an easy answer for that question himself. He focused on the candle floating on the lily pad first. He walked up to the reflecting pool, leaned out, and lit that candle again.

[Quick Study successfully analyzed Soothing the Beast. You partially acquired the Skill Soothing the Beast!]

Well, that's good, I guess. But what does it mean to partially acquire a Skill? Mina wondered.

She didn't have much time to think about that, though. In the moment when her vision was blocked by the notification, there was another murmur from the crowd.

She heard someone exclaim, "Look out!"

As the notification cleared, Mina saw Daltry turning to the stands again. Perhaps he hadn't heard the speaker properly, because rather than looking worried, he just raised a hand for silence with a stern expression on his face.

But Mina saw what the person in the crowd had warned him about. The tail. The snake's body, which formed the tail of the chimera, was moving. Apparently, despite the music, this part of the beast hadn't been soothed. *I guess that rules out the idea that it works like a tranquilizer.*

In the moment when Daltry had been turned away, the snake head reared up, opened its jaws wide, and sprayed a viscous, dark green liquid through the air.

Mina didn't have to wait to figure out what it was. Daltry turned back to face the chimera, but he wasn't quick enough to evade the green fluid. It landed on his face, robes, and other areas of unprotected skin. Everywhere the liquid touched smoked and burned.

Daltry went down in an instant, flailing and screaming in agony. Mina wished she could go help him. A few people around her forgot the rules of the challenge and tried to rush forward, only to run headfirst into the same shield that had protected them from the blood spray earlier. It sent them staggering backward on contact.

As Daltry writhed and screamed, the flute abandoned at his side, the other heads of the chimera awakened once more. The lion stretched, yawned, cracked its neck, and finally noticed the prey in front of it.

The flutist, whose face was now melted down to the bone in a few areas, stretched out his hands and fumbled for the flute. His acid-burned right hand found it. But before he could put it to his lips again, the chimera was upon him. It ripped his head from his shoulders and crushed it messily between its mighty jaws.

Darn. She turned away from the bloody geyser that shot out from the stump of Daltry's neck.

"Well, he was quite the performer," Charon boomed out. "I hope that one of you who remains can at least equal his performance. He got the closest thus far."

"That son of a bitch," growled Jose beside Mina. She turned to see his face. He looked absolutely livid. "Mocking how we die."

"The joke will be on him," Mina said. Jose looked at her. "When we win." She put on her best look of gritty determination, but she could tell it was far from convincing.

His anger seemed to dissolve into despair. "Yeah," he said softly, without conviction. "When we win."

"I volunteer to go next!" a voice declared from behind them.

Mina turned around. There was another non-Mage pushing himself forward through the crowd. He looked taller and stronger than the first volunteer had, but Mina doubted he could do better.

"Damn it, Fergus!" swore a woman beside him. They both spoke with noticeable Scottish accents, Mina noticed. "Let the Mages handle this!"

"It's pretty obvious magic isn't actually the key to the challenge." He drew a sword from his side and used it to point at the chimera. "You just have to deal with that beastie!"

"Good luck, Mr. Dalyell," Charon pronounced approvingly from his high perch. "We salute your courage!"

As the man stepped forward, Mina saw that he wore the distinctive armor of the Light Warrior.

Maybe he can do this, she thought. If he could move faster than the chimera. If he could inflict a fatal blow quickly. At least he could do some damage.

Or so she thought.

As soon as Fergus Dalyell had stepped clear of the group, he charged at the chimera, sword raised.

The lion's head rose from devouring the flutist, opened its mouth wide, and began visibly gathering bright yellow Mana in its maw.

As Dalyell got close, the lion let loose a bolt of lightning from between its jaws. It struck Fergus's sword and then visibly ran down to his hands and the rest of his body. Mina smelled his burning hair and skin. For a few seconds, he thrashed as if he was in the throes of a seizure. Then the warrior collapsed to the ground, unmoving.

"I think I know what to do," Mina said quietly. She had seen one ability from each head. That would have to be enough. No one else was likely to force the chimera to show more Skills, if it had them. There was only one piece she was missing.

Jose looked at her as she spoke. "What do we do?" he asked.

"I need you to show me fire elemental magic," she said.

He didn't ask any questions and simply began chanting.

The others in the crowd backed away, seeing Jose was using magic beside them. But it only took a few seconds for Quick Study to finish breaking down the ability she had already seen more than once before.

[Quick Study successfully analyzed Basic Elemental Magic: Fire. You acquired the Skill Basic Elemental Magic: Fire!]

"Do we have another volunteer?" Charon called down. "Someone who's so eager they didn't bother waiting to announce themselves?"

"The next volunteer is me!" Mina yelled loudly. The arena had grown so quiet that she could hear Leo and Yulia gasp in the crowd.

CHAPTER SIXTY-THREE

True Conviction

Mina avoided looking at Yulia and Leo. She had to make her final preparations for the fight.

"I'm ready, Jose," she added quietly after her announcement. "You can stop casting now."

"Right," he replied. The Mana dissipated from around him.

"The main event comes early," Charon said, sounding interested for the first time since the challenge began. "We knew you were the one who would best be able to accomplish this task, but I personally thought you would wait a little longer. Gather more information, perhaps." The last sentence came out almost as a question. A suggestion?

In any case, Mina ignored the implications the hound was trying to convey. She quickly read the description for the Soothing the Beast (Partial) Skill.

[Soothing the Beast (Partial): Music can calm even the most savage beasts. Using a musical instrument, alter the mood or state of consciousness of a monster. You lack musical Skills, which are required to make use of this ability.]

Okay, I think I might be able to pull this off. Plan A was to get hold of that flute and then get some distance from the monster. If she could learn a new Skill in such a short time with Quick Study, she was betting she could also learn how to play a simple melody. If that happened, she could put the beast to sleep as Daltry had and use Silent Spellcasting to light all of the candles from a distance. The snake wouldn't be able to spray her with acid that way.

It was a plan that only Mina could carry out, with her very particular set of Skills.

If Plan A didn't work, there was a Plan B and a Plan C, of course. Plan A was only Plan A because it kept her the furthest away from the chimera.

"I'm ready," she reiterated, raising her voice to be heard over the gentle murmur of the crowd. Other participants in the Orientation, both in the stands and in the field alongside her, were muttering conspiratorially in response to her and Charon's exchange.

"She could have ended this earlier," went one snippet of conversation Mina caught.

"Before anyone else died," came the reply.

Mina wanted to yell at the people muttering to themselves in the background. None of *them* had volunteered. But she forced herself to focus on the challenge at hand.

She remembered something James sometimes said: "Victory excuses everything."

That would have to be true since apparently her heroic reputation was taking some dents.

"You may begin!" Charon barked down. His booming voice silenced the murmurs.

Mina stepped carefully in a wide arc around the crowd of other people, putting them between her and the chimera. As long as they were around her, she was protected by Charon's shield. It would be like she hadn't started the challenge yet.

Once she had worked her way around to the back of the other competitors, she climbed up onto the stadium and began chanting, gathering wind Mana. The chimera seemed to take notice of her chanting. The lion head's eyes narrowed, it rose from the corpse of the previous contestant, and it let loose a fierce roar.

Mina almost lost her focus. The roar seemed to be a Skill of some sort intended to achieve that result.

But not quite. Her focus was made of stronger stuff. She had passed so many tests in her life.

Judging the Mana she had gathered to be sufficient, Mina released it. Wind whipped around her and then swirled around in a concentrated movement toward the chimera. It found the flute lying discarded at Daltry's side, and it began to pull at the instrument, trying to lift it into the air.

Mina's fists were clenched tightly as she watched and directed her Mana. The flute began to float up off the grass, then took off like a tiny rocket—and then suddenly the chimera was there, pouncing, trying to crush the flute under its massive lion's paws.

The paws missed, and Mina thought she could guide the flute quickly through the air to her, but then the tail struck. The snake caught the flute in its jaws and snapped shut hard, crushing the instrument between its teeth.

Well, that's Plan A down the drain, she thought. She tried not to let that discourage her. Although her backup plans were not her preferred solutions, one of them should still work.

She began walking around the stands, trying to work her way toward where Charon sat next to the first candle she needed to light. The chimera followed her with its eyes, and it took a few steps in the general direction she was moving, but then it seemed to hit some invisible border it was unwilling to cross. Instead of following her up into the stands, it returned to where it had sat near the beginning of the challenge beside the reflecting pool, sat down, and waited.

That eliminated one of her alternative plans, then. She wouldn't be able to get it to chase her and thereby lure it away from the targets it was guarding. That was fine, she supposed. The idea of making the chimera chase her had made her nervous in the first place.

But that only left the option of her going to it.

First, she lit the candle that stood next to Charon. Although she hadn't practiced Basic Elemental Magic: Fire, she found it was just as easy as handling water had been. It did feel different, though. There was something more pleasant about the way fire Mana felt. A warmth that seemed to radiate everywhere. Maybe it was just because she'd spent the last few weeks cold much of the time, but she immediately liked fire magic better than wind and, she thought, better than water too.

The hound stared down at her curiously as she moved. She took a moment to examine the stand the candle sat on before she left.

Yep, confirms I could carry this away with me if need be. But the difficulty wasn't the candle by Charon, anyway. There was no point in moving this candle. It was the other two that it would have benefited her to move. And they were guarded.

If she tried to move the other candles with magic, the chimera might destroy them. Then she would have failed the challenge for certain, and possibly for everyone else too.

Mina descended the stadium and prepared to execute her riskiest, yet perhaps most likely to succeed, plan.

She began gathering Mana around herself as she walked. Water Mana.

She had noticed the reflecting pool beneath the candles almost as soon as she reached the stadium. Though she didn't think she could do much offensively with water, the fact that there was some already there gave her a real advantage. Since the chimera was right between her and the water, it was ideally positioned for her to try something with the pool.

I can do this, she told herself. *No. I* will *do this. No one else will die here.*

As she approached, the Mana growing thicker and denser all around her, the chimera rose to its feet. It looked apprehensive. Defensive.

Mina hopped down from the steps back into the field, and she yanked a torch free from the sconce closest to her. She intended to continue using water Mana for most, if not all, of the challenge remaining. Having a non-magical source of fire nearby could be valuable.

At this movement, the chimera pounced toward Mina, making a huge leap through the air. Simultaneously, Mina released her Mana.

She seized control of the entire pool of water behind the chimera, and she pulled the water forward. With all the Mana she had infused into it, the liquid outpaced the chimera and surrounded it in an instant, grabbing it mid-pounce and pulling it to the center of the body of water.

The beast thrashed about with its paws and its heads, trying to find purchase in the water, to break free somehow, but Mina kept a firm grip. And she tightened it.

She kept the water in a similar shape to when it was in the pool: a rectangular prism, but one that grew smaller and smaller as she concentrated it.

Water molecules, close in, she thought. *Closer and closer together in the area surrounding the chimera.* Slowly, the molecules condensed around the chimera. The air around them grew colder as the pool turned into a massive ice cube surrounding the chimera. The creature still tried to move, but very slowly. Its energy was quickly fading as the water around it turned more and more solid. The snake head was already completely still, perhaps unconscious.

Mina kept her mind on making the ice colder and colder, but her body was already walking past the chimera. Her Mana would run out in the next few minutes, after all. She had to make each second count.

The pool water was now completely wrapped around the chimera, and the candle and the lily pad it had been placed on had fallen beside the chimera. She approached it, still giving the chimera as wide a berth as she could. She stood the candle up, keeping one eye on the chimera and the ice cube and only taking quick glances at what her hands were doing. Then she lit the wick with the torch in her hand. It took only a few moments to light.

Then she looked up at the candle that hovered off the ground, six feet in the air. That was the only thing she hadn't specifically planned for.

I could throw the torch at it, but what if I miss? I'd have to get another torch and keep trying, and at the same time, my Mana's running out. She looked around herself to see what she could use to get a better angle.

If she went back into the stands, she would be too far away. Besides the stadium itself, there were the dead bodies. She could pile them up and use them as a kind of stepladder, but her mind recoiled at the thought of doing something so disrespectful to the dead.

I wouldn't get high enough anyway, she told herself.

That just left—*Oh, duh!*—the frozen water from the pool.

She quickly ordered one of the frozen sides of the cube to form itself into stairs. The side that had the most space separating it from the chimera.

Then she walked up, her body bent, walking almost on all fours to avoid slipping and falling on the icy steps.

She managed to get to the height of the candle. Then she reached out with the torch and lit it.

Multiple notifications streamed in at once.

[You defeated Tri-Headed Mountain Chimera, Lv. 22 and passed Hecate's challenge! You gained 1200 exp!]

[Mage leveled up!]

[Mage leveled up!]

[Mage leveled up!]

[. . .]

Victory! She slowly walked back down the ice stairs, glowing inside.

I did it! I saved everyone. Thanks in significant part to the example of the ones who died, but I did it!

Yet there was something strange. The crowd was completely silent. No cheers.

As she reached ground level again, she finally allowed herself to look around.

She found Yulia and Leo's faces in the crowd. They looked strange; their faces were in the middle of changing expressions. From worried to happy, it seemed— raised eyebrows, mouths shifting into big smiles. But they were completely still. *Unnatural. Impossible. What's going on?*

She looked around, and she let out a sigh of relief. It wasn't just them.

The crowd was frozen. Not frozen in ice, like the Tri-Headed Mountain Chimera. Just still. Utterly still.

"Congratulations on your victory, Ms. Danailova!" Charon's voice boomed down at her. There was an obvious undertone of respect in his voice that she liked. "The goddess knew that you would triumph. You have saved every one of your fellows!"

"Um, what's happened to them?" Mina asked. She could barely raise her voice above a whisper. She found herself very suddenly, unaccountably tired. She released her control of the water, and she felt only very slightly better.

Charon's hearing seemed to be excellent, though.

"They're simply frozen in time," the hound replied. His voice showed signs of strain as well, and Mina noticed that the letters around his body were lit in a different color this time, a strange luminescent shade of gray. "Everything in the arena is frozen in time except you. I will repair the damage done to your colleagues, and then I will explain what you've done to everyone."

"Repair the damage?" she echoed. "You mean you're going to bring back the dead?"

Charon winced visibly. "No," he said, his voice a strained whine. "Bringing back the dead from the underworld is impossible, of course. But this is the in-between. No one dies here without the goddess's say so. Their souls remain in this space unless the Gatekeeper should release them. As long as the souls have not passed on, they are not dead. And so, it simply remains to reverse the flow of time a few minutes for each of them and put their bodies back together."

"That sounds difficult," Mina said carefully. Charon looked as if he was under strain every moment he spoke. She didn't want to make him use mental energy on her while he was supposed to be reviving her semi-dead colleagues.

In her peripheral vision, she saw movement, but she didn't turn. She could tell it was in the area where the bodies of the fallen challengers lay, and she guessed they were pulling themselves back together, something she wasn't inter-ested in seeing.

"Honestly, out of all the magic I have learned in the goddess's service, this one is the most difficult," Charon replied. "It becomes more difficult to manipu-late time if I try to do something beyond my capabilities, or if I engage in more than one manipulation at once."

"Oh." Mina realized that Charon was engaging in two such manipulations as he spoke. He was reversing time for the dead, and he was freezing everyone and everything else. "Why do you need to freeze the others?" she finally asked.

"To give you private time with the goddess," he replied, speaking each word carefully, as if they required great labor. "Go down those stairs." He pointed with his muzzle to the stairway that had been blocked by a translucent magical barrier earlier. It was unobstructed now. "There you will encounter the goddess. Lady Hecate has been waiting for you for longer than you know."

Hecate, Mina thought. *I finally learned the name.*

She dropped the torch at her side, turned, and without a word began walking toward the stairs.

When she reached them, she descended without hesitation, though they led into a pitch-black darkness that swallowed her whole. It felt like stepping into a deeper darkness than she had ever known, endless and black. A true night.

Mina smiled.

Coda

Alan found himself standing in thin air.

He dropped and instinctively braced himself for a rough landing, but he fell an extremely short distance. Just a few inches.

He was one of the luckier people. All around him, he saw a half-dozen people fall out of the air. He recognized every face he saw; they were his coworkers from Barry, Pesca & MacDougal. Three of them had been on the second story of the law office, so they dropped considerably further than Alan did.

He rushed over to where two of those who fell from the second floor had landed, but fortunately, neither appeared to be hurt.

They made it through Orientation too, after all, he reminded himself. *And without James protecting them. They're probably rather formidable. What happened to the building, though?*

He helped the slower moving of the two to rise to his feet. *Wait, are these all the survivors from the office?* Less than one-third of them had returned alive.

It seemed the System had been serious about cutting down on the human population.

Alan responded numbly, automatically to the equally formalistic "thank you" from the fellow he'd helped back to his feet.

Then he looked around for a moment, checking faces again.

Jesus, none of the partners survived except—

"Alan, how did you sur—I mean, so good to see you!" Dean Crocetti's voice cut through his thought process.

"Good to see you too, Dean."

A shame that only you and I survived, though. And "shame" was an understatement. He'd known Cliff and Brendan for decades. That long acquaintanceship had been snuffed out by this *System* in only a few weeks.

I'm just glad Mitzi and I are all right. The casualty rate for this thing was worse than any war I've ever heard of.

He turned and finally saw the firm's office. The building had moved, he realized. Perhaps the Earth itself had changed size and shape. The System's voiceover had said something about that when all this started, hadn't it? It was difficult to recall, and Alan's memory wasn't what it once had been, anyway.

Between the surviving firm employees and the building gaped a wide sinkhole. Alan peered into it, and he wondered how deep the hole went. Florida sinkholes opened up all the time, but he'd always thought the firm's building was set on a sturdier foundation. The possibility of a sinkhole could be predicted in advance by construction professionals, he'd believed. Something about a layer of limestone and erosion?

But maybe it was a waste of time wondering how it had happened. The law firm was no more, and most of his friends at the firm were dead. *I need to make my way to Mitzi. At least she's all right. That's the most important thing.* She would have teleported back home.

"Alan, are you feeling okay?" Dean asked.

"Are you, Dean?" Alan replied, cocking an eyebrow. "Knowing that only this handful survived?" He gestured at the precious few people left from the firm. He turned and began to walk away.

"Wait, wait," Dean said, catching up to him. "At times like these, we ought to stick together."

Alan turned to analyze his face, trying to read what Dean's intentions were exactly.

It doesn't really matter, though, does it? he thought. *Whatever Dean wants to accomplish doesn't matter. Because the ones I need to "stick together" with aren't here.*

The images that came to mind were those of Mitzi, Sierra, and James.

Timothy Rook found himself in the Planter High School cafeteria, surrounded by other high school students.

When the System transported me to Orientation, I was in the boys' restroom, he thought. *Dropping me here seems pretty sloppy.*

Then again, it was also rather convenient. There were dozens of other students with him here. Some of them were people he'd been thinking about killing before the System's announcements had caused him to hold off on the school shooting.

His trigger finger felt itchy, and he knew the Keres were hungry for sacrifices.

Now might just be the right time to make good on those plans he'd put off . . .

Damien Rousseau dropped headfirst into a trashcan in Orlando Central Park.

I was not in a fucking trash can! he thought exasperatedly as he pulled himself out. The System Homunculus had told him they were all being transported back to roughly the same places they'd left from. Clearly, that was slightly misleading.

But as he emerged from the can, he saw some people he recalled walking around the city block when he'd vanished. *Maybe the Earth's location changed, but the relative position of the humans on it, at least compared with each other, stayed the same. Which means . . .*

He glanced around for his cousin Philippe, but he wasn't shocked when he didn't find him. *We never got along, but I never expected him to die in circumstances like those.* Philippe had gone off with Nikolai Rostov at the outset of Orientation, despite Damien's expressed reservations. It was no surprise to Damien that the cultists had come to a bad end once he'd heard about what they'd gotten up to since he and Philippe went their separate ways.

I'm just grateful Aunt Camille never had to see her boy turn out that way.

Damien looked to the city center, which was only a couple of blocks away. Or had been. The center of Orlando was no more. The sidewalks and roads were shattered into lopsided chunks of asphalt, separated from each other by fissures of varying size. What was left of the pavement was littered with broken glass. The skyscrapers had almost all been utterly destroyed, probably as a result of whatever calamity had destroyed the roads.

An earthquake? Or did the planet grow larger or something? He supposed it didn't matter. All that mattered was knowing what to do next.

And that much was obvious to Damien. *Find James Robard.*

Wherever he was, that was clearly the place to be.

He was about to walk off in search of James's wolf pack, or anyone else who would know where to look for the leader, when he saw a familiar face. A young woman walking around in the wreckage of the former city center.

Damien decided the search could wait. He'd see if she needed help. And maybe she would know where to find James. *That girl was part of his group for longer than me, at the very least. And maybe longer than the Rodriguez family?*

He rushed over to the woman whose name eluded him.

"Hey, there!" he shouted as he drew close.

She turned at the sound of his voice and smiled at the sight of him. But Damien couldn't help but notice that the smile, pretty as it was, didn't seem to reach her eyes. The eyes were exhausted, impatient, frustrated—anything but happy.

"I didn't imagine I'd run into the team Werewolf so quickly," she said.

You didn't expect to run into me at all, Damien thought, *and the way I'm reading your smell, I make you a bit nervous.* He'd had his Werewolf senses for less than a month, but he thought he was adapting to them very well. A certain odor for fear, a certain odor for food, an odor for a prospective rival—following that instinct a little too closely had already gotten him into trouble—an odor for almost any situation. Living bodies were almost an open book now.

"I'm going to find James," Damien said. "I thought maybe you'd know where he is. You were traveling with him before, right? We could go together. Looks like this world isn't much less dangerous than the one we just left."

She let out a little sigh. "You're probably not wrong."

"But you don't want to go with me." It wasn't a question.

"I'm planning on going my own way for now. There are things I want to do . . . that wouldn't be of any interest to him." She swallowed and took a long moment to think, but Damien could sense she wasn't finished talking. "You tell James that I said 'Thanks,' all right? For the way he behaved in Orientation. He was more decent than he had to be. If we meet again, it will be as friends, as far as I'm concerned."

Damien simply nodded.

She went on her way, and Damien began his search for the wolf pack in the park.

The woman was already long gone by the time Damien realized he still didn't remember her name.

"S" something, right?

Luna and the wolf pack appeared in a patch of forest they didn't recognize.

Most of them had lived their whole lives in the Orientation space. Only the first generation, the Wolf King and his oldest pack mates, had ever been adults on Earth. They had lived in a wildlife sanctuary before the System changed them. Luna had been born there too, but her memories of Earth were fuzzy. And this forest was essentially fresh growth, anyway, though it looked deceptively well developed.

It was a new and wild world they inhabited. Deliciously unsettled.

Luna scented the wind.

Where do we go? asked one of the pack, a younger wolf, slightly runty.

She stated the obvious. *We go to find the pack leader.* James's smell wasn't apparent in the cool breeze that wafted over them, but she felt certain the bond that connected the wolf pack to their leader would pull them together again. She would see if they could find him with their collective tracking abilities, and if not, she would reach out telepathically.

Luna didn't want James to think she was the type of wolf who always wanted someone else to solve her problems.

But for now, she added, looping in the rest of the pack, *let's find some food.*

The wind hadn't carried James's scent, but the smell of other animals was strong and tempting in the air. These woods must be full of prey.

Camila Rodriguez smiled through tears.

"So many of us lost our lives in that horrible place, but I'm so happy that I got to see most of my family reunited."

When she had awakened in her tent in Orientation, the first piece of news her remaining family had given her was that all the able-bodied family and friends who had been left to guard them had been captured, or perhaps killed, by undead monsters. The second piece of news, given immediately after the first, was that James Robard was on his way to rescue them.

And now, here they all were, safe and sound.

The apartment complex where her family lived was in a strange condition. Some of the buildings had fallen down, while others had simply moved positions to be more spread out. Camila and her family had gathered in one of their apartments that was still standing.

The first few hours back home were a rotating series of reunions. First, the ones who had been captured came by to let her know they were okay. She squeezed them and doted on them until the next family members came.

Their cousins, the Sánchezes, and their neighbors, the Garcías, had fared much worse. In their Orientations, more than half of the population had died. Camila also gathered that despite arriving on the same day, they had somehow spent more time in the other dimension.

When they came, Camila and the other Rodriguezes shifted from rejoicing in reunion to commiserating over their shared losses.

While Camila was embracing her family and community, a few of the young men dug a pit in what had once been the front yard, to cook barbecue in. No one criticized them for ruining the landscaping. The Earth had shifted while they were gone, and none of the gas lines were functioning, even in the most intact of the apartment buildings.

That night, they all dined on a massive wild boar monster. Ángel García and Vicente Sánchez had caught it in the woods that had sprung up near the apartments while they were gone. There hadn't been more than a handful of trees there before. Who knew what else now lived in those woods?

Despite being a monster, it tasted just like the pigs Camila remembered raising in her yard as a little girl.

"We'll decide what the family should do tomorrow," she said to her cousin, Rafa Sánchez.

He simply nodded in agreement. His eyes looked distant and melancholic.

Cara appeared where she'd been before Orientation. She had been camping with a few friends. The tents were still standing, albeit strangely positioned, as if the campsite had been much more spread out than it actually was. Or as if the space had expanded? She didn't spend much time thinking about that. *Leave that to the brainiacs,* she thought.

Most of the friends she had come with had died in their respective Orientations.

Cara decided to spare the two who'd survived and simply walked off alone.

She was fairly certain they didn't even see her before she used her superior physical Stats to dash away.

Once she was a good distance away from her former friends, who she expected and hoped never to see again, she transformed back into her Wendigo shape. She felt more comfortable in a form that embodied pure power and ruthlessness.

And she covered ground faster too. She raced north, following the pole star. She had given the other Wendigos a common direction to travel in and a destination to meet at.

If they remained in the region formerly known as Florida, the hot, humid climate would sap their powers considerably. Instead, they would go to Canada, where winters were harsh. From there, they could gradually spread their influence and carve out their own slice of the world.

With their weather powers and the naturally cold climate, they would create a country where man had to consume man, and dog had to eat dog, in order to survive. A land of always-winter. A place where the environment would grind everyone down until they became monsters.

Like Cara and her new friends.

Detective Leo DaSilva reappeared on Earth just outside the police station he'd been sitting in when the world changed.

Surprisingly, although every building around the police station was ruined, the station itself was still standing.

Unfortunately, half of the police station was standing in one spot with part of a skyscraper embedded in its roof, and the other half was six feet to the left of its counterpart. Neither half of the building looked stable, though DaSilva took a moment to admire the remarkable skill of its construction.

In Florida, no one built structures to withstand earthquakes. The Sunshine State simply didn't have them. Florida architects worried about hurricanes, tornadoes, and thunderstorms instead. Clearly, the Earth had moved. But the police station, the most important building in the city in DaSilva's opinion, remained almost intact.

He decided not to go back in for his personal effects.

And even though he still had his car keys, he could see dozens of abandoned cars in the streets without leaving the police parking lot.

I guess I'll walk wherever I'm going, he thought. He still wasn't quite sure where that was.

But as Nana DaSilva used to say: "If you don't know where you're going, any road will take you there."

The detective started walking.

About the Author

D. J. Rintoul was born and raised in Orlando, Florida. He obtained his law degree from the University of Florida and subsequently returned to Pennsylvania, where he had met his wife and obtained his undergraduate degree. Rintoul now lives with his family in eastern Pennsylvania. He enjoys history, books, board games, Christmas lights, and, occasionally, sunlight.

Podium

DISCOVER MORE

STORIES UNBOUND

PodiumEntertainment.com

www.ingramcontent.com/pod-product-compliance
Lightning Source LLC
Chambersburg PA
CBHW020639120726

47906CB00001B/41